More Praise for
ACOLYTES OF THE DEAD

"*Acolytes of the Dead* is one of the best erotic horror novels I've ever read...offers plenty of thrills, chills and kills—everything you want from a horror thriller. There's a ton of racy content, since ancient sex magic lies at its dark heart... Reminds me of the best Richard Laymon and Edward Lee—full of adult situations and a plot that keeps you turning pages. Get cozy and plan to spend a long time reading because you won't be able to put it down!" —John Everson, Bram Stoker Award-winning author of *NightWhere* and *The Bloodstained Doll*

"(*Acolytes of the Dead* is) a modern mummy classic wrapped in archeological intrigue, ancient Egyptian secrets, shocking bloodshed, and kinky sex magick." —Brian Pinkerton, author of *The Perfect Stranger* and *How I Started the Apocalypse*

ACOLYTES
OF THE
DEAD

W.D. GAGLIANI
DAVID BENTON

JOURNALSTONE
YOUR LINK TO ARTIST TALENT

ISBN: 978-1-68510-160-2 (trade paper)
ISBN: 978-1-68510-161-9 (ebook)
The Library of Congress Control Number has been applied for.

First printing edition: September 19, 2025
Published by JournalStone Publishing in the United States of America.
Cover Design: Mikio Murakami
Edited by Sean Leonard
Proofreading and Cover/Interior Layout by Scarlett R. Algee

JournalStone Publishing
1400 North Wood Rd.
Murphysboro, IL 62966

JournalStone books may be ordered through booksellers or by contacting:
JournalStone | www.journalstone.com

Dedications

David Benton

For Jerry Kennon (RIP) whose kindness and creativity pointed the way, and Ed Rousseau, Bob Schneidler, and Shane Murphy for accompanying me on the first leg of the journey.

W.D. Gagliani

In memory of my parents and grandparents, who always encouraged my obsession with books and storytelling, and for Janis... as always a pillar of love and support.

ACOLYTES
OF THE
DEAD

Prologue
October 23

HIS FOOTSTEPS POUNDED raggedly down the concrete path. His running had started out that way and was now out of control. He was vaguely aware that his arms were windmilling as he fought to keep his balance and keep his feet on the path. His mouth was frozen open, and his scream of terror echoed in his head.

But only he could hear the scream. His mouth emitted no sound other than the rasp of his breath and the clicking of his tongue against his palate. He could hear that sound as well, and it reminded him of wood hitting wood.

He couldn't see where he was going.

He'd never see again.

His eye sockets were black holes. Tendrils of liquid gore that dragged across his cheeks were all that remained of his optic nerves.

The eyeballs were no longer. He had used an antique silver spoon to scoop them out of his own head. The pain hadn't hit until after he had finished.

He couldn't remember why he had done that.

He didn't know how he had found his way outside, out of the maze.

And now he was running down an alley, or a side street. He hadn't been out of the compound in so long, he had no memory of the nearby lonely streets.

No, he *did* know why he'd used the spoon to pluck out his own eyeballs like spoiled grapes. He knew what he'd seen, and what he tried to unsee. Knowing was no help now. The voices in his head had gotten louder, and after a full day he could no longer stand to not listen. He found he could no longer function now that he'd stepped across a line he had always imagined was uncrossable.

The voices told him what to do in every language he knew, over and over, as if they had been recorded in a loop and embedded into his brain. He'd tried blocking them out, but eventually he'd given up, snatched the spoon from the tea set tray on the long library table, and stabbed himself over and over. The dull spoon couldn't pierce skin easily, so even as his face bled from the many wounds, he set about prying first his right eyeball loose, levering it out of its socket until it lay like a slack full condom on his cheek, and then, following the voices' urging, he had attacked the left eyeball as well, greeting the sudden dark with something like relief through the sharp pinpricks of pain as the silver scooped gore and spread it like a cloud.

Then the voices had told him to run, and he had followed their guidance out of the Escher hallways and staircases, out of the compound, and down this street, or whatever it was.

Now the voices gave way to a strange baying.

The night's cold air stung his wounded face, entering his empty eye sockets like wind entering caves on a hillside. The baying came into focus, the sound of dogs, or wolves, or...

He couldn't see, but somehow he became convinced that what was stampeding in his wake was a pack of jackals, those lesser-known cousins of the dog. In his mind's eye, the only eye left him, he saw their long snouts and slavering jaws.

He ran faster, but they were so close now, their breath was on his neck.

Then he stumbled on a crooked cobblestone and he fell forward, his arms waving in front of him to try to break his fall, but he couldn't manage it and he shouted when his knees met the unyielding stones.

He heard a *crack*—he felt it, too, something shattering in there—and the pain spiked in his brain and he cried out desperately, but then the pack was on him, fangs and teeth tearing through his disheveled clothes, snouts digging for flesh, hot fetid breath in his face, and blood—*his blood*—splattering the stones and trickling into the caverns of his eye sockets. His screaming was drowned out by the jockeying of musky-reeking bodies as they struggled against each other to clamp ravening jaws on open patches of skin. Their claws dug, sharp, into his abdomen and opened it to the night air like a zippered sack. His attempts to fend off the hungry beasts soon faded to nothingness.

Then the alley echoed with the sound of feeding. The growls of pleasure and greed as they feasted.

Anyone who happened to be watching would have seen a broken man gesturing with his arms after falling, would have heard his screams and whimpers, and would have wondered what disease had ravaged his mind.

There were no animals visible around him, even as his life blood oozed between the damp cobblestones and seeped into the cracks.

But there was no one watching as Professor Ahmed al-Amani died, his mouth frozen in a terrible rictus. If he still had his eyes, they would have been crazed with terror.

PART ONE

Chapter One
November 6

THE WIND AND driving rain seemed to be on the verge of shattering the windows in his office. Based on the way the loosely caulked glass panes vibrated, Dr. James Blackstone figured he'd have to duck flying glass shrapnel at any moment. Yet he couldn't really move, for the stack of papers to grade was still too high and the windows were six feet tall and towered over his cluttered desk, the only place he could sit and work in his claustrophobic cube of an office on the third floor of Merrick Hall. A brief fantasy of escaping through a broken window played in his mind's eye. In it, he teetered on the wide ledge outside the row of windows, soaked by the violent rain being driven into him in waves, until the cement cracked under his feet and he went tumbling to the cobblestone courtyard below. His head would resemble a smashed melon.

He chuckled and shook his head. Thunder rumbled and the strobe of a nearby lightning strike illuminated his packed bookshelves, for a second convincing him they were about to collapse on him, burying him at his desk.

So much for focus.

Perhaps it was time to give up the noble thought of working late into the night. It was half past eight already and he had barely made a dent. His students' papers were pedestrian, uninteresting, unimaginative, ill-constructed, and poorly reasoned. He couldn't imagine a greater waste of his time than reading every word of every dreary essay.

Almost without realizing he was doing it, he reached into the lowest drawer of his massive desk, clearly remnant of an ancient purchase of Communist-gray monstrosities, and the half-full bottle of bourbon was in his hand along with his sticky but generous shot glass.

It was definitely a night not fit for man nor beast, but certainly fit for a tot of the good stuff. Maybe he could recapture his focus once his palate had been placated.

Thunder shook his shelves again, and when he turned in alarm ready to ward off a possible cascade of textbooks and artifacts, he was instead startled by the sight suddenly visible in the surreal strobe, a tall figure standing in his office doorway, a long face seemingly chiseled from blue ice and eyes glowing from within dark pits. A bundle over one arm could have been a cape, a body, a dead animal. Anything.

Perhaps a weapon.

Blackstone was frozen in the act, bottle in hand that he considered could serve as a weapon in a pinch. Then he relaxed slightly.

The lights had flickered and then his eyes had adjusted and his visitor was simply a tall man with a raincoat carefully draped over his right arm, continental-style.

Then again, Blackstone thought briefly, there *could* be a weapon under that raincoat.

Anything to conquer this damnable boredom.

Anything to keep him from reading more mind-numbing student attempts at prose, or from surrendering and heading for the garret he called home. All right, his mind corrected, it wasn't quite a garret, it was a fairly standard bachelor apartment--though he was regrettably married—with two bedrooms and a larger than average study, and he abhorred the thought of going there. It was worse than the thought of staying here in his office.

"May I help you?" he inquired of his silent visitor, shaking his head as he did so, driving the thought of his Hobson's choice from his mind.

"James Blackstone?" said the stranger. "*Professor* James Blackstone?"

"Yeah—y-yes, I mean." He almost stuttered. "That's what it says on the door." He sometimes deliberately added words to make sure he was pronouncing them correctly.

Have to watch that, it's been years.

The stranger's face made no motion, except perhaps a slight twitch of an eyebrow, the right one.

Silence always annoyed Blackstone. He held up the bottle. "Care for an artificial warm-up? We know alcohol doesn't really raise one's core temperature, but the illusion is rather nice." He raised his own eyebrow.

"No, thank you, we haven't time." The man's voice was ready for the gravel pit, low-pitched and almost a cliche for some Mafia leg-breaker. Fortunately, Blackstone had no memory of having borrowed from the local mob, though it had certainly occurred to him at one point, at his lowest. Not all that long ago, actually.

"We haven't?" Blackstone always felt rebellious when someone imposed some kind of limit. *He'd been rebellious most of his life, and look at him now,* he thought in the third person. "I think I might have, as I don't know who you are or what you want. What I want is a drink."

Blackstone poured himself a tot. Maybe a smidge more than a tot.

He knew he was covering up the embarrassment of having been caught drinking in his office, perhaps the poster for an academic career on the skids.

"Cheers!" he said with fake cheer and downed the portion in two swallows. The burning on his tongue and palate was sweet, and for a moment he forgot his visitor, closing his eyes with pleasure.

The visitor stood stock-still, apparently waiting for a wave of adult seriousness to wash over the down-and-out professor. Blackstone imagined his stock with the guy was dropping by the minute, whatever it was he wanted.

"So what do you want, need, that we haven't got time to get to?" he said. "If I may ask?" He half-smiled as if to prove he was exercising humor, but he sensed the leg-breaker didn't care. "And...who the hell are you?"

"My name is Batten. I'm here on behalf of someone who is in sudden need of skills such as yours. Your name has been on his list for some time."

"That's swell," said Blackstone, raising an eyebrow again. "But who is this someone? Why the night visitor routine? I mean, what is this about?"

Before the tall man could respond, Blackstone added, "Are you with the police?"

The question elicited a half-smile from the chiseled face. Perhaps a smirk. "I'm here representing my employer—"

"And what about this list?"

The man called Batten seemed about to lose his patience. "All in good time. My employer—"

"What the hell is *good* time?"

"Alton R. Chambers is my employer," said Batten, apparently committed to swallowing his frustration or disdain. "He has asked me to request your presence for a brief meeting, for which you will be remunerated." He frowned as if he didn't quite agree with the concept, not in *this* case. "All you need do is come with me, spend an hour with Mr. Chambers, and he will pay you one thousand dollars for your time." Now his raised eyebrow seemed to say, You could stay here and earn your negligible pay while drinking alcohol you can't afford, if you prefer.

"And you're not with the police?" Blackstone had been trying to think of what he might have done that would require an official visit. Not this year, anyway.

Batten ignored him. "Mr. Chambers is occupying his main dwelling a half-hour from here. Will you please join me before the storm worsens?"

Blackstone wasn't sure whether the reference was euphemistic, but he had to admit he was intrigued. Chambers. Chambers. Alton Chambers. Wasn't he some sort of reclusive billionaire? *What the hell does he want from me?* And then: *A thousand dollars?*

Batten said, as if reading his mind, "Mr. Chambers has authorized me to pay you in advance."

Well, that meant nothing. He could always be shot down and the money yanked from his grip at any time. Right?

Then again, a thousand dollars.

"All right, Mr. Batten," he said. "Let's go for a ride." He reached for his rumpled coat.

Chapter Two

THEY DROVE THROUGH the stormy night in silence. They were in the rear of a new black Lincoln Town Car, the reissue, with tinted glass. There was a driver up front, but Blackstone could only make out his silhouette through the closed glass, also tinted. It was a large silhouette.

Batten sat across from him, facing the rear, long legs relaxed and almost reaching Blackstone's seat. His face remained sober when he told Blackstone they'd reach their destination too soon for him to have a drink from the bar. Blackstone had requested one as soon as they'd climbed in.

"What's the point of a fancy car then?" he'd almost said, but thought better of it. Ten hundreds were folded in his pocket.

Batten deflected the few questions Blackstone mumbled as they skimmed over the wet streets while the wipers did their best. Lightning bolts that crossed the sky above were barely visible through the dark glass, and the rumble of thunder was a distant whisper in the soundproofed interior.

"You may ask questions of Mr. Chambers once he has spoken to you," Batten said, his tone discouraging further communication.

Thirty-five minutes later, they passed through an electronic gate set in an impossibly high wall overgrown with moss and climbing plants of some sort, and drove a short way. Blackstone saw in the lightning's strobe flashes a massive Southern-style mansion with a couple hefty wings anchored by turrets, a large colonnade in the center, and an outbuilding that must have been a four-car garage half-hidden to one side. It was large, but not as impressive as he'd expected.

The Town Car continued past the mansion.

"Gate house," said Batten by way of explanation.

Blackstone said nothing. If that was merely the gate house, then he was unprepared for how incredibly large the Chambers residence would actually be.

He thought he would have the answer five minutes later, when the car made a smooth ninety-degree turn and passed another house, except this one was twice the size of the first one and more of a severe Federal-style, also with long wings disappearing into the wooded lot that surrounded it.

"Guest house," said Batten, a smirk on his face. He was evidently enjoying this game, though his expression might have been similar if he'd been blasting birds out of the sky. Or people.

"Jesus," Blackstone muttered.

The car kept to the wide asphalt-topped drive as the woods thickened and the sky above them became a memory occasionally lit by a flash from above.

Blackstone desperately wanted a drink.

What had he got himself into, accepting this bizarre invitation from a known eccentric? He'd called his wife, Laura, and made an attempt at an excuse about a late meeting he'd been called to attend, and she'd sighed knowingly. He rarely came home for an early dinner, preferring to reheat whatever she'd left for him until it was slop and he could shovel it down with bourbon punctuation. To say they had grown apart was to label the Middle East's Palestinian problem a backyard squabble.

Sometimes it was a toss-up in Blackstone's mind whether reading student papers or passing the time at home was the more torturous. He longed for his early days of adventure, his digs, his notoriety and rakish good looks in khaki, and he resented his curator's career, which had come to a crashing halt due to...

His thoughts were interrupted by the smooth stop of the Town Car, which he only just realized had entered some sort of garage. Now that he thought of it, he'd noticed the slight angle, so this must have been an underground garage.

Batten silently swung open the door and extricated his long frame from the seat, unfolding himself like a lawn chair. He leaned back and held the door. "We are here," he said simply.

"I see," Blackstone said. He was stiff but pretended to be limber as he climbed out and stepped onto the brilliant white concrete. Along the distant wall, he could see a long line of classic automobiles parked like fighter planes on a runway. He glanced over the car roof and another line of cars, supercars and vintage sports models, faced center. He spotted at least three Ferraris, a couple Lambos, and he was almost certain there was an original Bugatti Type 41 Royale over in the corner, a huge boxy sedan worth millions. Only six remained, of seven built.

Chambers *was* loaded. Blackstone had no doubt.

The garage was not brightly lit, and he could see another row of classic cars along the back wall in the shadows. Maybe a McLaren and a couple Aston Martins there, but it was hard to tell.

Blackstone's saliva turned to acid in his mouth. His clothes turned to rags on his rangy frame. He could barely look Batten in the eye as he said, "Nice collection," intentionally downplaying it but knowing he was transparent as glass.

Batten smirked. It must have been his favorite facial expression.

They took one of two elevators—the small one for people, while the other was for cars—and emerged on what Blackstone assumed was the house's main floor. It was a great room with thirty-foot peaked ceilings and a row of skylights.

"This is the rear foyer," said Batten, his face screwed up in his typical sneer, as if reading Blackstone's thoughts. "The main great room is opposite us."

Blackstone estimated his entire apartment would fit inside the space twice over. There was incidental furniture along the perimeter walls, art in softly lit notches or on pillars, and a ballroom-style marble floor with a design too large to see from a standing position. He decided it would be clearly visible from the balcony that overlooked this wasteful atrium from above. Beneath the mezzanine there were at least three hallways, signifying different wings of the house perhaps.

"All right," he muttered, "I'm impressed. Now can we get on with it?"

"Mr. Chambers will see you in the main library."

Of course.

The skylights flickered with the remnants of the storm's lightning. Thunder was muffled. Blackstone followed Batten down a fair distance of the middle corridor. The library was tucked behind double doors at least ten feet high, Art Deco brass and dark exotic wood inlays. As they entered, Blackstone didn't bother to gasp, but he might have. He realized the room was probably its own wing. Two levels of books surrounded them, full bookshelves on the main level and nearly full on a second level, reached by way of two wrought-iron spiral staircases. And another smaller elevator, he noted.

But they were headed for the center of the cavernous room, opposite a fireplace that stole space from the book collection by reaching all the way to the ceiling forty feet above. There was a massive desk, a wide library table perpendicular to it that was stacked with books and papers and charts, and a computer workstation with three flat screens and a variety of keyboards, all forming a U. One screen showed continuously changing financial trading data, while the others seemed to be stuck on search engines.

Next to the desk stood Alton R. Chambers himself, casual in jeans and a black twill shirt.

The billionaire was taller than average and still muscular despite his age, though the skin of his neck and face gave away his secret. The tan was permanent, burned into him by many consecutive months of relentless sun in the Egyptian desert—this much Blackstone knew about the old man. His eyes were almost translucently blue, a stark contrast to the dark hue of his skin. His gaze burned with intensity. Below his eyes, a patrician nose played sentinel over thin lips and a Kirk Douglas chin. He approached Blackstone eagerly, his shovel-wide hand extended.

"Pleased to meet you, Professor."

Blackstone felt the strength in the grip and sensed Chambers could break bones if he chose to, but he was holding back. He gripped back and made a half-grin.

"Mr. Chambers," he said. "The pleasure's mine."

I hope, he thought.

"Excellent, excellent," said the tycoon, or whatever he was. "I'm glad you decided to accept my offer."

Blackstone wasn't sure how he'd made his fortune, or fortunes. He only remembered the Egyptian obsession that had gotten him so much press two decades before.

"Your man offered a monetary incentive that got my attention," said Blackstone. "I don't know anything about your offer."

"Yes, but your interest was piqued as well, was it not?" The man's smile was smug, maybe somewhat mocking. Maybe it was just the way his mouth was shaped, with its rubbery thin lips. It was hard to tell.

"I would be lying if I said I wasn't intrigued, certainly," Blackstone admitted.

"Good, good. Please sit." Chambers indicated a leather club chair that faced his desk from outside the U. It was one of a half-dozen scattered around the work area. "Care for a drink?" He turned to an elaborate miniature bar to the side that, on second glance, rested on four chariot-like wheels. It was well-stocked with high-end liquor bottles and everything needed for a thirsty tycoon on the move.

"Bourbon, rocks," Blackstone said, wetting his lips.

Chambers made a face as if he were holding back some critical commentary due only to manners and good upbringing. He poured into cut crystal from a well-known bottle shape and dropped in ice with silver tongs, frowning. It was an eighty-dollar drink in just about any bar.

Blackstone took it with no qualms. Free liquor, his preference. The first swallow was perfection on his palate. He sighed. Then: "What can I do for you that some purchased corporate division can't?"

Chambers chuckled as he poured himself two fingers from a different bottle. "That's a good characteristic, Professor. Get right to the point. Most of your fellow academics could learn a lesson, wouldn't you say? Wordy to the extreme, as if their salaries depended on it."

Well, to tell the truth, they do, Blackstone thought. *For the last five years I just haven't cared.*

His eyes traveled over the darker corners of the large room. Where bookcases were not built into the walls, more art rested on ledges subtly lit from above by Art Deco sconces. He realized all the art was actually Egyptian artifacts which, if real, were likely priceless. And would have belonged in their homeland, not in some tycoon's personal collection.

Then again, tycoons by nature do whatever suits them, laws be damned.

Blackstone figured it would have cost Chambers a small fortune just to smuggle the artifacts out of Egypt, let alone acquiring them. It was akin to secretly owning a Rembrandt or a van Gogh, especially if it had been stolen.

"Yes?" was all he said, then enjoyed another swallow of the excellent amber liquid in his glass. He could play hard to get. Whatever the old man wanted, he'd get around to it in his own time. Meanwhile, he could savor the man's booze.

"Speak your mind too," the old man added. "I appreciate that quality as well."

Blackstone nodded and sipped, quietly.

Chambers had poured himself something darker, almost bruise-colored. He sipped it as he gazed over the rim at his guest. "I would like to employ your writing ability, in fact," he said almost as an afterthought. "Your books on the Valley of the Kings and your digs there, as well as those tracts speculating on the Nile trade trends during different dynasties were eye-opening, as well as the lesser-known books you have self-published on your theories of Egyptian magic and myth."

Blackstone shrugged. But he was surprised. The latter books Chambers mentioned were largely unknown, ignored, and occasionally derided by some academic who stumbled on them. He stared at Chambers, his eyes meeting the old man's frankly. He said, "You've done some homework."

"I have people who do homework. But I read very widely."

Blackstone eyed the book collection. "I'm sure," he said lamely.

Chambers laughed. "This is only my public collection. A mere quarter of what I've accumulated. If we strike a deal, you'll see the rest of it."

Blackstone couldn't help feeling eager to see that other collection. But he wasn't going to get ahead of himself. *Hard to get*, he reminded himself.

"What would I be doing in your employ?" He added: "Assuming I'd be interested."

"I'd want you to ghostwrite my autobiography," Chambers said. "I've had an interesting life and it's inextricably tied to the wonder of Egypt, so someone like you would be the perfect writer."

"It's not really my field..."

"No, of course not, but I will feed you information about my family and me, and you will structure it any way you'd like just so it tells the story of our lives as they were shaped by the glory of Egypt and the digs we conducted over the decades."

Blackstone started to speak, but Chambers cut him off.

"Not only a book for you to write, but I also have need of an expert translator of hieroglyphs for a related side job."

At this, Blackstone perked up. This aspect of the job offer might be more interesting. But who considered hieroglyphics a side job? He'd spent his life learning the nuances. "What kind of translation?"

"I can give you more details later, but during our time in Egypt decades ago, my siblings and I discovered an unknown tomb and came into possession of a series of panels that, try as we might, we were not able to decipher. And I have also been unable, though I've spent decades and countless dollars trying."

"Came into possession?" *Stole, much more likely,* he thought. *Smuggled out.*

Chambers smiled. "Egyptian authorities were not always quite as avid in protecting their antiquities, you know. There were many years in which the right payments in certain quarters made almost anything possible to take home with no legal requirement."

"Ah," Blackstone said. He knew damn well what Chambers meant, and Chambers knew he knew. And both knew not much had changed.

"Yes, so in any case, I have a vault full of panels that need explanation, and which could become quite a feather in the cap of whoever translates them and presents them to the world. Of course, we would both benefit, as the Chambers family financed the dig and the research."

"What about the legal aspects?" Blackstone said. He remembered the thought he'd had a few minutes before. "Even if I were able to do the work, sharing it with the world would be like admitting to having stolen a Vermeer or something."

Chambers waved the objection away. "I've spent a fair amount back-tracking, creating a plausible paper trail with the right signatures and seals to prove I had legal backing to remove the writings, as well as much of the art you see here. And which you will see elsewhere when you work here."

In other words, you've bribed enough officials to provide yourself with cover in case anyone questions your ownership. Sure, another rich asshole perk.

"That was prudent of you," was what Blackstone said carefully.

"I've learned prudence the hard way," Chambers said with a throaty chuckle that implied multitudes. "I can see the translation has piqued your interest more than the autobiography. Perhaps I should be offended."

"It's not that," Blackstone said swiftly—the job could be lucrative, after all. "I'm not a writer first, but I am an Egyptologist."

"Indeed."

"I would be equally committed to both jobs, of course." Was he whiny as he backpedaled?

"Of course, I would expect nothing else."

Blackstone nodded and finished the bourbon. Added to what he'd consumed earlier, he felt slightly queasy. Only another drink would help. Fortunately, Chambers seemed to read his mind.

"Make you another?" he said, holding out his hand. He took the heavy tumbler and poured another generous portion, dropped in ice without making the face this time, and handed it back.

Blackstone took a healthy slug and barely suppressed a joyous sigh.

Chambers waited until he had swallowed, then said, "I would be prepared to pay you a half million dollars for the translation work, half of that sum when you begin and half when you complete. For the book, I would put you on a salary like my other employees. Is the sum of fifty thousand dollars a month, plus standard benefits, open-ended, sufficient to pry you away from your teaching duties?"

It was good that Blackstone had already swallowed the bourbon, because otherwise he would have choked on it.

Six hundred thousand dollars a year, plus at least a quarter million for starting a translation and that much again if he completed it... Currently his university job paid just under forty-five thousand a year with mediocre benefits. Chambers was offering to make him a millionaire—it would take him longer than a year to complete both jobs, and clearly the old man was willing to pay him as long as he needed to work.

His mouth dry, Blackstone managed to get out some words. "I'd like to think about it."

Chambers laughed as if they'd just shared a new and wonderful joke. "Of course! Take all the time you need. I should tell you that I have put out feelers to some of your colleagues with similar offers..."

Blackstone now did almost choke on the bourbon. *Who?* Who could Chambers have reached out to? Milton Thorpe? Jackson Hollander? Not Rasha Gulshan, she of the lustrous black hair and pointy tits who was known to have slept with the previous chairman of the department and was now making a play for his replacement, the man who had thrown Blackstone a lifeline?

Laura would slit his throat in the night if he passed on this opportunity while one of his back-stabbing so-called colleagues sucked up to Chambers and walked away rich...

No, this could not be allowed to happen.

But he had to maintain the illusion of weighing his options, of making a choice not based on mere money—even though *mere* money was the root of all his problems.

"That makes sense," Blackstone managed to say.

Lightning flashed rapidly like a strobe in the window. The rumble of thunder was muffled by the thick glass. He glanced at the tall window, now as black as obsidian.

Chambers was speaking. "Perhaps you'd like to see some of the main library before I leave you to ponder my offer, Professor."

"That would be excellent," Blackstone said, finishing his drink in a hurry. Suddenly he felt as if events were moving so quickly that he could be left behind, left with nothing, if he wasn't careful.

"Follow me," said the old man, as he took Blackstone's glass and placed it next to his on the bar cart. He waved them to the main door and held it, then led the professor down a long hallway lined with paintings and sculptures that were likely worth millions. Blackstone recognized several Egon Schiele sketches and other originals, mostly all small and expensively framed. Here in the hallway the art was eclectic, not Egypt-themed. But the library was different.

As they entered through two tall doors carved with rows of glyphs and cartouches, Blackstone was surprised to see a form lounging on a leather sofa in the center of the room, facing a blazing fireplace.

It was a woman with long salt-and-pepper (more pepper than salt) hair in a stylish wave, holding a long-stemmed chalice to wide, full red lips. Piercing dark eyes turned to fix the visitors with an interested stare, which ended with a raised eyebrow and a slightly mocking smile even as she sipped the bubble-infused liquid.

Raised eyebrows must be hereditary, Blackstone thought.

"Professor Blackstone, this is my daughter Alena," Chambers said.

There might have been a million books in the double-height room, but Blackstone could not take his eyes off the woman. She must have been late forties or even early fifties, but wore her age so well that from across the room she might have barely reached her late thirties. She wore a short black leather skirt and a silk blouse in a striking emerald green shade that complemented her eyes. Her lids were also a similar shade, and in fact she wore emeralds in her ears and around her shapely neck.

When she looked up, it was with some small amount of annoyance, obvious in her blade-like brows, but then her gaze fixed on Blackstone and her sudden smile was wide open and disarming. It seemed to say, *I'm not all that bothered after all.*

Blackstone took it that his appearance was somehow pleasing enough to change her demeanor.

His inner voice cautioned him to be careful. His inner voice was full of shit.

"It's very nice to meet you," he said when close enough to hold out his hand.

"The pleasure's mine," she said with a near-wink, gripping his hand briefly in her own and caressing the skin of his palm with the pads of her long, shapely fingers as she broke the connection.

Blackstone smiled and she turned back to the book she had open on her admirable lap.

Chambers beside him made some small sound, and Blackstone was reminded of his presence. For a moment, he had forgotten. He'd fallen into those dark eyes, hadn't he? She was most likely older than he was, but he couldn't help feeling attracted. The old man leaned in, conspiratorially, and confessed, "Alena could have been a top-notch Egyptologist, but decided to pursue a career in fashion..." He sounded apologetic.

"I own a small chain of boutique shops," she said. "Father thinks it's a waste of time, but my investors are quite happy with the results of my efforts."

"Enough so that they chose someone else to run the company," Chambers said, apparently determined to make his displeasure known.

"With my agreement, the board hired a well-regarded CFO. My duties as chair keep me busy and I don't have to deal with the daily minutia, so it was desirable all around." She directed her answer more at her father than the guest, using the opportunity to score points when he couldn't just overrule her.

"Do you live here?" Blackstone couldn't believe he'd asked. Certainly more forward than he was used to being.

She didn't seem to mind. "I have a small villa in the compound, yes, and an apartment in the north wing of this main house that I rarely use." She made a small wave at the ranked bookshelves. "And I do avail myself of Father's library, as you can see."

"Alena spends more of her time here than she realizes." Chambers frowned. "She can be quite the homebody, now that her business requires so little of her."

She made a face for a fraction of a second. "Good luck to you, Professor," she said as she arose and took her book out of the room.

Sounded like a dare, Blackstone thought.

He didn't want to get caught staring at her receding form, but he glimpsed that her *form* from behind was quite exquisite, age be damned. Blackstone filed away the thought, and the image.

Chambers cleared his throat and took Blackstone's elbow, pivoting him around to face the walls of books. "This is my main library, but there is a more focused collection in a room which you would likely occupy the most. That is next door."

With that, he stepped up to a tall bookcase and passed his hand over an invisible sensor somewhere off to its left side. The case moved silently on a hidden track and revealed a doorway as wide and tall as the case itself, leading into a study that was as large, with shorter bookcases lining all walls and stuffed with books from ancient to modern. Here was an L-shaped library table for working, and another table with a handful of huge flat computer display panels. And at one end of the room stood a large walk-in vault door, the same kind usually found in a bank.

"The floor is reinforced underneath, and the vault is fully encased in concrete on all sides. That is where I store the wall panels I removed from the tomb," Chambers explained, pointing as they stepped inside the space, which was larger than it first appeared. "For security, only I can open the safe. I also store high-quality photographs of the tomb's wall glyphs in the safe. Also for security, not many people have been allowed to see the actual walls."

"How many panels are there?"

"Exactly 367, of differing length and width. Most were five feet by four feet, which we split into two, but there are also other sizes."

"*Holy Christ!*"

Blackstone surprised himself with the outburst. But...

"That's about as large a trove of untranslated panels as any ever discovered in one place," he added. His left eye twitched as it sometimes did when his excitement blended with surprise and a sort of anxiety.

"Yes it is. Actually, larger. And I had them removed by the same people who moved the tomb."

"Did you say *moved* the tomb?"

"Yes."

"The whole tomb?" Blackstone shook his head, awed. "If I may ask, how were you able to *move* a tomb?

"You remember when the Aswan High Dam was built? Before your time, I'm sure, but doubtless you've steeped yourself in history."

"Yes, of course, early 1960s... Engineers moved the temple Abu Simbel from where it would have been drowned in the flooding of lower Nubia."

"A multi-national effort aimed at preserving the past! Yes, and the Chambers Oil Company later hired several members of the same engineering team for a special secret project."

"Secret?"

"Why yes, it had to be, in order to avoid running afoul of the dreaded Antiquities Service, those snobbish bastards. Changed their name a few years later to the Egyptian Antiquities Organization. Now they've elevated themselves to *Supreme Council* of Antiquities. Haven't changed a bit in decades, and they'll still take a bribe if you know whom to ask. Anyway, I was running the company by then and I hired some of the engineers who had moved Abu Simbel. They employed the same technique they used with the temple. They carefully cut the tomb into pieces, numbered them, and then a couple company ships ferried them here to the estate where very carefully it was reassembled. Somewhat like a three-dimensional jigsaw puzzle, as it were."

"Wait, it's *here*?" Blackstone looked around briefly as if the tomb would just appear in his field of vision.

"Yes, it's on the grounds," Chambers said enigmatically.

Blackstone wanted to pursue the matter. He wanted to know exactly where this tomb had been reassembled. He wanted to *see* it. He wanted to walk through it.

He wanted to fuck in it.

Unbidden, the image of Alena's form came into his mind's eye.

His memory of yet another exotic grad student in his past was of their cataclysmic tryst in Nefertari's tomb in the Valley of the Queens, that magical *wadi* on the Nile's West Bank. The bright colors of the magnificent wall panels swirled about them dizzyingly as they'd rutted like animals atop an empty sarcophagus. Blackstone remembered the girl's long blonde hair in his fist as he rammed into her from behind, her face lying sideways on the ancient stone, and then later sweeping across his face like silken strands from the marketplace as she rode him to mutual ecstasy for the second or third time, by then having turned their union into almost a religious experience. The gods of Egypt themselves had seemed to be watching, the many eyes painted on the walls open to their erotic performance. In fact, Time itself had stopped while they fucked in that most famous of tombs, but when they'd come out in the morning the police had met them halfway down the slope and Blackstone's greatest Egyptian dig had become his last.

Yes, Blackstone wanted badly to inquire more of his host.

But the images in his head had led to a most unfortunate condition that made him wish he weren't standing.

He forced himself to focus.

The wall panels. The job offer. The way it would change his life.

This large a cache of untranslated Egyptian writings—indeed, the entire damned tomb—would be classified a major find if anyone knew about it. When the results were published, there would be plenty of room for criminal accusations. Blackstone wiped his brow of a small rivulet of sweat that had started at his hairline.

The fact that no one knew about the tomb, and its panels, made the whole venture dangerous from a legal point of view. It appeared Chambers was well aware of the fact.

Chambers nodded as if he'd read his mind. "Yes, everything you're thinking is exactly right. A major find, unknown to the world. An unknown pharaoh, most likely, or high priest, to have had so much writing sent with him into the afterlife. I'm certain the glyphs are either an unknown dialect or a secret language. But now they are my secret. And I will keep it—and reveal it—at my discretion. You need not worry yourself."

In point of fact, Blackstone *was* worried. Suddenly and gut-wrenchingly worried. But he also knew that he was hooked. He was not just intrigued, he was convinced he was destined to know, to be involved, to see the colorful wall panels with his own eyes, to touch them with his own gloved fingers. He didn't even have to see them first, he knew that he wanted to...more than anything else right now. Cold sweat drying up as his body adjusted to the complex blend of emotions, he looked Chambers in the eye and said, "I'm not worried. I'm eager to get to work."

"So you've considered the offer sufficiently?"

Blackstone was caught in a trap of his own greed. He'd asked for time to consider the oddball offer—well, it had sounded oddball until he knew the specifics, including the pay and the panels of untranslated glyphs—but now he'd reacted rashly and given away his own transparency.

"Mr. Chambers, I'd be remiss if I simply lunged at the first offer to come my way. I must discuss this decision with my wife..."

"Of course, of course," Chambers said. "Mrs. Laura Blackstone should have a say." His gaze hardened. "But no details must escape your lips, otherwise the offer will be made to one of the others. I'm sure you understand."

The cold sweat started again. "Of course," he said, his mouth going dry. "It will all remain between us only."

He stepped forward and approached the large vault door, which was taller than he was and about three times as wide. It was modern, not an antique. It had a complex-looking panel with electronics that blinked red and green lights in patterns that were hard to discern. It was very impressive and, if it was as thick as it appeared to be, impenetrable. He touched it cautiously, almost as if he might be electrocuted by some unexpected defense mechanism.

If only he could at least *see* even just those photographs now. *That* would make up his mind.

He turned and jumped, startled to realize that Chambers had sidled up next to him silently.

"I'm sorry, you cannot see the photos—or the wall panels themselves—until you are my employee and have signed the paperwork," said the old tycoon, as if reading Blackstone's thoughts.

Thoughts.

Lusts...

Blackstone retracted his hand as if it *had* been scorched. His erection had wilted by now, thankfully.

Only later did he recall that Chambers knew his wife's name. In this day of social media—she had a definite presence on the usual platforms, Instagram and Facebook, at least—he supposed that wasn't so strange. Still...it had sounded slightly creepy. As if Chambers had wanted to make sure Blackstone understood that there were no aspects of his life that hadn't been explored.

"The vault, it's full of photographs and also the original panels?"

Chambers nodded. "And some smaller and very valuable, fragile artifacts, of course. I had it specially built, with large steel cabinets lining three of the walls. The cabinets are encased in reinforced concrete. Each wall panel is mounted on a vertical sliding drawer so it can be examined in detail. The vault is about twice the size of this room. It's impregnable, thick concrete all around, as well as climate-controlled. None of the panels or artifacts will turn to dust, I guarantee it." As if he decided he had to assure Blackstone, he added, "There are special steel pillars in the basement and sub-basement added only to support the vault, which may be the eighth largest in the world. You'll see, if you decide to sign onto the project."

Blackstone felt a strange pressure in his chest. It wasn't a medical event, but it was a sense of adventure rekindled as well as the tension of having to make changes in his life, and perhaps climbing out of the academic and financial holes he had dug for himself—or that others had dug for him.

"I'm flattered to be asked," he managed to say, his throat still desert dry.

Chambers said nothing.

Blackstone nodded as if there had been a response. He had nothing more to say either.

They stood in silence for a minute. Blackstone thought he heard thunder.

Finally, Chambers broke the uncomfortable dead air.

"Very well, Professor, please take some time to think about my offer. Only don't let it be too long. *Tempus fugit*, you know, and I'm at the age when it *fugits* faster every day. I want to live to see the work finished—*all* the work—and commencing as soon as possible would be desirable."

The old man led them out of the inner sanctum and back into the main library, where they stopped near the work area.

"I have all the paperwork necessary already drawn up, so it only needs your name and signature. Since you are interested, I can email you a copy so you may have it checked independently, but you will find that it's straightforward in the case of the remuneration. There is a standard non-disclosure clause, which would cover the writing of the memoir until its publication, after which you would no longer be bound. The translation job, however, would be covered for your lifetime by an NDA."

"Wait, are you saying I couldn't publish my findings?" Blackstone made a face. "The glyphs—the tomb itself—would have to remain a secret?" *That* wasn't very acceptable.

"Not at all," Chambers said, placating, with a hand up as if to request calm. "It would cover you for life *unless* we negotiated a new agreement with regard to how much to publish and how quickly. In other words, it would simply force us to be cautious, to avoid dumping the entire find and its elements. It would force us to formulate a plan by which to expose our find to the world."

Blackstone assumed with the use of *our*, Chambers meant him and his deceased siblings. Not Blackstone, as he was just a hired gun. It was all right, he was okay with that. A million dollars—or more—would buy whatever silence he needed to maintain, and perhaps a new agreement would shine forth and he'd manage to get some well-deserved credit for the translation, and... His imagination bloomed, and he realized he'd tuned out Chambers' voice.

A flash of lightning from outside interrupted his reverie. The storm was ongoing still.

"...these are all factors to be decided later, when the work is nearing completion," the tycoon was saying. "You agree, protecting the work while it's underway is most important."

"Of course," Blackstone said, his voice cracking. Was he giving away too much? But then, he would be *getting* so much.

"Very well then. Batten will see you home. I'll await your call, with whatever you decide. I bid you good night."

With that, he turned and stepped away down the wide corridor and into the depths of the house's wing.

Weird old bird, Blackstone thought. He turned, wondering how he was to take his leave, and was startled again by Batten, who was standing at attention as if he'd just beamed in from some other location. That place and its people were giving him the creeps. But creepy money's as green as any...

"This way, sir." Batten pointed.

They reached the great foyer and, as lighting strobed above them in the skylights, Alena Chambers exited a nearby room.

"It was nice meeting you," she said with a bright smile. "Father can be...stuffy...at times. Especially when it comes to his little Egyptian fetish."

Blackstone smiled. Nodding, he said, "It's all right, he's entitled."

"You don't know the half of it," she said, a pretty laugh punctuating the joke. "And you, Professor Blackstone, do *you* have any fetishes?"

He couldn't help it, her raised eyebrow and her wicked little smile gave him a response that was sudden and painful. And perhaps obvious.

His throat even more arid than before, Blackstone said, "I have many layers."

Lame, as his students would say.

"I don't doubt it," she said, and her dark green eyes flashed without the aid of lightning. She held out her hand, and when he shook it, Blackstone felt her give him that tiny caress again, and his shiver matched the rest of his physical responses, and suddenly he needed to be outside where he could breathe.

"I have the car ready, sir." Batten pulled the door open as if it were a prison cell door and waited.

Blackstone turned and headed down the steps to the drive. The air was charged, but there was no rain.

"Don't be a stranger," said Alena Chambers from the doorway. The door closed with a definitive slam.

Chapter Three

AFTER BATTEN HAD ushered out the washed-up professor, and his daughter had scurried away to one of her sanctums, Chambers poured himself a finger of good Cognac and downed it. He rubbed his hands almost unconsciously, set down the crystal, and headed for the elevator. Inside the brass-lined car only about wide enough for three abreast but much longer, he pressed a bulbous knob and the grate closed. He liked the feeling of dropping, closed his eyes and enjoyed it as the car went down two levels, and when the grate squeaked he opened his eyes and surveyed the foyer of the sub-basement.

Following the brick walls to the corridor on the left then down a side corridor, he came to a solid door. He tapped the black plate with his keycard and let himself into the Prep Room.

The near-gutted naked corpse of the previous professor lay on the metal dissection table, the remaining blood that hadn't run down the gunnels now dried under him.

Chambers donned gloves and leaned in close. He pulled down an overhead lamp and a magnifier and inspected the inside of the slaughtered corpse. He was humming a tuneless ditty, unaware of it, and smiled as he nodded with approval. There were few organs left inside the cavity, but the important ones were now in their canopic jars where they would be preserved for future use.

When he was satisfied, he pulled down a four-inch pipe and worked the valve with long practice. Opened, it allowed a cascade of cedar oil to spill into the abdominal cavity. It would liquefy what was left of the intestines and minor organs in a week or so, as well as take care of bacterial growth. He moved the pipe back and forth gently to allow the oil to spread evenly throughout. A rectal plug kept the oil from leaking out. A natron bath next to the table would eventually embrace the corpse as it prepared for its journey to the afterlife, though that step would last thirty days rather than the prescribed seventy. Chambers had spent decades perfecting the art of mummification; his method combined several described by Herodotus and others, which usually divided them by families' class and means. Since his purpose in their preservation was not as sacred to him as that of his own family, he allowed himself the luxury of experimentation.

Still humming his ditty, Chambers closed the valve and pushed the pipe and the lamp out of the way. The dead man's face was contorted with fear, frozen in mid-scream. That was all right, the bandages would cover it and the face would melt into a more bland expression with time. No one would ever see it again. The hairy nostrils were enlarged by the escape of the liquefied brain, which Chambers had accomplished just the day before after using a rod to break it up and raising the body by the feet so it could drain.

Pleased by the subject's progress along the path to eternity, Chambers dimmed the lights and left from the rear door, which led deeper into his sub-basement. In this direction the new addition would travel as well, until he reached the Tomb Room, where he would take his place along the wall niches Chambers preferred for those of less relevance and standing. Others would rest in simple sarcophagi, while family members rated much more elaborate quarters.

Chambers never worried about his own vessel to eternity.

He had other plans.

The lighting was low in this chamber, each wall lined with the previously prepared dead and all traveling the road together. The last step was the wrapping of bandages and the application of a resin mix that would seal the gauze and also help slow decay. Chambers walked deliberately around the large square room, pausing at each rank of wrapped mummies, luxuriating in the musty, aromatic spice smell of the preserved departed—some of whom had been nudged on their way to the afterlife by Chambers or his personal employees—and communed with them one by one, each of them indelibly engraved in his memory in one way or another. He imagined they were grateful for having been preserved this way, having been made more consequential in death than they had been in life, most of them.

He walked the perimeter of the room and acknowledged them all, young and old, male and female. Then he moved to the other doorway and continued on to the farthest reaches of his sub-basements. Massive systems kept the entire warren of chambers cool and dry, which was necessary to aid in the mummification process. He stepped out of the mummy rooms.

Here the wide corridor was lit by electric torches and ornamentation was provided by canopic jars filled with the organs of many of his mummified guests. Curved arches were reminiscent of ancient cities' sewers and had been laid lovingly brick by brick by a special international crew Chambers had secretly hired specifically for this purpose. They had done such a fabulous job that their bones now rested in several specially prepared nooks he had bricked over with his own hands once the overall job had been finished. He inhaled the stale, arid, slightly leathery scent of the bodies' eternal death and smiled.

Tonight his mind was on the guest who had drunk his spirits.

He hoped Blackstone was a good choice. The professor's work was impressive, more than most in the field realized, unfortunately overshadowed by his indiscretions and weaknesses, of which Chambers had identified many. He sensed Blackstone had a hidden but keen intellect, his books and papers were well-written (and he had written them himself, no ghostwriters), and he'd displayed a creative mind when Chambers had dug deep enough. He had a tendency to be his own worst enemy, with an endless ability to fuck up every single job.

Chambers reached the Grand Tomb.

The rounded brick arches now opened up above him and led him into a double-height chamber wider than several basements laid side by side and deeper that the mansion's own footprint—indeed, above ground this chamber extended far beyond the house proper and lay underneath the sculptured gardens, the guest houses, and the tiny temple replicas that dotted the Chambers compound. Here the lighting was a mix of real torches and carefully concealed electric strip lights. The ceiling was almost too high to be clearly visible, but one could see that smoke from the torches' flames had tinted the brickwork black over the years.

In two concentric circles, stone and wooden sarcophagi were arranged through the space like a strange Egyptian Stonehenge in which the slabs lay equidistantly parallel. Here were the mummified remains he had brought back from the tombs of Egypt as well as Chambers' own family; his late wife (Alena's mother), Alena's cretinous late husband, and the rest of his immediate nuclear family. Chambers' father and siblings were in worse shape than most as they had been early attempts and had decomposed before he'd had them exhumed. Now they were little more than skeletons wrapped in cotton linens. But Chambers was glad they were here with him and would soon witness his greatest triumph.

He entered the circles and reached the center, where the altar rose above the floor on its own dais. He climbed the seven steps to the top, over which an eight-foot obelisk portrayed Ra, the Sun God.

"I knew I'd find you here," he said. His voice echoed pleasantly among the mummified dead of his family.

"I feel so at peace here," said Alena, who reclined in a death pose on the wooden bier. "It's almost my favorite place in the compound."

"As well it should be," Chambers said. "It cost ten million dollars in sixties currency."

"Well, you can't take it with you," Alena said acerbically.

"That's what they say," Chambers said. "You look lovely in death, by the way."

"Thank you. Good genes."

"No, *great* genes. We've been fortunate."

She sat up and lowered her long legs to the marble floor of the altar dais. "Do you think this is the one?"

"He can't do worse than the last one." Chambers mumbled an oath. "Two years wasted."

"You should talk. You didn't fuck him."

"No, but I came very close. He was highly recommended. I had my hopes up, I'll admit that."

Alena chuckled as she stood, making room for her father to lie down in her place. He put his hands under his head, casually, and stared at his usual spot on the ceiling. There was a small painting there that he always used to center himself. The light scent of incense wafted over them and he sighed.

"What do you think, daughter? Could you live with him?" Chambers winked.

"He's certainly the most fetching of your would-be codebreakers. But then again, I haven't sampled the goods...*yet.*" She smiled.

"My research seems to indicate that he could be the right one," the old man said. "Blackstone has done some translations that stumped dozens of his peers. His biggest mistake was letting his weaknesses overshadow his brilliance. He paid for that, and that's what makes him prime for our purposes. He wants to make amends, but also to reap the rewards that eluded him before. And his appetites. If his appetites are any indication, not only could he be the right one, he might be the *chosen* one."

"Time will tell, Daddy Dear." Alena made a pout with her red lips and winked at him. "Time and money."

"Yes, well, I have much of one and not so much of the other. Make sure you're doing your share."

She stuck out her tongue at him, but his eyes were closed so he didn't see it.

She climbed down the steps and stalked away toward the main corridor, leaving him in repose among their quiet family members.

Chapter Four

LIGHTS WERE OUT in the apartment and he tripped over the ottoman that had been kicked in his way intentionally. He saw a thin blade of light from the rear bedroom and heard the sound of a television stuck on some program with an audience reaction, probably a mindless sitcom.

Blackstone stood still in the near darkness, his thoughts racing. He was home late—again— and his wife was displeased. Locked away in her own portion of the flat, which would have been a good bachelor pad if only he had remained a bachelor, she chose to interact with him in direct proportion to her anger with regard to any subject.

Being home late was definitely high on the list.

He turned and headed for the galley kitchen and tripped over a pair of shoes lying not as near to the coat closet as they should have been. He stumbled into the door with a thump and fought for balance, barely winning before he could tip over and likely crack his head on the baker's rack on his right.

The overhead light blared on.

"So, you're home," Laura Blackstone said from the bedroom door. "Great. There's food in the fridge. Eat it cold or heat it up, I don't care, but don't leave the goddamn oven on like last time."

It was you, you left the oven on the last time! He didn't say it, but he wanted to. She was always reversing things on him and then they'd fight. It really was better when he chose to not respond, even though it would also antagonize her. She recognized condescension even when it wasn't present, so he couldn't decide when to employ it or when to let things go. He let it go.

"Fine," he said. "Thanks." He thought he'd show some gratitude.

"Whatever." She was puffing a cigarette and that, in itself, rankled him. He hated the smell of smoke, and he believed she had taken up smoking again just to annoy him. "Working late every night this week?

When's it enough? I make dinner and you don't bother to call or text, let me know what you're doing. When are you going to be considerate of others? It's not all about you, no matter what your mother told you."

There she goes again.

But no, she just sighed with world weariness and turned, heading back to the bedroom and closing the hallway door behind her.

She probably let the silly TV show play in there while reading one of her disgusting religious coping books, trust in the Lord and He will walk with you, and so on.

Yeah, to Hell. That's where the old Lordy would walk with her.

Laura Blackstone had thrown in the towel. That was the way Professor Blackstone saw the situation they'd landed in after his *difficulties* had come to light and he'd lost his curatorship and the salary that had gone with it, and the money he'd made prior to that he had squandered on his own vices (and a few of Laura's, if there was full disclosure). The comedown had been hard, fast, and damn near close to public, though he had managed to salvage enough vestiges of his reputation to wheedle the professorship from a barely sympathetic colleague who had risen in the ranks to head the university's better-than-average Archaeology department. If it had been unfair that his problems had affected Laura, then it was also unfair that she would not let him forget it.

He shuffled to the kitchen and yanked open the fridge. Some kind of slop in an uncovered pot, stew maybe, was on the top shelf. He shuddered. It looked like congealed dog vomit. He pulled an IPA from a lower shelf, some questionable deli meat that he rolled into an untoasted slice of white bread, added a long squirt of yellow mustard, and sat alone at the kitchen table with his make-do dinner.

And a thousand dollars on the table in front of him. Ten crisp one-hundred dollar bills. Just to listen to the offer.

The offer.

He warred in his mind. To share the news—and the money—with Laura?

Or keep one, or both, to himself?

Old man Chambers was a funny fish, all right. Eccentric was a kind word, Blackstone figured as he munched the almost-sandwich and gulped down his beer. Certainly had plenty of money to splurge, buying experts when he needed them. But was the job secure enough for him to give up the safe prof's pay (and those goddamned essays and research papers)? Sure, Chambers was beyond loaded, but what if he changed his mind after a couple months, or didn't like Blackstone's work? What if he tossed him out on his ear, and then the university position was no longer available to him? What the hell would he do then?

Blackstone had no illusions. Writing the Chambers book would be a royal pain in the ass, but it certainly wasn't beyond his abilities. If anything, he'd be bored. Boredom with great pay is much better than excitement with low pay.

But then there were the mysterious panels Chambers had bragged about. He felt blood heating up his veins when he thought about it.

No touchee, not yet.

Now *there* might be a challenge worthy of his talents.

Blackstone chafed at the mere thought of getting his hands on those panels, secret though they might be.

He had little doubt the panels had been stolen from their own land, smuggled out in ranks of innocuously stenciled crates. This kind of arrangement, becoming someone's pet Egyptologist, had existed for over a hundred years. Usually it had been British wealthy colonialists and amateurs who sought out pet experts, but there was no reason to think Americans hadn't ever indulged their own vices. He shuddered to think how many artifacts sat in secret collections. Or, worse, how many golden artifacts had been melted and lost forever to greed and lust.

He chuckled. *My kind of game.*

He had requested time to ponder the offer, but he'd known as soon as he heard the figures involved and seen the two big libraries—and the panel vault—that he would accept. And then to come home to *this*.

He swallowed the last bite, gulped the last inch of beer, and tucked the bills into his pocket.

When he told Laura about his new position, and the pay, would she appreciate the newfound wealth it represented? Or would she mock him in her usual no-way-to-win approach?

Never mind.

Wait, wait. *Wait.* Chambers didn't want him to disclose any details. So why tell Laura the exact figures, the money he would suddenly find himself banking? Why tell her anything at all other than that he was done with teaching?

He started composing his resignation letter in his head.

No, better to make it a request for sabbatical. Or leave of absence due to family emergency. He might be grasping at a shiny lure, but that didn't mean he couldn't take some shears along to cut the line if needed. Chambers had offered a lot of gossamer promises, but there was no way to ensure any of them would come through.

And the last thing he wanted was to once again beg for a teaching job.

He would rather shoot himself—after shooting a select group of others.

Blackstone made his bed on the leather sofa, as he had many nights before.

His phone buzzed softly. Not his iPhone, his other phone. He rolled onto his side, pulled it from his pocket, and read the text.

Chapter Five

He awoke in bed.

Wait, wasn't I...on the couch?

As his thoughts coalesced, Blackstone realized that he should have been at home, sleeping on the sofa. He remembered throwing a blanket and pillow on the cool leather, stretching out, and sleeping. No, wait, not sleeping. He'd gotten a text.

His head felt like shredded cotton balls and he squinted, furrowed his brow, and tried to make out where he was. The bedroom was relatively bare, not cluttered like the master bedroom at his place, where Laura's clothes cascaded out of the closets like a talus slope out of a mine shaft. No, this bedroom was minimalistic and well-appointed, and slowly his memories of the rest of the night caught up to him. As did the inevitable tequila headache.

Shit, what did I do?

But by now he was starting to remember.

He'd gotten a text from Michelle, one of the grad students who worked for him in the department. She was grading the recent exam, and had texted a question expecting to find him still at the office where he'd been reading essays. Of course, he hadn't been there.

He texted a terse response, implying that his argument with Laura was approaching the last straw. Then she'd texted him a topless selfie in which she was licking her own right nipple with a wink and a smile. *Come over?*

He texted back, *Are U crazy?*

She texted a photo of her hand inside her panties, stretching them open. *Could be U.*

Now he remembered fully. He'd felt pressure in his groin, had sighed, and had gotten up, grabbing his coat and leaving the apartment as quietly as he could.

The streets had been still wet from the storm, but the thunder had retreated to where it was not so much a rumble but its long-distance echo. Trees dripped heavily as he headed for his car. They only had street parking for the apartment, and he'd managed a spot a half-block away after Chambers' guy—that strange, uh, Batten—had dropped him off at the university and he'd gotten his car. Now he started the six-year-old Camry and gave up the prime parking spot, steering through the late-night quiet neighborhood and the empty streets until he'd reached Michelle's place, a small Craftsman-style bungalow with red trim and window boxes and a back bedroom with a sex-swing.

She had opened the door wearing only black thong panties, served him tequila shots that he soon found himself lapping from the deep cleft of her navel, and eventually had climbed on him and rocked until his head spun, though with her nipples alternating in his mouth he'd forgotten to care.

Michelle.

His greatest find and his worst mistake.

One of the terms of his employment at the university, due to his faux pas, was to undergo counseling for his "sex and alcohol addiction." It was bullshit, but he'd gone along with it to appease the Board of Regents, and because he needed the job. There was nothing wrong with two consenting adults enjoying mutual pleasure, or with having a drink now and then (or now *and* then!). He'd gone to his sessions every week for over a year. Then he'd met Michelle.

She was the perfect combination of grad student and mistress, heavy emphasis on the mistress part. With enough kink to rev up his near-middle-age engine past its usual RPMs. They hadn't made it to the sex swing, but the center of her living room floor had sufficed as they sweated together through most of her various preferences, thereby hitting all of his. He thought he was highly sexual, but her appetites put his to shame. She'd played him like a prepared piano, with fingers, tongue, and *tools.*

Somewhere along the line, they'd ended up in her bed. He had no memory beyond that, not really. Only strobe-like images of more debauchery and tequila. There was an empty bottle in his sight line to confirm his memory. There might have been another on his side of the bed, and maybe one in the living room.

Michelle wasn't there, and he was glad. He'd be embarrassed by this current state of his.

He groaned.

Laura.

He held his head, willing it to stop throbbing.

He had to get home. His memory was returning deceptively fast, and he knew he had decisions to make. Some calls. He had to go to his office. God, his watch said he'd barely make his 11:00 am lecture, and then two office hours after that, and a mid-afternoon lecture.

Michelle opened the door. "You're up," she said. "Good morning, Professor." She advanced on him and even though he felt like the bottom of a shoe in an alley, when she reached under the sheet for him and found him, he realized he wasn't leaving yet. He groaned as she gripped his rising member in her red-tipped fingers...

Suddenly he was visualizing Alena Chambers holding him the same way, her own slender hand massaging him...

And he came all over Michelle's hand.

"Well," she said, making a frowny face, "*that's* a disappointment."

"Michelle, I have to leave!"

"Clearly, no reason for me to hold you back," she said acidly. Then she smiled, a bit of wickedness with her lips that usually got him going at least as much as her completely perfect ass and sundry other bits and pieces. "Come back later and we'll rectify the situation." She stripped the sheet off him and used it to wipe her hand clean.

"Maybe," he said. "Maybe. But I have a lecture soon, and Laura..."

"Hm, she doesn't deserve you. I do."

In the shower, washing off the grime of his drunken night's sex and alcohol session, he held his face in his hands. The Chambers offer was on his mind, but clearly his body was thinking of Alena Chambers, not Alton.

And the panels. There were panels too, and a huge paycheck. Slowly the realities of the last twelve hours came flooding back and he started to feel better. For the first time in, well, probably two years, he was facing a situation in which his worth had been recognized, and his skills were in demand. Laura would be happy too, and he did care about that. Didn't he?

For a moment, his brain slipped a dagger through his expanding ego. What if the whole offer was nonexistent? What if it was a giant prank? Would his colleagues go to the trouble to trick him into falling into a job that was too good to be true, because it wasn't true? What if they'd rented the window dressings and Alton Chambers was played by some unknown local has-been actor in need of a gig?

Had he fallen for an elaborate hoax?

Still wet from the shower, he sat on the cold toilet seat and fired up Google on his phone. No, the photographs of Alton Chambers, what he could find with a cursory and random search, all seemed to be of the man he had met. The compound was toured in one of those annoying slideshows. The grand foyer was there, as was the main library and some of the guest houses. There was a shot of a corner of the garage, merely teasing the cars stored there.

Only after he was finished scrolling did he realize that he had almost neglected to breathe.

It was real.

He dried and dressed in yesterday's clothes.

Michelle gave him a chaste peck on the cheek as he left, a surreal postscript to the night's definitely unchaste activities.

He made his lecture with three minutes to spare and winged it, dredging up as much of his dig stories and memories as he could, syllabus be damned. If his students noticed he was beat-up from a long night and straying from their prepared path, they didn't mention it. They were too busy staring surreptitiously at their phones or napping with their eyes open.

Blackstone himself stared at the clock through the lecture, then through office hours in which only one hapless student stopped by that he figured wouldn't last the term, and then he stared at the clock through the later lecture, which he blew by allowing his boredom to show.

By the end of all that, he had made his decision.

Laura was at home when he arrived hoping for a quiet early dinner and, perhaps, an announcement.

But she was on the warpath. "Where the hell did you go last night? Where were you all night long? Find another graduate student to pull you around by the dick? Did you get enough pussy?"

Her otherwise pretty face turned monster-ugly when she let herself rile to this level, and his silence only galled her. Seeing there would be no dinner, he set about making himself a sandwich. She kept egging him into an argument that he wasn't going to jump into, so her rage increased exponentially.

"I'm considering another job offer," he slid into a quiet moment between two of her verbal jabs. He was sitting in front of his untouched food. She was flying about on her broomstick.

"What, are you crazy? Who's going to hire you after what happened? Or are you considering that server's position down at the Hindu Garden?"

He wanted to smack her. It was so like her to fling arrows at him without even waiting for him to explain. He forced himself to stay calm. Under the table, his fingernails dug into the palm of his hand.

"I'm planning to go to work writing and...cataloging antiquities...for Alton Chambers," he said almost casually.

She paused between insults. "You mean *the* Alton Chambers? The oil guy? That billionaire asshole?"

"He's more than just oil. He's a philanthropist now." He wasn't sure that was true, but she wouldn't know. "He needs someone to ghostwrite his book, and to work on his Egyptian antiquities."

"And he asked *you?*" she said mockingly, as if it were the most ridiculous idea in the world. "He couldn't find anyone..."

"Anyone what? *Better?*" He decided to have his sandwich to settle his stomach, then call the Chambers estate. Batten had left him with a card. He took a tasteless bite. It would take a while to find the taste in food once again, after Laura.

What was he saying? Was he through with her then?

Yes.

She was chuckling wickedly, but a strange look had climbed into her eyes. "Yeah, better. How far down the list were you?"

She was clearly looking to antagonize him, bait him into a fight, but that look in her eyes also indicated that she was nervous. Perhaps he would leave her behind. He decided it was better to not engage with that possibility now.

"Listen, Laura," he began, trying to sound reasonable. "He sent a car for me last night. He showed me his library and his museum." He didn't mind embellishing. It was necessary with Laura, and he didn't want to get into particulars. "It's a job that might last a couple years or more, with excellent pay. You'll be amazed. We can move out of here and find a much better place, maybe a house. You always wanted your own green space..."

She was about to make a retort, he saw it in her eyes, then she pulled back. "Our own house?"

"Yes." He took a bite. Tasted almost like food now.

"How much? What kind of pay?"

This was it, the lynchpin. He couldn't tell her the figures Chambers had shared, but it had to sound better than his current wages.

He said, "Three times better than the university. With full benefits."

Her jaw dropped and she closed her mouth, caught flat-footed. "That's...that's very good."

"I know." Not too smugly.

"What's the catch?" she added, back to some wickedness.

"I'll have to spend a lot of time at the compound." Actually, he would most likely move in, but he didn't have to say so. And would he mind living apart from her?

"The *compound?*"

"It's a mansion and a bunch of guest houses. I'll have a place there, maybe spend weekends at home. Some nights. I need access to the Chambers libraries, the art and antiquities, and other resources."

"Like who?" she said, smiling crookedly and her eyes flashing suppressed rage. "You get a secretary? Bring your friendly grad student with you? What's in it for you? Other than some fine young ass?"

He tried to remain calm. "What's in it for *me*...is to be respected for my skills and knowledge again, and frankly, for all the mockery and disdain you toss at me daily, I would have thought you'd be happy to be better off without having me around all that much. Then you can shop to your heart's content and live the life of a kept woman."

His outburst surprised her speechless. In the moment, he took the advantage, tossed the remains of his food in the trash and the dish in the sink, then grabbed his coat and left the apartment, letting the door swing loosely in his wake, not giving her the satisfaction of a slam.

Chuckling, he headed for his office at the university.

The streets were wet again from some of the recent daily rains, but the fall temperature was milder. He parked in his usual staff spot. He hoped the *friendly* Michelle wasn't around. But she was, in the office down the hall from his (where he couldn't avoid it), and she stood up to intercept him as he tried to sidle past.

"Professor Blackstone!" Always formal first in case someone overheard. Then, quieter, "James!"

"Hello, Ms. Davenport," he said curtly, hoping he could get past her before anyone stepped into the hall.

Her face recoiled a bit, but recovered as she realized that he was just being cautious. At least he hoped that was what she thought. At the moment he had no interest in playing his usual games, locking his office door and bending her over the desk, diving between her buttocks while she encouraged him with all sorts of nasty talk. Finishing with her on her knees in front of him even as someone knocked on the door and he shushed her as she giggled around his erection...

What was he thinking? Usually that was *all* he'd had interest in doing. He enjoyed those games. He almost smiled then and waved her inside.

But he didn't. "I'm very busy right now, Ms. Davenport. I still have essays to read. Have you finished grading the exams?"

"Uh, no." Her eyes showed sudden hurt. "I have a few more to go."

"Time, Ms. Davenport. I need those done before I leave."

Now the look was cold, angry. "All right, I'll bring them..."

"Just put them in my mailbox, please. I can't be disturbed right now."

"Of course," she said stiffly. "I. Will. Do. That." Then she whirled and went to her own tiny office, her back ramrod straight and her steps like gunshots on the venerable marble floor.

He released his held breath, thankful no one had chanced upon that little scene. He regretted what he'd done to Michelle, but he could make it up to her later. Right now he had one important call to make and two less important calls. He felt the card he had slipped into his pocket earlier in the day, where it had almost caught on fire reminding him of its presence.

Damn it, he realized suddenly that it was evening and he was still wearing last night's clothes. Had Michelle noticed? Sure she had, she didn't miss a thing. Maybe he'd have to buy her a little gift to smooth things over. After all, Alena Chambers wasn't going to be available *all* the time. He chuckled.

He stepped into his office, almost expecting Batten to have beaten him to it and to be standing in the shadows over there, ready to scare him to death. But no, he was alone. He sat at his desk, cleared some space from the top, poured himself a tot to lubricate his throat, then fumbled with his phone. He tapped the screen and waited.

His life was about to change, and he felt a shiver of...expectation? Fear? Excitement?

Whatever it was, it disappeared when a stiff-sounding voice answered.

"Chambers estate."

Chapter Six

HE DROVE HIS car to the Chambers compound and immediately felt some level of embarrassment he couldn't shake after the gates swung open for him. The Camry was so out of place anywhere on the expansive concrete and gravel driveways, and finally parked on the slab in front of the cavernous garage's entrance, that he turned red as he slammed the screechy door and stepped away.

Batten let him into the great foyer with an air of displeasure, as if he'd come to the door with a sample case of household gadgets.

"Good day, Batten," Blackstone said as he entered, probably a bit too cheeky, but the driver, footman, valet, whatever the fuck he was, had really gotten under his skin with his superior attitude. Once Blackstone was employed by Chambers, they'd be equals, wouldn't they? Maybe that was the problem. He had to let the embarrassment wash off. There was greatness in his future, once he was given access to those panels.

"Mr. Chambers has the paperwork ready in the main study. Follow me, please."

Batten's back was ramrod straight and his pace military quick.

"Blackstone, there you are," said Chambers, all pseudo-British, *cheeri-o.*

They shook hands.

"I'm glad to take you aboard. I'm certain the work has met its match in you, Professor. Honored to have your expertise on the job. I assume you've checked over the papers, a rather standard employment contract except for the figures, which you must admit are better than average."

"Yes, sir, they are."

Chambers nodded, pleased. "Once you sign these forms in triplicate, and initial all the highlighted spots, I will sign as well, and here I have prepared a check for your first six months of employment as an advance of sorts. I expect you to spend a lot of time in the compound, and when you are here you will have room and board. If you'd like to bring your wife to weekly dinners, that can be arranged. If you prefer moving in entirely, I will send a truck to gather up whatever you need. Anything else will be provided. You'll be able to come and go as you please. Our security is top-notch, however, and you'll have to make sure you follow all our guidelines."

He paused.

Blackstone caught sight of the check. He kept himself from whistling in awe.

"Need a pen?" Chambers held one out.

"Shouldn't I sign in blood?"

Chambers stared at him a second, then guffawed loudly, a series of the *Ah!* barks Blackstone had already heard. He joined in and they ended in a long, companionable chuckle.

"Ink will do, Professor. Ink will do just fine."

"In that case then, it's my pleasure." When he handed the pen back, he was sure the old man noticed his clothing was from the day before. But he said nothing.

"When—"

"Feel free to take a couple days if you need to, then call Batten here and he'll set up any movers needed."

"Perfect."

The library door opened and Alena Chambers entered, a blinding vision in leather and silk and a multicolored scarf, with sparkling diamonds in her ears and on her fingers. He assumed she used her family name, but perhaps she'd been married.

"Sorry to interrupt," she said, seemingly not sorry at all. "Father, you're needed in the kitchen. There's something wrong with the delivery, and it's a different driver so they need you to sort it out."

Chambers made an apologetic gesture. "We're finished here anyway. Feel free to let yourself out, Blackstone." He held out his hand and they shook again.

"Nonsense," Alena said, forming a smile Blackstone couldn't take his eyes off, "I will let you out."

"As you wish." Chambers made his exit, leaving them in an awkward situation.

She took his arm and Blackstone was sure it tingled where her fingers encircled it gently.

"Please, come with me. But do you have to leave so soon?"

Was that a pout?

This woman was well into her forties, perhaps her early fifties, and yet she was ten times more alluring than either his wife or even Michelle the very kinky grad student. He'd never had a problem with older women, and in his late thirties now he remembered fondly a long line of them who'd been more mature. But none had been anything like Alena Chambers. She was like a cross between Morticia, or maybe Elvira the TV host, and some older porn star whose name escaped him. Jenna Jameson? Maybe that was the one, except with dark hair instead of blonde. Whoever she resembled, Alena's touch on his skin was electric.

"Well," he said, clearing his throat, "I have a lot to attend to now that I'm, uh, an employee."

"Don't be ridiculous," she said. "You're a guest."

"A paid guest."

"Nevertheless, no reason to put you on a different list. All Father's academic acquisitions have been guests first and employees second."

"As you wish," he said weakly.

"Very well then, why don't we have a drink? To celebrate."

"Um, fine, I know a place—"

She play-slapped his shoulder. "Silly! I mean right here. Why waste Father's very high-end booze on the old men he usually entertains? You're the youngest we've had here in a long while."

"All right," he muttered. Looking at her made up his mind. He could stand to look at her for a long time.

"Bourbon?" she asked. "I believe that was your choice?"

"Yes."

She poured him another of those hundred-dollar shots, give or take a twenty, then she poured absinthe for herself.

He wrinkled his nose. He abhorred it, but this was clearly the good stuff, imported and fully potent. She stopped at three fingers and brought the glass up to her lips, tilted it, and then poked at the green elixir with a pointed tongue.

"Cheers," he said, with a little shiver. He felt suddenly uncomfortable. He sipped; the smooth whiskey settled his stomach. Didn't do anything for his groin area.

"Cheers." She lapped the spirit like a cat then licked her lips. He smelled the anise and it made his head spin a little. Maybe her presence was making his head spin, or her glance over the rim of the glass.

They sat on the leather chairs and assessed each other. There was no other way for him to describe the session, as they sipped their drinks and appraised what each saw. He saw a highly attractive slightly older woman who gave off sexual vibes he could feel in his loins. He was adept at picking up such signals; his adeptness had led ultimately to the major scandal that had just about derailed his career. Of course, that was on top of several other indiscretions that had cost him much of his professional reputation even before the final straw, a particularly limber graduate student with advanced skills.

Now they surveyed each other like meals about to be devoured, checking each other's attraction through completely nonverbal means.

She had crossed one shapely leg over the other and the leather skirt was scandalously short and gave him a good view of a fair length of muscular thigh. Her heels were high without that stiletto look, but her feet were encased in sandal-like straps and her violet toenails added to his sensation.

"Mmmmm," she said, clearly referring to the absinthe.

Or was she?

He knew he looked rough right now, after a couple bad days, but he also had enough mirrors at home to know that he had a rakish Clooney-Pitt look with perhaps a hint of the young Clive Owen. That was to say, he knew he caught the attention of ladies who made appearances their first touchstone. Alena struck him as one. He smiled thinly.

"Yes, this bourbon is very nice." He didn't go as far as smacking his lips, but another sip for effect was in order.

"Well, we agree on the refreshments then," she said, her eyes sparkling. "There's something about the sense of *taste* that really...gets me going." She chuckled and lowered her eyes and batted her eyelids a little.

"I like the taste of good alcohol," he said, "and other fine things..."

"I agree."

The air between them felt charged and he almost expected his hair to stand up. But he hadn't showered in a while, so it was oily and stuck together in clumps. Thankfully he'd brushed its longer than average length back earlier.

He glanced around the library. "It must be something, living in a place like this. Having access to so many books, so much art, so much of everything."

"It has its moments. Usually it's boring as hell and I stay away for weeks at a time. I enjoy traveling, and staying here too long makes me feel a little too much like one of Father's artifacts."

He chuckled dutifully.

"I prefer a *faster* lane," she was saying. "I want to be kept young, and dancing—*all* kinds of dancing—helps keep me that way."

He wondered how metaphorically she intended the word *dancing*. The way her eyes were eating him up, unless he was imagining it, *dancing* might well be closer to what he and Michelle had done so energetically.

"Would you like to stay for dinner? I can have the staff add a setting without any trouble at all."

Blackstone truly did feel a tingle then. But he said, "Thank you, I'd love to take you up on that, but I really need to go home and to my office to determine what I'll need here. I'm sure your father wishes me to start as soon as possible."

She made another pouty face. "As you wish. You'll be here soon enough, and Father will expect you to have dinner with him most nights he's in town. And I believe he's planning a brief excursion to Egypt and one of our digs there, so make sure your passport is in order."

Blackstone wondered why Chambers had not mentioned an Egyptian trip. His blood sang through his veins. With Chambers' sponsorship, or perhaps the right *baksheesh*, he knew he could beat the ban.

"Sounds great," he said, aware that in her presence he tended to sound lame. "I'd better get going."

Almost as if on cue, the library doors opened and Blackstone turned, expecting to see old man Chambers, or the stealthy Batten.

Instead, the visitor made him almost do the famous double-take. He just barely caught himself.

The visitor was a carbon-copy or—for the sake of modern times—a clone of Alena Chambers, feature for feature, the dark eyes and full lips, the perfect shape encased in leather pants and suede tunic. The only exception was that while Alena's hair was lustrous salt-and-pepper, this woman's was lustrous pure black and longer, hanging halfway down her back. Her brows went up as she spotted Blackstone and Alena sitting with drinks, perhaps surprised to see anyone in the room.

"Professor Blackstone, this is my daughter Naira," said Alena with what seemed like just a hint of scorn. "Naira, Professor Blackstone is going to replace Dr. al-Amani."

"Uh, one of Grandfather's pet academics?" Naira shrugged, but her smile held barely any wattage. "Welcome, I guess. I'm sure I'll see you around."

Blackstone had stood as Alena introduced them and started to offer his hand, but after the summary greetings the Alena clone bypassed him on her way to a bookcase, where she started to scan titles.

Now Blackstone shrugged.

Alena stood. "Don't mind her," she said with a frown. "Kids these days, they don't know how good they have it. And their manners could use adjustment. My daughter's home from university at the moment."

Blackstone wondered, *In the middle of a term?*

He glanced surreptitiously at mother and daughter and registered that they were equally beautiful. The extra miles on the mother were barely discernible, such was her outstanding physical condition, but the daughter was every bit as stunning, with the added attraction of the youth that vibrated through her lush body and emanated around her like an aura.

Alena, Naira... At the moment, he would have had a difficult time choosing one as a partner. He realized with an inner chuckle that the best answer would have been *both of them*. Even from behind, Naira exuded a sexuality that almost stunned Blackstone—a man whose appreciation for such things had led him to numerous experiences, some of which should have made him blush.

"Well," he said, "it's a pleasure to meet you, Naira." There was no answer. He turned to her mother. "Thank you for the drink. I'll probably return tomorrow after settling some things at home and work. Your father said I could take several days..."

"Of course, of course," she said. "I'll show you out." She took his glass.

"No need," he said, but she shepherded him and he let her, especially after she took his elbow. His skin tingled where her fingers touched him. Despite the daughter's surprisingly fetching appearance, Blackstone was still quite taken with Alena Chambers.

"I guess I keep sweeping you out the door," she said, chuckling. She held the main portal open for him. "I really am more *welcoming* than this."

"I'm sure," he said. Their quick handshake was as charged as any previous connection, and then he was down the steps and walking the fairly long distance to where his piece of shit car was parked.

He was painfully aware that the thought of mother and daughter had given him an erection.

Chapter Seven

THE CALL TO his supervising colleague, Dr. Nathan Sanford, was amusing. Sanford was in the middle of a stint as chair of the department, a post he detested.

Blackstone wanted to hurl insults at the university, the ridiculous syllabus they'd foisted on him, the students, the faculty, the administration, and the goddamn parking lot, which was always full when he got there, forcing him to hike in like a man lost in the desert to reach the tiny oasis of his office.

"Wait, are you saying you're leaving? Just quitting your position in the middle of the semester?"

"That's right, Nathan. I'm accepting another position and I don't have time to give notice."

"What about your classes?"

"Perhaps you can get Gulshan to fill in..." *You can ask her while she's blowing you under the desk.* "Or maybe Thorpe, he's always looking for extra work..." *Or chairman ass to plant his mouth on.*

"But, but... James, this is not a very good professional move. I mean, if it's about your salary, I think I could—"

"Find an extra hundred a month? Just keep it, use it on the grad student party. In fact, Michelle Davenport could easily replace me in my classes. She's adept at many different subjects and she knows the syllabus and my every move..."

"I'm very disappointed—"

"I'll come for the books in my office, which as you know are pretty much all my own. Or send for them, either way."

"James, is there anything I can say, or do..."

Blackstone almost relented then. Nathan Sanford had been a good friend when he needed one most, and there had been no others. Certainly no one else who had actually helped him.

No, this is too good. I can't pass it up.

"I'm sorry, Nathan, my mind is made up." He paused. "Thanks and goodbye."

He clicked off and sat back in his seat. He looked at his watch, then checked the browser on his phone. Too late tonight.

He headed home, where he found Laura ensconced in the bathroom, probably in the tub.

An image of her in there, her wrists bloody and the water a deep crimson, appeared in his head, but he shook it off even though he would like to have lingered over it. Laura was too mean to kill herself—she'd kill *him* with hardly a wince, but not herself.

Quietly he packed a second bag, a well-traveled leather valise. He still had a go-bag from the very last dig he'd led (this one a lower-echelon Indian site near a backwater Wisconsin village, not the Egyptian one he'd badly wanted). Laura was still in the bathroom when he finished, so he plucked a dozen books from a bookcase and stuffed a briefcase too. He'd decided he wasn't up for a scene, so he was heading to a motel located midway between home and his office. Tomorrow he would begin moving his necessary office books, and he could shop for clothes if he needed to.

He let himself out and drove to the Holiday Inn Express, where the staff knew him from an occasional stay—recently a particularly athletic few with Michelle—and the clean room allowed him to clear his mind. He showered and dressed in fresh clothes, feeling almost human enough to venture out. He stared at the advance check after smoothing it out and placing it carefully on the desk, where he could stare at it for a while.

A bit later, Blackstone put the check in the room safe, then took his keycard and headed for his office again. It was now too late in the day for the notoriously early bird Nathan to be lurking the halls, and he needed to check on the books he wanted moved, perhaps boxing them if he could find a box or two. He hoped Michelle would have headed home too.

The old building had somehow missed the campus-wide renovation projects that had sucked up all the money, so it remained a Gothic old hulk with darkened portions of hallways and occasional blinking hall lights, doors and staircases to nowhere, and rooms piled with dusty ancient furniture that had been picked over and abandoned due to its advanced state of decay.

Like my career, Blackstone mused. At least until now.

There was no lightning blasting through the tall windows that lined the long corridors on his floor, though the sky outside seemed pregnant with rain again. He was secretly glad the mysterious manservant Batten wasn't lurking about, his cadaverous form casting frightening shadows to and fro.

Blackstone shivered. It was almost as if Batten *was* lurking about. His own footsteps echoed on the chipped marble floor. He looked around to make sure there wasn't a second echo, signaling an intruder.

Then he shook his head and chuckled.

Bit jumpy, eh?

He thought of his newfound money and career change and his fingers tingled at the thought, though he hadn't yet ironed out his plans.

He stuck the key into his office door.

"Well, hello again, *Professor* Blackstone..."

He nearly leaped from his shoes. The voice behind him had come from nowhere, for Michelle had not been in the hall seconds ago. How had she done that?

He turned, trying to wipe the surprised and startled look from his face, and his breath hitched in his throat.

Michelle Davenport was luscious, there was no denying it. Her features were classically beautiful, with just enough wickedness symbolized by the peeking tattoo on her neck and the diamond stud in her nose. She made his pulse race whenever he looked at her.

But what was she still doing here now?

"Come in," he said. He held the door for her and she sashayed inside, moved a stack of papers off a chair, and sat. He closed the door only halfway, a symbol of his lack of intent. "I'm sorry about earlier, Michelle..." He steeled himself for her wrath.

"It's all right," she said, waving off his apology. "I didn't realize you were going to quit!" Her eyes were open wide in some kind of awe.

"Something came along, something better," he said, starting to explain. "But how did you find out so quickly?"

She looked around and whispered, "Sanford stuck his head out of the office and called for Gulshan. Sounded serious. I was in the department office picking up my mail..."

"Which is right next to their offices, so you overheard everything."

"Let's say his voice carried more than usual. He was pretty mad. Called you ungrateful. A few less charitable names."

"Then what? Did Gulshan say anything?" Despite not caring, his curiosity was up.

"That old bag? Not to me. But I heard them yelling a little. And then there was no sound at all for a while. Then they laughed and Gulshan came out of there rubbing a spot on her blouse." Michelle cocked her head and made innocent-face. "She got all red when she saw me and dived into her office. What do you *think* that means?" Eyebrow raised, it made him smile.

So he'd been right, Nathan had been dipping his quill in the department administration inkwell after all. Bitterly he mulled over the fact that he'd lost nearly everything, but while others were also flying too close to the sun their wings were holding up just fine. He shivered at the thought of Gulshan's thin lips wrapped around his penis though. *That* was an image he'd like to unsee. *Maybe she's good at it,* he mused.

"Gulshan emailed me, said she's taking over your classes as of tomorrow," Michelle added. "I'm gonna hate working for that old battle-axe."

"She's not that old," he said absently.

"That's what makes her looks all the more tragic."

She leaned forward and put her elbows on his crowded desk, her perfect chin cupped in her hands. She fluttered her eyelashes. "You can't leave me here, James. *Please.*"

He'd been about to let her down easy, but then he changed his mind. "First of all, I'm not leaving the country, I'll still be around. And I still want to know what's going on in the department—you can be my eyes and ears."

"But I'd rather be your—"

"There might be a place for you with my new employer," he said quickly. He gave her a very concise outline of his new position. "And I think I can probably talk Chambers into hiring my brilliant assistant. So there, you see, I'm not abandoning you."

"Oh, James," she said, "that's so sweet. But he's going to have to pay me really well to live on that Waco compound of his."

"I'm sure all this can be worked out, Michelle." He glanced at his watch. He adored watches and couldn't abide by all those men who gave up classic timepieces for an idiotic app on their phones. "It's almost late. Can you help me round up a few boxes, pack up some books, and maybe have dinner?"

It was liberating. For once he didn't care what Laura would say or do. He wasn't heading home after dinner anyway, and she could rage around the old place all by herself. She'd think about what he had said, about his newly found pay and benefits, and she'd quiet herself down and long for him. Maybe he'd let her sweat a little, but he knew how he could keep her placated. Meanwhile, here was Michelle, staring at him with a smile breaking out on her model's lips...

"Will you tell me more about the Chambers estate? And what exactly he's having you work on?"

"I'll see," he said mysteriously. "Is that all you want to do?"

Now her eyes were sparkling. "Depends on dinner. Street tacos or a sit-down?"

In the end, he spent money that only yesterday he would have had to save. After loading some boxed books in his car, they had dinner at a popular steakhouse where the bill for two would have fed six average people. But he wasn't average anymore, was he?

By the time they finished dinner, Michelle had already put a hand down his pants under the table, giggling when someone seated nearby glared at them.

Soon she was riding him as he sat on Holiday Inn's uncomfortable desk chair, her hair in his fist as she pounded into him until they ran into the desk and stopped, laughing, and she turned her body around without letting go of him, and then they were finishing facing each other, nearly falling out of the chair. When her final sigh was finished, she asked him for a cigarette.

"It's a non-smoking room. You know I don't smoke. I want to live as long as possible."

She said, "Me, I want to go out with a bang." She giggled. "You know what I mean! Anyway, if I go young I'll leave a good-looking corpse. Wouldn't I, James?"

"I'd rather you didn't die young." He tweaked a tender nipple. Not the one that was pierced.

She said, "Everybody's going to die, and everybody's going to die of something."

"Why the obsession with death?" he asked as she snuggled her face on his shoulder. The chair creaked.

"You're kidding," she said. "You're an Egyptologist—a damn good one!—and you're accusing *me* of being obsessed with death?"

She had a point.

"I like the *little death*," he said.

"Oh, me too," she replied, reaching down for him. "What's *he* think, is it time for another one?"

"I think we can both manage."

The chair barely survived.

Chapter Eight

HE PULLED THE shiny pewter Aston Martin Vantage to the curb in front of their building, miraculously getting a VIP parking space, and caught his wife just as she was entering the front door with grocery bags in hand.

He was amused. At first Laura glared at the sleek interloper, then realized who was driving it and her jaw dropped visibly.

"What the hell...?"

Pushing the button, the engine shut down with one last growl. He climbed out of the low, wide sports car.

"Hello, Laura."

"I can't believe this is the first thing you do when money comes your way," she snapped, her face a mask of disgust behind the grocery bags. She was crushing them to her torso, hands whitening as she squeezed.

Blackstone ignored the signs. "Chambers gave me the use of this company car," he lied. "It's not costing me anything. But I did put down a deposit on that new Mustang you were drooling over," he said. "All you have to do is go and sign on the line." He grinned. "Chambers said we should afford to upgrade a few areas. You know these rich assholes and their image..."

She turned away with a swift motion and let herself into the front hall, and the door slammed behind her.

That hadn't gone well.

He'd thought he could exploit her greed and jealousy, using the new Mustang as bait, but maybe she was going to play hardball. He stepped into the hall, slid an envelope with her new car papers into their mailbox, and was climbing back into the Vantage within minutes.

Let her be a bitch. He had other things to do.

He plucked out his phone and called the compound. That damnable Batten, the ubiquitous manservant and henchman, picked up. "Chambers estate."

"It's Blackstone," he said. There was no response. *Bastard.* "Please let Mr. Chambers know that I'll be happy to come for dinner. Ms. Alena invited me," he added.

"Very well, sir," Batten said as if it wasn't. "I shall tell them."

Click.

He made sure the connection was cut. "*Fucker.*"

Pressed the starter button and savored the car's purr.

Michelle would like the car very much. He imagined her face down near his groin as he shifted gears on the freeway. After last night, he could put *automobile head* on the agenda.

Damned Laura. He would wait a few months, then he would find a way to shed her as easily as he'd shed the crappy teaching job, the style-less clothes, and the piece-of-shit wheels.

He squealed away.

His mind's eye replaced Michelle's face with Alena's. And then the granddaughter's.

Naira?

An exotic beauty if ever he'd seen one. That was more like it.

Life was looking up.

He left the car on one of the empty slabs in front of the super-sized Chambers garage. At least now it fit in with the fantasy-car collection within.

Batten let him in, his face set in what might have been a smirk.

"Good evening, Batten," Blackstone said with a nod.

"Yes, it was."

Asshole.

He was led to the library, where Alton Chambers waited. He stood at the tall window, staring outside as if there was a desert vista out there. At least, that's how it looked to Blackstone, who made a mental note to use the image in the book. Although, would it work in an autobiography?

"Dr. Blackstone," Chambers said by way of a welcome as he turned. "A small aperitif, perhaps?"

"Thanks, Campari with rocks."

"Ah, so European." Chambers smiled as he glided to the bar and poured the deep red elixir into a tumbler and dropped in two large ice cubes. "Soda water splash?"

"No, thanks. I've spent time there."

"Of course. Your digs in Egypt were punctuated by long spells in the, ah, more exciting European cities."

Blackstone grinned. "Sand gets into everything. You need time to shed the desert."

"And you were on an expense account."

Blackstone's smile faded. Chambers had done more than his homework. His wrist-slapping for overages on the old department credit card had been hushed-up. Or so he had thought.

"I wasn't particularly more of a spendthrift than most of my colleagues." He took the glass but kept himself from sipping. The bittersweet Campari was likely to taste off after the veiled accusation.

Chambers waved a gnarled, liver-spotted hand. "Water under the bridge, I'm sure. Your predecessor in this job had absconded with half his department's funds and used it for his own dig. You are hardly unique. Funding is hard to come by. Accounting has to become, er, creative. I see it as ambition and enterprise. Resourcefulness. In my employ, I make sure you have all the funding you need."

Blackstone relaxed. He sipped the Campari and nodded. "Everyone fights over the scraps these days. Universities aren't as fluid as they once were."

"Indeed." The old man looked up as Batten opened the door. "Shall we? Dinner."

He was led down the corridor to a huge dining room. On the way he registered at least a half-dozen artifacts he was certain were solid gold.

A fortune.

All probably stolen.

He forgot about the artifacts when he surveyed the long and richly appointed table and saw that both Alena and her daughter Naira were waiting, wine glasses in their slender hands.

"There they are," Alena said, smiling. She held up her glass. "We've a head start."

Did she put a little emphasis on the word *head?*

He was clearly fantasizing.

Naira giggled and the two women sipped their red wine. Perhaps it was some kind of ritual in-joke.

Blackstone tried to chase the surprise from his face. He'd expected Naira—due to her youth—would have had other things to do. This would be painful; he would have to pinch himself in order to listen to his host.

"Please, sit." Chambers held a chair out for him, across from the mother and daughter. He sat at the head of the table, between the other three.

Blackstone concentrated on his aperitif, trying to avoid staring at the women across from him. The pleasantly bitter drink settled down his stomach, which had been fluttering.

"Welcome to our home," Chambers said, his gravelly tone grating when compared to the gracious words.

"Thank you."

"Professor Blackstone," Alena said, "are you planning to move in while you do your work for Father?" She gazed at him over the rim of her glass.

"Please, call me James," he said. "I guess I will move in at least part of the time... I don't really know yet..."

Chambers interjected, "James, we haven't talked about it yet. I have a suite for you here in this house, or a guest house on the grounds. The suite is essentially an apartment with a full bathroom and kitchen. The house is larger, with three bedrooms and three baths. Your choice. Batten can show you."

"I'll take the suite," Blackstone said after a moment. "I'll be closer to the work. I work crazy hours, not a normal schedule at all."

"A night owl, are you?" said Alena.

"Or do you party long into the night and call it work?"

The granddaughter's a smarty-pants, he thought. "It's *work* late. I get a second wind after a good nap and I can work all night."

"Hm," said Alena, but swallowed the rest of her thought with a slug of wine.

"I bet," Naira said, smirking.

This is some mother and daughter act.

"Grandfather," Naira said, turning abruptly, "are we going to Egypt now that Prof–James, I mean–has come to work for you?" Her limpid eyes expanded, and for a moment she looked like a little girl.

"Possibly next year, after my work in Washington is underway," Chambers said as he took the first platter that the staff had carried in and placed on the table. "First priority is we will work on my special research, and then I hope we can make some progress on the book. If both those things are well on their way, then yes, we will visit the digs." He took spiced meat onto his plate and turned toward Blackstone, passing the dish. "We have two on-going now. One is in the Valley of the Queens, and the other is...in a secret location while we determine exactly what it is we've found."

Blackstone took a small amount of meat and passed the platter. It sounded as though, like a business with two sets of books, Chambers had an officially sanctioned dig and a concurrent, undercover dig facilitated by greased local magistrates and officials. He'd heard of the technique. It required endless funds to pull off. The Chambers family was awash in oil money, so *that* was a given.

Both women passed on the meat.

"You'll expect me to accompany you?" He took another platter, this a vegetarian spread in a fragrant sauce. He spooned it liberally onto his plate and passed it on. He noticed both women also preferred this to the meat. He repeated the process with a grain pudding or salad, he couldn't tell. He wasn't all that much into food other than for fuel, but he remembered he had eaten like this when he had been on his own digs, with locals running the camp kitchen and the larder.

"You'll be welcome to come along, of course. With your expertise, you'll be the senior academic and we're likely to benefit from your presence. Extra pay, of course. Not a *per diem*, but a company salary for the trip's duration."

Blackstone's head was almost spinning at the thought of how rich he could get, working for Chambers. The dude was eccentric, but his money was by no means tainted by eccentricity.

Alena filled his wine glass and then Chambers was passing more platters, eventually leading to sweet desserts made from spiced, gooey dates and other Egyptian delicacies including a more than passable *basbousa* and the best *kanafa* Blackstone had ever had outside of Alexandria. When he tasted the *Umm Ali*, a hot raisin cake bathed in the traditional milk, he became convinced that Chambers had hired Egyptians to cook for him.

Blackstone lost himself in the sweets, an obsession few were aware he had, and in this household they seemed endless. There was rice pudding, and *kahk,* and a *baklava* better than any he had ever had. The sugar and honey and sweet dates and raisins went to his head. The wine Alena had selected paired well with the desserts, and soon they were onto a second and then a third bottle.

Blackstone noticed that Chambers ate sparingly but across the wide spectrum of foods, and he drank mostly water. Alena happily imbibed as much of the wine as she could, and somehow the number of empty bottles a silent staffer removed from the table became as much of a blur as the conversation.

Blackstone felt his head growing thick. If he'd been walking, he would have staggered. If he'd been talking, he would have slurred.

Suddenly he realized he *was* slurring his words.

Chambers stood and bade them good night, somehow disappearing from sight without Blackstone noticing exactly when. Soon after, Naira claimed her traveling had exhausted her. She edged away from the table, eyeing her mother and smiling crookedly at Blackstone, whose vision was wobbly at best.

Batten stood at the door and frowned as Alena finished pouring yet another bottle into their glasses.

"What's wrong, Batten?" she said sharply.

To Blackstone's ears, her voice was almost a buzz.

"Madam, your father has requested that I show Professor Blackstone his suite." The disdain when he said *professor* was obvious even to Blackstone's fuzzy ears.

"Well, Batten, I am quite capable of showing him the suite. It's in my wing," she added, turning to Blackstone with a tiny smile.

"Ah," he said in response, not trusting his tongue.

"Very well, madam, I will leave it to you and retire then." He pulled the doors closed quietly.

She put a finger across her lips for a minute. Then: "I wish he *would* retire, the stodgy old buzzard," she said conspiratorially, succumbing to a case of the giggles immediately after.

They finished their wine. And soon another bottle that Alena found among the table debris. The staff hovered, waiting to clear the platters and dishes. Finally, Blackstone couldn't stand it.

"I'm afraid I need to use a restroom," he whispered hoarsely.

Alena chuckled. "Down the hall to the right. Like the song." She dissolved into laughter.

He was vaguely aware of what she was talking about, but his bladder was too insistent for drunken cleverness.

When he returned, she was waiting for him outside the dining room. The staff was finally able to clear the dinner debris. She was still holding a half-bottle of wine and their glasses. She raised her right eyebrow and held up the bottle.

He nodded and she filled it, then hers, then handed the empty bottle to a harried kitchen staffer, who studiously avoided looking at either of them.

They drank standing there. Blackstone's legs felt as unsteady as when balancing on a ship's deck. "I think I should find that suite," he said apologetically.

Alena led him out into the foyer and down a side corridor, where they stepped into a small but plush elevator to the second floor. "This is the east wing. I'm just down the hall from you."

He shrugged, filing away that bit of knowledge.

They walked down the carpeted corridor which reminded him of a fancy hotel. Art was ubiquitous here, too, but had been selected with an eye toward eclecticism. There was some of the obligatory Art Deco, but that was the extent of the Egyptian influence.

She opened the wide door and led him inside, where a light went on automatically and revealed a well-appointed living room furnished in exotic woods and leather. Presumably the room led to bedrooms and a kitchen for a total of twice as much space as his own apartment.

He pushed the door shut and when he turned Alena was standing there with her face only inches from his. Startled, he backed up against the door.

Alena leaned forward and kissed him, her red lips surprisingly soft and supple. Before he knew it, they were staring into each other's eyes. Their mouths opened and Alena leaned into Blackstone heavily.

When they separated, breathless, he stuttered: "Uh, Ms. Chambers... Alena, uh, that's not a very good—"

"Shhhhh," she said, placing a finger on his lips and wiping off some of her bold lipstick. "There's no one within the length of a half-mile. You might as well allow yourself to relax."

She leaned on him, more gently this time, and their lips met again. Blackstone inhaled deeply of her scent and when her tongue sought out his, he felt his passion rising despite the wine and the haziness he'd felt since dinner. They remained clasped, their mouths busy, their bodies fused together.

"Surely, Professor, you are acquainted with the story of Isis and Osiris," Alena said. Suddenly she was on her knees in front of him, her hand tracing the hardness of his cock under his pants.

"Uh," he said nonsensically and leaned his head on the door itself. His hands found the top of her head and the silk of her hair went easily through his combing fingers. "*Alena...*"

"You see," Alena cooed, "once upon a time, Set murdered his brother, Osiris, chopping him into tiny pieces and scattering them to the four corners of the Earth. Osiris's sister, who also happened to be his wife, went around collecting all the pieces of her lover, and reassembled him so she could bring him back to life. Unfortunately, she couldn't find one *very* important piece..." She squeezed Blackstone's erection for emphasis, eliciting a groan from him. "So she molded a new one out of clay..." Now she rubbed him more fervently, imitating the mythical work of Isis. "And then she blew life into him, and so performed the world's first blowjob."

Before he could comment, she placed her mouth on his twitching flesh where it was corralled by the single tightly-woven wool layer.

Her hands were there now along with her lips, and she shifted him gently under his clothes and put pressure on him also with some very effective caressing.

Blackstone couldn't very well stop her, so he patted her head again and prepared himself for what he'd been fantasizing about all day.

Then the pressure suddenly decreased and her hands and lips were off his rock-hard flesh and she was standing again, her mouth stretched in a mocking smile.

"Welcome home, Mr. Professor," she said in a fair Marilyn. She fluttered her eyelashes. "It's not your birthday. Yet."

She swept past him, opened the door a crack, and let herself out. He heard her laughter fading as she disappeared down the hallway. He closed the door.

He glanced at himself and saw that she'd left a perfect dark crimson ring on his light blue trousers.

"*Bitch.*"

He stumbled through the luxurious suite, found the master bedroom, used the huge attached bathroom, then stripped and fell into the king-sized bed.

Damn, that is one sexy woman. He rolled over and wistfully thought about what might have been. He thought about relieving his condition, but strangely he enjoyed the pressure and decided he was too drunk.

There's always tomorrow...

Right then his head pounded as the wine seemed to seep into the veins that threaded through his brain.

He rolled and tossed sheets and blankets to the floor as if angrily casting nets from a leaky boat.

His dreams were peopled by bird-headed entities and expanses of sand dotted with half-buried temples. The sand was red with blood. His hands and feet were encased in sticky red clumps.

The autumn sun cast a weak beam across his face. His eyes twitched open painfully. His head immediately commenced throbbing.

Muddled thoughts took a few moments to clarify.

The Chambers estate. *My new home?*

His eyes were shocked open when he realized the window had been covered by the silky draperies last night.

And the suit he had tossed all over the floor was now hanging—pressed?---—and presumably clean on an old-fashioned gentleman's valet stand across the room, one which had definitely not been there last night.

His leather valise, which he had left in the car, was sitting on a hotel-style luggage rack next to the full-size desk.

Sitting in his underwear on the destroyed bedclothes, paranoia gripped him. Someone had entered the room while he slept and walked around. In fact, they'd been in there twice. Or more. The suit, the stand, the valise. The drapery...

He groaned as he rocked himself off the bed and staggered slightly to the door. There was a lock on it, and he would be damn sure to use it from now on.

As he stood at the door, medium-loud rapping on it startled him.

"Yes?" he said, his voice a bit of a croak. His mouth tasted like wet barroom sawdust.

"Breakfast, sir. Twenty minutes." It was Batten. *Always Batten.*

Was he the midnight visitor? Had he stood and stared at Blackstone as he slept fitfully, only barely clothed, his bedclothes scattered to the wind?

The fine hair on his neck stood up. He kept the sudden rage out of his voice as well as he could.

"Twenty minutes, got it."

"Very good, sir."

Blackstone extended his middle finger at the door. Somehow the gesture cheered him.

The hangover did not.

He swallowed three aspirin from his overnight kit, then stood at the massively tall windows that lined one side of his bedroom. A thick grove of pines and colorful maples with a swathe of open grass was visible across his field of vision. He was in his briefs and felt a chill coming from the radiator under the window. He scratched himself absently while gazing at the gray sky.

A flash of movement caught his attention. It was Naira, astride a chestnut mare, her long hair streaming behind her as she rode at a gallop across the screen of his window. She was wearing tight white jodhpurs, knee-high black riding boots...and apparently only a black sports bra covering barely a portion of her toned torso.

Blackstone eyed the erotic vision hungrily, remembering last night's boozy interlude *interruptus*. Then he watched as she steered the horse onto a path through the tree line and disappeared into the woods.

Disappointed, he turned away and set about exploring his new digs. The shower alone was as large as his old apartment's whole bathroom. He took care of his *problem* under the hot spray, but it was barely satisfying though mother and daughter both made appearances.

Twenty-three minutes later, showered and wearing casual khakis and a navy light wool pullover from his valise, he entered the dining room.

The conversation between Chambers and his daughter stopped and they looked up.

"Here he is now," Chambers said. "Seat yourself, Professor. There's fresh fruit, and platters of Western-style fare—eggs, sausage, potatoes. I only make the cooks prepare Egyptian dishes for dinner."

"And a whole lot of lunches," Alena added. She turned to Blackstone. "Were your ears ringing?"

"My whole head is ringing," he said, sitting across from her. The lustrous salt and pepper hair was a cascade on one side of her face. She looked as fresh as if she'd slept the whole night. He knew how rough he looked in contrast. "What was in that wine?"

"Honey. It's an old Egyptian formula. The honey goes right to your head. Tastes good going down...but not so good coming back."

He was noncommittal. How did she mean *going down*? Was she toying with him again?

Something touched his foot under the table. He hadn't seen any pets, so he looked straight into Alena's eyes and saw the humor there.

His smirk told her all he needed to.

Chambers was asking him about moving his things into the suite.

"I only need a few changes of clothes as well as my books and my dig journals. I plan to take notes on all the work as I used to, when I...when I worked in the field."

"Very well, but the notes can't leave the compound."

Blackstone agreed. "When can I see the tomb?"

Was he childishly over-eager?

"All in good time," the old man responded. "First will be a few photographs of wall panels. I'd like to compare your translations to those of your predecessor."

"A test?"

"Of sorts. Now eat. I've a feeling it will be a busy day."

Blackstone dug into the food. That and the aspirin he had swallowed soon chased most of the hangover away. Too late he realized he could have had a screwdriver or a Bloody Mary. Many had been the time one of those resurrectors had brought him back from the dead, so to speak. Now he was too embarrassed to ask. He filled a plate from the family-style spread in front of him, loading up on protein and its best friend, grease.

He looked up and saw Alena watching him with a faint smile. He remembered how close she had been to him not so long ago, and he felt himself responding. And she knew it. He could spot it in the way she curled one eyebrow up only a fraction of an inch, but it might as well have been a mile.

He felt like agitating. "I saw your daughter out riding this morning."

"I bet the little tramp wasn't wearing much," muttered her mother.

"She was—er, she looked just fine."

"I'll bet," she said, and looked away. "Keep your eyes peeled, you might see her riding nude. A nutcase Godiva."

"Huh," he grunted. Damn it, he knew that now he would indeed stare out that window every chance he got. He chuckled and filled his mouth with food. Full, it couldn't get him into some kind of trouble.

For his part, Chambers was silent, occupied with the meal.

Blackstone wondered what he was missing. Would this job include outrageous levels of drama? Well, the pay should alleviate his feelings regarding any inconvenient facts. Like in the rest of the world, what right did he have to expect facts to hold up here in this closed family ecosystem?

He put his head down and finished his food, then helped himself to fresh fruit and a dark and sweet Egyptian coffee that brought him right back to Cairo.

They had finished, just waiting for the staff to arrive, when Chambers started to spin a story from his youth.

"Hold that thought, sir," Blackstone said. "We'll need that anecdote in the book and I don't have my notebook."

Chambers shrugged.

Just then, the door was jerked open and a wide-armed dust devil swirled into the room.

"Good morning, Grandfather!" said Naira as she swept over the table. She glanced at him. "Professor Blackman..."

"Uh, it's Blackstone, dear..."

"*Mother!* I'm sure he can speak."

Alena turned to him. "My daughter the queen has arrived apparently, James."

"Do you hear how she talks to me, *James?*" Naira pouted through the process of shoveling eggs and bacon from a platter onto her dish. Followed by a single large grape. Then she gulped from a huge glass of orange juice, setting it aside half-drained.

Before Alena could take the bait and say anything, Naira jumped back in. "Oh, I'll bet you tried your patented oral argument. Works every time, doesn't it, Mother?" Naira turned to Blackstone and smirked, then gave him a secret smile and an eye roll.

She was still wearing her form-fitting jodhpurs and boots. But for the sake of modesty she had thrown a silk blouse over the black sports bra, which was still visible under the white material. She had carried in with her a pleasant, downright erotic blend of clean sweat, skin cream, and horse leather, with maybe a note of subtle cologne, and Blackstone sat back a little and tilted his head so he could examine her surreptitiously. She was a clone of her mother, though her hair exhibited no salt yet, and she was just perhaps a little slimmer and slightly taller, her face basically a carbon copy except her lower lip was fuller. Secretly he admired them both without rotating his head.

Yes, they were both creatures of fantasy.

And now they were bickering in a sort of bad *Dynasty* parody. Naira popped the grape into her mouth and pushed away the rest of her untouched plate. Chambers turned to Blackstone. "They're lost to us now, James. Please follow me and I'll start your employment with some small revelations."

Reluctantly, Blackstone gave the women a slightly mocking salute, with a shrug as if to say, *I have no choice, have to go.* They didn't seem to care as they pecked at each other with well-practiced vitriol.

The men headed for the library in silence, and through the secret bookcase entrance Chambers had shown Blackstone. "I'll leave it unlocked for your use," he had told the professor. "Always make sure you lock it on your way out." Now Blackstone followed as Chambers entered the large inner study, past the library table and the computer monitor array table, and strode up to the vault. He called forth some kind of scanner lens from inside a sleek box and stared into it until it recognized his retina. Seconds later, the huge vault door hissed open. It was at least a foot thick.

"Your first look, Blackstone. I was going to wait but... I've changed my mind. Wait here."

Chambers was gone for a minute or two and Blackstone heard a metal drawer being pulled out, then closed. When the old billionaire stepped out of the vault, he held out a large professional-quality color photograph.

Blackstone took it and stared at its subject, a portion of wall panel with its clear hieroglyphs arranged in tight horizontal lines. His lips moved silently as he translated, though some glyphs were new to him and therefore he had no words for them.

But there was something else he wasn't used to seeing.

There was one cartouche that identified the person who occupied the tomb. Whether a pharaoh, high priest, wealthy merchant, or some other individual of high station—enough to deserve an elaborate tomb with such wall carvings—the cartouche should have enclosed the glyphs that would identify him. It had at one time, but the glyphs had been painstakingly chiseled off until they were illegible.

"It's as if they wanted to strike his name from history," he said to Chambers. "Perhaps a wealthy man who was also a criminal? Or a rogue pharaoh, one we've never heard of?"

Excitement was rising in his gut. This could be a huge find. An incredible story.

If he were allowed to tell it someday.

Chambers was noncommittal. "I'm not as interested in the name as I am in translating the rest of the panels. This one is rather simple, as you can see. I can read most glyphs—taught myself over the years. But there are others that are completely unintelligible, glyphs no one's seen before. I have had other scholars attempt, but none have cracked the code. I have also kept a close eye on research being done all over the world, even by less than prominent scholars. There doesn't seem to be a Rosetta Stone for this one singular tomb."

"And you expect me to somehow manage to do it?"

"Blackstone, you're one of the best. A criminally unsung talent. Your books are prominent in my library. If I'd found you sooner, I wouldn't have bothered with the others. Unfortunately, your...er...difficulties...kept you from my view until recently."

Blackstone felt his cheeks warming.

"Yes, my *difficulties* were unfortunate." He wondered how Chambers had heard of him and his work. His *real* work, not the shenanigans.

The old man waved his hand dismissively. "I don't care who you screwed, where, or how! All I care about is this translation." He added, "And the book, of course. But if you can translate the portions of the wall panels that interest me especially, you will have achieved greatness. And you will be rewarded handsomely for it."

"May I?" Blackstone gestured and Chambers concurred, so he took the photograph to an elaborately carved side table and slid it under the lamp. His finger traced the glyphs as he mentally made note of what the familiar symbols meant, but the gaps—where the glyphs were unknown—piled up, and by the end of the passage he concluded that he could only hint at the content.

"It seems to indicate the tomb's resident was greatly feared by his house staff, but that's no surprise. It doesn't refer to him as pharaoh, but the fact that he was represented by a pharaoh's cartouche is puzzling. A sort of he was and he wasn't situation."

"Perhaps he held the power of a pharaoh without the scepter? I have considered for decades that he might have been a rogue leader, someone with a claim for the throne but opposed by...other family members perhaps?"

Blackstone nodded. "That's an astute observation. Perhaps like one of the Jacobite rebellions in more recent history, he pursued the throne and was rebuffed, maybe more than once. And maybe he was a Colonel Kurtz-like figure who had created his own shadow kingdom until he was taken down by the established pharaoh or his proxies. Or perhaps *her* proxies."

"I'm glad to hear your on-the-fly thoughts mirror my own. I think your work here will be quite enlightening. To us both." His hand reached for the photograph and Blackstone reluctantly surrendered it.

If only he could be given access to the vault this very minute, he would immerse himself in all the panels. Not the photographs, but the very words painted and scratched on rock. Chambers might well be the only amateur who had managed to slice the glyph-laden panels from the interior of a tomb. Blackstone had never heard of such a thing.

"May I inquire," he said as Chambers locked the vault, "whether there was care taken in marking the tomb's remaining blank walls so that panels could be seen in their original context?"

Chambers made a face. "Of course, that was my first concern! Every square inch of the painted walls is photographed and catalogued with context and location foremost in everyone's efforts. There are multiple wide-angle photos that will prove valuable for the context you seek. My experts were the best, and they knew what they were doing."

My experts? Hadn't Chambers been barely out of his teens? He'd have to revisit the story for the book project. He wondered how factual the old man's stories would turn out to be. But what did he care, as long as he was paid as promised?

"I'll have to see the tomb itself. The photographs will help, but there's something about a dig, being within the chambers of the tomb itself..."

"Don't worry, Blackstone, you'll be welcome to see it for yourself. Only a handful of men have seen it, and that is how it shall continue. Once we've hit a certain point in the translation, a visit to the tomb will fulfill all your needs—and perhaps all your dreams, as well."

Chambers took a framed photograph out of a drawer, turned it over, and handed it to Blackstone.

"What's this?"

"The first step to fulfilling your desire."

Blackstone took the frame. The photograph was color, but faded. A much younger Alton Chambers, dressed to look like a junior explorer, face smudged with sand and dirt, stood proudly in front of a low squared-off arch with glyphs carved and painted in rows all around it. Beyond the doorway was darkness flecked with floating dust caught in the glare of the flash.

"This is the tomb itself?"

"Not the main entrance, as some of the outlying portions were destroyed when the rig broke through the roof. This is a side entrance and leads to one of the main passages once you are past the foyer, so to speak, the anteroom to a chamber in which a long shelf held the jars that contained the organs of the occupant's family and retainers. You can't see those in this shot, but I've always been partial to the way it portrayed the find."

And how you looked finding it, Blackstone thought with more than a hint of snark.

Blackstone brought the frame close to his eyes so he could trace the glyphs that were visible. Most weren't because the flashbulb had overexposed the film and some of the colorful symbols were lost in the blinding glow.

But what Blackstone could see was incredible. He'd never seen anything like it in any of the dozens of tombs he had explored.

Suddenly his eyes unfocused and Blackstone was back in the tomb of Nefertari, the same

place he had been busted with the naked grad student straddling him on the sarcophagus.

But now he was there with Chambers' granddaughter Naira, and it was *she* naked on top of him, her hard nipples poking into his chest while his hands roved over her bare back, and his head was spinning—or maybe the tomb itself was spinning on its axis—and he could almost feel the wet warmth of her enveloping him, her eyes open above his and seeming to change colors as he thrust upward and she urged him on, ever faster.

Suddenly Blackstone thought he was fainting. He grasped the nearby table edge, stumbling slightly until he recovered his balance.

But still he felt the cool stone surface under his back, the musty air and dust motes swirling around them, and the pressure of her thighs on his as she rose and fell on him, riding him like a steed galloping over sand dunes.

And his loins felt it too.

It was as if his memory of that tryst in the tomb had blended with his fresh memory of Naira on her horse, her skin glowing with sweat and health in the chill weather. As if she'd shed her riding breeches and black sports bra just before climbing on top of his ready and willing flesh on the funerary bier of one of the greatest Egyptian women in history.

As if he'd been courting *her* instead of letting her mother seduce him in the great Chambers mansion.

Blackstone swallowed, his mouth and throat as dry as if he were indeed in that tomb in the middle of the worm-tunneled hills, the aura of death all around him.

He was still on the edge of fainting and gripped the table more tightly, his throat closing up now, and Chambers standing out of focus before him, his lips moving with no sound.

He heard voices whispering and some kind of wind instrument playing a strange, otherworldly melody that nevertheless seemed familiar. The voices spoke in a different language, but he felt close to the edge of understanding, as if the meaning was just out of reach but nearly in his hand.

Instinctively he realized that the voices were speaking the language of the glyphs and, in the way of dreams and visions, he understood it perfectly as if he were a living contemporary to whoever was buried in the tomb, whoever he was whose name had been erased.

Although in the vision he understood, the current Blackstone was not privy to the words and their meanings, and as he slowly regained his balance and knew he was not going to faint after all, he saw Chambers speaking to him and his words became intelligible.

"Are you all right, Professor?"

"Yes," Blackstone said after a moment. "I-I-I-I am just...overwhelmed," he stammered. Damnit. He hadn't stuttered since he was a child. What was happening?

"You looked almost sick for a moment."

"I-I'm fine," he said, concentrating on forming the words.

But Blackstone's head was throbbing, his throat was dry, and he could still hear the faint echo of the ancient language as it was spoken by those who had painted the walls. He could still *almost* understand it, and something about it terrified him.

Chapter Nine
November 15

BLACKSTONE ENTERED CHAMBERS' study—which was really the mansion's library—where just a few days before they had started meeting evenings after dinner to conduct the interviews that would at some point congeal into the biography Blackstone had been employed to create. *Autobiography*, to be more exact. Chambers wanted it to sound like his own voice, recounting his long and interesting life.

But Blackstone's mind wasn't really on work. Instead, the last days he had found himself increasingly distracted by Chambers' mysterious and alluring daughter.

And, to his surprise, the college-age granddaughter, who was every bit as attractive as her forty-something mother.

It was no help that both were flirting with him shamelessly. He remembered the first night he had spent here in the mansion, and how Alena had almost gone down on him inside his suite. She hadn't quite reached that level, which was probably due to the sweet wine of which they'd drunk way too much, but he kept hoping. He wasn't afraid of Chambers; after all, he and Alena were adults. And Chambers wanted too much for the work done to kick him out just because he and his daughter became involved. If it was his granddaughter though... Blackstone put that thought squarely out of his mind right now. Even he knew to observe some limit, a sense of moderation.

One at a time.

Talking to the old man had proven to be something of an unanticipated pleasure, and tonight it might be a needed distraction from his thoughts of Alena and the curves of her resplendent body, which she displayed for him unapologetically every chance she had. That, and the high-class alcohol the two of them would consume while engaged in the story—which lubricated their conversations—undoubtedly made the walk to the library well worth the effort. So far Chambers had spoken only of his childhood, but it was obvious he wanted to move past those years.

Tonight when Blackstone approached, the old man was already standing at the rolling bar in anticipation of their nightly conversation. He had pulled the cart closer for convenience, barely having to stand at all to refill their tumblers.

"Bourbon, Blackstone?"

"Yes, please," said the professor, a bit of a grin spreading across his face.

"I'm getting to know you too well," Chambers said as he decanted three fingers of top-notch Kentucky whiskey into one of his monogrammed cut crystal rocks glasses.

Blackstone went directly to the old man and took the drink from his hand. *I'm getting to know your daughter well*, he thought. *But not well enough yet.*

"No ice?" Chambers raised a bushy eyebrow.

"Not tonight. If you're getting to know me too well, then it's time to throw you off the trail." He took a long sniff of the spirit and enjoyed it.

Chambers laughed. It was one clipped-off *ha*, similar to the sound a dog would make if suddenly roused by a noise from a dead sleep. "You'll find it more difficult than that to throw me off your trail." The old man smirked and winked at him. For some reason it pricked at the skin at the base of Blackstone's neck. Did he know about him and Alena and all the heavy flirting? Would she have told her father she was interested in him? And would he admit it to the old man? Alton Chambers was a hard man to read. Clearly he was well-practiced at playing his cards close to the vest.

After Chambers had filled a glass of his own—his usual snifter of Cognac, a bottle of which most likely cost more than Blackstone's old car when new—the two of them made their way to the pair of high-backed leather chairs that sat at ninety degrees from each other, a small circular mahogany table to rest their drinks set perfectly between them.

"Well now, Blackstone, where were we?"

Blackstone pulled his small notepad from the breast pocket of his shirt. Though he had a magnificent memory, he liked to note the most minute details, like dates and times, to maintain the accuracy of the accounts. He scanned the past few pages. "We have a good basic start on your childhood, so now I'd like to know where you got your interest in Egyptology."

"You mean my obsession."

Blackstone cocked his head and nodded. "Yes."

That was no surprise; Blackstone himself had been obsessed. When he was young and brash and full of big dreams.

"Well..." The old man drew the word out as if he were pulling a sword from its sheath. "I presume—no, in fact, I'm certain—it started in the summer of 1958 when my father sent all of us —my brothers, my sister, and myself—to Egypt, to be exact. Father did not believe in *coddling* his children. He was bound and determined to make oilmen—and one woman—of us. Certainly it's true he was also grooming Junior—my eldest brother, Charles Chambers Junior—to be the heir to the Chambers Oil Company throne, and I'm sure there would have been room for the rest of us at the table. This, of course, was many years before the family diversified into shipping and real estate. Back then the kingdom still had all of its resources firmly rooted in the petroleum industry, and in those post-war days that meant working in Egypt or Saudi Arabia.

"So he sent us to Marsa Matruh, a northern city in Egypt on the Mediterranian Sea where we could help oversee—and by oversee, I mean watch people who were actually qualified to do so, and thereby learn—the drilling of exploratory wells. This was so soon after the war, you could still see the physical remainders of Rommel's forces.

"Now, at the time, I was a young man—a teenager in fact—and as such I had hoped that we would be travelling to the Nile Delta, or Alexandria, or Luxor, or even colorful Cairo itself to seek the kind of adventure a young man craves. But no, our father actually expected us to work! So instead of those more glamorous destinations, we travelled out into the western desert straight south of Matruh to help drill for oil. But, as it turned out, we found an adventure waiting there for us..."

Chambers went on, warming up to the requested subject, as Blackstone took an occasional note. Both stopped to sip amber liquid as necessary.

Chapter Ten
1958

THE BATTERED, DENTED, and sand-blasted Series II Land Rover cruised over the dunes. There may have been a road there somewhere, but if so, the drifting sands had hidden any trace of it. Alton sat in the last row of seats, beside his brother Harrison. They both wore Legion-style billed *kepis* with the white drape protecting their necks, long-sleeved button-down bush shirts over cotton t-shirts, long cargo pants, and sturdy hiking boots. But even with all that to protect them from the desert environs, Alton could taste nothing but sand. It crunched under his teeth and abraded his tongue and palate.

They'd mostly given up trying to talk. Yelling over the whining engine, creaking suspension, and wind-driven particles that *ticked* against the sides of the Rover like miniature meteorites, had proven exhausting. So they watched out the half rolled-up canvas and plastic windows as they traversed the seemingly endless desert. Alton thought it looked like a beach that had gone on forever, until it had become an ocean of its own.

"Not long now," Jack Houston yelled back from the passenger seat. Jack was a Texas oilman, transplanted to the Middle Eastern team. It showed in both his name and his accent. Not to mention the wide-brimmed cowboy hat he wore rain or shine. He didn't have to worry about rain most of the time—he managed the Egyptian exploration crews and was going to be their guide while they learned this portion of the family business and the field work itself.

"How can he tell?" Harrison muttered, mostly to himself. It was a commentary on the complete lack of geographical landmarks other than shifting dunes, the desert stretching out around them unchanging since the city of Matruh had blinked out behind them long before.

Their driver, Hemeda, was a local hire, a scrawny, dark-complected Egyptian who spoke near-perfect English and apparently a half-dozen other tongues heard on the international wells. He helped work the fields, as well as driving and translating. In fact, there wasn't much he wouldn't do for Jack, if asked. "A real asset to the company," Jack had told the Chambers siblings. "Your father was lucky to find him."

In the second row of seats sat Alton's two older siblings, Charles Jr., who was the eldest, and Cynthia, their only sister. Today she was a tomboy and was dressed like her brothers, for the field.

Before long a gangly derrick could be seen in the distance, hazy through the wind-blown sand. Alton had seen them several times before, in outings with his father to the oil fields where he had grown up, near Dallas. He could tell that there was something amiss even before he heard Jack Houston exclaim, "What in tarnation...!"

The double-stand derrick was cocked at an unusual angle, perhaps thirty degrees off its normal vertical position. As they approached and pulled to a stop, it was clear that the mobile drilling rig that Chambers Oil Company used here when searching for reservoirs was off-kilter, its front wheels off the ground and leaning to the right, while its rear wheels were hidden from sight, as if being sucked into the sand below them.

Jack Houston jumped out of the Rover as soon as it came to a jarring stop. The Chambers siblings leaped out behind him, keen to hear what would be discussed. It was clear something bad was happening. Hemeda followed behind after making sure the Land Rover was parked far enough from the derrick so it wouldn't be damaged if the rig toppled. At the moment, that seemed a definite possibility. The slow, painful screech of twisting metal wove in and out of the wind's howl.

"What the hell happened here, Gram?" Houston strode up to the on-site foreman, a tall red-haired Scotsman in khaki safari shirt and shorts who stood with hands on hips, examining the drill rig up and down. A scowl was carved on Graham "Gram" MacNair's ruddy face.

"We found a reservoir all right, Jack. But also what seems to be an empty pocket. Maybe got leached out by water some thousands of years ago when this shit wasn't desert. Weakened the rock around it, and now that layer's giving way under the weight o' the damn derrick." His native brogue was enhanced by the urgency in his voice. "Either way, looks like it collapsed in on itself and it's tryin' ta drag the rig down with it. We're just trying to figure out how to move it outta there without gettin' anybody killed. Salvaging as much of the steel as possible."

Nearby, several other trucks with *COCo* stenciled on them sat parked in a row. They were assorted military surplus and contained supplies—provisions, parts, the equipment needed to construct a more permanent derrick in the event oil was struck, and most importantly gigantic barrels of potable water. There were also several sleek aluminum-skin travel trailers intended as housing and office space, and a number of tents that fluttered in the wind for the indigenous laborers. This wasn't a one-day operation, it was a caravan travelling from site to site and drilling exploratory wells, seeking the rich black gold that fueled the world. Alton estimated that there were at least three dozen men on the crew. He knew they were called *roughnecks.* And they did look rough, as though they belonged in a street gang more so than on a company crew.

Jack and Gram shouted orders and supervised as their men moved one of the heavy trucks into position and tethered the rig's front axle to the truck's trailer hitch with a length of thick chain. The crooked derrick swayed in the wind like the mast of a tall sailing ship at sea, threatening everyone nearby.

During the commotion, Alton, who was young and curious—his father would have said *foolhardy*—inched forward to get a better view. Sand had been piled on four sides of the well and the derrick rested on a layer of exposed rock. But that layer had turned out to be thinner in places than their instruments had indicated. It had cracked under the derrick and the drill angled until it had caught something and seized up. The explosion had equaled a dynamite-based blast, and now he could see injured workers off to one side being checked by a medic. The shrapnel wounds seemed mostly minor, but there was a copious amount of blood nonetheless.

Houston pointed out the former military medics Charles Chambers had hired and what they were doing. "This is a major setback!" he said then, meaning for the fledgling oil company. The price tag on the accident would probably be over a hundred thousand dollars in equipment destruction. Any loss of life would increase the cost, with families to be taken care of and other medical costs. And then there would be the inevitable insurance squabbles.

Alton imagined Houston would hate the task of informing the Chambers patriarch of the accident.

Beneath the weight of the collapsing rig, whatever the auger had struck had opened a sinkhole that pulled the piled sand through the void in its center as if it were being poured through an enormous funnel. Alton—who currently fancied himself a burgeoning entomologist—

thought it looked like the trap of an antlion, albeit an aberrantly large antlion. He could almost see the elk antler-sized mandibles protruding from its lair at the bottom of the pit, waiting to snare anyone who ventured too close to the lip of its trap.

Lost in thought, Alton barely heard the metallic shriek as a corner of the rig suddenly keeled toward him, the steel scaffolding popping and screaming as it began to collapse.

"Get the hell outta there!" Houston hollered, breaking Alton's reverie.

The youngest of the Chambers brood finally noticed his predicament as tons of twisted steel began careening down at him. Instinct and reflex took over in the face of certain death, and he leaped forward an instant before being crushed beneath the weight of the falling scaffolding.

He had jumped from one crisis to another. Alton immediately realized that he was now in the bowl of the sinkhole and was quickly being drawn downward. The loose cascading sand was like a waterfall pulling him deeper and deeper, down toward the hole in the earth. There was nothing to grasp, so his struggles to clamber out only seemed to hasten his descent.

In a matter of moments he had gone from nearly being mashed beneath the ruined drill rig to being sucked beneath the dunes like an insect getting washed down the drain.

Before he could even register it, he was through the lip of the pit. The last thing he saw was the broken-off drill bit, a length of steel pipe twisted into a half-pretzel.

He fell into the darkness, landing hard on the pile of sand that had emptied—and was still gushing—into the cavity. Here there was great danger of being buried by the tons of shifting sand, like sitting in the bottom of an hourglass under the bottleneck drain.

"Can you hear me, laddie? Are ye all right?"

Dizzied by the rapid slide, Alton heard the Scotsman's voice but faintly due to the rumble. He sat up and slid back down a little farther. Sand still raining down on him from above, he wiped his face and gingerly around his eyes and shook his head to get the granules out of his hair. He had lost his *kepi*. He spat, trying to clear the grit from his mouth and from between his teeth. "Yes," he yelled upward. "I'm okay!"

Thankfully this pocket beneath the surface wasn't too deep. He estimated that he had only fallen about eight feet before landing on the loose pile.

"We're gonna get you outta there, Alton. Just hold on," Jack said, his voice carrying faintly above the white noise of the sand that continuously poured into the cavern.

Alton got to his feet, standing on the conical mound of sand that had flowed into the pocket from above. He waited.

As his eyes adjusted to the limited sunlight that shone down like the narrowing beam of a spotlight, he was able to make out the portion of unbroken roof of the empty space above him. He marveled at its unnatural smoothness, which was obvious to him as he was an observant young scientist-to-be. Before long he was able to take in more, and as he became increasingly acclimated to his surroundings he realized that the surfaces weren't just smooth, they were also perfectly flat where they hadn't been damaged by the ruined auger. In a short time, he was able to make out the entire area around where he sat. It wasn't a cavern at all. It was a room, a cubical chamber comprised of massive stones laid like huge bricks. An unexpected splash of color from the walls popped out at him as his eyes continued adjusting.

"Hey!" he called up, his throat almost closing with the grit. He spit some out.

"Aye, laddie," Gram yelled back. "We're comin' for ya. Hold on."

"I've made a discovery," Alton said, cupping his hand near his mouth to help project his voice upward. "This isn't a cave. It's some kind of huge room. It's manmade, and I can't even see the end of it."

Making his way down by sliding to the bottom of the sand pile—where only a wide dusting covered the stony floor—Alton put his hands against the nearest wall. He was astonished. He traced the seams between the gargantuan blocks. His heart raced, though he wasn't sure if the feeling was caused by his two consecutive scrapes with death or the thrill of discovering this chamber beneath the sands, or if the two experiences back-to-back compounded the awe of both.

A shiver worked its way through him, starting at the back of his head and working its way all through his extremities.

Beneath the gentle *hiss* of the sand that perpetually sifted down from the desert above him, he could have sworn he heard voices whispering to him in a strange tongue.

"What?" Alton yelled up toward the surface. The hole didn't seem quite as large, but he was unable to see it clearly due to the dune that had been created inside the chamber.

There was no response.

Perhaps they couldn't hear him now that he'd slid down to the floor? He knew he could never climb the sand dune—it was too fluid, and it was too high. If not careful, he'd end up buried by it.

He shivered again.

Has to be in my head, right?

Yet the whispering persisted. Maybe the way the still-falling sand echoed in the chamber. Or maybe how the wind blowing above swept over the open hole in the roof?

Something cold grasped his arm and Alton's hand jerked there reflexively, but there was nothing, only cold.

It wasn't just cold.

It was ice cold.

Certainly it was cooler down inside the chamber than it had been up above, beneath the blazing desert sun, but not like this. His arm was freezing. Or was it his hand?

Suddenly panicked, Alton stepped away from the wall, which felt as if it were closing in on him. "Hey," he called up again to the others, hoping to hear a response.

Was the opening up above getting smaller?

No, it couldn't be.

Could it?

His boot kicked up something solid, half-buried in the massive sand pile that reached two-thirds of the way to the ceiling like a brand-new dune. Even in the partial light, he could clearly make out the object. It was a human skull. He picked it up and sand poured out of its orbital sockets and nasal aperture. He felt a tingle in his fingers, almost like a slight electrical shock.

He dropped the skull onto the sand at his feet and, when he looked down, realized there were others there as well. Other skulls and parts of skulls. More bones too, half-buried underfoot. He crunched down on one and it snapped like a gunshot and broke into shards.

His whole body went cold.

Fueled by fear and adrenaline, Alton ran-climbed up the sand slope, his feet sinking and slipping in the loose particulate, sliding back a couple feet for every one gained, but he didn't give up until—almost impossibly—

he found himself crawling up the mound like some sort of desert beetle. For a moment he was convinced his hands felt old dry bones everywhere beneath the top layer of sand. He clawed frantically, fear causing the acidic burn of bile to rise in his throat. He tried to yell out for help but instead gagged.

When he finally reached the top of the sandy pyramid, a rope dangled waiting for him from above. He looked up to the opening and saw Gram's face there, eyes wide and looking down at him. "There you are," said the Scotsman. "Tie the rope 'round your waist so we can pull ye up and outta there before the roof's a goner!"

When he climbed out of the hole, carefully stepping over the cracked stone slabs that had been hidden under the thick layer of sand dunes, those nearby broke into spontaneous applause. Alton stepped out of the rope sling impatiently and Gram helped him up and over onto safer ground.

"You can't imagine what I've found, Gram!" Alton's eyes were bright diamonds.

He was shivering.

Chapter Eleven

HIS FIRST CHAT with Blackstone in the vault room had grown into a full-fledged conversation over the span of days. It was like the several chats they'd had for Blackstone's book, during which Chambers had spun his tale of the young explorer who'd fallen into a tomb in the desert so long ago. Of course, he only told the factual parts, the parts that didn't hint at what he had truly experienced.

The magic he had found. And which had found *him*.

No, he definitely had not been disclosing *everything*. But he enjoyed reliving those days in his mind, and the days they would soon lead to.

He smiled at the memories.

Now Alton Chambers poured himself another Cognac and pressed a hidden button, sliding open another well-disguised panel that led from the main library into a short hallway and then into a second highly shielded, hidden room. It was originally intended as the home's defensive redoubt, an early model panic room, but over the years he had slowly altered its function. It was impregnable, and while the room with the vault that he had shown Blackstone was the perfect place to store his treasured wall panels, this secret chamber was the center of his private security system.

He approached the long table at one end of the room and its array of large flat monitors, each of which was split into eight smaller screens that showed various views of the mansion and the guest cottages and outlying portions of the compound, both indoor and out.

He snatched up one of the various wireless joystick controllers and found the appropriate screen. A few clicks and keystrokes and he was watching a video of Blackstone and Alena shot some nights before from above and to the side. The professor was backed up against the door and his lovely daughter Alena was just getting on her knees in front of him.

That didn't take long, he thought wistfully, as he appreciated the Cognac. It was never too early for Cognac, in his world. He sipped again, ready to enjoy the show, his finger hovering over the zoom feature.

But he was surprised when she seemed to kiss his trousers in just the right place, but then stood up and flirted her way out the door. Chambers chuckled at the tactic. *Leave him wanting more.*

A sound behind him made him turn, but he'd already smelled her scent.

"Alena, you're both quick and give up too easily," he said. "This didn't end the way I thought, but yet I was surprised."

"Hm, yes, I realized I've already got him captured. Suddenly I felt a little like having caught the big fish too easily and had the damn thing chew through the line and get away. Best to keep him on the line, where he can wriggle but he can't get away."

"You may be right. This one wants to be here badly. But I doubt he'll be able to focus on the job at hand if you keep him in this state. A well-sexed man is easy to control, but a frustrated one..." Chambers chuckled again. "But then, you know how to play your game better than I. It is, after all, *your* game."

"It's not as if you don't have some game yourself. Don't worry, Father, I'll keep him squirming on the hook easily. And if I can't..."

"Yes," he said, as his joystick brought up another camera view of Blackstone in his shorts staring out the window. Another screen showed Naira on her horse. The time stamp told the tale. "There's always Naira. Her beauty has already captured him too."

"Well, then I'll have to work harder."

"Do I sense some jealousy?"

Alena shrugged. "It's hard not to be. To be young and firm again. With all the work I have to do, all she needs to do is walk into the room to have men eating from her hand."

"Once he translates those texts, that young firm body will be yours, daughter. And his will be mine. Don't distract him too much. I want him translating to the maximum of his abilities. He is brilliant, you know, probably more so than he himself realizes. Even if he is a weak, weak man."

"And pretty, too." She stared at the still frame of a disheveled Blackstone in his briefs.

Chambers nodded. "Yes, he is, isn't he?"

"Make sure the cameras are working in my suite."

"My dear, of course they will be. I want to see the moment he is ours."

"Father, you had him when you mentioned the money." She rubbed her fingers together needlessly.

"That may be true. He didn't even look at the contracts he signed, he was so busy thinking about the money and your ass. But once you're whispering in his ear, or licking the inside of his ear, he'll work harder for me. For *us*." Chambers replayed the video of Naira on her horse. "Although, if you're not careful, she will take him from you. He likes them young."

"Don't worry, I can handle it. Between the three of us, he'll have no reason to stray from his labors."

"Carefully, Alena, carefully. We are so close to achieving everything we have worked for all these years. That *I* have worked for most of my life. There isn't much time left to me."

She took his liver-spotted hand, brought it to her mouth, and began to suck on his fingers.

"Don't start something you don't intend on finishing, dear."

"Who said I didn't intend on finishing?" she said, before getting down on her knees and giving her father what Blackstone had been denied.

Chapter Twelve
1958

AFTER FINALLY HAVING been rescued from the tomb, Alton couldn't think of anything else.

Harrison, Cynthia, and Alton waited in one of the trailers while Charles Jr., Houston, Gram, and the rest of the crew fought to right the crippled drilling rig. Even inside and out of the elements, the sand seemed to permeate everything. Alton could feel the grit abrading his skin beneath the fabric of his clothing. His feet inside the thick socks felt as if someone had taken a file to them, and his underwear had also been infiltrated. But all this was just a minor distraction to the young explorer. His mind was filled with images of the chamber beneath the dunes, and he was impatient to drop back down and explore it more fully, with lights and proper gear to investigate the improbable space.

What he had seen—glimpsed, really—was scratching at his brain. He wanted to examine the colorful strips of alien art that told ancient Egyptian stories. Was it a tomb? Had they discovered a tomb far away from the Valley of the Kings? And if so, whose tomb was it? Why was it so far away from the usual places explorers found tombs?

He wanted to jump out of his skin at the thought of lowering himself down without anyone to bother him. And yet, a tinge of anxiety sparked through his frame, and the remnants of whispering voices echoed somewhere in the back of his head.

A diesel generator powered the small refrigerator and electric lights in the trailer, and from the fridge Cynthia had poured Alton a cold glass of *qasab*. The icebox was stocked with ranks of sweaty Coca-Cola bottles, but Alton had developed a taste for the juice made from sugarcane that was common in the region.

"How are you feeling?" Cynthia asked. "Are you all right?"

"I'm fine," said Alton. "Physically, I think there's nothing wrong. Maybe I'm a little shaken from the experience, but mostly I'm excited to get down there and see what else might be discovered." Even as a young man, Alton was serious and acted older than his years. And he spoke like an adult, which sometimes amused people until they realized he was indeed their equal.

"Tell us about it," Harrison prodded. "It seems much more interesting than drilling for oil."

Harrison did not have the zeal for the oil business that their father and Charles Jr. did. He was more of the artistic type and hoped to make it to Hollywood someday to try his hand at acting on the silver screen. But he had caught some of his younger brother's new enthusiasm for the mysterious chamber.

"There's not much to tell. It was dark and..." Alton brushed his sleeve for dramatic impact, "...sandy. But it was definitely a room with squared-off corners and flat walls. It wasn't a sinkhole or anything like that. I heard them talking of water leaching the sandstone, but that wasn't it. A room—like the room in a tomb." He didn't mention the things he had heard, or the bones he had crushed under his boots. *Were there actually bones? Had there been whispers?*

"D'you think Jack will let us go down there?" said Harrison.

"Of course he'll *let* us. I discovered it, didn't I? Besides, we're his boss's children, which means we outrank him."

"Boys!" Cynthia said, feigning exasperation. "Aren't you two much too old to play in the sand? If I'm going to play in the sand, I'd rather go back to the beach at the hotel and enjoy modern civilization."

"Think of it, Cynthia," said Alton. "This could be the discovery of a lifetime. We may have just stumbled upon the tomb of some long-forgotten pharaoh. There could be countless riches down there!"

"And maybe a mummy," Harrison said. "A mummy of the pharaoh!"

"Oh, and *maybe a mummy*," Cynthia mocked them. "I think father has enough riches already, don't you agree?"

Before long the trailer door opened with a squeak and Charles Jr. entered. "We got the drilling rig up and out of the hole," he said, shaking the ubiquitous sand out of his clothes.

Jack Houston and Gram MacNair followed shortly thereafter, their own clothing covered in patches of grease and oil to which a layer of sand clung stubbornly.

"It's starting to get dark," Houston said, heading to the refrigerator. "We won't be able to assess the damage until tomorrow." He opened a Coca-Cola bottle and drank greedily.

"Aye," said Gram as he caught the bottle Jack tossed him. They were speaking to each other, ignoring the Chambers youths.

"When can we explore the tomb?" Alton often blurted out what was on his mind.

"Hadn't given it much thought, Alton," Houston drawled. "We've got more important things to worry about. Besides, it might be too dangerous. Who knows when the whole thing might cave in now that the roof's been compromised."

"Without the weight of the rig on it, it should be quite safe," said Alton. "My calculations show..."

"I don't know..." Houston shook his head. "*Calculations?*"

Before Alton could defend his position, Gram chimed in. "Me, I'm curious meself. I wouldn't mind getting down there and havin' a look about. I doubt it's a tomb, we're too far from the Nile. But it could be a temple of some kind, or a building used to house supplies or grains. Either way, it's worth a peek. I can take the boy down tomorrow for a wee bit."

"I'd like to go too if you don't mind," said Harrison.

"Count me in," Charles Jr. added. He couldn't have his bravado outdone by his younger brothers. His ego, straight from their father, wouldn't stand for it.

"Okay then, as long as you're takin' responsibility for them," Houston said.

"Aye," said Gram, "I'll watch over 'em. Maybe we'll find some old clay pots or spearheads down there. Tomorrow, eh, lads?"

Darkness settled in over the arid land, and Alton stepped outside for some cool desert air. Excited about the next day's activities, he knew he wouldn't be able to sleep at all. The wind had died down and the night was as quiet as death itself. There were strands of electric lights strung around and between the trailers and tents, bobbing on their wires and looking every bit like the mythical will-o'-the-wisps. Alton shivered. As hot as the desert was by day, it was easy to forget it was equally cold by night. He spotted Hemeda standing nearby, puffing on a hand-rolled cigarette.

Stepping away from the trailer, Alton approached the gangly Egyptian and nodded in greeting. "You wouldn't happen to have an extra one of those, would you?" he asked.

"Yes, of course," said Hemeda, passing his already lit smoke to Alton before fishing a tobacco pouch and papers from his pocket and beginning to roll a second cigarette.

"Chilly out here," Alton said. Always intense, he made conversation with some effort.

"Yes. It is always cold in the desert at night. It relieves the hot skin."

Alton took a drag and gave Hemeda a twisted smirk, shrugging. The tobacco was exotic, strong, and Alton fought to avoid coughing. Somewhere in the distance, he heard high-pitched howling punctuated by short, clipped barks, almost yelping.

"Coyotes?" said Alton.

"Jackals," Hemeda corrected. "But I have never heard them this far out in the desert before. They know we will have food remains."

Alton shivered again, though this time it wasn't because of the chill. He was about to comment when screams erupted from the tent encampment where the local laborers were turned in for the night. One of the Egyptian laborers burst through his tent flap and fell to the ground, rolling and shrieking as if he were on fire.

Hemeda and Alton both rushed to his aid. Behind them, others exited their tents to see what was happening but held back, frightened by the screams.

Between his unintelligible howling, the laborer was yelling something that Alton couldn't understand.

"*Burj aleaqarab! Burj aleaqarab!*"

Alton learned quickly.

Possibly scores of large scorpions clung to the man's long, traditional *gallibaya,* and seemed to burrow into his hair, or perhaps it was his head.

The laborer's log-rolling, frantic kicking, and arm-waving dislodged or crushed most of the oversized arachnids, but the rest were like a black wave breaking across his features. Alton's long sleeves protected his arms as he swiped across the screaming man's head, face, and body, and scorpions fell to the dirt, allowing Hemeda and him to stomp them into black goo with their boots. When the last armored insects had succumbed to the onslaught of weighted leather, Hemeda and Alton helped the blubbering man to his feet and looked him over—he, whose eyes were still wide-open in panic—to make sure there were no more of the creatures clinging to his flesh or hair.

Movement in the corner of his eye caught Alton's attention. He turned and stared at the poorly lit ground. There, he noted one of the armored bastards scurrying toward him like a miniature tank. Alton's anger exploded and he struck with his hiking boot, ground the attacker into the sand, then bent down and picked it up by its tail. The remaining portion was curved like a quarter moon or the blade of a scythe. It was at least three inches long, quite a bit larger than the only other scorpion he had ever seen, when he'd been with his father at a drill site in Texas—which had been easily dispatched—and it was a strange yellow color, save for the black stripe that ran down the length of its back.

He held it up to the light. Its legs curled in on its body as if it had tried to hold onto its soul as it fled the segmented corpse. Of course he recognized it. *Androctonus Australis*, the southern man-killer. Otherwise known as the Egyptian fat-tailed scorpion.

Suddenly there were more screams.

Alton dropped the insectoid corpse. The screams seemingly came from a number of places, and Egyptian workers ran or filed from their tents all over the wide encampment, some brushing their arms and legs with their hands, others helping their fellows do the same. On the ground, the black wave that seemed like oil rolling on a beach was immediately revealed to be countless giant arachnids. Boots hit the ground everywhere as laborers and company employees stamped the creatures into grotesque blobs of goo and venom.

A trailer's door burst open and Houston stepped into the light. "What the hell's goin' on out here?!"

"Scorpions, Jack!" Alton yelled. "We must've pitched camp in some kind of nesting area!" Alton ground another of the arachnids under his boot, then another. His feet were nearly numb.

"Well, kill 'em and go back to sleep!"

"You don't understand, it's an infestation! And they're deadly."

Even as he responded, Alton heard other men's panicked shouts.

"Well, son of a bitch!" Houston blared. "Everybody get inside shelter then!"

The laborers abandoned their tents, roughly half of them piling into the trailer where the Chambers siblings, Houston, and Gram MacNair were housed for the night, the other half streaming to the second trailer where the roughneck crew slept.

It was not an orderly retreat, but the number of scorpions still stampeding through the camp was just too large to subdue by boot alone. A steamroller might have done the job, or a flamethrower.

Once they were safely inside, Cynthia passed out paper cups of cold water, while Gram tried to help the few who had actually been stung by the deadly arachnids.

"Is there anything we can do to help 'em?" Gram asked Alton, deferring to the young science enthusiast.

"No, not really." Alton's voice was barely louder than a whisper.

"Why can't they breathe?"

"The venom of the Egyptian fat-tail is a neurotoxin. It causes paralysis of the diaphragm, which eventually leads to suffocation. There's really nothing we can do to help them except hope that they didn't receive a potent enough dose to kill."

"How the hell do you know all this?" said Houston, who had stalked over to them.

"I've been curious about insects and arachnids, so I researched the local species when I learned we would be coming to Egypt."

Where Charles Jr. was the businessman, Cynthia the socialite, and Harrison the artist, Alton took his scientific endeavors very seriously.

Hemeda stepped up, interrupting. "The men are saying this place is cursed. They want us to leave here."

"Well, you tell 'em that if they want to leave, they are welcome to do so. It's about a three-day walk back to Matruh," said Houston coldly. "I don't believe in curses or any such things. We just had a bad day. Tomorrow will be hard work."

Tomorrow. Alton had almost forgotten about the tomb in all the commotion. As soon as the sun rose, they would be able to climb down and investigate whatever he had discovered the day before.

But tomorrow will also be a day of death, Alton thought.

Everyone bedded down as well as they could. Whimpers from the wounded kept everyone awake.

Now that the trailer was so cramped that he couldn't possibly sleep, a wave of exhaustion washed over him and he entered a fugue state, awake yet somehow unconscious and dreaming.

Visions appeared in Alton's head—likely due to his thoughts being consumed by the hidden chamber he'd found beneath the sand—and he saw himself descending into the mysterious space. He imagined finding a secret passage, its entrance disguised as part of the wall of the chamber, and going through it. The passage led to a second chamber, a treasure-trove filled with the riches of ancient Egypt. He imagined discovering a lever-activated trap door which opened to the tomb of one of the most powerful pharaohs to have ever lived. The images were lucid yet dreamlike.

He started alert when the shouts of the others in the trailer roused him from his stupor. Two of the laborers had died of asphyxiation during the early morning hours, and several others were close to death. Before long, the death toll increased, and soon those felled by the deadly wave of crawling horrors numbered eleven.

The keening began.

Death.

Alton stared at the covered bodies. He imagined them being prepared for mummification, which interested him greatly. The process, the wrappings, the somber handling of the mortal remains. But death itself... He found that he did not like the thought of no longer *being,* whether or not there was an afterlife as they taught in the Sunday schools of his youth. There was something troubling about the concept of your eyes closing for the last time, a hitched breath taken before the final sigh, the death rattle...

No, he was interested in the Egyptian custom, but not at all in the death that awaited everyone so inscrutably.

I would choose not to die. Ever.

The thought surprised him. It seemed to have bloomed in his mind of its own accord, like a bud suddenly flowering. As if it hadn't been his own thought at all.

But that was a silly idea, born of the excitement and death of the day. He tried to sleep, but similar thoughts swirled inside his mind and he squeezed his eyes shut, hoping to also squeeze the thoughts out of his head.

Soon the sun's earliest rays began to shine through the dirty blinds on the trailer's small windows, staining the walls with an orange glow.

This day would not see any work done on the damaged derrick or anything else, except the transporting of the ragged dead back to the city, where hasty funerals and burials would be arranged and grieving families would receive the minimum amount promised by the Chambers Oil Company, a meager legacy for their lost loved ones.

Alton was distracted. He tried ignoring his thoughts from the night before. He visualized the interior of the tomb—*for it had to be a tomb!*—throughout the somber proceedings.

Tomorrow, someone whispered into his ear. *Tomorrow.*

And: *There will be many tomorrows.*

Chapter Thirteen

BATTEN WAS STANDING in front of his door when he opened it, and Blackstone had to work hard to avoid showing he'd been startled. "Yes?"

"Sir, the gate has just rung up. There's a Miss Davenport to see you." He sneered. "Shall we let her in?"

"Please do," Blackstone said. "I'll meet her in the library."

"Very good, sir." Batten's expression said he did not think it was.

Blackstone turned away. He had broached the subject of hiring an assistant with the old man. He'd sensed Chambers wasn't thrilled, but he had made a strong case for having help—Michelle could work with his book notes, and she was well-qualified to help with the glyphs too.

Plus there was the extra-curricular activity. Alena was flirting still, but he was frustrated with how slowly she was moving. Having Michelle around part of the time would stir the pot. He'd done this on digs too, loading up the personalities and the rampant sexuality until something interesting happened.

He headed for the library as if that was where he'd been going when Batten had indeed startled him.

In a few minutes Batten led Michelle into the room then walked away, his back ramrod straight with disapproval.

"Hello, Michelle."

Her eyes were wide, but she played cool very well. "Nice work if you can get it. Look at this house!" she said. "Doc, you're traveling in some pretty great circles to land here. I got the sense this homestead's about the size of a city. I want to explore it!" She gripped his hand with both of hers, her inner child beaming.

He nodded. "I haven't even had a chance yet to see the whole compound. There's at least a dozen separate buildings, most of them like mansions. And this house, this is like a castle."

"So gothic," she said.

You don't know the half of it, he thought.

"Are you interested in my offer? You'll still have to pass an interview with Mr. Chambers himself, of course."

She smiled. It was one of her best features. *Visible* features while clothed, he amended. "Of course," she said. "I think Nathan's going to have me shot once I walk away. Gulshan's sex appeal can only go so far."

He laughed. "About four inches. That's probably his size."

"Perfect for her then. So...you can recruit for this work here?"

"Not exactly," he said, "but since I'll be doing two jobs essentially, I realized I'll need help."

"How's the pay?"

"I don't know, but he has deep pockets. And you're worth it."

"Oh, that's so sweet," she said in a little girl voice. "I know just how to repay you..."

"We'll talk about that. Have to be careful here though. There's a daughter and granddaughter and servants and...Batten."

"That Frankenstein's creature?"

"Indeed." He shrugged. "And I don't know who else. People can come out of the woodwork in a place like this."

He wanted to tell her about the tomb Chambers had spirited away from Egypt in the sixties and that it was located here, somewhere, but he was bound to not say a word. He hoped he could share the information if Chambers hired her.

Speaking of whom, he thought, *when is he going to show up?*

As if on cue, the tall doors opened and Alton Chambers strode in, looking much younger than his many decades.

"Ah, you must be Miss Davenport, the assistant I've heard so much about," he said charmingly as he extended his hand.

"Yes," she said as they shook. "Thank you for seeing me."

"Oh, delighted," said the old man. "Professor Blackstone speaks very highly of you."

"He knows all my strengths."

Blackstone blanched. *Hope she's not going to blow it by playing games.* He really could use an assistant, besides her other talents.

"You seem to be very reassured, very self-confident. I like that in a woman. The professor gave me your CV, and I've already called your references." He looked her up and down. "I don't see any disqualifying features or behaviors. You may start tomorrow, or whenever Blackstone would like you. There'll be some papers to sign, an advance on your salary, which will be three times what I'm told the university is currently paying you. Your access to the compound will be unlimited, within reason. Is this acceptable?"

She was speechless.

"Blackstone?" Chambers turned to the professor.

"I think Michelle is processing it all," he said. "Right?"

"Uh, yes, yes. I'm more than satisfied. I just didn't think—"

"It would be that simple?" Chambers laughed his *Ha!* bark. "I've gotten far on my gut instinct. Today my gut says you'll be quite valuable."

"Thank you," she said, blushing. They shook hands again.

"And now I must finish some tasks I set for myself today. Please excuse me." He nodded at them, then left them in the library.

"Wow. No wonder you took the job. Who wouldn't?"

"I know. So, tomorrow? Bring your laptop and anything personal you might need. You'll have a desk in my workspace." He didn't mention they'd be working next door, in the vault room. It was becoming his office, and as it was between the vault and the library proper, it was perfect.

Before he could say anything more, Batten appeared at the door.

Like a goddamn ghost, he was.

"He'll see you out."

"Okay," she said, still awestruck. "Bye."

Blackstone watched her jeans-encased ass as she walked away.

Let the games begin.

PART TWO

Chapter Fourteen
November 22

THE FIRST WEEK Blackstone was in residence at the Chambers estate, he set up his office within the inner library, gazing with eagerness at the vault door. Michelle Davenport helped by bringing more boxes of his books from his vacated office to join those he brought from home. In a matter of days, Chambers gave him a thin folder of high-quality photographs of the panels from the mysterious tomb, as well as photos of the tomb interior itself. He was also given a series of digital files so he could use the current technology to peruse the glyphs on a huge monitor.

He spent two days familiarizing himself with the photos, wondering at the incredible nature of what he was seeing.

"And these were on wall panels within the tomb you fell into while playing at being an oil man in your father's company?"

Chambers had bristled visibly but held his anger in check. "Yes."

Blackstone shook his head. "This tomb is fairly easy to place timewise. It's probably early to mid-Eighteenth Dynasty. A fair amount of time before Tut, but strictly speaking it's pretty late."

"Yes." Chambers seemed to be peering within Blackstone's eyes as if he could perceive something beyond the obvious.

Blackstone made a face. "But this writing, it's not from that period."

"No."

"It seems...it seems much earlier. It's not even normal hieroglyphics as we know it."

"Now you see the dilemma. Why would those who buried the occupant of the tomb use such early writing? They shouldn't even have known it."

"Exactly."

Chambers waited to see where Blackstone would go, how he would rationalize the mystery.

"It almost looks like Sumerian cuneiform, but..."

"But?"

"But it's too primitive! It's complex, but it looks like an earlier step, an earlier period. But the Sumerians did the earliest writing, so..."

"So?" Chambers prodded.

Blackstone looked at Chambers quizzically. "So why do I sense that you already know the answers?"

"I know some of them. One is that this writing—"

"Predates the Sumerian?" Blackstone said. "That's impossible."

"Is it?"

"How does such ancient writing—hell, even Sumerian—find its way into a tomb this recent? No one would have known it. I mean, even if it's much older than Tut, the chances that something this old would be inscribed on the walls... Unless..."

Chambers was impatient. "Yes?"

"Well, I guess the tomb itself could be much older than the burial."

"Eventually I had the tomb and the walls and the traveler's effects carbon-dated. The writing, the painting and carving itself, was not only contemporary to the construction of the tomb, but also to the burial."

"Huh." Blackstone rubbed his head as if the brain inside hurt. He rubbed his eyes as if digging for dirt. "It would be like me having runes carved on my tombstone. It's not impossible, but it begs some questions. For instance, finding someone who could do it." He indicated some of the photographic samples. "This is much older than what would have been current, in relation to runes versus our writing. It would be even more impossible to have someone around who could do it."

Chambers shrugged and said, "Well, whatever the circumstances of how the writing came to be there, what I really want—and I assume your curiosity demands—is that you manage to translate the writings by working your way backward. Or any way you prefer. *But I need these panels translated to the best of your ability.* And the sooner, the better. The stakes are great, greater than I can say."

Blackstone stared at his new employer. There was no way for him to quantify how strange his response had been just now, how intense. As if the old man's life depended on Blackstone's successful work. Granted, he was well past seventy, probably pushing a very spry and healthy eighty, but how could the translation mean quite so much to him?

Blackstone thought then that he could understand. Chambers was seeing the end of the road, the sand quickly running through the middle of the hourglass, and he wanted to be able to bask in some fame, perhaps tainted by notoriety, but as an eccentric rich guy he'd be happy anyway as he faced his final road.

Sure, that was it.

But then why insist as he had that he would allow none of Blackstone's work to be published? Why command that Blackstone's success in this venture could not be used to bolster the disgraced professor's career?

And why all the secrecy?

The answer was simple eccentricity, wasn't it? It could be ignored, worked around. Sometimes it's best to ask for forgiveness than permission, so what he would do with his work he'd think about later. There was that ironclad NDA, sure, but that's what lawyers are for. As far as the work itself, Blackstone didn't necessarily have to break the code, he only had to make the eccentric boss happy. As long as the paychecks flowed into his account, did it matter?

Blackstone hated this line of thought, because it left him feeling slightly dirty, like a hooker after the john's left the premises. But in this dynamic, who was using whom? Who was the hooker and who was the john?

"What are the stakes? What is your hurry?"

Chambers lowered his voice. "I'm running out of time, Blackstone, that's what the hurry is all about. I want to see it done before...before the end."

"What about the book? That'll take time too."

"Ideally, both projects are important, but the book is secondary. I want you to run with the translation, but we'll continue to do interviews so when the translation is proceeding apace you can also devote some time to that project. The book can be published after...my death."

Blackstone nodded. Whatever Chambers wanted. He understood his position here. He was being used to puff up the old man's ego, maybe help him impress someone. Maybe the old guy had politics on the brain... No shortage of ego-filled pus-bags there, people who lusted after power for its own sake, or for fattening their wallets, and most likely both. Maybe the old man was dying.

Chambers had meandered over to the window and now looked out as if over a sea of sand.

One other thought struck Blackstone.

Maybe the ancient writing had been kept alive by a small group, a cult. Maybe the Occupant, as Chambers referred to the subject of the burial, was a cult leader, and that explained the scratched-out cartouches and the secretive burial.

Blackstone wondered what else he would learn about the guy who had made such an impact on the Chambers family, and Alton especially. Impact from the grave.

A shiver worked its way down his spine.

And would he *want* to learn everything? In the end, what would be the result of his labor? And what else would Chambers demand from him?

Blackstone continued to shuffle through the photographs. "And what are these?" he asked aloud, though he wasn't sure Chambers could answer him.

A number of the panels (a rather large number) bore pictographs of people engaged in sexual activities. Much like the glyphs, they were arranged tightly in horizontal lines, and some of the panels had nothing but varieties of sexual positions while others were broken up with lines of hieroglyphics. When Blackstone had first seen them, he and Michelle had laughed and compared notes on how many of the positions they had tried, but he couldn't shake the feeling that they were somehow integral to the meaning of the panels.

Chambers pulled himself from the window, returning to look over Blackstone's shoulder at the photos. "No one's been able to give me a conclusive answer to that question, Blackstone. Sex magick was well practiced in ancient Egypt, as I'm sure you know, but why this Egyptian pseudo-*Kama Sutra* was painted onto the walls of a tomb, I have no idea. That's why you are here."

The old man's eyes betrayed an eagerness that was almost difficult to define.

For once, Blackstone felt some sympathy for a man named Faust.

Chapter Fifteen
1958

THE DAWN CAME with a splendor that belied the recent horrors.

As they filed out of the trailer with night's chill still pushing back against the sun's heat, all of the deadly scorpions seemed to have gone back into hiding, only the husks of the ones they had squashed remained.

Alton was afraid that the night's horrors would derail his plans to investigate the secret chamber beneath them, but to his surprise Gram seemed as enthusiastic about the discovery as he was.

"We'll begin after we 'ave a bit of brekkie," the Scotsman said. "I'm keen to get down there and see what we've found." He winked at Alton.

"What about the laborers? The men we lost last night?"

"We can help the crew handle 'em. Then they'll have to cart 'em back into town. Poor fookin' devils. We best take a small group down below later, while Jack and the oilers look over the damage done to the rig."

This sounded like a fine plan to Alton.

Though his stomach was knotted in anticipation of their expedition beneath the dunes, Alton was still able to put away a plate of *ful medames*—the regional stew of fava beans, local spices, and in-season vegetables.

They all pitched in, wrapping bodies in tarps, then loading them and whatever possessions the departed had brought with them into the rear of one of the military surplus transport trucks after they'd unloaded the cargo of drilling supplies. They stood watching as the grim convoy ground its gears and rolled away.

Soon Alton, Gram, Charles Jr, Cynthia, Harrison, Hemeda, and one of the local laborers whose name Alton did not know, were all headed into the ancient site below.

Most of the adventurers were equipped with heavy-duty Big Beam portable lanterns strapped over their shoulders, with their giant rectangular battery hanging under the handles. They were all wearing hard-hats with built-in headlamps. In addition, Gram carried a duffel bag with a selection of tools that might come in handy.

They made their way carefully down the sloping sides of the titanic mound of sand rising up from the floor of the chamber. Adrenaline coursed through Alton's veins as he half-walked, half-slid down the sand pile. He dug his hands through the grains, wondering about the bones he had felt there the day before. There had been bones, hadn't there? Now he felt nothing but sand, cool against his skin. Soon they reached the bottom of the pile and stood on a flat stone floor.

Gram swung the beam of his light around the space. "Pure barry!" His voice was filled with awe. The walls of the chamber came to life beneath the light of their lamps, and what Alton had taken for simple stone walls were in fact covered from floor to ceiling with painted scenes of ancient Egyptian court life. Though muted with the passing of centuries, the colors were still vivid.

"You've found something extraordinary here, laddie," Gram said to Alton. "It's the find of a lifetime."

"What do you think it is?" Alton asked.

"Could be a pharaoh's tomb, or maybe a palace or temple. Who the 'ell knows, maybe it's a whole bloody city been buried beneath the sand."

The seven of them slowly made their way around the room, gazing at the walls in silent astonishment.

"What's that over there?" Cynthia said, pointing.

At the far end of the chamber, the most distant wall from the sand heap and the opening they had slid down through, the beams from their lights dispelled just enough of the shadows to make out what looked like a doorway cut into the stone.

Without a word Gram strode from the ornately painted walls to the door-shaped anomaly. The others followed. There they found a single slab of recessed stone approximately eight feet across and twelve feet high set into the wall. The blocks framing the slab were covered in hieroglyphs.

Gram studied the ancient writings intently. At length he said, "It's a prayer to Osiris."

"How do you know that?" Charles asked.

"Before I enlisted in the army, I studied Egyptology at Oxford. That's why I stayed on here after the war, my fascination with *this place.* And look here, this cartouche has been chiseled away into obscurity. Apparently someone felt this big yin should be lost to history. Let's see if we can get this open." The Scotsman put his shoulder to the slab and tried to get it to budge. Nothing. He felt around the seams with his fingertips.

He opened the canvas duffel he'd set aside while he inspected the door, taking out a small pry bar. Wedging the bar between the door's frame and seam, and chipping the stone in the process, he levered the barrier so that a crack appeared and widened until it was large enough for him to slip his fingers in. Gram set aside the pry bar, slid his fingers into the opening, and pulled back on the slab. "Give me a hand, would ye?" he said with a grunt. Charles stepped forward, knelt near the Scotsman, and lent his strength to the effort.

In spite of the stone portal's immense size, it gave way and soon was open wide enough so that Alton was able to step into the gap and help, pushing as the other two pulled.

The door moved more easily than Alton expected, having been perfectly balanced and set into some kind of track system of ancient design, undoubtedly the height of technological advancement of its time. Soon the opening was wide enough that they could proceed.

Alton's lamp illuminated a space that hadn't seen light of any sort in many centuries. The others followed. It was a second chamber, much smaller and less ornate than the first.

"Careful, everyone," Charles Jr. said authoritatively. "These old tombs are filled with booby traps."

"Ha!" Gram replied. "That's a myth made up by movie directors and pulp fictioneers, laddie! There may be some pitfalls, as ye would find in any old and decaying structure, but I can assure you there are no booby traps."

The walls of this rectangular room were comprised of enormous stone slabs that stretched from floor to ceiling, each about eight feet wide and of indeterminate thickness. The seams between these stones were hair-thin and barely detectable. Otherwise, the space was utterly bare.

"Was this some kind of storage space, Gram?" Cynthia asked.

"I canna tell ya, lass. I've no idea."

"What's that noise?" said Harrison.

Alton heard it too, but he hadn't said anything. After the strange voice-like sounds he had heard down here, he didn't want to mention anything for fear of appearing insane, but it was clear now that he wasn't the only one hearing things.

This wasn't the whispering sound that had chilled him to the bone the previous day though, this was different. It sounded like stone grating against stone. Similar to the noise that the opening of the stone door had emitted, but quieter, as if it were coming from behind something. But it was getting louder.

"It sounds like..." Harrison began.

"Quiet," Gram shushed him. "Listen!"

Not only could Alton hear the harsh scraping sound, but he could feel it as well, as the floor began to vibrate.

As if all of them had located the source of the grating in unison, they all stared at the chamber's back wall.

The wall was *moving*, and doing so with increasing speed. In fact, it was falling, tumbling forward.

Toward *them.*

"Run!" Gram yelled.

Alton bolted toward the door before Gram had even finished his panicked command. It seemed as though he had just exited the chamber when its back wall hit the ground with an earth-shaking *boom* that echoed in his ears.

With his heart still trying to pound through his chest, Alton turned and saw with relief that all of his siblings had made it out in time—as had Gram and Hemeda.

But the other local laborer who had joined them was gone.

Mostly.

Only his hand and a bit of his forearm remained, roughly severed from the rest of his body which had been flattened into non-existence. Tendrils of black blood began to weave through cracks in the stone and the floor, widening from the point of impact.

Cythia gasped, sobbing and shaking her head.

"We must go back for help!" Hemeda called out tremulously, nearly weeping.

"Help?" said Gram grimly. "There's no *help* for him. The entire crew wouldn't be able to budge that stone. And even if they did, what they scraped up wouldn't even be recognizable as a man."

"We can't just leave him here!"

As Gram and Hemeda argued their next move, Alton focused his light into the depths of the second chamber, over the severed limb and eighteen-inch-thick slab that had crushed the poor laborer.

"Hey, look, everybody," he said, pointing. "It keeps going."

Behind the collapsed wall there was a second wall—ornate and similar in style to the walls of the first chamber—and set into it was a second doorway, this one open and yawning into a black abyss.

Alton felt a shiver. It wasn't fear—the air was suddenly very cold.

Gram stopped arguing and gazed at Alton's new find. "A hidden room," he mumbled, mostly to himself.

"I told you we needed to watch for booby traps," Charles Junior asserted.

"This was no trap, lad," said Gram. "It looks like they tried to conceal whatever lies beyond this point."

"It might be a treasure trove."

"Indeed it might be, young Alton."

Gram stepped up onto the stone slab and re-entered the room. The others followed. Hemeda whispered a prayer for his fallen kinsman beneath his feet before joining them. The stone that framed the second door was also covered with *bas relief* hieroglyphics similar to those that marked the first doorway.

Carefully they made their way through the opening, Gram taking the lead with Alton in tow and the others following.

Inside there was a long corridor flanked with statues, some as tall as a man, other smaller ones set upon short pillars. Some were full figures, others merely busts. Alton noted most of the more well-known gods: The ram-headed Amun, Anubis with the body of a man and head of a jackal, the cat-headed goddess Bastet, the wise Thoth with his Ibis head, Ra with his hawk head and disc of the Sun. Alton also recognized Osiris, Horus, and Seth. There were others that Alton had never seen or heard of before: a man with the head of a crocodile, what looked like a pregnant woman with the head of a hippopotamus, a frog-headed man, a woman with the head of a cow, a man with a beetle's head, a goat-headed woman. And some others he saw were downright bizarre—a man with an octopus for a head, another had a snake's tail, or perhaps a single tentacle, in place of his head, and another who looked like a toad with the head of a baby. All of them—whether grotesque or more mundane—were either cast in precious metals or carved from valuable stone. Some had large gems set into them. The light from their portable lanterns and headlamps cast wicked shadows of the statues onto the walls, making it look as if they were surrounded by a host of demons dancing in the infernal pit.

Silenced by awe, they continued on.

Another door awaited them at the end of the corridor. This second portal was covered with more intricate carvings. On one side was a man holding a dagger in one hand and a chalice in the other—his arms crossed in the typical way a pharaoh was portrayed, with a flail and scepter—the bright disc of Ra above his head. On the opposite side of the door, numerous smaller figures were depicted in ranks, kneeling and bowing toward the man with the dagger and chalice. Perhaps they were his subjects, servants, or acolytes. A seam down the center divided the door in two, and in its middle was set a large seal covered in smaller hieroglyphs that had been pressed into the soft clay prior to hardening.

"It's a warning," Gram said, studying the seal. "It says something like, *Whatever right bastard breaks this seal, will unleash a plague of death upon the whole land o' pharoahs.*"

"Never heard the likes o' *that*," he added, rolling his eyes.

Grinning, Gram swung the pry bar, shattering the seal and turning its center into dust. "Shall we?" he said, and pushed on the surface. With some effort, he was able to move one of the stone slabs incrementally. Taking the Scotsman's cue, Charles Junior heaved his weight on the other side and the crack between the hinged, double-hung doors slowly widened.

Their lantern beams cut weakly through the pitch-black darkness in a chamber that hadn't known light for thousands of years, if it had ever known light. It was a large room, not as massive as the first chamber, but large enough that even their Big Beams couldn't manage to illuminate its farthest recesses.

Shadows seemed to flit in and out of the beams like lace and gossamer. Strange dark shapes grew behind the swirling.

But there was no real movement other than ancient dust swirling in their lights, and what those feeble rays settled upon finally was a wealth of artifacts that cast those shadows.

"Good lord," Gram marvelled. Even the usually garrulous Scotsman was near speechless.

Statues of gods and animals that dwarfed those they had seen lining the outer hall, plus urns, basins, chests, and sarcophagi in numerous shapes and sizes, were arrayed in ranks across the floor and perched on a wide ledge built into the wall.

Alton was so amazed that his voice failed. Yet what he saw seemed somehow familiar, as if it had all come to him in a particularly vivid dream. He felt himself almost falling, suddenly suffering a bout of vertigo. Perhaps it was the strong sense of *deja vu,* or perhaps it was something else altogether. His mouth hung open and dust from the air about them found its way in, tasting of dust and chalk and...*the skin and bones of dead people.*

The tickle suddenly caused a paroxysm of coughing and Alton doubled over, trying to simultaneously suck in air and get the taste—and the thought—of the decomposed out of his palate.

Gram pounded his back until Alton thought his spine would break. Finally he was able to stop his hacking cough. He spit out as much dust as he could, but he couldn't help feeling as though he had been *invaded* by the dust, as if it had filled in the spaces lining his young lungs until they felt musty and old. It took him a few minutes to regain his breath. There was also another sensation, one young Alton was only recently becoming accustomed to, a tingling arousal in his loins.

Meanwhile, Charles Junior had crouched over a bulging ornate basket. "Look! It's gold! And jewels!" He reached down and pulled up a handful of shimmering stones and chains and bright yellow trinkets carved in various shapes. "It must be worth a fortune! This will easily make up for our losses with the drilling rig."

"You cannot take this!" Hemeda warned. Obviously still upset at the too-quickly forgotten death of his friend and countryman, his glare was dark and menacing. "This treasure belongs to the people of Egypt!"

"This was found by us under our legal drilling operation!"

"It does not matter, you do not own every grain of sand—"

Alton stumbled forward, dizziness overtaking him even as his ears began to ache. The argument growing louder between his brother and Hemeda was lost in a wave of deafening white noise. Voices in the stone chamber became strangely muffled. The room's darkness closed in on him, his vision tunneling. He heard a faint noise that came from inside his own head and quickly grew into the sound of voices chanting in some long-forgotten tongue. The same *voices* he had heard in the first chamber, the previous day. He had almost forgotten about them. They washed out the sounds of the exploration party, making the angry chatter of his siblings and Hemeda and Gram sound as if it came from another room, from *somewhere* else. He felt strange, as if he were sleepwalking into one of the dark corners, barely noticing his surroundings or the lack of light. And his member was unexpectedly engorged, stiffening painfully beneath his trousers. Suddenly he was about to collapse. Reaching out blindly to try and steady himself, he grasped a nearby solid object. He couldn't tell what it was and he didn't care. Whatever it was, it shifted with his weight, and he was immediately plunged into darkness more complete than any he had ever experienced.

And he was falling.

Again.

He had no time to cry out.

He landed with a hard *thump*, instantly clearing his head while also knocking the wind out of him. A white-hot flash of pain shot through his back. Not only had he landed on a hard stone floor, but his Big Beam lantern—which he had hung with a thin leather strap over his shoulder—had been sandwiched between his right flank and the floor, hard, smashing the bulb and bruising his kidney. The pain there was sharp as shattered glass and he thought he felt hot wetness.

He had fallen, all right. Into some type of room tucked *beneath* the treasure chamber. And now he was in utter darkness. His headlamp must have also been knocked off and broken as he fell, because he could no longer feel its band around the top of his head. The lack of light anywhere was immediately frightening beyond belief and his breath caught in his throat.

He couldn't avoid the thought that lanced through his brain.

It might as well have been his own tomb.

Perhaps it would be, for he was cut off from his fellow adventurers. The opening through which he had fallen had closed somehow, and was invisible.

He tried to breathe, but instead sucked in air that was mustier than above in a slow and painful wheeze. Gradually he was able to manage a cautious standing position. He had no idea how far he had fallen, but apparently he could stand upright.

And then he realized...

The voices were gone, as was the dizziness. And his erection. Reaching back, he tried to massage some of the pain from his bruised and battered flank. His shirt was soaked and he hissed at the sharp jab through his innards.

But moments later he forgot about his pain.

A dull *thud* broke the eerie silence. Followed by another. And there was another sound, too, like something scraping—or being dragged. The two noises followed each other rhythmically, *thud, drag, thud, drag.*

It occurred to Alton that they were like the sounds a man with a bad limp might make as he staggered across a sand-covered stone floor.

He froze, terrified. How could it be? What else could be down here, alive in a sealed chamber with no light or water or anything, after all this time?

Thud...drag...thud...drag...

He stilled his pounding heart and listened carefully. It was moving away from him, bearing from right to left. Alton could barely draw a breath, afraid that whoever it was would hear *him* in the deathly silence. That whatever it was would *show an interest* in him.

Because it was *alive.*

But how could it be?

Thud...drag...thud...drag...

Now the sounds were getting louder. Whatever it was moved in a circle. As if it was...*pacing the tomb.*

It drew closer and closer now. Louder and louder. *Thud...drag...thud...drag...*

Alton held his breath and bit his lip to keep from crying out. *It was coming directly toward him.*

He shivered as if a cold wind had swept up and down his spine, curling around his vertebrae and clamping onto his heart and organs until he thought the chill would freeze his breath in his lungs.

The steps drew very near, then they stopped. Directly in front of Alton.

And he heard the *breathing.* Long, hissing, gasping breaths. Not only did he hear them, he felt them warmly upon his face. Warmly and wetly. And the smell... Horrid, like the smell of death. Which might have made sense if it had smelled like old death, but this smelled like *new,* fresh death, like a stray dog on the side of the highway. Or like whatever it was that had drawn closer had rotten meat lodged between its teeth. Or that whatever it was, was itself rotting even as it stood there, wheezing.

Alton froze in place for what felt like an eternity, face to face with something he could not see—and which he did not want to imagine.

There was a long scraping sound from above, and then suddenly a beam of blinding light flashed past him.

"Alton!" It was Gram. "Are you all right, lad?"

Even though he had to squint, Alton now saw he was alone in a rough-hewn circular chamber. In the center rested a huge, dark sarcophagus. There was no one walking, or staggering, in a circle. There was no rotting breather, or creature, or anything that looked either alive or dead.

He turned to face Gram, who was being lowered down through the trick stone trapdoor on a length of knotted rope. "Yes," he said simply. He could find no other words.

"It took a wee bit for us to find the trigger for the damnable trapdoor. Thankfully your sister saw you go down through the floor, otherwise we may never have found ye."

Now Gram stood on the chamber floor beside Alton. His boots scraped as he came closer. "Are you sure you're all right, my boy? You look pale. And you're trembling!"

Alton tried but couldn't speak. He realized he was still trying to hold his breath.

Looking past the youngest Chambers, Gram eyed the sarcophagus. "My Lord," he said. "Your luck of falling down and discoverin' things is unbelievable. This is unlike anythin' I've ever seen, or even read or heard about."

In the light of Gram's headlamp, the sarcophagus wasn't dark. It was dark *red*, and apparently made of countless red jewels, like rubies or perhaps the red spots on bloodstone.

It was a gigantic crimson sarcophagus.

And it was standing up on its feet.

Facing them as if to welcome them...or threaten them with its ruby stare.

Alton's stomach clenched at the thought of who, or *what*, might lie— or stand—within it.

Chapter Sixteen

CHAMBERS HAD HIS hands in her soft hair as he reclined on the wooden dais-like altar set in the center of the sarcophagus circle. She was pleasuring him with the particular skill she had developed early in life, and now even though she was older she was still as accomplished in it as ever.

"Alena!" He grunted as she took him all the way to the base of his manhood, swirling her tongue around him despite his girth. "Oh, my *dear* girl..."

She looked up at him and smiled as much as she could, bearing down on his stiffened flesh and then backing off. She was expert at taking control and dragging out the act, taking him to the edge and then sliding back, as long as she felt like. But eventually he would be at that edge and no longer wish to back off.

Now he placed his hands on her ears and held her head steady so he could thrust gently at first, then more insistently, into her wide-open throat. Her response was a gargling moan, and then he felt the climax slowly erupting from far down below and increased his thrusts until he was finishing, letting her take care of the mess the way she liked to do.

Alena wiped her lips clean then joined him on the dais and seductively spread her thighs wide apart. "My turn, Father," she said, her voice silky.

And he slid down to his knees and began pleasuring her. She rested her legs on his shoulders and for a while they were alone with the dead, fulfilling another of the rites called for in the directives by which Chambers had lived for decades. As he had learned, mostly through trial and error, Egyptian *sex magick* was of a particular strain, and the translated rituals functioned just as well as when he had struggled through them as a lad with less ability in linguistics than he wished. Over those decades, he had recouped all his investments in learning, having taken instruction from a long line of scholars he had purchased with his vast resources. Chambers now considered himself a high priest of Thoth—a reincarnation of Thoth himself, he suspected, returned to the world to fulfill a greater agenda—and he sensed that Alena was the reincarnation of his wife and consort, the alluring Nehmetawy. Perhaps the goddess had taught Cleopatra her reputed skill.

As he worked on her now, the volume of the whispering in his head, which was rarely completely absent, increased until he thought his head would burst. Alena's hands on his head, caressing his balding scalp, seemed like electric charges arriving through electrodes, making him hiss with the pleasure-pain that was his life.

He led Alena through the same path, roughly attacking her swollen sex until she screamed, and her scream merged with the whispers until they were one.

"Ah," she sighed. "Father... *Husband...*"

They kissed as passionately as teenagers, and as he held her he wondered if the time had truly come, if his life's work was about to be fulfilled.

When they were ascending, clothed again, she kept to the opposite side of the elevator car as if she wanted no part of him. The results of *sex magick* and passion were different for each of them. He could have ravaged her yet again already.

Arriving on the main level, and after wishing his daughter a good evening, Chambers found his manservant waiting.

"Yes, Batten?"

"We have a visitor at the gate, sir. I believe it is Laura Blackstone, and her voice indicates she is very distraught. Shall I send her on her way, or alert the authorities?"

Chambers rubbed his chin. He smelled Alena on his fingers, on his lips, and he was certain Batten did too. He smiled at his majordomo, enjoying the man's discomfort, which he went to great lengths to disguise. Batten really was indispensable.

"I think I should speak to her, but no farther than the foyer. Let her onto the grounds, Batten."

"Very well, sir."

Batten spoke softly into the intercom, which squawked with her grating voice in response. As Batten buzzed open the gates, Chambers had no doubt why Blackstone was such a bounder.

When Batten opened the main door, Chambers was there to greet her.

She was not an unattractive woman, if a bit severe in profile which she chose to not soften with cosmetics. Perhaps that was a mistake, Chambers thought as he extended his hand.

"Mrs. Blackstone," he said, smiling. "Welcome to my home."

She barely held his hand a second before dropping it like overripe fruit. "Yeah, well, I came to speak to my husband. *Professor* Blackstone. He's here, isn't he? That damn car of his is parked out there."

"Have you tried calling his phone?"

"What do you think I am, an idiot?" She was red in the face now. "I have called and I have texted and I have left voicemails, but the jerk is refusing to call me back."

"Madam, I have no control over that—"

"Since he's here, and being paid by you, it seems to me you do have control over that!"

"I assure you, I have nothing to do with whom he wishes to talk to, or avoid. Professor Blackstone is either in his office or in his suite, my dear lady, and he's not to be disturbed. He works late nights, and needs his sleep. He may be working or he may be sleeping, but I shall not disturb him either way. You may tell me what you would like to say to him, or if you'd like to leave him a message..."

"I want to talk to him. *Now.* Or I'll call the police."

He laughed politely, as if she had made a mild joke.

"The police? My, my, dear lady, whatsoever for?"

"I think you've kidnapped James. Or...brainwashed him, or something. All of a sudden he tells me he's quitting his job at the university and becoming your own personal...what, *assistant?*"

"Professor Blackstone is a highly regarded scholar, and I assure you nothing of what you suggest has happened. I have hired him for a more than fair compensatory wage and he has decided to spend much of his time here in the house while in my employ, because of the size of my collected materials. It's as simple as that, dear...Mrs. Blackstone. Your *husband* is here of his own accord."

Chambers realized he might have smoothed things over, if he hadn't slipped and twisted his emphasis on the word "husband," revealing his feelings on the subject of husbands in general. Instead, her eyes blazed and her mouth turned into a sneering grimace.

"Just the way you say that..."

"I'm sorry if I've offended you. I meant no such thing. I merely wanted to oppose your characterization of him as an assistant. As I said, he is here to lend me and my corporation his expertise in all things Egyptian, especially hieroglyphs and hands-on excavations, of which I have sponsored many over the years. I assure you, he is here of his own free will, with a generous salary, and is free to come and go as he chooses."

She had started nodding, but not in an agreement mode. Her nodding was sarcasm about to bubble over, rage about to burst forth.

She leaned into his space, her index finger under his chin.

"I. Don't. Care. About. You. And. Your. Little. Projects." She collected herself but spittle had reached his personal space. "I want to talk to my husband. Or I will call the police." She brandished a smartphone.

"Perhaps it would be better if *I* called the police," Chambers said, waving his own phone. "After all, you are intruding into *my* house. Let us see who the authorities would believe, the crazy woman in my foyer or the wealthy taxpayer whose peace and well-being are being threatened by her."

She took a menacing step in his direction and he held up the phone, showing her that he had 911 on the screen, ready to touch.

She was too close now, but if she backed off, her advantage, such as it was, would be lost.

Chambers refused to step back, and if he had been wielding any weapon, a fireplace poker, a candlestick, anything, he would have smashed it into her skull over and over until her voice ceased to make his ears ache.

Instead, he said, placatingly, "Mrs. Blackstone, I beg of you. Here is my card. Please call during the day and ask for James, er, Professor Blackstone, and you will be connected to him straight away." He took her elbow. "Now please, dear lady, I implore you—"

She yanked her arm away as if he were a leper. Snatched his card, mangled it, and threw it underfoot. "Don't implore me, just... Damn you, I know what kind of a crooked business you're running, and I promise you this isn't over!"

"Of course not, it will be over when you call and speak to your husband. *Tomorrow.*" He looked off to the side. "Batten, please escort Mrs. Blackstone to the gate. Good evening, Mrs. Blackstone."

Batten approached, his gargoyle-hard features just frightening enough to widen her eyes. She stepped away from him before he could get too close. She grunted and whirled, opened the front door with some difficulty, and stepped outside, followed all too closely by the stolid manservant. Chambers heard her swearing at him until she was out of earshot and then he turned away.

Alena was standing at the arch that led into the great room. She had fixed her clothes and makeup.

"Will she cause trouble?"

"Oh, I doubt it," said Chambers. "However, the professor had best humor her before she does become an obstacle."

"I'm afraid he will not do that," she said, smirking. "I'll be surprised if he even takes her call, if she bothers to call. He's too much into me now..."

He frowned. "Hm, perhaps you snagged him too quickly."

"I thought you said we had less time. *Father.*"

"Yes, yes, whatever you say. We are stuck with this man's problematic behavior...if only he'd been a bachelor."

She looked at her nails, one hand at a time. Her lips curled. "Well, I don't mind saying that I'm happy to know I still have *it*..."

"We'll figure something out." He grunted. "We'll have to. I fear that woman will not just fade away."

A few minutes later, alone, Chambers checked the cameras in Blackstone's suite. The professor was lounging in his underwear, reading from a stack of books. Completely unaware of his wife's visit to the house and how it had ended.

At least the man was on the job, studying rather than mooning over Alena. Or Naira. Or his *assistant*, with whom Batten had confirmed the professor had been having a rather torrid affair for months. The quietly efficient all-around Odd-Job type had reported the two had been known to cavort in his university office, in her office, in empty classrooms, in her apartment on a sex swing, and in various hotels. Apparently Blackstone didn't know how to be discreet.

Well, he was working for his employer at the moment. Chambers went to turn off the camera feed.

But then he swore.

Blackstone was reaching into his shorts.

The old man switched off the camera view and considered throwing the monitor against the wall.

Chapter Seventeen
1959

CHARLES JUNIOR PULLED the key ring from the pocket of his suit coat. A single skeleton key and a tag denoting his room number were all that hung from the ring. Room 412. He had trudged up the stairs irritated at how few of these old European hotels had elevators. Even the most opulent of Old World accommodations lacked the modern convenience. He couldn't imagine a hotel in New York City not having an elevator, but here in West Berlin only the most recent construction allowed for it. The cornerstone at the front of this building read *1891*.

Slipping the key into its hole, he disengaged the lock and stepped into the darkened room. The only light came through the windows from the streetlamps below. He toggled the switch by the door, lighting the floor lamp near the bed, and dropped the key on the small table beside the front door.

It had been a long day and tomorrow he had an early flight back to the States. He peeled off his suit coat and tossed it haphazardly over the back of a chair as he made a beeline to the bar cart in the corner of the diminutive room. He pulled the stopper off a crystal decanter and took a whiff. It was some kind of whiskey, maybe some Irish swill. Definitely not Scotch. He poured himself a short glass, which he downed in one gulp, then poured a second and drank it more slowly before carrying the glass to the bedside table and sitting on the edge of the bed. Wearily he took off his shoes. His feet were aching, the patent leather digging into his heels and ankles. He felt like he'd walked for miles when in fact he'd been at meetings most of the day.

He poured and drank another inch, and then another.

Maybe not so much a swill after all.

The meetings hadn't gone well. *Not well at all.*

No one had budged. No one had stuck out a hand and smiled. No one had pulled his fat out of the fire, as Charles Senior was wont to say.

He ran his hand over his greased-back hair. That the meetings hadn't gone well was low on his list of worries, really. It was just the final nail in the coffin lid. It was just the final straw that took the camel through the needle's eye, or whatever the fuck...

He drained the glass again and, blinking rapidly, thought, *What the hell,* and poured another two-three fingers.

Recently he had begun to wonder if he actually wanted to run an oil company, or if he had taken on a bigger role in the family business only because it was what his father wanted. He had been groomed from an early age to eventually take the reins completely; everyone knew it. It was time to step up his training. But was it what he wanted?

On top of that, his family was beginning to come undone. It was like a ball of yarn spinning out of control and creating a hopeless tangle. *There, that was better.*

He drank and it really tasted pretty good.

His sister, Cynthia, over the past year had gone from being a budding socialite to verging on turning into an embarrassing party girl, to becoming a full-blown recluse. His brother, Harrison, had taken to drinking hard regularly (*see, I'm not alone!*), and Charles feared he was into the junk along with all that *beatnik* shit. And his kid brother... Alton had become utterly obsessed with Egyptology, almost to the point that Junior considered it a form of madness. It seemed that ever since they'd traveled to Egypt, they had all lost their innocence. Perhaps lost their way. No matter what he called it, everything had changed over the course of a year and he didn't like it.

He took a smaller sip of his whiskey. And another. Then he drained it.

Better cut it out. Early flight.

They had cut out his heart, that's what they had done with their superior Teutonic smiles and polite dismissal.

Fuck me.

The harsh words sounded strange to him; they were more what dear old Gram would have said.

And fuck it.

He poured and the trickle went into the glass, barely covering the bottom. The empty decanter tipped onto the nightstand and he left it.

After briefly massaging his aching feet, Charles rose and stepped over to the blond wooden Grundig cabinet. He turned on the radio and the tubes hummed with life, immediately bringing in a broadcaster's voice speaking in German. Charles Junior frowned, then turned the dial through bands of static and garbled signals, finally finding a station where a crooner was working his way through a Sinatra song. But he was singing it in *German*, and instead of an orchestra or big band, he was accompanied by an accordion player.

A goddamned accordion player.

Charles turned it off.

He approached the narrow window that looked down onto the Ku'damm, the city's bustling shopping district. The street was full of both cars and buses and pedestrian traffic, walking from store to store, gasthaus to gasthaus. Neon strips located the occasional night club between the beer halls. If he didn't have a flight to catch in the morning, he probably would have joined those people, but his wake-up call was slated for 4:30 am and he was already dog-tired.

And shit-faced, Gram would have said.

Draining the dribble left in his glass, Charles set the tumbler down on the cart on his way to the bathroom where he quickly completed his nightly voiding, splashed some tepid water on his face, and prepared for what he wished would be blissful slumber. If not blissful, at least restful. If not restful, at least unaware.

Donning his silk pajamas before exiting the bathroom, he turned off the lamp, closed the curtains as tightly as he could to eliminate at least some of the blazing exterior light, and settled into the stiff bed. He struggled for a while, but then found his way into a chasm of deep, empty, semi-drunken sleep.

A noise roused him. Groggy, dry-mouthed, his eyes gummy slits, he lay motionless, hoping to return to the dark void. He was still half-asleep, and he felt it was possible he would succumb once more to the welcome dark.

But instead, a sudden shuffling noise, perhaps like the sound of something being dragged across the floor, caused his eyes to open and his heart to flutter. Then he heard a wooden groan, a soft whistle.

"What in the hell?" He sat up on his side, propping himself up on one elbow as he tried to unstick his eyelids. The room was as dark as when he'd gone to bed, so he really could see nothing, but his ears picked up soft sounds he couldn't identify. Slowly, his eyes peeled open and the outlines of the room's sparse furniture took shape. There was a tall wooden cabinet in the corner, but in this light it was first a menacing sarcophagus and then an innocent wardrobe, and also an elaborate desk and chair, a telephone table, the bar cart, and an overstuffed armchair.

A sudden stab to the heart made his chest ache, and his breath caught in his throat.

Someone was sitting in the armchair.

Motionless.

A shadow among other shadows, but the oval shape of a head had not been there earlier. And now it floated where a person's head would be if sitting squarely in the center of the scarred old chair.

Charles felt frozen. Transfixed with liquid fear. He could barely snatch a breath, and his heart or his lungs, or both, hurt when he tried. Inexplicably, he felt his bladder strain to contain itself despite having emptied recently.

When he found some semblance of courage, he scrabbled for something, anything, to fight with, but the lamp on his nightstand was too far out of his reach. *The bottle!* But it, too, had slipped out of his reach. His hands found an extra pillow, a heavy thing with stiff cloth ticking holding in straw or hay or maybe some of those new polyester balls. It wasn't much of a weapon, but Charles grasped its corner and threw it with all his strength at the shadowy interloper.

Before the pillow had even struck home, he managed to leap unsteadily to his feet. The chair was in his way, so he ran to the window and violently drew open the curtain.

The neon outside bathed the room in harsh crimson glare.

And he realized his possible assailant was no person at all.

By all appearances, it was the jacket of his suit, which he had carelessly tossed on the back of the chair when he'd first arrived. It had bunched up, and in the dark it had looked like a head.

Junior's shoulders slouched, and his hand went to his chest where his heart still pounded in double-time, his lungs straining at his chest wall as if they could never get enough air.

He laughed aloud in the darkness.

Relieved, and grinning at his own stupid fear of the dark, he picked up the thrown pillow and tossed it back onto the bed. He was just about to crawl back under the blankets when he stopped to listen.

The noise. There it was again.

It was the same sound that had awakened him. Something being dragged across the floor, or against the wall? He listened intently.

The room was still dark, but the glow from the uncovered window gave it a blood-red tinge.

He followed the sound, letting his ears lead him. Inside his room? *No.* In the tiny bathroom? *No.* Was it coming from the floor above? Impossible; he remembered this was the uppermost floor of the hotel. The sound grew louder, more insistent, and led him to his door. The scraping, dragging, whatever it was, came from the hallway. He placed his ear against the door, listening.

It was some kind of scratching, and it wasn't coming from the hallway actually. No, it came from something that scratched slowly, achingly slowly, *at his door.*

In a fit of anger and more than a little fear, Charles grasped the knob, twisted, and pulled the door open in one swift motion.

"Who—?"

Standing in his doorway was a child, dressed in rags that smelled of disease. Its loosely wrapped bony fingers had been scratching insistently on the door.

For an instant, Charles wondered how this waif had found his way into a relatively high-class hotel. This was the rich, urban portion of West Berlin, and the figure now at his door belonged in an alley at the edge of a slum. Certainly it couldn't have been the offspring of one of the other guests. Suddenly, before he could shut the door, the child shuffled forward and into his room.

He stepped back, recoiling at the stench the small body carried with it like its own atmosphere. Uncomfortable, Charles considered simply pushing the kid back into the hall. But as he raised his hands to do just that, he began to realize it wasn't a child at all. It was a shriveled old man almost completely wrapped in tattered old, smelly bandages.

His mind nearly snapped shut when he suddenly remembered seeing *it,* or something like it, before. *In that damned tomb—Alton's big find.*

It wasn't a child or a man at all. As the figure moved slowly toward him, Charles could see more of its hideous features, now tinted lurid blood-red by the light in his room. It was nearly a skeleton, with skin stretched and dry like rawhide pulled over its bones, half-wrapped in ancient yellowed linens that crumbled to dust as the thing slowly ambled forward, reaching for Charles like a beggar with its arms outstretched for a tithe.

It's impossible.

It's a Goddamned mummy...

Impossible!

Charles lashed out to push the cursed thing away. It was as small as a ten-year-old child and moved as feebly as a geriatric, so it should have been easily overcome. But as soon as he touched the thing, Charles regretted it.

The mummy—for that was what it *had* to be—was so cold, so piercingly bitter in nature, that it burned to the touch, like picking up a piece of dry ice. Charles squealed as he pulled back his shocked hands. His stomach dropped to his groin and a cold shiver flowed through him uncontrollably when Charles looked at his hands in the red light to see that they had actually atrophied and blackened from touching the mummy's icy hide.

His hands had been scorched by the mummy's touch.

In a blind panic, Charles backed away. The room was too narrow for him to move around the damned thing without touching it. The corner on one side and the desk on the other effectively blocked him, and the only direction was backward to the bed on one side, and the outside wall on the other.

As the thing moved slowly but steadily toward Charles, backing him into the corner made by the end of the bed and the window wall, he reached back and painfully wrestled open the window with his damaged, scalded hands.

"*Hilfe!*" he called down to the street as he turned. "Help!"

But the street was now empty, night finally having cleared it of shoppers and revellers. And it was too many floors down.

"*Hilfe! Help!*"

He tried again, but was answered only by the echo of his own pleas.

It was right behind him now, and Charles could feel the cold radiating off the damned mummy-thing. Fear screaming through his belly, he climbed up onto the windowsill and stepped out on the narrow ledge that ringed each floor of the building. If he could make it to the next room over, get in through their window and find his way out to the hall...

Then what?

Worry about it—and whatever people might think—later. Right now, he knew he had to get away from that...that *thing.*

Shimmying along the stone ledge with his back to the building, he had to ignore the excruciating pain in his hands as they hugged the rough outside wall behind him. Wobbling precariously, looking down on the barren street through the red neon glare, Charles inched his way to the next window. He glanced back the way he had come, feeling himself teeter in the imaginary breeze.

And the mummy-thing had followed him out onto the ledge.

Its diminutive size allowed it to move relatively unhindered across the ledge. In fact, balancing on a high ledge didn't seem to slow it down in the least. It came at him as steadily as it had in the room. It didn't even have to walk sideways as Charles did. It almost *floated* above the ledge.

But that wasn't possible!

None of this was possible!

Maybe I'm having a nightmare.

No, that was wishful thinking. Deep down, through all the pain, Charles Junior *knew* it was no nightmare. He knew something dark and menacing and evil had followed him from Egypt.

"*Hilfe!*" His words were carried on the wind and scattered over the deserted sidewalks. A boxy German car went by slowly, but no one in that car would be looking up at this hour. "*Hilfe! Hilfe!*" he tried anyway, but the words dissipated like gossamer.

Out of the corner of his eye he saw the thing approaching, moving faster than he could, so he scrabbled to quicken his sideways gait—ignoring the danger of relying on his near-useless hands.

Suddenly he realized he had reached the neighboring room, which was as dark as a grave.

Luck, such as it was, was with him: the window was unlocked!

Somehow Charles managed to scratch at the jamb with his bloody, throbbing fingertips, and wrenched the narrow frame open—

—*just as the creature's claw-like hand grabbed the sleeve of his pajama shirt.*

The shirt was covered with paislies, he remembered.

As if it mattered...

And—

—the next instant was stretched out in his mind, so the moment itself was as clear as crystal and lasted an incredible length of time.

Charles fought to free himself from the creature's grip, but by now it had grasped and squeezed the shirt's fabric and was making his forearm sizzle with its cold burn.

Teetering again on the ledge as his arm seemed to turn to stone in the creature's grip, his foot caught on the bottom edge of the opening window just as he was bowing his head to enter the room. He was suddenly thrown off-balance. Swinging his free arm, he tried to regain his footing, but instead he slipped off the window ledge, trying to turn into the wall, grabbing at bricks much too neatly laid to allow any sort of purchase...

He fell backward.

Away from the mummy-thing, which was no longer there.

He saw the empty ledge above him in that split-second, but it was too late. His hands barely worked, and they grasped nothing but air.

Charles fell, plummeting down the four stories to the unforgiving concrete sidewalk below.

Blood filled in the paisley pattern of his shirt.

* * *

Young Alton was on his knees with his pants and underwear bunched up around his ankles. In his left hand he rubbed a small strip of ancient cotton linen that he had taken from the artifacts they had collected in the desert. It crumbled to dust as he pressed it between his fingers and thumb.

With his right hand he stroked his erection fervently.

On the floor in front of him, between his knees, was a photograph of his eldest brother, Charles Junior.

It was the last thing he wanted to look at while pleasuring himself, but the voices were insistent.

His lips were moving and he was making sounds. Sounds he didn't understand. The voices were repeating them over and over, so Alton did the same. They were like words, but nothing that he had ever heard before. Only the voices knew what they meant.

When he spilled his seed and spattered his brother's picture, the voices stopped.

Mostly.

Chapter Eighteen

"TODAY IS THE day, Blackstone," Chambers said, sweeping into the inner sanctum—the vault room—that had now become Blackstone's study, open to him at any time. "Follow me."

The professor set down the magnifying glass he'd been using to scan one of the hundreds of photographs he had so far logged and translated to the best of his ability. The story that was taking shape had been eating into his sleep, keeping him up later and then keeping him awake.

Sometimes Alena slipped into his suite and before he knew it she had thrown the covers off and either straddled him or wrapped his manhood with her hand, or even better, with her lips. And then, in a fever-like state, he became less a lover than a plaything, but he couldn't bring himself to complain or question Alena's aggression—or her needs. He had his own. After she left, he would try to drop off again, but his mind and body fought sleep and instead he ruminated over the glyphs he had studied all day. By morning he would be bleary-eyed and weary, but ready to scan more photographs.

Other days, Michelle would flash him her breasts and they'd share a slippery interlude after which both would need a shower, which would help to wipe away his fatigue. Michelle was almost as adept as Alena at some sex sports, but went further in others. In fact, both women were well beyond what any of his former lovers were willing to do. Despite the complications, he considered himself very lucky indeed.

But today he followed Chambers to the vault, a different kind of excitement rising and wiping out his exhaustion.

"It's time," said the old man. "Your most recent translations are very interesting. I want you to see the panels themselves."

Blackstone's breath caught in his throat.

"Wait here," Chambers said, as he always did when he entered the safe.

When he exited a few minutes later, his white-gloved hands were cradling a narrow jagged-edged panel chiseled from a wall of the famous family tomb. "There are gloves on the table," Chambers said.

Blackstone hurriedly donned a pair, his hands trembling with expectation.

When Chambers handed him the panel, Blackstone felt tears squeezing out from between his lids. He blinked them away. "It's beautiful!"

And it was. Though the back side of the panel was jagged, having been cut from its wall by some sort of specialized saw, the front was smooth and the colors of the bas-reliefs eye-poppingly vivid. There were fine cracks in the painted surface, but Blackstone decided they were cracks in the surface paint, not the panel itself. The glyphs were bold yet delicate, lines of characters and pictograms starting to sing in his brain, though he still couldn't read them as he did most others. This was different in nature than even the photographs he'd studied for two weeks.

"What do you think?" Chambers asked, acting the proud father.

Blackstone's tears suddenly flowed freely. And his voice was hoarse. "I don't know what it says, but it's reaching into my gut."

Chambers stared at him as if uncomprehending. "I had some cradles specially built to hold the panels," he explained. He bent at the waist and deployed one like a keyboard drawer. "Lay this one in here."

When they had arranged the panel in the cradle so it could be examined hands-free, he used a magnifying glass to check the brush strokes that filled the glyphs which had been painstakingly gouged from the stone panel thousands of years ago.

Damn the old man, how could he not understand the emotion of the moment?

For all his flaws, Blackstone prided himself on being truly devoted to archaeology and the understanding of ancient civilizations.

"I haven't made enough headway to translate this yet," he said as he checked the lines and color whorls with the magnifier.

"I'm confident you will," Chambers said. "Though perhaps lessening your distractions would help."

Blackstone felt his face warming and knew it had reddened.

Did the old man know? About whom? And how much did he know?

No way to tell now, but Blackstone sensed that he needed to be more careful, with both Michelle *and* Alena. He didn't want to lose the gig so shortly after scoring it. Did he?

"I'll leave you alone with it for a while," Chambers said. "See that it's not damaged, Professor."

Blackstone swallowed his retort. All he wanted to do was examine the chunk of wall that was changing his life.

He spread out his books, several notebooks filled with copious notes written in his exacting hand, and swung a laptop closer. Then he got to work.

Three hours later, he raised his head, felt his neck crack, and realized the weather outside had changed, darkened, and his bladder was uncomfortably full. But his excitement kept him from moving.

The panel was, in part, either a description of or an actual incantation to some deity he had not yet identified. The words and phrases he had translated seemed to be part of a greater ritual. Ignoring his screaming bladder, he consulted some of the photographs that documented the remainder of the larger panel, and nodded with sudden understanding.

It *was* an incantation!

Instead of the more typical historical context given by most tomb writings, this segment was part of a religious rite.

What it intended to do was as yet unclear. Blackstone needed the rest of the wall panels that completed the whole. His excitement gave way to his bladder's need, however, so he pulled off the gloves and abandoned the study.

Exiting the main bathroom for this wing, he nearly collided with Alena. She was resplendent in tight black leather pants, knee-high boots, a black silk blouse, and red kerchief tied around her neck. Blackstone noted that her nipples were visible through the sheer silk.

"Professor, I was looking for you."

He had insisted they keep their public meetings somewhat formal. The creature named Batten often lurked nearby as if he'd been tasked with keeping an eye on Blackstone. Perhaps he had. But the professor did not want to give the manservant, or whatever he was, anything to report.

"You've found me, Alena. I'm afraid it's a busy day today, since your father finally decided to make the panels themselves available to me."

She sneered. "Of course, I wouldn't want to interrupt your orgasmic seizure over those chunks of painted rock."

"That's not fair, Alena. He's paying me well, and I am obligated to give him my best effort, unlike whoever was here first."

"They did their best," she muttered. "It was merely not good enough."

"*They?* There was more than one? What happened to them?"

"Fired, or they left. I don't know, with most of them they weren't even aware of me."

Blackstone laughed. "I find that hard to believe."

She thrust her chest at him without shame. Whoever had done the work was a masterful technician—her breasts were firm and perfectly balanced, capped with splendid nipples. "They might have noticed, but they were not... Let's say they didn't have your *attributes.*"

"Flattery will get you every little thing."

"And some not so little?"

His face warmed again. "I doubt this is a good time. Your father expects me to get further than I have, and today has been a huge step forward."

"Lest you think all I wanted to do was play games with you, I was merely letting you know that dinner will be ready soon."

Blackstone sighed. "I must have lost track of time."

"I can help you with that whenever you want."

"I know."

She reached out a hand and caressed his cheek in an almost motherly gesture.

But then her hand fell down, across his chest, and to his groin, where he was already straining.

She leaned into him and whispered in his ear.

"After dinner, there's dessert...and then *dessert.*"

By the time they were seated at the dinner table, Blackstone had cooled off. Naira was being quiet, while Chambers did all the prompting of both Blackstone and Alena. She winked at Blackstone occasionally, reminding him about his personal sweet course later. Halfway through the otherwise bland meal, Michelle was shown into the dining room.

"I'm sorry I'm late," she said as mother and daughter glared at her.

"In this house, no one is ever late!" Alena tossed her head at Michelle regally, scolding and dismissing at the same time.

"Nonsense!" said Chambers. "Welcome, Miss Davenport." The old man was almost effusive. Perhaps he thought her presence would spice things up.

Or more likely, perhaps having a lovely new woman to ogle was doing it for him, Blackstone thought with a secret smile. He tried to catch Michelle's eye, but she was too busy being in the crossfire.

Based on the looks exchanged by the three women, spicing things up was an understatement. Blackstone looked on, bemused, as they started sniping almost as soon as all three had taken their places at the table.

"Mother tells me you're an assistant," gurgled Naira, placing too much emphasis on the start of the word. "Now what does that entail?" She smiled widely after also overemphasizing the end of that particular word.

"It entails doing things you can only dream of, sweetie," Michelle purred.

"Oh, I doubt that."

"Naira, mind your manners!" Alena didn't seem all that upset, however her words might have been a scolding.

"Mother, I'll mind mine when you and the professor mind yours. Although I'm betting yours have been minded pretty thoroughly by now."

Chambers had been smiling up to now, but the look soured as he realized the meal was not going to end well after all. "I apologize for my daughter and granddaughter's behavior. It appears I've failed as a father, and that failure was passed on to the next generation. Please help yourself to some of our Egyptian fare, or skip it and the staff can prepare something less exotic."

Michelle speared two *kofta* sausages from one platter, *Lahma Bin Basal* stew from a large wooden bowl, and folded a wide *Saboob* flatbread. "I'm quite happy with all this, Mr. Chambers. Reminds me of Cairo." She dipped the *Saboob* into the stew. "It's very good!"

"I have very good chefs."

Michelle nodded, mouth full, and spooned up some spicy lentil soup into her bowl. She looked at Blackstone and winked.

The professor saw that his women—as he was increasingly thinking of them—didn't appreciate Michelle's affability and refusal to embarrass herself by ordering something as banal as a hamburger. He winked back.

Alena's features hardened and she stood abruptly. "I've lost my appetite," she announced and stalked from the room.

"What the fuck's wrong with her?"

"Naira!"

The younger Chambers turned her innocent face to Chambers and pouted. "I'm sorry, Grandfather, but Mother uses language like that all the time."

"So do roughnecks on my rigs. I'll tolerate no such language at my table, in front of my guests!"

"I've lost my appetite too," she said, standing dramatically before sashaying out of the dining room, her buttocks swaying for Blackstone's benefit.

"Really good!" said Michelle around a mouthful of stew.

Blackstone had to stifle his laughter with food.

Chambers glared at them and ate in silence.

Blackstone wondered if there would be some repercussion for the lapse in decorum.

Chapter Nineteen

BUT THERE WOULD be no dessert from Alena that night, for when she turned the knob on Blackstone's door, she found it locked. She leaned her head and her right ear closer to the door, and when her skin touched the cool wood she could hear faint sounds from inside.

It was rhythmic screaming, the orgasmic kind, from Michelle, who sounded as though she was being pounded.

Alena ground her teeth as she listened. She could go to her father's security set-up and spy, or she could pound her fist on the door, or she could even use a master key to unlock it, but through her anger she knew it would all backfire.

No, it would be best to prove to Blackstone that Alena would be the better liaison, not that she hadn't already gone out of her way to make that case. But they hadn't planned on the professor's shameless promiscuity—call it what it was, perverted male randiness and shameless exploitation of female bodies...which made her smile a little, for wasn't she guilty of the same, but in reverse?

In any case, it was more difficult to stand out when the object of her attentions could find the same or better with someone else. Alena thought she could make him forget the Davenport woman, but she hadn't planned on his asking her father to hire her. Or that her father would have done so! He did love to play games, didn't he? All one had to do was take a look at this house. Charles Senior had built it, but Alton had made it his own, turned it into a castle with many secrets, and that was half the fun.

Alena frowned at the thought of her father drooling over the scene inside, staring at one of his monitors.

Suddenly she realized that she was really doubly jealous. Michelle right now was winning, stealing from her both her lovers, albeit in different ways. She didn't need to see Blackstone fucking Davenport's ass to know that was what was happening, and to be certain her father was enjoying the spectacle.

Alena stalked away to her own suite, furious at everyone involved, including herself for caring so much. Even though her use of the professor was part of the plan, she had started to enjoy his company during their torrid trysts, and that this turn of events bothered her so much enraged her further in a cycle of rage that very little could lift her out of.

She slammed her door twice as hard as needed.

From down the hall in a spare room, Naira watched as her mother stalked into her place and jumped, startled, at the anger released in the door slam.

What was up with the old bitch?

She chuckled. She knew what it was. The professor was probably drilling that Michelle bitch right now, keeping her mommy dearest from her *dessert after the dessert.* Naira had been just down the hall eavesdropping when her oversexed mother had just about ripped Blackie's clothes off earlier. The dude must have been on a glyph-related high, it had taken him a while to understand that she wanted to jump his bones, and then her mother had flipped the whole thing neatly by forcing him to put it off.

Must've really pissed off Mommy that in the meantime Michelle Davenport had appeared to offer up her tight ass.

She recognized the challenge. Trying to get Blackie to go for *her* pants when he had both other women doing somersaults to fuck him would be difficult, but she'd seen him watching her and thought it was inherently possible she might have an inside track—her youth.

Mommy was pretty great sexually for her age, but she was older than Professor Blackie. Davenport was way younger than Alena and just as inventive and skilled, so it was natural that he'd want to hang onto her.

But Naira was everything the two of *them* were and more, and on top of it she was the youngest. She had sensed right away that while Blackie was a dog who'd mount anything with a hole or two, he was particularly struck by youth. After all, why else was he teaching when he could have been graverobbing like her grandfather had done all his life? Yeah, Blackie liked 'em young, and teaching gave him his pick every semester.

She'd seen the file Batten had compiled on the old Indiana Jones lookalike, and it sounded as though he'd fucked his way through several years' worth of students and assistants until he'd fucked one once too often and in too sacred a place, and then he'd been lucky to land this position at a much lower level in a lesser college. But even lesser colleges have a plethora of young flesh-merchants willing to offer sex for grades, and Blackie had fallen right back into his pattern. Maybe the selection was a bit less fresh, but then Michelle Davenport had simply stood out as the best and most fuck-worthy.

Naira laughed at the thought of her mother in her dingy suite, probably maneuvering one of her countless sex toys into herself, in a rage that it wasn't her pal Blackie.

She'd heard some strange conversations between her mother and grandfather though, and she was still trying to process what she thought she'd heard. Was her grandfather pimping out his own daughter to the professor for some sort of greater goal?

WTF? she thought, not for the first time.

In fact, she wondered what her grandfather was doing *right now*, while Blackie was plowing Davenport's furrows.

She thought she knew.

Naira redoubled her commitment to snag herself a chunk of that professor hottie and see what the fuss was all about. If in the process she could piss off her mother, all the better.

And if she could figure out what sort of game Gramps and the bitch were up to, that might be something she could use at some point to dangle in front of Blackie.

There was *always* a use for blackmail in the Chambers family.

Chapter Twenty

WHEN THE INTRUDER alert went off, Alton Chambers was in the Prep Room checking on his newest creation, the late Professor al-Amani, which was coming along rather well. Batten's voice on the old-fashioned intercom unit interrupted his supplication to the gods of the Nile, which he recited whenever working on a new mummy. It was a form of respect, and Chambers had nothing but respect for the dead who traveled the eternal path.

"Sir, you'll want to see this, from camera six."

Chambers sighed.

He composed and whispered an apology to the gods for the interruption.

At a nearby workstation hidden inside a cabinet, a large screen allowed a view of most feeds from the house and grounds cameras. Batten had fed the monitor a loop from camera six of a shadowy figure in black jeans and black jacket climbing over the wall in one of the most wooded areas of the compound. The figure landed on its feet inside the compound and crept toward the main house. Then another camera had picked up the intruder, and then another, and soon the figure was at the side of the main house. The intruder kept to the shadows and carefully approached every window.

As Chambers watched, a bit of overhead light from one of the external lamps caught the person's face for not more than a second or two. And anyway, other cameras were infrared and would have revealed her identity before long.

It was Laura Blackstone, the professor's wife.

Chambers smiled, amused. He went back to the intercom.

"Is she still on the grounds?"

"She is trying to breach one of the basement windows in the east wing."

"See if you can help her, Batten. Encourage her to find an open window. The right one."

"Very well, sir."

Chambers reviewed the loop. What was Laura Blackstone doing here? Was she merely coming to protest that the Davenport woman was also here, or that her husband was being paid a fair sum more than he had told her? It wasn't as if she were attempting to rescue her husband. More likely she wanted to catch him *in flagrante*, hoping to extort his newfound income in some revenge-driven divorce settlement.

He went back to the dessicated al-Amani with an apology on his lips... The gods demanded respect, and he well knew how important it was to grant them what they wanted. They could be very generous indeed. But they could be merciless, and he had shown them that he, too, could be. He had seen enough to know the gods listened and paid attention.

He had spent most of his life paying them homage. Since that awful and wonderful day in the tomb he had found, where he had also found his destiny. It was getting closer to the time he would get what *he* wanted.

But right now, there was the matter of Laura Blackstone.

Nothing really. A mosquito, to be brushed off with minimal effort.

Ten minutes expired and the intercom buzzed quietly. "She has, er, taken the bait, sir." Batten seemed to taste the unfamiliar phrase.

Ah, as any naive and essentially lazy human would have done, she had accepted the unlikely proposition of one open window. How painfully predictable.

"She is trying to orient herself with a compass or device of some sort," added Batten. He waited for instructions.

Chambers wanted to just have her removed, swatted like the mosquito she was. But he felt a pressure in his loins that clamored for attention.

It was clearly a message from Min, one of the most prominent fertility deities.

Prominent especially because he is always depicted with an erection, Chambers thought with amusement. He whispered a prayer to Min now, as he touched himself and understood what the god wanted of him.

He heard a voice in his mind, a guttural voice speaking in staccato chunks of sound that formed themselves into clusters of words he could understand. He shivered with joy at communicating with the Other. He listened, nodded, and whispered a brief response with similar sounds.

"Bring her to me in the usual place, but make sure she's asleep first."

"Sir." Batten clicked off.

He considered. Did he need to know what Laura Blackstone was attempting? No, he did not. Batten had told him she had spent time in the university library, reading old microfilm and making a ream of photocopies she had clipped into packets. Chambers had been amused. Clearly she planned to expose something of what Chambers was thought to have done over the years, perhaps giving her husband the "proof." She *was* trying to woo the professor away, wasn't she? Blackstone was too greedy to believe what she provided. No, at this point it would help Chambers more if she just disappeared. And Blackstone himself would probably not care that much. Chambers had done his research well, and things weren't so great back at Blackstone Castle, were they?

Blackstone was brilliant, a master at translation and a highly accomplished writer. He was a passably good teacher when he put his mind to it, and he knew how to conduct a dig. But he was a weak man with too many vices, the greatest of which was the sloping delta between women's thighs, followed by the rounded globes of their buttocks and the shape of their lips.

He wasn't altogether different from Chambers himself, except that the sad-sack professor couldn't keep from being caught and his peccadilloes exposed. Chambers had learned while young that problems were best solved when they went away, disappeared, and were lost in the dust devil of history. He had operated on that principle from the earliest days that followed his falling into the tomb... And when the true destiny of the Chambers name had been revealed to him, rather quickly he had begun to take control of problems until he had none.

Now he turned away from the screen and attended to al-Amani once again, caressing the nicely desiccating flaps of skin he would lovingly sew together before final wrapping with the ceremonial bandages.

He bowed and engaged with the voice in his head.

Rather, he listened while fussing with the body he was preparing for its forever journey. He listened as he had for decades, and for a moment he was taken back to that earlier time, in the desert, when his father and siblings were still alive. He remembered so very well those first years after the tomb became the most important thing in his life. And he remembered how heady those early days of the project became.

He bowed and prayed to Min again, knowing he would need the god's help soon.

Al-Amani had been on the verge of a breakthrough in the work, but when he had reached the critical point, he had—somehow, Chambers was not certain how—begun to suspect what he was translating, the nature of the writings and their purpose. He suspected Alena, his ambitious daughter, had clued the elderly professor into the realization. Perhaps one of those times she had reawakened his mostly waned sexual capabilities.

She has a talented mouth, that one, especially when she's not using it to speak.

Perhaps she had thrown her not inconsiderable talents into recruiting an ally against him, her father, and the Occupant—the god who spoke to him. Perhaps it had all been accidental.

In the middle of his incantation to Min, Batten intercomed the news that he had *prepared* the Blackstone woman, as he put it. This meant, in part, that she had been dosed with a careful blend of Rohypnol and GHB.

Chambers had not observed this time, but the standard procedure with such interruptions was to isolate the intruder or guest in a room that, once entered, seemed to have no exit. This was an illusion based on a trick passage Chambers had found in the tomb, and which indeed had been used in numerous pharaoh's tombs to trap and eventually kill graverobbers. Once seemingly locked inside the square space, the side walls had begun to move rapidly together on near-invisible oiled tracks until the subject—in this case, the intrepid Mrs. Blackstone—was forced to flatten sideways, usually at the door end of the room. Of course, by then she would have been screaming herself hoarse at the very real expectation of being squashed flat like an insect by the moving walls, but the room was soundproof even as it compressed itself to sixteen inches in width. At that point, thanks to an oft-updated computer program controlling such estate functions, the walls would have stopped their internal movement.

The exhausted subject, screamed all out of breath and ready to accept any proposition, moved closer to the door and—when in position—a small square hatch set into the door's center slid open and Batten simply reached in with a hypodermic needle and delivered the dose before the subject could begin to understand the significance of this new development, and by then the hatch had slid shut once again.

Once the exotic blend of modern potions had spread through the subject's bloodstream and the body had flopped to the narrowed floor, it was no effort for Batten to release the walls to their original position, reach inside, and scoop up the burden in his deceptively strong arms.

Chambers made his last salutations to Min, bowed in obeisance, and took his leave of the mummifying professor.

Down the main corridor, inside the great crypt with its concentric circles of sarcophagi, on his favored altar was splayed the currently inoperable body of Professor Blackstone's annoying spouse. Her eyes were wide open, facing sideways, so she was able to see Chambers when he climbed the steps to the dais and entered her limited field of vision.

"Welcome, my dear Lady Blackstone," he said with mock cheer. "Welcome back to the Chambers estate. I must say, your efforts to gain entry would have been less taxing for you at the front door. Oh, but you *had* attempted that mode of entry, hadn't you?"

Laura's eyelids were paralyzed so her gaze gave nothing away.

"Don't worry, I know you're unable to speak right now. I'll do more than enough talking for both of us. I suspect you sought entrance by way of our windows because again you wished to confront your esteemed husband at his new place of employment. He is well, and I think he is otherwise occupied at the moment. He has been working hard on translations for me, you see, and he and his assistant have been inseparable as they work through the nights. Burning the midnight oil, you might say. Burning the candle at both ends. They've worked tirelessly—and I mean sweat-inducingly *tirelessly*—to do the job before them, the job *I* set before them."

He glared at her. "Now that they are on the verge of a discovery for which I've waited nearly my entire life, I will not allow their work to be derailed by the intervention of a disturbed individual."

Laura tried to blink repeatedly. The drug was beginning to loosen its control of some minor functions, and her horrified gaze was centered on his ceremonial vestments. He'd been communing with Min, so now she was staring at the solid gold ankh he wore as a pendant. And she had noted the dagger on his sash-like belt, sheathed in gold with its intricate golden grip topped by a jackal-head crystal. Her lips moved a bare millimeter, as if she were working up to a supplication.

"Now now," Chambers cooed, "this was inevitable. In fact, I'm glad you came to me, here, like this. You're really making it much easier for me, my dear."

Chambers put a hand on the dagger's grip. He unsheathed the exceedingly sharp blade shaped from meteoric metals.

"I think it's safe to say that we can all agree you should have just left that cheating bastard years ago."

Laura managed to blink once. A tear squeezed out of her left eye and dropped to the altar.

He undid the sash over his robe and slowly lowered it to the stone floor of the dais. Then he spread his vestments. He was naked underneath, his elderly body in surprisingly toned shape for its age, with knotty muscles and raised veins. And his manhood rampant, bobbing in her view.

As it should be for this offering to Min.

He stepped forward and Laura's eyes released a torrent of tears. The blinking increased, eyelids fluttering. He needed her to see him, to *watch*, and so he held her head down on the altar and deftly maneuvered the sharp tip of the dagger. The tears turned bloody. Her eyes would watch now. Then he pried her lips open as far as they could go, knowing she could not control them.

Chambers chanted the holy incantation which served the double purpose of calling forth the deity and covering the young woman's unintelligible sounds of terror—and, later, more pain—while he circled the altar and took his pleasure in the name of Min in a variety of ways. It was all part of the ritual.

Time passed, and when he was finished, completely finished, then he scooped up the dagger from the floor.

By now Laura was catatonic. Her eyes, lidless and glazed, were ringed by the congealing blood.

It didn't matter. Min was sated, and so was Chambers.

Then he went to work again with the dagger, making his cuts and thrusts with surgical precision. Eventually life left her and he was sure he saw her *ka* appear, briefly, before it was consumed by the Occupant.

Chambers always enjoyed this phase, when the flesh was still warm but cooling. He handled the dagger with practice and a pure love of the ritual.

The collection vessels filled swiftly.

Chapter Twenty-One
1961

THE CAT WAS cautious, eyeing Cynthia with suspicion as she crouched down with the bowl of food. Its long orange fur was matted and tangled, disguising its emaciated frame beneath a tabby-printed facade.

Cynthia made kissing sounds as she pushed the bowl toward the skittish animal. "Aren't you hungry, baby?" she asked in a sing-song voice, as if she were speaking to a child.

The cat turned away, pretending to not be interested.

"Okay, well, I'll leave this out here in case you change your mind, okay?"

The orange tabby was not the first stray or feral cat to stumble along to her house, it was just the most recent.

Cynthia stepped through the doorway, absent-mindedly letting the screen door slam behind her. She flinched, imagining that it was what the cat did when the door crashed shut.

She had no idea where all the cats had come from. She had no idea that there were so many cats that needed a home. She supposed it was her own fault for feeding them. Once she had fed the first one, it must have told its friends, and from there her legend must have spread through all of catdom, because it seemed as though more arrived every day.

Cynthia strode into the kitchen, still wearing her breeches and riding boots. She'd spent most of the day at the stables, and had taken Starbeam out for a ride through the compound's back acreage. Her love for all things equine had been persistent and had only deepened over the past couple years. Her party girl years were behind her—she guessed she had just outgrown the phase. She had moved her things from the main house to one of the smaller guest houses to be closer to the stables. And to get away from all the testosterone in the big house. Being the only woman living with her father and three brothers—well, only two now—plus a mostly male staff was just too much. She needed softer surroundings. And a space of her own.

She sat at the opulent dining room table, her tall-stemmed glass of Mouton Rothschild 1945 resting before her. She took a sip of the red grape while reaching for the sparkling clean crystal ashtray at the center of the table. Pulling it close, she removed the book of Chambers Oil Company matches from its bottom and took a Newport from her silver case. She put the cigarette in the corner of her mouth, struck a match, and took a deep drag, the flavorful smoke playing on the notes of the wine.

A thump at the window snatched her attention away from her simple pleasures. A big gray tomcat—the one she called Silver—had leapt up onto the window ledge and now had begun pacing the narrow sill, its tail swishing wildly.

"Yes, I'll feed you guys soon, Silver," she said mostly to herself, as the cat had no idea what she was saying.

She turned her back to the window so she could finish her wine and cigarette without further interruption.

After grinding out the last ember of her Newport beneath its filter, she took one last swallow of wine and headed to her bath. She made quick work of it, washing off the dust from a day in the saddle and in the horse barn. Later she would walk to the main house for dinner with the family, which was their custom, so she wanted to look nicely put together. Finishing her bath, Cynthia dressed in her room, opting for the sleeveless powder-blue suit dress that made her feel like Jaqueline Kennedy. She carefully applied her makeup and made sure her hair was presentable, already looking forward to retreating back home for another glass of wine and cigarette after dinner. She checked her appearance in the mirror one last time and smiled to herself. Maybe the party girl was still in there somewhere.

She paused in the hallway to look at the solid gold statue of Bast—the cat-headed Egyptian goddess—that rested on a short pillar against the wall opposite the staircase. It was her only keepsake from the ill-fated trip to Egypt she had taken with her brothers two years earlier. It seemed like a lifetime ago. A year later, her elder brother, Charles Junior, had taken his own life. Seeing the statue now made her sad. Usually she walked past it without taking notice, but tonight for some reason it had caught her attention, as if she were seeing it for the first time. The figure of the goddess stood stalk-straight with her arms crossed over her chest.

Hadn't her arms been at her sides before now?

Cynthia shook her head. What an outlandish thought! It couldn't be, statues don't move.

But it did seem different somehow.

And unnerving.

She took a deep breath to calm her nerves. The memory of the Godforsaken trip and of her brother's death rattled her for a moment. *Statues don't move.* And Chambers women don't get rattled.

She was on her way out the front door, concentrating on dinner with her father and brothers in order to push the discomfort from her mind, when she noticed Silver still perched on the windowsill.

The cats! She had nearly forgotten them.

Cynthia scurried to the kitchen and wrestled a half-full bag of kibble out of the pantry. Cradling the bag in her arm, she headed out the front door. A group of cats had crowded together there, and began to serenade her with a chorus of meows as soon as she stepped outside.

"Oh, I'm sorry, babies. How could I forget about you?"

The swirling group of felines followed underfoot as Cynthia stalked to the side of the house where the six bowls she filled daily sat waiting among another throng of anxious strays, their tails waving like flags at the Olympic opening ceremonies.

"Okay, okay. Here I am, everybody relax," Cynthia said, and began pouring some kibble out into the first of the bowls.

Patches of earth-toned fur twitched and flipped and squirmed between, around, and over her feet as the number of cats seemed to increase by the moment.

"Ouch!"

There was a painful sting of needle-sharp cat teeth against her ankle bone. Cynthia jerked her foot away. Though she looked down, the offending cat was impossible to differentiate from the others in the throbbing feline mass below her.

Damn, it hurt. She felt blood on her skin.

This has never happened before!

Before she could even process the thought, a claw found her other ankle. The feline's sharp nails snagged on her pantyhose as Cynthia pulled away quickly. Clumsily dancing backward to escape the cat-chaos, she dropped the bag. Dry pellets scattered across the lawn when the bag struck the ground and burst.

"There, have it!" she said, anger bubbling up. "Have all of it!"

She looked down and noticed that her hose were torn, and blood trickled from both scratches.

The cats ignored the strewn kibble, choosing again to encircle Cynthia's feet. Their meows were changing in intensity, becoming more hostile, some devolving into loud hissing.

Changing tactics, Cynthia took a more aggressive stance. "Get outta here. Get! Go! *Shoo!*" She stamped her foot and clapped her hands hard.

The cats paid her no heed. In fact, now they were openly swatting at her legs, their claws extended. It would have looked like play, except for the claws.

Retreating, suddenly she saw cats coming from all directions. More than the number that she'd been feeding. Far more. It was as if every cat in the county had descended on the property, merging on *her.*

A sudden stinging pain on her thigh hijacked her attention. A particularly sickly-looking feline clung to her leg. It had buried all four sets of claws into her flesh, even through her skirt and hose. She kicked to dislodge a second cat that had leapt onto her foot as if it had been a rat, while grabbing by the scruff of the neck the nasty beast clamped painfully onto her thigh. But it seemed to give way far too easily. A sound rather like sackcloth being ripped filled her ears. And there was a cool gush of fluid over her hand.

And the smell.

Dear God, the *smell.*

If she hadn't been fearing for her life, Cynthia would have fallen to her knees and vomited at the stench that engulfed her.

Looking down, she could see that she'd pulled all of the fur and skin off the little monster's head and shoulders. Its skull remained, covered in graying decay. It looked up at her with raisin shrunken eyes and pantomimed a meow.

"Oh my God!" Cynthia screamed, swatting the abomination off her leg. It took a long ribbon of bloody skin with it.

She turned to run. At this point her body overruled any debate and set itself into motion, driven by the pain of those wounds she'd already suffered.

The path she normally took to the house in the evening was long and curving. She cut the corner and ran headlong through the woods to save time. Thus she'd skirt the edge of the pond and emerge on the other side, close enough to the big house that they could help her. Though she had thankfully elected to wear flats rather than heels, it was still rough going, the smooth-bottomed shoes slipping and sliding on last year's discarded leaf litter and the fine carpet of pine needles.

Cats converged from all around her. Some were yowling, some meowing, some hissing. It sounded like they were everywhere. In front of her and behind her. Flanking her. Occasionally one of the beasts dashed in and attacked her legs with either teeth or claws, but for the most part, as long as she kept moving and they couldn't corner her, their attacks were mostly ineffectual. Still, bites and scratches added to her catalog of pain, and she ran as if pursued by the devil himself.

It was almost as if they were driving her in a certain direction.

A clearing appeared in front of her. She was near the duck pond, where the trees thinned and reeds grew thickly, overspreading the pond's banks. She pushed through them, still under feline assault.

The snapping reeds almost drowned out the hideous sounds made by the cats. They were not normal cat sounds. These were terrifying, unnatural sounds that echoed through the clearing and over the pond. Yet, for now it seemed she had left most pursuing cats behind. Had she outrun them? Or were they sliding stealthily between the tall thin stalks, as all large cats do in the wild? In Africa she had seen lions and leopards stalking prey through reeds very much like these. Invisible until suddenly they pounced.

The reeds grew taller near the pond, and it didn't take long before they towered above Cynthia. In every direction all she saw were reeds, and now she heard what sounded like countless cat bodies stalking through the growth, growling and hissing as if they were communicating. She plowed her way through, hoping she was heading in the right direction. Her wounds throbbed.

The ground suddenly gave way before her, her foot slipping off the muddy bank and into the pond itself. She grabbed at the reeds, both hands clutching a desperate fistful, to keep from tumbling face-first into the water. Some balance restored, she pulled back her wet foot.

She'd misjudged her angle through the woods. Now she'd have to walk around the pond's perimeter, sticking to the water's edge to keep from getting lost in the tall reeds. The reeds were so much thicker here, and their tangle—in addition to the wet, muddy ground—made for slow going.

Not much farther, she told herself.

Suddenly she realized she could no longer hear the cats. Their unearthly yowls and growls had given way to the chirping of the crickets and frogs. But Cynthia wasn't about to slow down. Her heart was still pumping hard, adrenaline coursing through her veins. Lightning pains from her cat-inflicted wounds reminded her that for some reason she'd become *prey.*

She wasn't sure how, or what that meant, but she had no trouble remembering the scorpion stampede at the Chambers Oil Company drilling site where Alton had fallen into that damned tomb. She had no trouble remembering the death caused by the strange infestation.

And right now she felt the same way she had in Egypt. *Terrified.*

Rounding the upper edge of the pond, she tripped over some unseen obstacle. She tumbled forward and landed hard on a pair of large stones that jutted out near the water's edge. She struck the first stone with her elbow, hearing it crack just before her head snapped down and hit the second stone. She sat up with difficulty, trying to shake off the excruciating pain. Reaching up with her good arm, she touched her forehead where warm slick blood leaked from what had to be a severe gash. She felt the parted skin and bit her lip at the painful jolt.

Then she heard the sounds.

What—?

Her breath caught in her throat, the new pain almost forgotten.

They emerged from the shadows of the reeds. Moving like cats do, slowly. Purposefully. Barely stirring the tall stalks with their movements.

Cats. Dozens of them.

But these weren't Cynthia's cats. Not anymore. They may not have been cats at all. Their eyes were dead and staring through her and into the great void beyond. They opened their mouths impossibly wide, stretching from ear to ear, exposing concentric rows of sharp pointed teeth.

Maybe someone at the house would hear her...

She opened her mouth to scream.

They tore into her.

And this time they weren't just scratching.

* * *

Alton had his head buried between the young housekeeper's legs, her panties pulled down and her skirt pulled up. She was, in fact, several years his senior, but still barely in her twenties. It was his first time with a partner.

He was chanting the words—the sounds—but through his mouthful of housekeeper it sounded more as if he were humming some circular melody. The act of forming those sounds with his tongue and lips seemed to control his mouth's movements, which in turn seemed to incite the young woman's pleasure. In fact, he was almost certain that she was chanting them as well, rhythmically, between her gasps and moans.

Alton had been speaking the chant since he'd arisen in the morning. The cadence of its syllables followed him throughout the day. It had been on his lips when he killed one of his sister's stray cats, the little beastie's head now residing in an ancient fired clay bowl that they had brought back from their Egyptian expedition, resting in the top drawer of his dresser. He'd been repeating the words when the pretty housekeeper had noticed him and led him by the hand to his bedroom.

He didn't understand the meaning of the words, but he could feel their power. He could hear them whispered inside his head and he had a vague notion of their intent.

Their intent to grant *him* the power of the eons.

The power of wealth.

The power of Pharaoh.

Chapter Twenty-Two

BLACKSTONE PULLED THE Aston Martin up to the curb, aware that someone was peering at him from behind the drapes of a second-floor window.

Probably wondering what the guy driving that car was doing at this dump of an apartment building.

He keyed himself into the front door and minutes later was staring at the dim interior of his apartment.

Laura wasn't home. Had not been home in quite a while. A week, maybe, judging by the mustiness of the air. The shades were drawn. She usually left them up.

But it was worse than that. It seemed some things were missing, her things. Personal stuff, knickknacks and, when he entered their bedroom, about half her clothes were gone. He checked the top shelf of her closet and one of her suitcases was also gone, the hideous one with the floral pattern.

What the hell?

Had she left him, or just left?

He found the paperwork for the Mustang on the kitchen table, so she had at least looked at it once. He went back into the bedroom and checked the dresser. There was a jewelry box, and when he lifted the lid it seemed to him it was half-empty, as if she had scooped up some pieces haphazardly and tossed them in her suitcase.

But that wasn't typical of Laura.

She would have selected items carefully and placed them in a set of zippered travel cases she had spent way too much on. She wouldn't have just grabbed jewelry willy-nilly. It was too important to her, and her approach to it was a more studied one.

He found an errant sock on the floor, at the bottom of her main closet.

That wasn't typical either...

In the coat closet off the living room, he spotted several empty hangers. She had also snatched coats and jackets at random?

Blackstone stalked from room to room, still trying to put it all together. What had she done? Instead of accepting that he'd now be able to earn more than ever before and letting herself share in his windfall, she had decided to... To what, *exit*?

She had no parents to run to, no siblings that he was aware of, so where?

This made no sense.

Yeah, she was definitely bipolar, but she was as greedy as the next person, and why would she pass up a chance to at least try to have a better future? Did she hate him so much that she would leave just when he was finally able to provide for her the way he had always promised but never delivered?

Blackstone had given up trying to understand his wife, and if she wanted to leave him then he would be fine without her. Part of him understood that his infidelity had soured their relationship years before, but despite the knowledge that he was yet again engaged in faithlessness, he refused to accept that she had walked out on him.

Had she been kidnapped?

But who would grab a suitcase full of clothing for a kidnapping victim?

No, that couldn't be it. Only happened in movies.

She'd left as if the house had been on fire, just grabbing randomly while running for the door. Maybe in a fit of anger or depression.

He really couldn't blame her if she'd left. They'd both checked out emotionally a while ago. Really, hadn't he been the one who left? Packed up his bags and left to work for Chambers?

Still, his heart panged a little bit. Maybe he just couldn't handle the fact that she'd left *him*.

He poked his nose here and there, seeking her treasures throughout the space they had shared so long. There, too, he saw signs of her bipolarity. Some treasures remained, others were gone. There didn't seem to be any logical reasoning at all. Speculating was meaningless. There was no sign of a struggle with anything other than a negative attitude, so it wasn't likely she had been dragged out by thugs.

Blackstone wrote a brief note and left it on the kitchen table in case Laura returned to stay, or for more of her things. He didn't really know what else to do, and if he were to be honest with himself, his mind was on the old man's panels and their secrets, which formed the core of his life right now, and then there was the pleasure to be found between Alena and Michelle's thighs. Could he really care if Laura had decided to leave him?

He shrugged. There was no one to see him, but he felt as if he had made an effort and Laura had abandoned him.

Really it would be for the best if she was gone. Now he could keep all his newfound riches and spend however he pleased, with no one to hound him if he decided he needed a new car or anything else that might strike his fancy. He could bed any woman he wanted and not have to hide it from anyone. Not have to feel the omnipresent guilt that hovered specter-like in his deepest recesses.

And now it was time to get back to work.

Locking the door behind him, he felt almost as if this was the end of a chapter in his life. The new chapter was in the Chambers compound, and the conclusion would include his discoveries, and his plan to make them public whether or not Alton Chambers agreed.

Blackstone grinned mirthlessly as he headed back to his car, his mind rife with possibilities and, at the moment, not much thought of Laura.

She probably just wanted to stab at him. Scare him a little.

She'll be back just to hound me. She can't stand to have me succeed.

Chapter Twenty-Three

"BLACKSTONE, THERE YOU are. How goes the translation?" Chambers was swirling a snifter of expensive bourbon.

The professor had just entered the dining room and headed for the table, which was set for dinner. "Tough day. My eyes are watering. I need a break."

"Joining us for dinner? I'm told the cook has prepared a fine prime rib roast."

Blackstone exhaled forcefully as if he'd been holding his breath. "I guess so."

Chambers nodded and his lips formed a smile-like rictus. "You seem distracted. Drink?"

"Sure, why not." The professor used his fingers to comb his hair into place. "It's just a frustrating set of panels that I'm on now, and I've been a little freaked out since my wife left town. I haven't heard from her at all. I'm not sure what to think."

Chambers poured a few fingers of his bourbon for Blackstone then turned away, staring out the nearest window into the darkening evening. "Perhaps the infusion of, er, capital was too much for her and she has taken a trip, or some kind of pilgrimage."

"Her only religion is shopping, so if that's the case I'll need a raise." He drank half the portion much too quickly.

Chambers chuckled dutifully. "I'm sure she'll turn up." He glanced at his watch, a vintage gold Rolex Oyster Perpetual. "Speaking of turning up, I see my daughter is punctual as usual. Have you seen *her* today?"

Blackstone stuttered. "I-I can't recall. No, I don't think I have."

Chambers nodded. "How about my granddaughter?"

"No, not seen her either."

Except he'd watched her ride her horse back and forth all afternoon from his window. In his underwear. Did that count?

Chambers mumbled something noncommittal.

The door flew open and Alena strode inside, her face glowing.

"Speak of the devil," Chambers said.

"How predictable, Father Dear," she said as she sashayed up and planted a kiss on his cheek. "I've been called worse. By you, even." His only response was a glare.

"Professor, very nice to see you again," she said, making herself a quick drink of Bombay gin with two ice cubes and taking her seat at the table. "We don't meet often enough."

He nodded. *We met well enough just a short while ago. Though we didn't see much of each other's faces.*

He sensed Chambers knew he and Alena were more than just housemates, but if they wanted to keep their *sessions* private, who was he to argue? They could engage in their own affairs, here or anywhere else.

The meal was served a minute later, and they ate in silence until they reached the second course and Chambers requested a report on the translation's progress.

"I'm making headway. Not getting a lot of sleep, but I really can't sleep when my brain is engaged and committed. I'm intrigued by the small portions I've managed to decipher, but they're not indicative of the whole work. They seem to be some sort of screed against the Occupant's enemies. I'm hoping they'll shed some light on the Occupant's identity. At this point I can't tell if he—I'm pretty sure it's a *he*—was a pharaoh, a priest or head of some cult, or a wealthy landowner. The pictograms are...*ambiguous.*"

"Maybe it was a transgendered person."

Their heads swiveled toward where Naira had slipped silently into the room and now headed for the table. She walked behind and past Blackstone. He watched her ass, encased in the thinnest and most skin-hugging leggings he had ever seen.

You could bounce golf balls off her buttocks.

Sometimes Blackstone felt ashamed at his appreciation of the female figure. Sometimes he chastised himself for being so corruptible, so easily swayed by the pretty face or the nice ass or the flirty undergraduate manner. He recognized it was a flaw in his character, and he also knew it was what kept him in academia... Where else could he face a roomful of potential conquests daily? He wasn't cruel and he didn't think he allowed his weakness to influence grading, but he'd learned the hard way that others did not see it that way. At least he had most recently limited his hunting grounds to graduate students only, and

Michelle was the latest. She was also the most uninhibited and experimental sex partner he'd ever had.

In his employer-encouraged counseling sessions, the therapist had told him that sex was his way to cover his buried and lingering feelings of inadequacy due to the cruel mockery of his childhood classmates. He had confided in her that they had frequently taunted him with chants of *J-J-J-James.* Even now the thought made him bristle. *Kids can be such cold-hearted bastards.*

He had pledged more than once to mend his ways and stop indulging his lusts, and he had decided before the Chambers job came along that Michelle would be his last dalliance. He would try harder to build a better life with Laura, who was really not as bad as he had come to think of her. If he ever saw her again. She had simply begun reflecting his stumbles, and he had not been able to keep himself from stumbling. His pledge would have taken hold on the day after he shut things down with Michelle, whenever that would be.

But when faced with the Chambers mother-daughter act, all that pledging had gone right out the window. He'd never seen a mother and daughter so alluring, and he had fallen right back into his worst habits.

Now watching Naira bouncing around the dinner table to her place, her lithe body seeming to call out to him, the coy smiles and little eye-widening moments making a subtle connection, he knew he was unlikely to resist.

The same way he was already not resisting her mother, for fuck's sake.

Exactly for fuck's sake...

"They didn't *have* transgendered people!" snarled Alton Chambers at his granddaughter.

She smiled mockingly. "Didn't they though? Sure looks like it with all those made-up males and females on the walls. And in the movies, like that porny *Pyramid* series!" She turned to Blackstone and winked. "Once I caught my mommy and some *man* watching that."

"Naira! How dare you!" Alena's cheeks flushed and she turned to stare at her daughter.

Jesus.

He'd seen those movies too—given his interests, he'd been curious, and one of his earlier teaching assistants had shared them with a grin. They *were* hot. He stifled laughter now as old man Chambers looked steamed. Blackstone winked back at Naira and she smirked.

He saw Alena take notice of the winks too, her own eyebrow raised. *Retreat, retreat!*

He shook his head. And Alena's glare made him regret getting between the beautiful women, especially at the Chambers family table. He was grateful Michelle wasn't here to make things worse.

"Well, just sayin'." The granddaughter shrugged with exaggerated naivete.

Blackstone started to chuckle but bit it back, trying to wrangle the conversation back to a serious subject. "Yes, well, so far I'm putting my money on a high priest or maybe the head of some obscure cult. Many of the glyphs are new to me and don't seem to belong to any dynasty I'm aware of. It's slow going..."

Chambers nodded. "But I don't have forever."

"No, you don't," said Alena.

Blackstone didn't know what to make of that, so he kept silent and dug into his food.

Tension was good only for indigestion.

Chapter Twenty-Four

AFTER DINNER CHAMBERS went to his study, fuming.

He wasn't sure he'd welcome the sex-starved professor tonight if he showed up for their interview session. Frankly, right then he was inclined to tell Blackstone to fuck himself, not his daughter.

And the bastard was making eyes—and more—at his granddaughter now!

Not that the little slut wasn't encouraging him. She was just like her mother, spitting image in more ways than one.

Alena was his, and even though he had set her onto Blackstone, and indeed onto the other experts they had bought before him, after all was said and done she was still supposed to be *his*.

Alena had one problem. She enjoyed the assignments he gave her a little too much for his taste. And she had really been enjoying this one, once she'd had a look at the promiscuous professor. Blackstone was a handsome devil, as his father Charles Senior might have said, an undeserving inheritor of good genes and the looks of about five current and past film and television leading men squashed together to make one delectable piece of man-candy.

At least, that was the way Alena had described the professor after meeting him. He'd purposely neglected to ask her which leading men.

Alena would have told him in colorful detail.

He shook his head, a strange mixture of awe and disgust playing through it.

He had seen the two of them engaged in an elaborate session of *soixante-neuf* on the professor's bed a mere two hours before dinner. Clearly Alena had sunk her hooks into him deeply. He had watched them writhing, their bodies erotically entwined, unwilling to admit he was feeling the sting of jealousy. Alena made it worse by playing to the cameras, the placement of which she was quite familiar. She'd laughed in his face as the professor's ejaculate spilled from her lips and down her chin.

He knew she enjoyed taunting him, and she had taken Blackstone in her mouth again with a wink that she knew her father's very good camera would pick up. He had shut it off in anger, rage building. Only a session with the latest mummy down below had returned his balance.

He had to keep reminding himself that she was just taking his body out for a test drive. If things went as planned, Blackstone's Hollywood good looks and virile physique would be his. And Blackstone himself would unlock the code that would make it happen. There was some justice in that.

But then he had watched Blackstone, alone now that Alena had drained him, spying on Naira as she rode one of her horses again, and the professor hadn't been so drained that the sight failed to arouse him. He'd stood in his underwear, clearly wishing to find a way into Naira's jodhpurs. Clearly hoping he would.

And Chambers had snapped at Batten to tell his granddaughter to get her ass in for dinner, which was probably why she'd put on such a display when she arrived.

Not to mention the professor's supple *assistant* whom he had allowed to be hired. Chambers could only blame himself for that.

He cursed Blackstone's libido. The plan was to have the man wrapped around Alena's little finger, but it seemed that Blackstone's seemingly endless sex drive and bountiful stamina had turned the tables on them. Instead, now he had Alena barking on his command and all three women jockeying for top position on his roster.

At least he'd taken Blackstone's soul-sucking bitch of a wife out of the picture. That was one less thing he had to worry about.

Now Chambers poured a double Cognac and considered a cigar, a nicely illegal Cuban, and decided against it.

The voices he had heard while in the mummy room still echoed in his head, and he knew the cigar smoke would give him a headache. His head always felt soft after these sessions, and it was so easy for that strange softness to lead to an all-out assault of a migraine-like infliction that nothing could relieve.

He sat in the dark, the only light the harsh glow from the rear property spots leaking through his curtains.

He knew there wasn't much time. He had to spur the professor on to success, for his own sake. For his physical and mental well-being.

* * *

"I've seen how Alena looks at you, and how you look at her—and also her daughter! Blackstone, you're a sex-hound, damn you."

Michelle turned away and stared out the window. There was Naira, damn *her*, on her fucking horse again. She turned back to him. "You can't see what they're doing to you. It's all about this damned translation and those two women, with you. If you're not fucking the young one yet, I'm pretty sure you will be. They look at you like a frog staring at an insect on a leaf, James, and maybe you're not aware of it, but they're not thinking of what's best for you."

"And you are?" He had just poured them drinks, but neither was drinking.

She recoiled as if he had slapped her. "I've cradled your head whenever your wife kicked you to the curb, you bastard," she said with a growl he'd not heard before. "You certainly seemed to think I was thinking about the best for you *then*."

She stared outside again. Naira was walking the horse back to the stable. Her figure was impossibly perfect.

"Or maybe you just like my sex swing," Michelle added. "And what I've let you do to me on it."

"I think you're overreacting."

"Don't patronize me!"

Her few dinners with the Chambers household and Blackstone had rankled. She'd been surprised, and annoyed, at how the two women who looked more like sisters than mother and daughter openly competed for Blackstone's attention. And before she knew it, she had found herself tacitly agreeing to the competition.

"I'm really not trying to be patronizing, Michelle," Blackstone said, reaching out and caressing her hair. "I need this job, and I want this job because of what I'm learning, but in order to keep it I feel obligated to let those two do whatever they want, even if it's to flirt so outrageously. And they do."

"Sure, in public." She drew away enough so that his hand fell off her hair and he tucked it onto his lap. "In private, I'm pretty sure you've more than met that obligation. The older one looks at you like a pastry she intends to lick the inside out of, then swallow the rest whole."

He laughed nervously. That *did* rather describe Alena.

"It's not funny. She's older than you, and she's using you. And," Michelle added, "if you're not careful, she'll lose this job for you that you're so desperate to keep."

"Michelle, I'm just playing along, playing her game."

"Yeah? Do you realize the old man's playing some kind of game too? Do you know they seem to be on the same side? I think they're downright creepy, those two. Add that geezer Batten and the chickie-chick and you've got a worse Addams Family than anyone could ever draw up."

"That's not fair. They're eccentric, sure. Rich people always are. But how else would I ever get so close to solving the mystery of these glyphs, and the tomb, and whatever the hell Chambers wants to get out of it?"

"Sure, stay here. Write his book. Maybe he'll run for president, using your book as a platform. You're gonna talk him up, make him seem a lot better than he is. And you're gonna cover up all his creepiness because that's where your bread is buttered. Meanwhile, you're gonna butter—"

"You know you're sexy when you get mad?"

"I'm not falling for that! You know I'm right..."

"I know you're right that Alena's too old for me, sure, but you have to admit she does look a lot younger than she is."

"Yeah, but I bet her soul is a wrinkled old prune. And so would her heart be, if she had one."

Blackstone took her hand and gently placed it on his lap. "See what happens when you get angry? It really turns me on."

"Water out of a faucet turns you on," she said, scoffing. But she didn't take her hand off his rising flesh.

"It's all those pipes and all that gushing liquid," he said.

She chuckled and slid down to her knees. She finished her drink in one swallow, then worked down his zipper and reached into his trousers.

"I'll show you youth's advantage," she mumbled.

In a minute, Blackstone set aside his drink and concentrated on her lesson. It was very convincing.

* * *

Elsewhere, Alena was watching the monitor. The angle wasn't perfect, but she could guess what the damned girl was doing to Blackstone. His hands on the girl's head more than hinted at how she was handling him.

Alena resented their agreement that she was too old for him, but damn them, it was true that she didn't have the firmest flesh anymore. It was true that she was watching her life trickle through the neck of an hourglass, the bottom now much fuller than the top. It was true that her stamina was starting to fail, although she made up for it with inventiveness and an experimental spirit second to none.

She could show that damned girl a thing or two.

She'd install her own sex swing, damn her, and by the time she was done with him he wouldn't know where he was, or who Michelle Davenport was. And maybe he'd have forgotten all about Naira, who seemed to have set out her own trap for his slippery eel. Maybe it was a daughter's competitive spirit, or maybe Naira just hated her, but she'd seen the girl ogling Blackstone, and of course Blackstone had noticed. He routinely fucked girls Naira's age, and Alena cursed all the gods—and her father—for having allowed *tempus* to *fugit* quite so fast. When she had him, he was under her control, just as her father wished. But when she didn't have him, damn the randy bastard, then he was distracted by every short skirt, every set of buttocks encased in tight riding breeches, and every wink followed by licked lips.

Alena turned her attention toward the monitor again. She swore. Now the Davenport girl was bobbing up and down backward on Blackstone's lap, her cries making it clear that she was being satisfied.

She felt the wetness in her panties and swore again.

But soon, oh so soon, Alena would possess Blackstone's body with Alton's mind. Then he would be all hers. And, of course, she would have Naira's firm young body.

She took a deep, consoling breath.

Surely she couldn't actually be falling for Blackstone. The horny rogue.

What she really wanted was to win. To win the competition between Naira, the Davenport tramp, and herself. She wanted to feel like she wasn't just another hole for the professor to fill. She wanted to own him the way she owned Alton. And she didn't want to be challenged.

Chapter Twenty-Five

BLACKSTONE STEPPED OUT of the university bookstore with a bag in hand, having found a text by one of his colleagues he thought would shed some light on a set of glyphs he was working with at the moment. He hated giving Jackson Walters any royalties, but no one had to know.

This was really his favorite time of year on and around campus. Most of the leaves were still clinging tenuously to the tree branches in a spectacular array of yellow, orange, and red hues, while the crispness in the air was offset by the warmth of the sun. Before long, these streets would be blanketed in snow that would linger for months until life was resurrected in the spring.

He was walking, head down, back to the parking structure when a voice called out to him.

"Hey, Blackwell!"

He snapped up his neck and turned in the direction of the sonorous voice and groaned inwardly.

"Huh, Naira, isn't it?"

"Yeah! Good memory for an old guy..."

"It's B-Black*stone*, you know."

It sounded lame even to him, but he was tiring of the girl's ignorant act.

He couldn't see her very well at first, since she was half-sitting on a concrete parapet that abutted some of the university's currently denuded floral beds. He slowed and she came into focus. She resembled a statue there, posing like a model for some alcoholic sculptor, her jacket opened to the chilly air and her blouse buttons undone to a dangerously low level, the fabric bulging in just the right way so he could see an expanse of creamy breast and darkness where her lack of a bra made all the difference. Her long legs extended to the pebbled concrete flooring, her thighs mostly bared by a short leather skirt.

His route to the parking garage would take him past her perch, so there was no avoiding her.

"I know," she said, grinning. Her eyes were dark and heavily shaded in gold and blue, but they seemed to twinkle at him, like stars or diamond bits. Her shiny lips curled upward and twisted in her typical half-wicked smile, and he couldn't help but grin back.

Damn her.

He was defenseless against her charms. She'd learned well from her mother, presumably.

And he, he apparently *never* learned.

"Are you between classes?" He was trying to be polite, but really preferred heading out on his way back to the compound where he could study the relevant portions of the text he had bought.

"No. I'm just hanging out."

You can say that again...

"Well, nice seeing you," he said, sidling away.

"My mother's using you, you know," she said quickly, before he could get himself out of earshot. He slowed and looked at her as she put on an innocent look as easily as zipping up a jacket.

"What do you know about it?"

She giggled. "You'd be surprised."

He didn't think he would be.

"Look, I'm heading back to your grandfather's. You want a ride?"

"Leash getting a little short? You know, you might be about as far as you can go."

"Listen here," he growled, unwilling to let this young filly get the upper hand on him. No matter what she knew. "You need a ride, or not?"

"Oh, I guess I could sit in your very cool car for a while. My grandfather will be *so* grateful."

She was annoying enough that he almost walked away and left her. "Let's go," he said.

They were silent as they entered the waffled structure and rode an elevator up with another faculty member Blackstone recognized. He was hoping she wouldn't say anything embarrassing. As it was, he felt warmth on his cheeks as the elderly prof gazed at Naira's young but highly developed assets on display.

Blackstone could sense her grin and chose to ignore it.

She jumped into the passenger seat without making a fuss, and for that he was grateful. He climbed in and he put on his belt in silence. Maybe he could get out of this without too much trouble after all.

Before he could start the car and pull them away from the garage level's parapet, she displayed how limber she was by suddenly leaning over and sticking her head in his lap. Then her hands were on his fly and parting the fabric of his pants, and, in a fair bit of disconnect, while his head wanted him to say "*Stop!*" his body betrayed his brain's better sense and responded with abundant acceptance.

"Well, lookie here, Black*well*," she muttered into his rising flesh, "looks like you're not as uptight as you seem to be."

Then her warm mouth enveloped him and he nearly hit the auto's low-slung roof.

He couldn't banish the sudden thought of a scene from De Palma's *Carrie*—which his father had adored and shared with him at an early age—that flashed through his brain. Then he forgot all about John Travolta and Nancy Allen as Naira's tongue started to flick around and around, and while he knew his best bet was to leap out of the car and stalk away, he simply put his hands encouragingly on her bobbing head. He reached down and flicked a switch and his seat backed up and reclined enough to give her more space.

Footsteps echoed outside and he glanced in the mirror and saw a man's torso, perhaps someone who had stopped to admire the Vantage. He willed the guy to walk away, but the girl's mouth on him took up most of his attention. Then the man gasped audibly, and the footsteps hurried away as whoever it was declined to watch once he realized what was happening. A few moments later, a much humbler engine down the row started up and a car rattled hurriedly toward the exit ramp.

Bet he's considering putting a down payment on one of these, he thought before Naira distracted him again by taking him deep down her throat, grunting until he was all in. Blackstone was proud of his stamina in most positions, but in this one he was enslaved by Naira and her expert control of his sensations. She made sure he could see what she was doing, her gold and green eyelids fluttering and putting him in mind of a movie Cleopatra practicing her reputed art, or those *Pyramid* pornos she had mentioned, and with that his stamina peaked at barely five minutes.

She's done this before.

As she ramped up her attack, he pressed his hands on her head but she stayed with him precisely as he wished, increasing her tempo, and took his explosion without hesitation while making little sounds of pleasure.

He thought he would break his back thrusting as she finished him without opening her lips, and then her hands were tucking him primly back into his pants and he realized that here he was Travolta, but what did *she* want from *him*? Nancy Allen sure had had wicked plans, after all...

"My turn," she said primly, looking up at him with lust-filled eyes.

"What!" he blurted out. "This is a parking garage!"

"So?" she said.

He'd seen her limber athletic body in action before, but he suspected he was about to see more.

Naira pushed herself up from his lap and curled up in the tight cockpit, and before he could figure out how she did it, she had swung her hips up and her thighs straddled his shoulders. She stretched her torso backward over his body until she was on him like a blanket. Her head barely fit over his thighs, but he had the steering wheel set high and she wasn't very large.

Her hands fluttered upward and he was shocked to see that under the black leather miniskirt...she wasn't wearing panties.

I should have guessed.

She squirmed her lithe body sideways and back and forth, crawling up on his reclined torso, and suddenly he was more or less trapped by her shaved mound which was tantalizingly within reach when she spread her thighs farther, her legs dangling over his shoulders like a strange sort of sex-starved trapeze artist.

Jesus.

No saviors needed.

Her pleasant musky scent immediately turned him on again.

What had Michelle said about a gushing faucet?

Michelle who?

Fully aware of his weakness, cursing himself for succumbing so easily to this overt assault on his defenses, he bent his mouth to the task at hand with more than a little enthusiasm. In a minute or two, her body's vibrations signaled that he was reaching all her preferred spots.

Hell, even Laura had enjoyed his skill in this particular area. She'd jokingly called him a *cunning linguist*, back when things were good between them.

Laura. A lightning bolt of guilt struck and he tried to ignore it.

Naira moaned from down below where she had melded her body to his. She grabbed his hands, moving them to her breasts, which had worked themselves free of the blouse and oozed downward, quivering, over her collar bone. He found her supple nipples with his fingertips and her body tightened over his as he squeezed them. She knew what she liked, that was certain.

Can't believe it.

This was a first even for him.

At this point he didn't care if anyone saw them, though being rousted by a campus cop would surely ruin his day. Blackstone put his mind and skill to work along with his tongue, zeroing in on what he needed to do to get her off so she'd finally release him from her prison of corrupting flesh.

In mid-groan, she let out a surprised squeak. "Wow, not only are you good, but I think we're awakening something down here too!"

Her head was resting on his groin and thighs and there was no doubt her pleasure was causing new blood to pump into his own flesh. She reached behind her head and massaged him through his trousers while he carried on pleasuring her in this awkward but incredibly sexy position.

Muscular thighs tightened more and more on his neck and head and he sensed she was close, her abs and limbs vibrating and transmitting her approaching release. Grabbing her narrow waist, he bent to the task, enjoying both its own nature and her obvious pleasure. When she came, it was violent and loud and he prayed there was no one nearby to hear her squeals. She ended with a long sigh and he grinned because it really had been an amazing experience—being in public with the danger of discovery, the weird position, the unexpected nature of the encounter, and Naira's own natural sexy quality...all of these combined to push Blackstone over the top a second time, this time into his bunched shorts, with barely a touch from her.

At the end, he thought he was seeing the inside of a tomb and a golden throne, and he was perched on the gold seat with her lithe body splayed over him exactly as it was here, except they were both in ancient garb and he smelled some kind of incense that mixed with the heady smell of her sex, and they were united in their pleasure.

But were they alive or dead?

Christ.

Where the hell did *that* come from?

"I've gotta go, Blackwell," Naira said as she performed a dismount over the center console worthy of Simone Biles and somehow unscrewed herself from the seat and out the door, smoothing her skirt back down over her bare assets and tucking her breasts under her jacket just before a couple unaware students walked past the car. "Thanks for the ride, old man."

"Get in," he said. "Ride home with me." He hoped it didn't sound desperately whiny. *Needy.*

"Nah, I have to go study," she said, smirking. She leaned into the car like a hooker negotiating with a john. "But I think we'll meet again. OMG, say hi to my mom!" She closed the door with a slam. "See you back at the ranch," she mouthed, and blew him a kiss then sauntered away, presumably pleased with herself.

Now what was he going to do?

Blackstone realized he had trapped himself into a corner from which he could not easily escape. He needed to work for Chambers quite a while to become financially independent, but meanwhile he had allowed himself to become entangled not only with his graduate student assistant, which certainly wasn't his first rodeo or his first filly, but also with the two women in Alton Chambers' life...and that might not be such a good idea.

Just how weak am I?

The cold wetness in his briefs said he was *very* weak.

If Chambers found out not only about his daughter, but also his granddaughter, there was no telling what he might do. The contract stated Blackstone could be dismissed for any of a dozen reasons, or no reason at all. And if that happened, he was certain he'd not be welcome back at the university, not the way he'd walked away with the bridge burning and collapsing behind him.

So what should he do about it?

He started the Aston Martin and for the first time took little pleasure in the engine's purr.

He wanted to finish the translations now. No, he *needed* to finish. Regardless of what Chambers wanted, Blackstone was now in it for himself. Something was driving him to figure out what those damned panels said, what their story would turn out to be, and even more importantly, how he could parlay this job and its results into a great career enhancer, a move toward possibly a major curatorship or perhaps bestseller status on two books: the one he would write as the Chambers autobiography, and his own outlining how he had struggled and eventually translated the strange hieroglyphs. And maybe a tell-all too.

He drove away, distracted by his thoughts of greater success. And by the strange feeling that he was merely a pawn in someone's game.

But whose?

Chapter Twenty-Six

WHEN CHAMBERS ARRIVED in the vault room carrying a bottle of wine, Blackstone hoped it wasn't to hit him with it.

Dinner had been a quiet affair, with Alena arriving late and avoiding most of the technical conversation between Chambers and Blackstone. She gave him a funny side look and tapped his foot under the table a couple times, but when he turned toward her, she feigned lack of interest. She ate sparingly of the vegetarian fare, while Chambers indulged in a bloody steak with gusto that was almost revolting. For his part, Blackstone partook of the fairly good Egyptian Sirah and kept quiet as Chambers rambled on about his boyhood adventures, which culminated in the discovery of the tomb.

Blackstone nodded or grunted in the right places, hoping the book he would write might be of interest to anyone. Listening to the ramblings of his host, he wasn't so sure.

He tried to catch Alena's eye without success, and moved some meat and dough concoction around on his plate. If Chambers expected him to remember any of his increasingly drunken banter, he was sadly mistaken, because Blackstone was barely listening.

With the car sex between him and Naira, he was surely too pained to face Alena, but what was worse was that she seemed to be angry at him. Perhaps Naira had spilled the beans? If so, wouldn't she have taken a shot at him with one of the vintage guns locked in a case in the massive den?

After the uncomfortable dinner, he excused himself with a muttered, "Have to get back to work..." and made a quick exit. He thought he heard Chambers harshly address his daughter as the door closed, but he didn't care. She was a grown woman, and if she couldn't hold her own against her father, then that was too bad.

Blackstone enjoyed his time with Alena, but he was willing to admit to himself it was only because of the borderline fetish sex and her abandon while practicing it. Not that she needed practice. Apparently it had become a case of "like mother, like daughter," and he really was confused about everything.

Now the patriarch had come visiting with his opened bottle of wine and two glasses, holding one out to him. "Take a break, old man."

That's something, coming from you.

"Thanks," Blackstone said.

"Sit for a minute."

Blackstone nodded and dropped into a nicely worn leather club chair near the worksurface scattered with open books and notes and his flickering laptop. In the nearby cradle was the latest wall panel torn from inside the tomb, which he'd earlier removed from the vault. Several weeks of daily work had made the panels seem more commonplace. But if he thought about them, he was still awed by what they represented.

He waited while Chambers half-filled the glasses, handed one over, and sat in the other club chair. Chambers tasted and made a face. "It's too sour," he said, staring at the desk light through the red liquid.

Blackstone shrugged.

The wine was fine, nothing great, but Blackstone knew he didn't have a wine palate. Usually it was beer and whiskey for him. But this was wet, alcoholic, and tasted better than water. He was realizing that he enjoyed being buzzed as often as possible while working for the old man. Although, it seemed that was the old man's objective, too. Just about every large room in the mansion sported a small bar cart for just that reason. Yet he never seemed even slightly tipsy...

"It's time we took a walk back a few millennia," Chambers added.

"Huh? What did you say?"

"You're making progress. I see your increasing success and I believe you should experience what I did, all those years ago. Drink up, we're going for a walk."

Blackstone hastened to drink the remaining wine in three gulps. "Ready."

Chambers took longer with the ochre liquid, then he stood and motioned for Blackstone to follow.

In a different elevator hidden behind an anonymous doorway panel in the hall, after Chambers closed the old-school brass grate, he smacked a black plate with a keycard and pressed the bottom button. They rattled and shook on their way downward. Blackstone wondered just how far below ground they were being carried. And just how many elevators wormed their way through this house? What the *hell* was this place? What was under the skin of this dowdy mansion?

They stopped with a muted *thump* and Chambers opened the grate.

"I had this elevator transferred from my father's original main house," he explained as if he'd read the professor's thoughts. "It stood on this site during his middle years. There are four other elevators, one each for the main wings and one that is private."

Blackstone followed him out of the car and into a well-lit, round foyer-like space with art on display all around. A corridor crossed the foyer and extended in two opposite directions. Chambers chose the right corridor and Blackstone kept pace as they walked silently for a few minutes. The walls for about a hundred feet were paneled in a medium-dark wood, but then the paneling ended and the rest of the passage was seemingly made of painted cinderblock.

As if all this weren't confusing enough, there were other corridors crossing in front of them at right angles, leading Blackstone to think that a visitor left to his own devices might never find his way back to the elevator. He wished he had some white chalk in his pocket.

Blackstone shivered. The air was markedly chillier here.

They reached a wider chamber and the walls turned to red brick, the ceiling twice as high and vaulted like something from that *Phantom of the Opera* show. Blackstone was certain this corridor was older and had been connected to the newer passage from the elevator. They crossed through the rounded chamber and continued onward, though he sensed there was a slight bend they were following, leading *away* from where he thought the mansion should be above them.

Just how many tunnels existed beneath the monster house? This one put Collinwood to shame.

How much time did Chambers spend down here? How large was this warren?

Up ahead was another intersection of corridors, and this time Chambers turned left.

Blackstone chuckled silently. He had a sudden sense that the maze might be smaller than it appeared and perhaps now they were returning to the space immediately under the house.

It's meant to confuse, he thought.

But the red brick had to be older, like construction from the late nineteenth century. Water dripped visibly. Up above, the ceiling was higher and supported by brick arches that seemed about to collapse on them as they passed through below. Here and there was a small, broken brick talus spilling across the floor, which itself was beginning to show signs of buckling.

Jesus!

The professor wondered how safe the whole tunnel complex might actually be. He'd never been claustrophobic, but this weird combination of low and high ceilings, narrow and wide corridors, both dark and well-lit, could induce a bad case.

"Prepare yourself," Chambers whispered as he slowed suddenly, turning to fix Blackstone with a glittering, hard gaze. "Prepare yourself to experience what I experienced in my youth, the very thing that has shaped me to this day."

"All right," Blackstone said. He hoped he'd kept the amusement out of his voice.

But then Chambers steered him forward into a new chamber and his mouth opened as if he'd lost all control over it.

"Behold, the tomb!" Chambers beamed. "As it was before it was buried by the dunes, then found by our oil rig, and then by me, when I fell through the roof and into its center."

Blackstone was struck speechless.

The chamber seemed immense, and immediately in front of them was the low entrance of a classic tomb that had once been buried in the desert sands of Egypt. Its threshold faced them as they edged into the chamber. The tomb's portal was all that was visible—the rest was buried in what might well have been the original sand from the desert dunes. That sand appeared fine, similar to copier toner dust except it was silica. The mound over the entrance reached almost to the chamber's arched ceiling.

It was a tomb buried in a dune that itself was buried in a sub-basement chamber under a gargantuan mansion.

It defied credulity.

Blackstone tried to swallow. His mouth was dry and he tasted sand, as motes of the granules were visibly floating in the artificial lighting of the chamber.

Just like in the middle of the desert.

He approached the entrance reverently, feeling awe and an irrational fear that arose suddenly and raised the hair on his neck. The transom was decorated with more of the symbols Blackstone had managed to translate over the last few weeks. As he would have expected, the saying was a curse of sorts, reminding him that if he plundered the tomb its Occupant would not rest until vengeance had been visited on the interloper and his family throughout the ages.

Or words to that effect. He was still struggling to master the entire vocabulary he'd opened up, but he was getting close. And this curse was a standard affair, the sort of thing any noble with money or even a relatively unknown minor pharaoh would have used to protect his afterlife journey and his take-along riches.

Although, if Blackstone's reading was correct, the inscription implied that the tomb's Occupant *himself* would wreak vengeance throughout the ages. *That's different.*

"I must enter," he muttered. He'd meant to ask, but his words betrayed him. He felt *pulled* into the entrance.

His host chuckled. "Please do." His tone was prideful, as if the tomb had been created as a shrine to *him*. He handed the professor a small but powerful LED flashlight and flicked on another one.

Blackstone lowered his head and stepped through a small sand drift, distantly wondering whether there was artificial wind in this chamber, and found himself in a square foyer with colorful glyphs on three walls. The ceiling here was low and he had to hunch. Also, he could barely turn his sizable body in each direction, but he did in order to see each panel. The two flashlight beams lit the space harshly.

"Chambers, I thought you said you had all the wall panels removed."

"I removed those most relevant, Professor."

"Ah."

How did he know what was relevant? And relevant to what?

Blackstone traced some of the lines of pictograms. He'd learned enough to be able to make sense of the writings, which appeared to be a list of the tomb Occupant's accomplishments—wins in battles Blackstone had never heard of, subjugation of races he didn't recognize, and the creation of temples no one else had ever written about. There was reference to a long journey and arrival, and Blackstone understood that to mean the Occupant had predicted arriving in the afterlife.

"This is...*unbelievable.*"

Softly Blackstone related his on-the-fly translations to Chambers, whose head was all that fit inside the foyer with the professor.

Blackstone wasn't claustrophobic. A good thing, because the tiny chamber's area was barely larger than that of a standing sarcophagus.

The thought formed a shiver that ran up and down his spine and settled somewhere in his groin.

He wasn't sure why the image was so vivid in his head, but it chilled him much more than the chamber's cold air.

"Your translation is impressive, Professor," Chambers said. His voice seemed to come from his floating, disconnected head. "How accurate?"

"I'd give it sixty percent at the moment. I'm just not sure about the timeline. And the nature of the journey that's being described."

Chambers displayed his excitement even though he was trying hard to rein it in, but whatever he heard in Blackstone's sketchy translation had clearly stoked his engine. His complexion turned ruddy, at least in the strange lighting, and his heart rate might have been pumped if the pulsing vein in his neck was any indication.

"The nature of the Occupant's journey interests me very much," he said, "but I am also interested in other aspects of his life. I'm certain there is much to learn from the writings that he ordered left behind with him."

The *Occupant?*

But hadn't Blackstone himself referred to whomever resided in the tomb in the same way?

"You sound as though you know more about him than you're letting on, Chambers," Blackstone said, forcing a grin.

"Perhaps I do. When I come here, he speaks to me. In a way..."

"You spend much time in this tomb?"

"Yes, I would have to admit that I do."

They were so close together in this chamber that Blackstone, for one, was becoming uncomfortable.

"I suppose if one has an entire tomb cut apart, shipped over the ocean, and then reassembled piece by piece, one might be forgiven for choosing to hang out in it. Like your own personal playground."

"It's not a sandbox, Blackstone. It's a shrine. Of sorts. And it cost millions even back then. Now it would be billions." He seemed to have cooled on the professor's attitude. "Follow me, and I'll show you where I do some of my best thinking these days."

They switched places so that Chambers could lead the way. Blackstone waited for him to move before following into the impossibly tight foyer.

Chambers turned and faced an inner passageway barely two feet wide that forced him to walk sideways. He gestured for the professor to come along, then started to edge farther into the tomb, their bright lights playing about like children's lightsabers in the dusty atmosphere.

Blackstone followed awkwardly, feeling the strangeness of facing one wall and feeling another wall at his back even as he stepped sideways. In a minute, they'd walked at least twenty feet, maybe more, and the long corridor seemed not yet close to coming to an end. Blackstone could no longer see the opening that had led them here, and in a flash of understanding he realized that the narrow passage was ever so slightly curving. Not enough to easily notice, except when shining his light to where they'd just been and not being able to see the low foyer from which they'd started.

Blackstone's breath suddenly became labored.

The silica in the air, he thought, as he struggled to inflate his lungs. *It's like breathing in particles of sand, just smaller.*

The floating silica didn't seem to bother Chambers.

The wall in front of him had been stripped of its colorful panels, and he assumed the wall behind him as well. The brickwork that peeked through the plaster was solid, but he thought he could see the seams where the cut-up portions had been mortared back together.

"It's a marvel, this corridor," said Chambers, pausing to wait for him.

As if he's reading my mind, Blackstone thought. *Again.*

"You may have noticed that it's not altogether straight. Rather, it's taking us in a long, lazy spiral."

"Yes." He coughed.

The old man went on. "When we found the tomb, we also found that this corridor was a death trap."

"*What?*"

"Yes, once a graverobber was in it, stones weighing a half-ton each were set to roll into place, blocking both ends and trapping an intruder inside, almost like a long and narrow standing grave. The air would have staled quickly, and the floating silica particles loosened by passage would begin to clog the intruder's airway and lungs, leading to quicker asphyxiation. Of course, unless you had a light, as we do, you would have died a dark and terrifying death. If you had a light, then you would have died with your last sight the beautiful images on these walls."

Blackstone coughed again and couldn't stop for a long minute. His lungs ached after the spasm, and it seemed sand was tickling his throat and forcing him to cough again. He leaned forward and hit his head on the wall.

"Here, drink some water," Chambers said, producing a flat flask from somewhere.

Blackstone could barely stop coughing, but awkwardly he took the flask and drank, hoping the water could somehow cleanse his throat of the minuscule particles that seemed to be coating it in layers. He coughed again, and drank again. His eyes were burning.

Chambers chuckled. "I thought you'd be more at home in a tomb, Professor."

"Oh, I am, but this one—this one is different." He regained his composure. "What about the rolling stones?"

Chambers chuckled again. "Your humor is back. Good. You might be surprised to know that I'm aware of the Rolling Stones—in fact, I have taken my friend Mick through here, once, on a visit during one of the band's tours in the nineties. He was suitably impressed." He waved a hand at the wall. "These rolling stones though, we had them locked in place, so they can no longer roll over the apertures. We passed one already. It's what made the entry so narrow. The other one will be noticeable too, but neither is dangerous. Let's keep going, there's more I want you to see. And better air."

"The panels? They're all removed?"

"From in here, yes. You've already been working on them."

"Ah."

They started moving sideways again, forced to shuffle in the narrow passage.

"Wait a minute, is this tunnel narrowing?"

"Very perceptive, Professor. Yes, by the time we get to the end it'll be a good thing neither of us is a corpulent fellow."

Blackstone was still wheezing, but he followed Chambers and soon he felt the wall touching his shoulder blades. In front of him there was barely a hand's worth of space. And then they reached the end of the passage and squeezed through an aperture barely wide enough for a suitcase. Blackstone noted the trap stone, off to the side and presumably no longer able to slide over the opening and seal anyone in the tunnel.

Then Blackstone realized something else.

Their flashlights weren't needed, because the chamber in which they now stood seemed to have its own light, yet he couldn't see any cables or bulbs. The eerie effect gave the walls a red tint that reminded him of freshly spilled blood.

"You noticed the lighting?"

Blackstone nodded, uncertain. "Yes."

"It's a wonder, isn't it?"

"Where is it coming from?"

"The center of this vault. Look up."

Blackstone did and realized the ceiling was much higher here, and something else... There was a wall separating them from advancing any farther into the large space. It was like a barrier, but he could almost see over it. It stretched in both directions and curved, like the narrow tunnel.

"Follow me." Chambers led the way to a nearly invisible notch in the wall, and into what seemed to be a six-foot high maze, with walls crisscrossing and sometimes ending in dead ends. "Some of these have pits that held snakes," Chambers said. "We filled them in with sand, of course."

"Of course."

"There's one cul-de-sac that ends with a slide to a lower level, where you would have been sliced open by rows of spears set into the final wall." He pointed to the right. "Don't go that way, Professor."

"Surely you've removed the spears."

"Surely not! I love their ingenuity. These features of the tomb are part of what makes it so much...*fun*. Don't stray from my side."

"I guess that explains all the hidden panels in the house."

"Ha! There's more than just hidden panels, Blackstone. You shouldn't stray there either."

He has to be kidding, right?

Blackstone tried to note the direction they took and memorize it, but there were at least twenty turns. *Should have brought some chalk.*

Suddenly they were standing in a circular center, and there in front of them was the source of the red light.

Blackstone blinked hard. The silica in his eyes sent tiny jabs through his head, but he could barely focus on the pain.

Above there was a strange roof, which looked like a slightly open trapdoor. But his eyes were drawn to the center of the maze.

The sarcophagus.

So Chambers hadn't just moved the tomb, he had also moved its Occupant.

No greater crime existed in the laws of Egypt, and indeed in international law regarding religious antiquities. The days of mummies shipped to Europe by the shipload had been long over even when Chambers had committed this...*atrocity*.

It stood over six feet tall, as far as Blackstone could tell, and it was sheathed in red glass. It was rendered almost blurry by the multiple reflections it cast about itself.

As they approached, Blackstone amended his assessment. The sarcophagus was covered by countless rows of what appeared to be deep-red rubies or similar gemstones. They caught the artificial light and reflected it in all directions, turning the very air of the chamber blood-red. He touched it, felt the rough stones with his fingertips, surprised how sharp they were. And surprised, too, that the sarcophagus lid seemed to vibrate under his touch.

What the hell is this?

He thought at first he heard the sound of an air shaft, maybe where the faux wind was coming from, and that was causing the vibration, but no... Then he realized it sounded like many voices whispering.

He took his hand off the rubies, but he thought the vibration continued under his feet.

The sound rose and fell and imitated the cadence of a chant. If he listened carefully, he could almost hear and see the words of the chant, words that up to now had been merely glyphs on wall panels owned by the old man whose eyes were closed and who seemed to be having an orgasm as they stood there.

Blackstone wanted to refute the image, but then he realized that he, too, felt almost a sexual arousal. His groin ached and his flesh strained at the fabric of his trousers.

The whispers grew to a howl and made his ears hurt.

Chambers said something he couldn't hear, and the world became a blur. And then it became darkness.

When Blackstone opened his eyes, he was lying on the large bed in his suite.

Alena was prone between his thighs, her mouth on him. Her eyes staring into his were made up like those of an Egyptian woman on a wall painting, the lids bright lapis lazuli and around her right eye black liner with red and blue edges formed a perfect Eye of Horus. Her full red lips, distended on his engorged flesh, reminded him of sister-mother Isis bringing the dismembered Osiris back to life by blowing into his clay replacement penis.

Slowly engulfing and then liberating his cock, a loving and yet somehow dominating ritual, Alena's lips reminded the professor's scholarly side that sex was once the core of Egyptian religion. Priestesses in their temples conducted sexual rites to cleanse men and celebrate their fertility. It might have been a myth that Cleopatra herself had fellated one hundred Roman men in one night, but right then Blackstone could have believed it—Alena play-acting Cleopatra with him, proving she was also a talented fellatrix.

They exchanged no words as she dragged him to the edge a half-dozen times only to let him suffer without her attention until he could take it no longer, and then the swallowing commenced again. When his climax finally arrived, it shook his body and soul, and as he lost consciousness he heard the whispering chants rising again around him as Alena withdrew slowly from his spent flesh.

When he awoke, he was hard again, thinking of the dream he had enjoyed and the strangeness that surrounded it. He started. Blackstone was sitting in a club chair in his cluttered workspace in the library. Slowly he remembered Chambers bringing in two glasses of wine. Or had that been part of the dream too? It seemed so lucid. Had any of that really happened? The red sarcophagus?

Indeed, he had *touched* it, hadn't he?

And felt its vibration.

Blackstone thought back to Alena as Cleopatra. Had it all been just a dream? Was there really a full-blown tomb beneath the house with booby traps and a ruby-encrusted sarcophagus? He *must* have dreamt it.

He got up and made his way to his room to get at least a couple hours of proper sleep.

When he was about to climb into bed, he saw the blood-red streaks on his clean sheets.

The exact same shade that had been on Alena's lips.

Chapter Twenty-Seven
1962

THE MUSIC ROSE up through the floorboards. Muted though it was, quieted by its journey from the club below, Harrison Chambers could still make out the melody. "Straight, No Chaser" by Thelonious Monk.

He forced his eyelids open. They were heavy, but through the slits he could make out his surroundings. He knew the room well. A small apartment above *Birdland*. The furnishings were sparse and decrepit. The room was lit by a single bare-bulb table lamp that left one side of the room bathed in painfully bright light and the other half immersed in shadow.

His arm felt numb.

Looking down, Harrison remembered he still had the tourniquet wrapped around his bicep. Leaving it made finding the vein easier. He loosened the strap and flexed his hand, making a fist a few times to get the blood flowing. The tingling sensation made him crack an addled smile.

He rose slowly off the bruised and battered couch he'd been sitting on. He was wearing a white undershirt, his brown suit pants, and patent-leather shoes, all of which were noticeably well-worn. They'd been brand new when he had first arrived in New York City.

Harrison's eyes scanned lazily around the room. He found his button-down shirt thrown over the back of a stained and tattered armchair, his neatly folded suit coat beneath it. With sluggish movements he shoved his arms into the shirt sleeves, while the musicians one floor below played feverishly.

He didn't live here, near Midtown West. No, he'd taken an apartment in Greenwich Village. That was where all the young and upcoming stayed, even though it was a shithole.

Stumbling while reaching for his jacket, Harrison smiled. The heroin had turned everything beneath his skin into warm, comfortable goo. He was dream-walking.

After his brother's suicide and his sister's strange but accidental death, Harrison had decided that life was too short to wait for a perfect opportunity, so he had moved to the infamous Big Apple to pursue an acting career. Of course, his father could buy him into a role with a couple phone calls, but Harrison wanted to get somewhere on his own. By his own merit. He wanted to feel as though he could be good at something, anything, besides simply being rich.

That wasn't going so well.

But he had hit it off with the local jazz musicians. He was quite fond of their music and kinship. They were fond of his money and their shared cravings for the junk. The kind of relationships with which Harrison was familiar. They had come to feel somehow more like family than his actual family.

The low notes of a double bass reverberated through the room while the piano keys deftly moved through the chord changes and brushes on the drum kit kept the beat. Harrison slowly wove his body to the unlocked door. The music buffeted him as he moved to the stairs that would take him to the bar below. Absent-mindedly he checked his suit pockets before taking the steps. His cigarettes and lighter were in the left pocket; in the right, a mostly finished half pint of gin. He tucked the gin away for later and lit a smoke before heading carefully downstairs.

The staircase seemed to go on forever, like a room in one of those halls of mirrors. Suddenly feeling dizzy, he looked down at his feet to keep the vertigo at bay as he descended. They almost didn't feel like his feet at all. He watched them march down from stair to stair. It seemed to go on much farther than it should have.

Harrison chanced an upward glance to see how far he still had to go before reaching the club's back entrance. There was no door anywhere to be seen.

"What the hell?" he muttered.

He continued his descent, clutching the rail with both hands. One foot after another. The landing had to be coming up soon.

The band was playing "So What" by Miles Davis. He stopped in his tracks. Somehow, the music was coming from above him. He must have missed the landing, but how? Walked right past the door to the club? His heart fluttered. He stared up and down the staircase. There was no door to be seen, just stairs ascending to the heavens and descending into the abyss. *Just stairs.*

He sighed, shook his head, and began to climb. This time he counted his steps. *1...2...3...* He glanced up at regular intervals. *7...8...9...* Where was the damn landing and doorway? *14...15...16...* It had to be close.

The music was still audible and now seemed to echo up and down the stairwell, sounding as if it came from above and below him at the same time, circling round and round.

Still, he counted steps.

22...23...24...

Harrison stopped and took a deep breath. He clung to the rail, his hand in a death grip, and looked up and then down.

He should have been back upstairs by now. He was confused. He must have missed the landing again. *Right?* He *had* to have missed it. *But how?*

He decided he would just turn around and head for the bottom. There *had* to be a bottom. These goddamn stairs couldn't lead to China!

Forcing himself to look around as he went—his vertigo be damned—he descended, one careful step at a time.

The music was fading out of earshot, but it was no longer jazz. Now it sounded more like a distant, distorted circus calliope calling to him with promises of the ring toss and cotton candy stands. Slowly even that faded out entirely, until all Harrison heard was the sound of the soles of his shoes slapping against the wooden steps.

Long after he'd stopped counting, he finally saw light at the bottom of the stairwell. He was still quite far from it, but the sight gave him hope and quickened his pace. Only now was he beginning to notice how hazy it was. Perhaps it was a good sign. It looked like the kind of cigarette haze that hung in the air at any good night club.

When he reached the end of the stairway, he stepped onto the floor and stared. He turned around and looked in every direction.

This wasn't *Birdland*.

A long rectangular room stretched out in front of and behind Harrison, somehow bathed in a soft orange glow that danced along the walls in irregular patterns. It was reminiscent of an empty warehouse. The walls themselves were soft gray and seemed to swim, or shimmer. There was something at the far end, an object of some sort—perhaps a fountain, or a statue? It was the only thing in the room. Full of trepidation, he approached the thing, somehow curious enough to set his fear aside.

The thing was a center beam balance. A scale. A *large* scale reaching about waist-high, gold in color.

The pan on the left side hung low, as if a heavy weight were sitting in it. The other was therefore held aloft. Harrison recalled a teeter-totter at the park when he was just a boy, his now-deceased brother Charles Junior sitting with his seat on the ground while their younger brother, Alton, sat perched high in the air. The thought made him smile weakly and he felt a pang in his heart, remembering his older brother. What had happened to them all? Where had it all gone so wrong?

He tried to shake the strange thoughts. Talk about *strange*. This whole evening was strange.

When he was close enough, he examined the scale. And it appeared to be made of solid gold. But Harrison knew gold, and this was the real deal.

The bottom pan was empty. Harrison touched the beam resting on the fulcrum to see if the apparatus was a working scale, and it indeed seemed to be. When it moved, something rustled in the upper pan. It was a feather. A single white feather, lying in the center of the pan. The beam's movement caused the feather to flutter lightly as if ruffled by a breeze.

A dull, heavy *thud* startled Harrison and he took a step back. It sounded as if it had come from the other side of the wall, behind the scale. Then he heard it again, and again, in an off-kilter rhythm. It sounded like slow, methodical footsteps.

But...heavy, massive footsteps.

The wall moved and undulated as the footsteps drew nearer. Harrison stared in disbelief as he realized that what he had thought was a solid wall was actually some sort of mist or smoke hovering before him. The smoke began to part as some *thing* emerged from within the cloud.

Harrison stumbled rapidly backward on his feet, tripped, and fell on his tailbone. A lightning bolt of pain shot through his lower back, but his eyes remained glued to the form that was now materializing in the shifting fog. His already precarious grip on sanity threatened to crumble to ash. Because the thing was not human, and it was no known animal as far as he could tell.

And yet it was *there*.

It was a horror show.

Its enormous head resembled that of a crocodile, a long snout and a huge mouth filled with ugly, pointed teeth. As the beast pushed forward, displacing the mist, Harrison made out more of its stout and bulky body, which looked much like the trunk of a hippopotamus. Its muscular forelimbs ended in lion-like paws. As unlikely as it seemed, he had the oddest sensation that he'd seen this thing before. Perhaps in a nightmare, or...

His brain racing a hundred miles an hour, he was both trying to get away and still figure out where he had seen its likeness before.

And then he remembered back to his youth. Not that long ago, for he had grown up fast.

He *had* seen its like somewhere. It was in the hall chamber in the ancient tomb beneath the shifting sands in that damned desert. A statue in a long line of statues. A simulacrum of this very demon had stood among those artifacts, he was sure of it.

Still not quite believing he was really seeing the creature, Harrison nevertheless crab-walked backward, away from the monstrosity. The thing opened its horrific maw and a deep rattling *hiss* emanated from its throat that reverberated through the room—a sound Harrison felt deep inside his entire body.

He tripped and rolled over, scrambled to his feet, and began to run. Glancing over his shoulder, he saw the beast was giving chase, charging like an angry bear, its bulk knocking the scale aside as it passed.

But now the room he'd been in was gone, replaced by a hellish landscape obscured by rolling clouds of smoke and raging fires. The door that led to the stairs was also gone, leaving him little chance of escape.

How can this be happening?

He heard the creature's footfalls growing louder behind him. The thing let out a bellow, or a growl, or whatever sound it made, and Harrison's legs melted, weakened by the low-pitched vibrations. His knees buckled and he fell forward.

Into a door.

He struck his head hard, and when he woke up, if he'd actually been out, he was lying on the landing in front of the jazz club's back door. He leapt to his feet, head spinning, and looked around urgently.

Nothing was amiss. Except his head throbbed.

Where was the thing, that grotesque monster thing that had stormed over the golden scale and chased him across the strange room?

Had it been there at all? Had the room?

Above him stretched the staircase, appearing not so long now. In fact, he could easily see the door that led into the upper apartment. His heart was still racing at an improbable pace.

If he survived the night, he would never shoot up again, he promised.

He straightened out his suit, reaching into the pocket for the remainder of the half pint. He drained the gin in one gulp and dropped the empty bottle on the floor. Then he reached into his other pocket for his cigarettes and lighter. He put a smoke in the corner of his mouth and struck his lighter. His hands were trembling enough that it took him several tries before he could hold the flame still enough to light his square.

The club door swung open. A friend of his held the door open a wedge, a saxophonist nicknamed Sticky. He looked Harrison up and down.

"I thought I heard someone out here. You okay, Harry? You look like you seen a ghost."

Harrison pushed past him without reply.

Manically, Harrison hustled through the club in his rumpled suit, cigarette clamped between his lips, a puff of smoke issuing out with each still-panicked breath. He paid no attention to the music oozing off the stage. He ignored the other patrons whom he brushed past without acknowledging. When he'd made his way through to the exit, he pushed open the doors and nearly stumbled out onto the busy sidewalk. He stopped, took a long drag off his smoke, bent over and rested his hands on his knees, then exhaled a billowing blue cloud.

He stared at his hands. They were still trembling.

It couldn't have been real. Just some crazy thing he had made up in his head. He must have passed out and dreamt it. Sure, it had to be a smack-nightmare. The beast was the junk, the stuff he'd shot up. But...he could still smell that sulphurous smoke in his nostrils and even on his jacket.

From somewhere nearby—behind him, perhaps—he heard the beast's low, throaty roar. He jerked upright. He looked at the other people walking past him up and down the sidewalk. None of them batted an eye. It was as if they hadn't heard it. Or they were pretending they hadn't. But he could hear it, and it was getting closer.

Gripped by sudden panic, Harrison dashed between two parked cars and into the street. He *had* to get away from the club. From the beast.

Then he saw it again, coming for him quickly from his left. This time the demon took the form of a pair of bright, luminous eyes. He screamed, trying to avoid the beast's angry glare.

The loud squeal didn't sound like the beast though.

The bulging taxi tried to stop but struck Harrison dead-on and flung him high into the air. He came down hard on the pavement and curb, and finally rolled to a stop twenty feet from the impact point. A broken mannequin, his limbs crooked and bent out of shape.

Harrison tried to look around, but his neck wouldn't allow it. His eyes focused, and even though it was a sideways picture, he now could see the car that had smashed his body to the point where he could barely feel anything other than the pain. In fact, he hurt all over. His knees, hips, neck, back, spine, skull...all of it hurt, but the worst were his shoulder and chest.

He blinked and now he saw the monstrous crocodilian head slavering drool and licking its chops.

* * *

The words came out of Alton's mouth, the syllables accentuated with each thrust, timed perfectly with the grunts of the stable boy bent over before him, both their trousers dropped to their ankles. Words in a language he didn't speak or understand.

In his hand, Alton clutched a single white feather. He believed it was an ostrich feather, procured from Alton's father's collection of oddities acquired in his travels. The feather had called to him in whispered voices, and Alton had found it among a menagerie of things housed in boxes in the estate's basement.

The voices told him many things. They told him what to do. They told him how to do it. They told him what he wanted. They understood Alton, and he understood them.

Chapter Twenty-Eight

"I'VE HAD A breakthrough."

Blackstone had an old-fashioned legal pad in one hand and an iPad Pro in the other, and he waved them now in celebration.

Michelle turned her head and managed to smile through the exhaustion visible on her features. They'd had a full week of late nights, cross-checking dozens of works in search of clues and ideas, trying one alphabetic overlay after another. Blackstone had created several dozen of them, but after being able to consistently translate a series of glyphs, there was always a point at which the consistency fell apart and the translation with it.

They'd begun to think the whole thing was some cosmic joke being played on the gullible.

Most nights, after giving up squinting at charts and tables and lists of variations on glyphs known and unknown, they'd end up on the bed and find enough of a second wind to merge their flesh in new and ingenious ways thanks to Michelle's endless sexual imagination. He didn't even miss her sex swing.

After eventually collapsing in true exhaustion but sated, she would take herself through the dark wings of the mansion—often taking some time to explore the exquisite estate, she had confided to Blackstone—back to her own smaller suite. Chambers had offered it to her right after meeting her—*ogling* her, Blackstone had later amended—so they could work as late or as early as they wished. Most nights they wore each other out, but Blackstone wasn't likely to mention that on days Michelle didn't drive to the compound, Alena might well knock on the suite's door and shortly they would ravage each other in entirely different, but also infinitely inventive ways. Alena's tastes ran to the more fetish-oriented, and she surprised him with skin-tight latex outfits she sometimes wore beneath her own clothing, and a wide and surprising assortment of related accessories.

He never mentioned the tomb dream—had it been real?

Nor did Alena ever mention Michelle Davenport.

If either of the women knew about the other, neither let on except for glares and smirks and frowns. Michelle had studiously avoided the daily dinner table, though she partook of an occasional lunch as often as not delivered to the study. There was still a chill in the air, but the women usually tiptoed gingerly around each other, leaving the professor almost exhausted in his attempts to avoid cross-contamination. It was something to which he'd become accustomed.

But this week Blackstone had rebuffed Alena's efforts to distract him and he had worked harder and with more intensity than usual. His focus had somehow improved and, though it wasn't yet sharp enough, it seemed to be increasing in resolution.

He felt as if something was just on the edge of his vision, or his understanding, and if he concentrated hard enough he would be able to reach out and grasp it. The glyphs and their meanings would finally align and he would have his Rosetta, a tool with which to make sense of the more esoteric meanings he knew were eluding him. He had worked nearly around the clock, hadn't shaved, had barely bathed or eaten—he had requested food be brought in, and a stone-faced Batten had appeared at his door with small silver trays on a cart, his glare enough to convey his feelings about the barricaded professor. Blackstone had barely glanced at him, eaten a few bites here and there, drunk copious amounts of water, iced tea, and more top-shelf bourbon than was wise, and forced his way back to work.

Until finally something had clicked.

He'd used old and new photos, taken his own photos, traced actual glyphs with gloved fingers, pored over long lists of small conquests and insights and more than a few guesses, and eventually he had found himself actually *reading* sections of a ritual.

The breakthrough had been discovering that the many panels depicting sexual exploits on the tomb's panels were actually the key to understanding the heretofore indecipherable glyphs. Somehow, through bleary sleep-deprived eyes, he noted how the painted orgy participants' bodies were intertwined in such a way that they resembled the triangular marks of stylus on clay tablets. They were in fact highly stylised representations of Sumerian cuneiform. Comparing the sexualized "writing" to the hieroglyphs he knew, with considerable effort he was able to begin deciphering the bits that had been previously out of reach.

And yes, it *was* a ritual—one of hundreds of such incantations he suspected had adorned the tomb walls.

There was plenty of Egyptian magic—and *sex magick*—from throughout the ages, most of it well-documented. He himself had been first to document some of it, although he had never considered there was anything real about it. It was merely mysticism, folklore, a religion perhaps, primitive attempts to make sense of a complicated world and the end of life, as is the case with most religions. But here, he soon realized, here was some new mysticism. Something that seemed to have sprung separately from everything else, some other place and some other time, but had meant enough to someone to make a full record of it throughout the tomb Occupant's final repose on his journey—or *hers*, he supposed, though he didn't think it was a woman who occupied the key position of the tomb complex.

On this day, when Michelle arrived Blackstone had been working at least three days straight without a break or a full meal. He was bearded and dirty, uncombed, and wild-eyed.

And when he told her he had made a breakthrough, he resembled nothing so much as a homicidal hermit, another Unabomber scribbling out a manifesto. Or a crazed genius crowing on a street corner about having solved the mysteries of the universe.

Perhaps that *was* what he'd done. He tried to remain calm even while he felt he was stepping over the line to manic euphoria.

"What?" she said. "Show me!" His excitement was infectious.

He laid out page after page of notes, read out his translations piece by piece, and eagerly showed her how far he had come in a short time. It was perhaps only ten percent of the tomb's contents in terms of writing, but it would serve as a Rosetta template and lead to more, which in turn would lead to even more.

"In a few weeks," he said enthusiastically, "I can imagine we'll be over fifty percent!"

"This is fantastic," said Michelle, touching his arm. He seemed to be vibrating. She shuffled through a few sheets of his notes. "What is it about? What was it for?"

Blackstone laughed, a bark that imitated Chambers' own laugh. He'd been doing that a lot lately.

"It's about immortality! Surprise, surprise. That's all these ancients thought about, you know. But there's more, from what I can tell. The ritual is intricately connected to another, a side ritual of sorts, I guess. This other one is about body-switching."

"Body *switching*?"

"Second only to immortality!" Blackstone crowed. "What else, it's just more bibbidi bobbidi boo, isn't it?"

"Bibbidi bobbidi *huh*? What?"

"You know, like from the movie. Wave a wand or a twig or a dead petrified snake at the darkness and conjure up some fantastic result."

"Magic?"

"Sure, what they thought of as magic. We think of it as folklore. Mysticism. Strange cultural quirks. Like I said, these guys were obsessed with living forever in some form or another."

"Have you been hydrating?" Michelle asked suddenly.

"Hydrating? Who has the time?"

"*Bibbidi bobbidi boo!* You can just make the time!"

They laughed, but their laughter was fragile.

Blackstone wondered whether he was losing his mind.

Their manic laughter died out uncomfortably.

"The pictograms were the key. After I spent hours studying them, it turns out they're a primitive type of cuneiform. The participants in these pictorial orgies are placed where a stylus would have marked a Sumerian clay tablet. It's not Egyptian at all, but an old Mesopotamian dialect."

"How did you figure that out?"

"Hours of staring at it, I guess. I don't really know, it just came to me. In a dream maybe..." His mind drifted wistfully for a moment.

"No surprise you'd be the one to look at pictures of people having sex for hours," Michelle said with a wink.

"I'd much rather be doing it than studying pictograms depicting it."

"Well, Professor, maybe you'd like to take some time off so we can make some magic of our own."

"Not now, Michelle. We have work to do. Let me read some of it to you..."

* * *

In his voyeur's control room, Chambers watched and listened to what Blackstone was showing his lovely and flexible assistant. He heard the words Blackstone read slowly at first, and then faster as he gained confidence in his translation. Chambers heard it and he knew Blackstone had done it.

For he had heard similar words in his head that first day in the tomb, back in 1958 when he'd fallen in, and every day since then.

He'd heard the words, but he hadn't been able to make sense of them. Or repeat them. Or dig out a meaning he could use.

But now it seemed he was on the verge of what he had waited over sixty years to do.

Blackstone had done it. He had created a ten percent translation that would take him through to the end.

Chambers beamed as he heard Blackstone's reading of the text. He knew it was true, and the awesomeness of the moment threatened to choke him with his own tears.

But then he heard them mocking the words, laughing at the very heart of what he had given up his life to discover. He heard the mocking words of Blackstone, the bastard, and his little whore.

Laughing.

They were *laughing.*

Laughing at the words, but also laughing at *him.*

Bibbidi bobbidi boo, indeed.

His anger almost sidetracked his delight at the success that was now within his sights. He had to calm down, let the anger dissipate. For the moment...

Because there was something more important to contemplate. Chambers now felt a certain vibration inside that he had not felt since he was a child explorer, falling into the tomb.

His blood sang through his veins, and he felt age sloughing off like skin he no longer needed.

He looked down at himself and saw that his loins had responded as well. He was as hard as a teenager, for the first time in years he felt himself ready to burst forth from his center and fuck the universe.

If Alena had been within reach, he thought he would have fucked her to death.

Literally.

He could see it in his mind's eye, her body unzipping like a duffel bag and spilling out its bowels even as he thrust into her orifices repetitively, furiously, and the light left her eyes but the smile never did...

Voices in his head aligned and he could almost understand the words they spoke, or sang, or chanted. They seemed to do all those things at once.

And the visions came from the same place as the voices, which urged him on.

His heartbeat was thunder in his ears. His chest seemed hardly capable of containing the swelled, pumping monstrous muscle that resided there.

Someone spoke.

"The time has come..."

It took a few minutes before Chambers realized it was his own voice, but the words came from someone else.

Chapter Twenty-Nine

Walking into Ashton Hall gave Blackstone a pang of nostalgia. It hadn't been long since he'd been here, but already it felt like years. Michelle had mentioned that his office had been reassigned already. As if he'd never even been on the faculty.

He sighed.

He wouldn't be here at all except for Sanford's call. "Say, James, when you get the chance, you might want to pop in and grab some mail. Most of it is junk, publisher circulars and the like, but there's a thick envelope...huh...from your wife."

"What?" Blackstone said. "Laura? It *is* for me?" *What's she doing writing to me there?*

"Sure, I have it right here. Manila, about a half-inch thick, addressed to you care of the department." Sanford paused. "Is everything all right? I thought you'd accepted a new, more lucrative position, and therefore I expected you and Laura would be..."

"Doing better? Patching things up? Getting along?"

"Uh, no, sorry, it's none of my business. I just thought... Well, in any case, this envelope is here for you when you can come pick it up, unless you would rather I forward it?"

Blackstone enjoyed Sanford's discomfort and let the silence drag on until he thought the prof would burst a vein on the other end of the line.

"I'll come get it," Blackstone said. There was an audible sigh of relief and Sanford coughed to cover it up.

"I'll leave it with the secretary. Sorry for bothering you."

"No bother at all."

But Blackstone *was* bothered. Why would Laura send him a letter at the university, when she knew he no longer worked there? Why not just send it to him at the Chambers place, or better yet deliver it herself? And, in fact, what did it mean that she had mailed this and then disappeared? And it was more than just a letter, wasn't it?

His mind immediately went to one answer.

Divorce papers.

Like in the movies, maybe she'd seen an attorney and then wanted to put the ball in his court. She had no one to go crying to, however, so where would she have gone?

The department secretary, somehow still efficient despite her 80-year-old appearance, handed him the envelope when he asked for it without waiting for him to identify himself. Her eyebrow was raised, but he just smiled and thanked her.

A few minutes later, sitting in his car away from prying eyes, Blackstone slit open the envelope. What he worked out of the tight fit was a thick sheaf of papers, mostly photocopies from the look of them, along with some print-outs from the Web.

What the hell?

It was a dossier of sorts centered on one Alton Chambers, the so-called "eccentric billionaire." *As if there are any non-eccentric billionaires,* Blackstone thought. But as he flipped through the papers, he could see right away that Laura had spent some time digging deeply into this particular billionaire's background.

More than just newspaper stories, she seemed to have found strangely sourced materials he had very little expertise in identifying—something like online background check companies, or maybe like what a private investigator would dig up for a client, as well as various articles from alternative and activist presses. Clearly she had even paid for some of this product.

As he glanced at the articles, he frowned.

There were allegations of corruption, mostly in the form of huge payments to certain politicians' campaigns or so-called super PACs, there were naked bribes to officials in the governments of a dozen countries, there were lists of lawsuits that had been squashed with out-of-court settlements or long-winded appeals, and there were news stories of various thefts of antiquities from museums around the world, along with several depositions and affidavits obtained in the courts of witnesses who pointed the finger at Chambers Industries and Chambers Oil as having supplied either funding or manpower or both. Chambers Shipping was implicated as well.

And then there were the generic articles published in the world press that offered up hazy but compelling arguments portraying Alton Chambers as a fraud and a criminal entity who allowed no laws to stop his acquisition of whatever he set his mind to. The articles painted a thoroughly unflattering portrait, barely any seeming to be aware of his Egyptian fetish.

Blackstone knew Alton Chambers was despised in some quarters, as most wealthy men tend to be, but beyond the usual gripes there was also a definite theme of people objecting to some indefinable quality in the old man that set Blackstone's teeth on edge. And yet, he was willingly employed by this possibly monstrous human being and broke bread at his table almost daily.

In spite of himself, Blackstone shuddered.

There were some carefully worded stories about the Chambers fortune itself and how Alton Chambers had come to be its sole owner and governor. The writers speculated in so many words that the old man had come into his directorship through subterfuge and perhaps out and out crime. More than one story went so far as to suggest that some of Alton's siblings who had perished in highly unusual circumstances were the victims of criminal acts.

Murder. They're talking about murder.

Blackstone remembered Chambers' narratives of the family history he had heard so far, and when he overlaid this new filter on them the result was indeed disturbing.

But this was so clearly speculation and less-than-expert detective work that he couldn't subscribe to the conclusions drawn. Sure, Chambers and his highly sexed female brood were eccentric, maybe bizarre. They were unusual—how could they not be, living in a mansion that rivaled television's Collinwood and contained within it an actual Egyptian fucking tomb?—but was that enough to tar them with the same sloppy brush?

He shrugged.

His bank account was healthy for the first time in years. He was doing important work, even if for a decidedly weird boss; he might well resurrect his career and reputation because of it; oh, and he was awash in sexy women who lusted for him.

What's not to like?

He knew he wasn't complex...just an amalgam of lusts and vices and some professional talent. But he wasn't a bad person really, was he?

Using the surface of the steering wheel, he reshuffled the papers into an orderly stack and wiggled the whole thing back into the envelope.

Laura was... What, looking out for him? Trying to blow up his gig? Jealous? Pissed off?

He slid the envelope under his seat.

Now that he was close, very close indeed, to actually solving the riddle of the ritual incantations, he had to decide if he was going to let whatever motivated his estranged wife affect his work and his relationship with his employer.

He shook his head.

No way.

He started the car and let the engine purr for a few seconds before shifting and peeling out of the parking slot.

What had happened to Laura? The thought darkened his mood, but he set it aside.

He had work to do.

Chapter Thirty

HE WAS STANDING at the window again.

Blackstone's attention had been drawn by some kind of movement, and he made a beeline to the huge glass pane. The day had started brighter, if not much warmer, than the last few, and now he squinted in the weak but direct sunlight.

His pulse quickened as he immediately focused on the movement—the Chambers granddaughter, *oh-so-exotic* Naira, riding her horse across the prairie-like rear of the property, wearing only black leggings and a fairly wispy white sports bra, proudly leaving behind silvery puffs of frozen breath that matched those coming from the beast's flaring nostrils.

It was primal, it was elemental. Or perhaps *she* was elemental, supernatural, a creature born of a union of nature itself and the universe of all things.

Blackstone was enthralled.

His mind conjured up the description, and while he chuckled on the one hand at the silliness of it, on the other hand he felt some sort of awe at how her image made him feel.

He remembered how she smelled, how she tasted, how her body molded itself to his.

She had a smart mouth and a sarcastic edge he normally would have found annoying, but for some reason she had gotten under his skin. And the fact that she was probably using him to smear her mother's nose in a kind of sloppy revenge pie didn't deter his lust in the least.

Naira reached the tree line at the left of his view, expertly wheeled the horse about, and raced back the other way as if she were being pursued by a hellhound, but she was so graceful on the horse's back that she seemed to *be* the horse, a strange but lovely melding of the human and the equine right out of mythology's best pages.

Blackstone stared at her, watching her breasts heave under their thin harness and her dark hair streaming behind her like a cape. He licked his lips.

He was leaning so close to the window that his nose fogged a round spot on the glass.

A loud, wet *smack* against the pane in front of his face made him jump back, startled. He glimpsed a pair of eyes, a sharp beak, and an explosion of feathers, which immediately disappeared but left behind a bloody art-style Rohrshach splotch.

A large bird—some kind of hawk, he thought—had kamikazed itself against the window as if aiming for his face.

That's fucking weird.

His pulse slowing again, he refocused his gaze on the hard-riding beauty who had brought him here to the window in the first place.

Smack!

Another bird, a large one, maybe another hawk or an owl, followed the first in its suicidal dive, leaving another splatter pattern and an errant feather or two on the outside of the window. And then yet *another* bird aimed for his face and sacrificed itself in the attempt.

Smack! Smack!

Two more, followed immediately by others, a half-dozen, dying as they dove for his face and sliding downward and out of sight, leaving a bloody landing zone target for those that followed them.

Smack!

The violent, wet collisions drove him backward. He forgot about Naira and her horse, transfixed by the seemingly endless squadron of hawks and eagles and a couple crows that destroyed themselves on the transparent wall in an attempt to...what? To attack *him?*

What the fuck?

He stepped a couple feet to the side, and two more birds adjusted course and found the spot in front of his face, splattering blood in picturesque explosions. Another bird flattened itself in the blood of its peers and flopped downward, and finally Blackstone stumbled to the side where he worked the rope and closed the blinds, hearing more collisions against the glass he could no longer see. But it was as though they could still see *him*, and they aimed for him despite the protective glass.

He stood, panting, and stared at the blinds.

He hoped the glass would hold.

A large straggler hit the outside of the pane with a louder explosion of ruined body and organs, and Blackstone imagined the glass smeared with its blood. And that of two dozen or more other avians.

All dead because of him.

The suicidal massacre seemed to have stopped.

He stumbled to the bed and sat down hard, his head bowed, trying to figure out what had just happened. He held up his right hand and watched it tremble. He tucked it between his thighs and *felt* it trembling. He couldn't stop the tremor.

After a short pause, Blackstone stood up gingerly and made his way to the credenza, where several decanters were lined up along with glasses—one of the necessities Chambers had made available to his guest. He poured three fingers of a fine-labeled bourbon, stared at the glass silently, then drank it down, barely feeling its bite. Refusing his urge for a refill, he set the glass back on the tray.

He took his leather coat from the closet, left his suite, and made for the huge front foyer, crossed it without seeing anyone. He wasn't exactly sure how to get to the back door, if there was one, so he opened the front door and let himself out onto the level, planter-lined tiled patio that presumably extended around the entire mansion. It seemed a long walk around that side's wing of the castle-like dwelling to where he reached the corner. He stopped, seeing that he was now facing a slice of the same wide prairie that Naira used to exercise her horse. He continued on, turned the corner, and came to a quick stop again.

Perhaps a hundred feet away, close to the exterior wall, Batten was bending over a pile of bloody corpses, all birds that had killed themselves on Blackstone's window.

He gazed up from where Batten stood. His window was indeed straight above that very spot. There were no dead birds on the patio anywhere other than below his own glass pane. He could see the blood splatters from here.

He tried to retreat quietly before Batten spotted him, but as he started to move, the prickly majordomo straightened after sweeping a red-speckled, feathered carcass onto a huge dustpan. Suddenly he raised his head as if sensing he was being watched and fixed Blackstone in a flat stare that the professor felt low inside his gut.

They stood that way for seemingly endless minutes, Blackstone and Batten staring at each other, the broom held mid-motion in the bastard's hand, until Batten's mouth turned from a straight line to a slow smirk.

Then Blackstone turned away and started his walk back to the corner, hearing the sound of sweeping and the broom's clatter against the dustpan behind him. He heaved a sigh of relief when he was out of sight and heading for the front of the mansion.

His throat was dry again and he wasn't sure if he needed more bourbon or water, but he knew that something had just passed between him and the Chambers hatchet-man.

Just what it was, he wasn't sure.

He reached his suite without seeing anyone, and for the rest of the afternoon he avoided his window and the study, making himself gradually drunk on the old man's top-shelf liquor as he sat hunched in a leather armchair. Dreading dinner. Dreading seeing anyone at all.

Just...*dreading.*

* * *

Alena knelt on her bed, naked. Her eyes were outlined in that lovely lapis lazuli shade she loved, and her engorged nipples were painted a contrasting shade of crimson red. She moved the purple gyrating vibrator in tight circles around her most sensitive spot, an assortment of feathers spread out between her knees. A sheen of scented sweat shone on her golden skin.

Jealousy was not an emotion that Alena Chambers was accustomed to. But then again, her father's other hired academics had not been James Blackstone. No one would have wanted them, any of them, but Blackstone was well put together and his genius and roguish good looks made him a catch for any woman regardless of age. Or *all* women.

Alena had spent a lifetime toying with men, both physically and emotionally, playing them as a well-seasoned grifter should. Now she felt as if the tables had been turned and she was the one being played. No, she wasn't liking the game.

And her own damned daughter had her hands all over it.

She mumbled an esoteric incantation as she plunged the vibrator inside herself, riding the waves of pleasure to her climax.

Soon Blackstone's body would belong to her lover, her pharaoh, her *father,* and yet it would be hers alone. And she would experience the ecstasy of him from within Naira's firm young body. *For eternity.*

With that thought in her mind's focus, she reached her shuddering orgasm. The feathers floated off the bed, colors shimmering as they twirled around and around. And the energy surrounded her like a golden cloud. She laughed and laughed as the wave rippled through her system, and she closed her eyes.

She wished she could see Blackstone right now.

Chapter Thirty-One

BATTEN SWEPT UP the dead birds and deposited the corpses in a waste basket. He figured he knew how this mess had happened, and he knew just what to do with them. The full, stinking basket in hand, he proceeded through the house.

He'd worked for the old man since forever. It had been such a long time that he barely remembered his life from before he had met Alton Chambers.

He had been nothing more than a street thug, a young ruffian living from hustle to hustle. Muscular Ricky Batten—they called him "The Bat," not because he looked like the night flyer, but because he preferred that blunt instrument to pay back those who crossed him—had worked part-time as a collector and *motivator* for a small-time loan shark, but he spent some of his nights perfecting his mugging technique for quick scores in the alleyways of Whitechapel. Until the night he decided to rob an obviously rich old man who'd been unfortunate enough to cross his path. That was his typical thought process at the time, and he had faced off against the well-dressed tourist. It was a night that changed the course of Ricky "The Bat" Batten's life, but he could barely remember how it had happened. He could still hear the echo of Chambers' words, "If you want to make some real money, come with me." Then the strange old guy had spoken some gibberish in a foreign language, and Ricky had tossed the bat aside and followed. It was as if his legs had grown their own brain, and in his mind there had been no alternative route.

Once in America, barely aware of how it had all happened, his first job for the old billionaire was helping to dig up his deceased wife's body, throw it in the boot of his car, and carry it down to what the old man called the *preparation room* below the gigantic family manse. Chambers put him on his generous payroll and a long string of illicit deeds began, interspersed between the more mundane aspects of Batten's duties. His total loyalty had been won early on, and it had never flagged.

As Batten rode the north wing elevator down to the basement holding the basket filled with avian corpses cradled in the crook of his arm, all he could think about was how much he would enjoy choking the life out of the smart-mouthed, cocky, arrogant professor. That jackass had just waltzed in and probably gotten a better salary than Batten's after nearly a lifetime of service, even though he was just another low-rent academic. And those women all fighting each other just to get a piece of him! Even Naira—whose tight ass Batten had been admiring since long before she was legal—was making eyes at the so-called professor. Maybe even more than just making eyes. Yes sir, when the time came to get rid of this phony, Batten hoped that Chambers would let him do the honors.

He had been promised much, much more.

Until then, he'd just have to bite his lip and bide his time.

Batten stepped out of the elevator and strode down the hallway to where Chambers kept his *pets*. Some of the old man's eccentricities were more terrifying than simply strange. Batten thought Chambers himself could be terrifying too. Sometimes the old man seemed to be different people housed in the same body. One was a proper old gentleman. That was the face he used on those occasions that he was in the public eye, or when he was trying to impress someone. Another was a spoiled child inclined to frightening temper tantrums and violent outbursts. And a tendency to bully others for fun. And then there was that third one, the one who...

Better not to dwell on *that* one. Batten had seen enough to know what his employer was capable of doing.

In the early days, Batten had wondered if his employer might suffer from one of those multiple personality disorder things. The old man would talk to himself at times, but not just normal internal monologues that had slipped his lips—no, these were full-fledged conversations where he answered himself too. Was that two personalities speaking? Or was Chambers talking to ghosts? Was he insane? It wasn't Batten's job to care, and his pay bought complete loyalty.

Eventually his pay bought more than loyalty.

Eventually it bought complicity.

Batten reached the door, tapped the keycard, and heard the lock disengage. Slowly he pushed open the door.

Inside, the room glowed red from the heat lamps that burned continuously in their fixtures above. It was warm and dry inside, and almost a foot of sand covered the sunken floor, tapering up to the doorway. An array of large stones and old dried-out tree limbs lined the perimeter, and Batten could hear the hiss of shifting sand behind them. The serpents liked to hide in the corners.

Chambers was so enamored with the bloody tomb he'd discovered that he had even made an effort to recreate the treacherous snake pit from within it. He'd gone so far as illegally importing deadly Egyptian cobras to make it more authentic.

Crazy old bastard.

Then again, *crazy* was only the tip of the old iceberg, wasn't it?

Realizing that it was feeding time, several of the more daring snakes began to cautiously approach Batten. He secured the door behind him and took a four-foot-long snake-hook from the rack near the door, as well as a pair of snake tongs. Batten reached into the death basket with the tongs and grabbed up a dead bird. Carefully, with the tongs he swung the avian corpse in front of one of the longer asps, shaking it so it appeared almost lifelike. While the snakes were accustomed to live food, mostly rats that Batten ordered through a local shop, he was able to fool them into going for the dead birds too. With the hooked pole he kept the other serpents at bay.

The snake rose up, interested, displaying its hood. It followed the corpse's movements as if it were a snake-charmer's flute, its head moving from side to side as it approached closer, closer...until it struck and pulled the bird into its coils.

Batten continued to feed the others in a similar fashion. He had worked with the snakes often enough that he had no real fear of being bitten, though he remained respectful of their capabilities. And he wore thick boots and reinforced trousers for this task.

This was a feast. When he had handed over the last of the dead birds, he stood and watched the snakes dislocating their jaws to swallow their meals whole. There was something mesmerizing about the beasts and their appetite.

A thin smile spread across his ruddy face.

Chapter Thirty-Two

BLACKSTONE THREW HIMSELF into the work. After all, he was being paid handsomely, and the only way to continue earning was to show some success.

And he *was* successful. Little by little he expanded the vocabulary and increased his understanding of the strange language—he'd come to think of it as an archaic dialect. Chambers was hot to have the panels translated, and as Blackstone succeeded bit by bit, the results continued to suggest religious rituals with some bizarre aspects.

Bizarre?

He knew from bizarre, didn't he? What the fuck was the bird mass suicide, if not bizarre? What drove the goddamn birds to do a Jim Jones on *his* window?

And there was Batten. The silent man *was* bizarre. Since the bird event, Blackstone had gone out of his way to avoid the Chambers family hatchet-man. It was an arrangement that worked, and if Chambers noticed he didn't say.

Blackstone might have left right then, walked away from the job and the two crazy women and gone back to bickering with his wife and screwing his teaching assistant on the side, and perhaps everything would reset back to where it had been. It was an attractive option, though an impossible one.

Despite his troubled personal life, Blackstone had started feeling the excitement of discovery, and he planned for the day when he would defy his employer and find a way to seek the accolades that would be due him. He worried that someone else would beat him to it, but Chambers insisted that he owned all the actual glyphs that had ever been discovered—by his father's company, and in his own youthful adventure. The family's unfortunate legacy of death had left Chambers holding all the marbles. There was more to that story, Blackstone figured, but riding along on the old billionaire's coattails wasn't the worst gig ever, even though if the papers Laura had sent him after she'd left were accurate, the old man may have been a murderer. Or at least an accomplice. *If* the papers were correct.

And he was honestly curious about the old man's motivation. What did he expect to gain from Blackstone's work? If he wasn't interested in publishing, then what?

Blackstone had been thinking about it while he worked on the translations. Almost everything in the tomb, almost every panel, every set of related glyphs, basically almost every "paragraph" he translated seemed to be a ritual, some of which had fairly nefarious purposes. For instance, some were meant to kill enemies in various ways. Some were meant to further the spellcaster's ends, whatever they might be. Some were anchored in the ways of vengeance.

Other rituals seemed to be about immortality, which wasn't a surprise. Everything about the Egyptian way of death was about immortality. But this seemed to be actual immortality, not only metaphorical or generational. Actual ways to prolong the life of one's body. There were references to the consumption of blood, for instance, that Blackstone found problematic. Some of them demanded that blood be drunk *"while the sac emptied and the ka departed."* If he gave Chambers those translations, would the old man attempt to kill people to consume their blood? Had he already attempted it?

And then what about those even more bizarre incantations? He'd kept these even from Michelle. Much of what he'd shared with her of the translations was indeed sexual in nature. Egyptian *sex magick* was well established, and he himself had done his share of screwing willing partners while at least considering the possibility that they were willing due to some ritual he had recited. He was never sure whether the women were so pliable because he was so handsome—*and dashing, don't forget dashing*—or because something in the words he had spoken had influenced their wills. If he *had* influenced their wills, would he be likely to stop?

This was in part why he had felt a certain kinship with the old billionaire. Chambers did what he wanted, how he wanted, when he wanted. He never worried about cost, and he never worried about criticism. He thought social media was a television invention. He only cared about fulfilling his own every wish...and Blackstone was ready to admit he, himself, had lived life that way. *Only without the billions.*

When women had responded to whatever spark they sensed in him, he allowed it. He never pushed them away and he never backed down from a tryst that was granted to him. Alena was enough to occupy his time when not with Michelle, but her daughter Naira was also desirable, and if she wished to partake of his rampant libido, then who was he to refuse? He believed in equality, and if they wanted him—without him forcing himself on them in any way—then he was not likely to opt out.

The fact that it seemed strange that both mother and daughter desired him was not lost on the professor, however, and while he did not lose sleep over it, he did consider the reasoning behind it. Perhaps it was being in Alton Chambers' orbit that made Professor Blackstone so desirable. Maybe it was just the Chambers family dynamic. Hell, he felt like he was a character on *Dynasty*. Or maybe it was this damned loony bin of a house. And its secrets.

He shrugged it off. He was earning his keep and the rest were fringe benefits.

Sexy fringe benefits.

Chapter Thirty-Three

SHE'S DEAD!

When Blackstone turned the key and entered, he felt a strong puff of air blow past him and he stumbled, suddenly convinced that it was his wife's soul escaping from their apartment. His brain provided the words and his guilt set them on repeat, like a dark mantra.

The door had swung open on its own almost as if someone was standing on the other side, letting him in after he freed Laura's spirit—or soul, or *ka*, or whatever.

He steadied himself against the door jamb and waited for his pulse to slow.

There was no one behind the door.

Nothing had left the apartment except air made stale by having been shut in for some time.

The stuffy smell told him Laura hadn't come home. She had always regularly opened windows to keep fresh air circulating even when the outside temperature was low. But the place had been closed up and he knew she was gone.

Still gone. Maybe gone forever.

He scolded himself for the thoughts, but as thoughts do, they kept coming no matter how hard he tried to stem them.

Feeling rising tension in his neck, as if his muscles were seizing up, he wandered the apartment absent-mindedly, trying to suppress the wild thoughts.

She's dead!

No, she isn't!

He forced himself to make a sweep, noting that everything was as he had left it. There was the canned and boxed food that always spilled out of the cramped pantry cabinet, there were the skillets and pots stored on the stove and hanging overhead, there was the same modern clock with the rotating pendulum—

He stopped mid-step, realizing his mind's eye had provided the clock, a near-transparent rectangular glass column with the rotating gears of the movement visible on all sides, right there on the gas fireplace mantel...

It was a... He thought about it. Maybe a Howard Miller? Howard-something. Expensive, anyway. It had been a gift from her parents. He could see it in his mind's eye.

But the clock *wasn't* there.

And it had been there the last time, which he knew because he had consulted it before leaving.

So Laura *had* come back!

Blackstone stood uncertain for a minute, then shook his head.

Would Laura return only for her *clock*?

He quickly checked the rest of the apartment and noticed a couple subtle differences from his last visit. A bookcase in the corner of the living room contained a smattering of eclectic titles, some of them the romances Laura read incessantly. In front of a row of novels were some ceramic figurines and some examples of "depression glass" passed down from her grandmother—and half of them were missing, perhaps two of each. He stalked into the bedroom and noted that one of Laura's jewelry cases sat on the bureau, but he could have sworn it had been inside last time. He opened the lid and it was half-empty.

Had she returned for a clock, some low-end jewelry, and a couple figurines and colored glass?

Then again, why not? She'd come back and taken a few items of personal significance. Gifts from family and friends, reminders of happier times. Maybe they were the only things she wanted to remember about their marriage.

He strode back toward the living room, perplexed and unsure what to think, whether to worry or be angry. Laura had tied up his emotions the last few years as she had begun to close herself off to him—and it was his fault, surely—but essentially he still loved her. Her departure had hurt him, but she hurt him every day she stayed too. He couldn't figure out whether he had caused this crisis or if she had gotten into trouble.

All indications pointed to her having left.

But then what about the letter and the deep research on Alton Chambers? Why try to convince him that Chambers was some kind of evil genius instead of benign?

And if she wanted to do that, why disappear?

Suddenly there was a scrape outside the apartment door, as if someone had tripped and caught himself by grabbing the jamb. He remembered there was a subtle curl in the hallway carpeting where two sheets were unraveling apart in opposite directions—he had tripped on it himself more than once. But then whoever it was seemed to have stopped moving. He heard no steps, no other doors opening. It was as if someone had tripped, then stood in place so as to avoid making any other sounds.

Quietly he tiptoed to the door, stood off to the side and took the knob in one hand and, since he hadn't locked it, counted to three then turned the brass bulb and snatched open the door.

She was standing there as if she'd been waiting to knock, but her pupils widened and he was certain she was surprised.

"What are you doing here?"

Naira smiled, mocking, and winked. "Came to see the professor's digs." She looked over his shoulder. "Nice. Bland, but nice. Kind of empty. Describes you, doesn't it, Professor?"

He snatched her hand hard and yanked her inside, closing the door on the hallway he knew had big ears.

"*Ooooh*, Professor Blackwell!"

"Would you just stop playing games, Naira?"

"He knows my name!" she said, sulking.

Even sulking, she was beautiful.

"Listen, do you know anything about Laura, my wife? She's...huh, disappeared. Left me, I guess. But it's strange..."

Naira blinked rapidly in surprise. "Sorry, Professor, can't say that I do. I never even met her. Are you sure?" She looked around the apartment innocently.

"How did you follow me?"

"I have a friend who drives Uber. I said, *Follow that Aston Martin!* It was very Bond. You don't look like Daniel Craig."

He didn't know how to respond. "All right, I can give you a ride back."

"Another ride?" she said, her eyebrow wagging. "I could go for that."

He felt heat on his cheeks. Truthfully, he was still tingling from the last *ride*.

They were closer together than he realized, and she leaned forward and pecked his lips with hers. Cinnamon and other exotic spices. He couldn't help himself, he held her in place and made it a proper kiss. They lingered, yet it was chaste compared to what they'd done before.

"Oh shit," she said, her eyes closed. "Take my pants down, would you?"

"Here?"

"There's a bed, isn't there?"

Blackstone hesitated. *Laura's bed?*

But Naira was already peeling her leggings down and stepping out of them, and the sight of her panty-less was too much for him. She went for his belt and he kicked off his shoes, and in less than a minute they'd found the bed after all and Naira was on all fours, urging him on, and before they knew it they'd torn the comforter and sheets to shreds, and by the time they were finished most of the bedclothes lay on the floor in a heap.

Blackstone lay on the silk explosion while Naira caressed him lazily, her head cradled in his ribcage, and stared at the ceiling. This was some sort of watershed moment. He had strayed plenty, but never in his own— *their* own—home. He felt as though a thunderbolt could shatter the window glass at any moment and skewer him with high voltage and a quick trip to hell. Or that Laura would come home and find them like this, fly into a rage, and leave the walls and sheets splattered with their blood and random bits of flesh.

Thing was, he deserved it.

But now Naira's hand was circling his rising flesh and the rest of the images in his mind went fuzzy as his loins reawoke under her attention. She was putting in some effort below his navel.

Then his thoughts drifted and the rhythm of the moment took over again as they melted into a series of challenging positions. Naira was nothing if not adventurous, enjoyed posing as if there were a camera, and he was forced to keep up. Which normally wouldn't have bothered him at all.

The niggling, disturbing thought that Laura might *never* come back ruined his pleasure.

As did the creepy feeling of fucking in this bed.

Chapter Thirty-Four

BLACKSTONE WENT NIGHT-WALKING the halls of the Chambers estate. But he was investigating, not merely wandering. He was wearing cargo shorts and a Talking Heads t-shirt, high-top sneakers, and carrying an empty carafe.

It was after dinner, and as far as he knew Chambers was away, Batten was out and had not returned. Alena had not joined them. And he hadn't seen Naira since breakfast.

He'd formed a strange obsession about the off-limits area below, and the reconstructed tomb chamber. He wanted to see it again. Now that he was translating words and phrases and entire rituals, he *needed* to see the bizarre red sarcophagus again. The need had been eating at him, especially when he and Michelle were coupling. There were strange tendrils of...*something*...swirling in his brain during those moments, and he suspected the ruby-covered coffin was somehow involved.

If confronted while on his walk, he would claim was looking for milk or juice and had gotten lost, and had stumbled onto the elevator. He'd been tempted, and...there it was, he had simply wandered into the underground area.

Yes, he *had* taken the elevator down. Was he not supposed to?

He figured the dumb act would work. *Once*, it could work once. What would Chambers do? Sic his attack dog Batten on him? That was a possibility, but as long as Chambers wanted something from him, he'd be fine. Wouldn't make sense to hurt the very person you desperately needed help from, would it?

Hurt?

Would Chambers have him hurt? What if it was worse than that?

But what was *worse* than being hurt?

He chose to stop worrying about it.

Blackstone looked at the elevator buttons. He was certain this car didn't even resemble the one he had ridden with the old man, did it?

And what the hell, there were *two* levels down below? He was hazy about which button Chambers had pushed on their journey to the bizarre tomb chamber, and so now on a whim he tried the lowermost button. It lit up briefly then went dark. *No access.* The black plate next to the call box mocked him. So he pressed the other button, and the elevator mechanism engaged noisily.

Once he'd arrived at the uppermost lower level, the art on display captured his attention. Then he really *had* wandered until hopelessly lost in the maze of corridors that seemed to go on forever. Was this an old mine shaft? How had it been dug? His mind whirled.

The lobby area outside the elevator door was like a small gallery with Egyptian gold artifacts displayed on stands and long glass display cases. The nature of this collection indicated that the items had been smuggled. They were nearly priceless as artifacts, but were also very valuable as simply pure gold. It was no wonder Chambers kept them down here, where only he could enjoy them.

And, presumably, also his family of weirdos.

He wondered momentarily if the old man had really offed his siblings, as was more than implied by the stories Laura had dug up. And if he had killed them, what about the Chambers paterfamilias? The research she had given him was worrisome on several different fronts, one of them overtly political. Just how badly did Alton Chambers want to become a senator? Or...*president?*

Speaking of weirdos, he imagined Alena wandering these halls like a ghost. A horny ghost.

And he remembered her Cleopatra moment, with her mouth on his manhood. He felt the lust rising. If that had been a dream, it was a keeper.

This level seemed more recent, architecturally, or at least had been renovated. But it was very confusing. Blackstone hoped he could find his way back to the elevator.

He thought about his previous visit to the family underworld, crypt, catacomb, whatever it was.

When Chambers had shown him the tomb—*the entire goddamn fucking tomb he secretly had cut up, moved across the ocean, and resurrected here in the bowels of his crazy-old-rich-fuck mansion*—Blackstone had been so awed, so star-struck by the life-size artifact, that he'd been transported back to the Valley of the Kings...

He had stared at that red sarcophagus at the center of the tomb and had stepped out of his own mind, he knew that now. Eventually he had followed Chambers out of the tomb and through the numerous corridors, and his mind had been in a haze.

And thus he'd forgotten all about how to find the tomb again, or how to find his way back from there.

So now he was wandering this eerie sub-basement, the corridors steadily changing in character from modern, paneled, painted and well-lit, to fieldstone fitted together like puzzle pieces, with those occasional brick arches that swooped overhead and made long curved slices of shadow only partially held at bay by weakening electric lights strung on ancient wiring along the corniced ceilings. Occasionally he heard water dripping, a hollow sound just like in a cavern.

Actually, the corridor *was* becoming more of a cavern, with slick rounded walls and pocket-like depressions that seemed to have been scooped out of living rock with pickaxe and trowel. Though he'd been here, or at least somewhere nearby, he seemed to have lost the ability to navigate strange locations. He thought he remembered the tomb well enough, but everything else—such as the way there—seemed to have been erased from his memory like audio tape run over a magnet.

Was the tomb one level down, where the elevator wouldn't take him?

He slowed his pace then stopped, quite lost.

For the first time, he sensed danger he couldn't quite identify, but which seemed to be approaching from behind and breathing over his shoulder.

But it wasn't really the first time, was it? If he thought about it, he'd felt a sense of impending danger since he had moved his things into the Chambers manse. The place was certainly strange, and its occupants more so. He couldn't put his finger on what the danger was, even though he sensed *something*.

The birds.

What about the suicidal birds? That had been horrifying, even though they hadn't attacked him. But they had shown a strong desire to do so.

He had difficulty sleeping well, it was true, but perhaps that was due to the hours he spent on the job...and the hours he spent in carnal pursuits.

And Laura had either left him in the most un-Laura way, or something had happened to her. That research she had mailed him spoke volumes. Or did it? It might have been a carefully planned hit piece.

From Laura?

Why would she go to all the trouble of faking the printouts and photocopies? No, they had to be real. Were they accurate? That was an unknown. Like the layout of this sub-level... He came to a corridor crossroads and stood still for a minute, trying to pick a direction out of the three.

This is ridiculous.

The underground couldn't be *this* large. It had to extend way past the outline of the house itself, which made him imagine this as some sort of natural cave complex that a Chambers ancestor had chosen to build the house on top of, like the tip of a hollow iceberg.

A sudden thought almost short-circuited his determination to locate the tomb. The underground might be expanding even as he walked its corridors. But it *couldn't* be expanding, that was impossible.

Wasn't it?

The incantations he'd already translated had seeped into his subconscious. *Something* strange was happening in the basement of the Chambers house.

He shivered.

Besides the bizarre thoughts, he was also cold. The air seemed to chill around him, and his breath turned frosty as if he were outdoors. He wished he was wearing more than shorts and a t-shirt. Rubbing his hands together vigorously, he continued straight ahead by choosing the center corridor.

The lighting was steadily diminishing. Bare bulbs strung on a loose wire had grown farther apart and the pockets of darkness they created became longer and more intense. An occasional niche in the rocky walls held some artifact that normally he would have wanted to examine, but he found that he was starting to stumble as he walked faster. He felt more and more lost.

A mental image of his bleached skeleton found someday in this sub-basement hurried him along as he turned and faced the way from which he had just come. Shivering almost uncontrollably now, he stepped carefully to avoid tripping over the uneven flooring which had become rocky and slippery.

Have to try to go back.

Soon he stood at another crossroads, but this one was made up of one straight choice and two that angled into the main corridor diagonally.

But those angled tunnels hadn't been there when he'd just passed by, of that he was sure. He would have noticed. Wouldn't he?

The thought that the tunnels could be expanding struck him again and he shuddered. If that was true, then...

Then nothing was real.

He chewed the inside of his cheek until it hurt. Should he stay on the straight route, assuming that was where he'd come from? He decided to try that way, and almost immediately the tunnel looked *wrong*. Its lights were spaced even farther apart, and the artifacts in the niches were different from those he had noticed just a while earlier.

Starting to panic now, Blackstone cursed his host...and cursed himself for this stupid excursion.

Suddenly he heard what sounded like baying.

A pack of hounds on his heels now?

Maybe there was some sort of security down here? Was Chambers toying with him?

But...*dogs?*

He remembered many a desert dig in Egypt where just outside the flickering light ring of a campfire they had heard the howling and yipping of the jackal packs that roamed the night seeking free meals.

These were jackals. He'd have bet on it.

Jackals?

They were drawing rapidly closer, baying, growling with hunger as if they'd just homed in on some helpless prey.

Wearing only a t-shirt and shorts, Blackstone actually *was* helpless. He grabbed a heavy bronze statuette from a nearby shelf and prepared to protect himself. He whirled just as the pack should have come into his field of vision, no more than a few yards away.

But there was nothing there. Only the sound of the ravenous pack.

Invisible jackals? This had to be some sort of audio trick.

Then he felt teeth clamping on his ankle.

"What the fuck!"

The pain was intense, ripping his skin and tearing a jagged wound with teeth that might have been invisible but were altogether too real and viciously sharp.

He hefted the statuette. Timed his move. He used the elongated statuette like a baseball bat, put his weight into it, and whipped it in a wide arc that connected with *something.*

The fucking thing was real enough to squeal. Blackstone swung back again and connected, and again.

Another thing had swung around and flanked him. He brought the statuette down on where its head might be and smashed it over and over. Then he turned his attention toward whatever was advancing on him.

Blackstone searched his memory. He'd been blessed with a superb one for words and translations; he had learned Shakespeare by heart easily in college. He had just worked on a simple incantation last week... How did it go?

The words rolled off his tongue easily, though he was unsure about the accent. But he spoke loudly as he held off his attackers:

"Night's creatures cannot be without /
The Voice of the Master /
Who speaketh the spell; and now /
Must return whence they came /
With their pain and disfiguring /
Jaws to the lands of the Dead."

Almost instantly the howling, baying, and growling was gone, and Blackstone knew he was alone. His ankle wound was gone, too, though his body still remembered the pain. But it was fading even as he touched the skin that had been torn.

This is what Chambers wants.

The spells. The incantations.

There were already spells he had learned that frightened him, suddenly, with their potential. For if one or two magical incantations worked, then why wouldn't they *all* work? Once it was proven magic worked, you had to adjust your world view, didn't you? Blackstone had always been willing, because he had translated plenty of Egyptian spells and rituals. None had ever worked that he knew of, but now that world had been altered.

He rubbed his ankle where the attackers had inflicted damage and pain and set off again to find his way out. He wasn't cold anymore. Now that he knew there was a sound basis to this Egyptian magic...Chambers' motives were suddenly a lot more suspect.

Finally he reached a more modern area of the tunnel. The walls were painted cinderblock and had a hospital basement look. The elevator had to be nearby.

Suddenly its door opened and he reached for the button. But when he tried to push it, the door became his own door and he was stepping inside.

Then, in the strange logic of dreams, he was lying on his sofa and Alena was draped over him but backward and offering him her shaved sex while she put her own skills to work on him, and as he glanced over her back at his legs he thought he saw the scratches made by the jackals, but there hadn't been any jackals, had there? Then the scratches were gone, and there was only his mouth on Alena and her mouth on him, and at some point he screamed as the orgasm pulsed through him. He could tell that she had reached the heights, too, when her muscles tightened and they both finished each other like cats in heat.

When she turned to smile at him, she wasn't Alena at all. It was a desiccated corpse, turning to dust right on his body.

He opened his mouth to scream.

But then he opened his eyes, suddenly realizing he was in his bed, tearing at his pillowcase with his teeth, like a dog.

The sheets were wet with sweat and his own sticky nocturnal emission.

He stood, unsteadily, and went to the bar. He tossed off a stiff bourbon with a single swallow, enjoying the burn. Light in the window indicated it was already day. His head was spinning. He poured another shot, then opened the shade. The day was gloomy and foggy, and when he turned away there was a sudden movement he caught with the corner of his eye...

It was Naira, a vision out of another wet dream, riding her horse, galloping from one side of the expansive pasture to the other. As usual, despite the chill in the air she was wearing only black riding breeches and a matching black sports bra.

Blackstone was caught between Naira's animal sexuality and her mother's undeniable beauty and more adult charms.

Yeah, until she turned to dust.

Jesus, I have got to get the fuck away from this job.

The bourbon burned all the way down.

Chapter Thirty-Five

IN THE CIRCLE'S center, Chambers stood with his arms raised in prayer while Alena lay waiting on the altar.

He'd spread his arms in prayer to Min every day the last week and now once again in order to cement his understanding of the professor's translations. As the whispering in his head increased in volume, and his tumescent flesh hovered at the portal of Alena's sex, he uttered the memorized words in the Occupant's language that he hoped would connect the two of them in preparation for the ritual.

"One upon the journey /
Awaken O Tefnut bringing /
Forth mist which /
Lays the ka to the sands /
Away from the eye of Ra..."

As he entered his daughter-wife, the words seemed to echo in the space, whistling between the many sarcophagi that held his family and others of value.

An uncanny wind picked up silica grains and whipped them around the altar. Chambers went on, intoning what he believed was the final command in the guttural language.

Blackstone's translation read: *"Sleep for the journey is long / Sleep though the Voice has called / Sleep and repose and awaken once more!"*

Alena groaned in pain and pleasure as his rock-hard penis penetrated her and magnified the powerful words. Chambers had learned to exploit Egyptian *sex magick* over the years, steered by the whispers in his head.

Whether he was accessing the power of the deity Min, or the Occupant, or both, or perhaps Ra and his daughter Tefnut, Chambers felt all-powerful. He knew he was on the cusp of realizing every plan he had worked toward for decades, searching for the right experts and finding some who were promising, but many more who simply lacked the knowledge and understanding and experience he required. James Blackstone had changed all that, perhaps *because* of his weaknesses instead of in spite of them.

The old man felt his power grow as he thrust inside Alena, her thighs wrapped tightly around him. When he was ready to finish, his hand slowly reached for the dagger under his robes and caressed the hilt. The sensation of lightning flowing between his hand and the weapon, between his body and the blade, nearly made him draw it from its sheath...

Using the blade to slit his offspring Alena's throat while his own spear of flesh thrust into her warm *sheath*—as the Romans would have it—would likely have granted him powers he could barely imagine.

But no.

It was better to wait. There would be greater reward with patience. *Much* greater.

Alena was screaming as his body, much leaner and stronger than anyone his age had any right to be, pounded into hers. When he finished spectacularly, she rode along with him, her *sheath* squeezing him dry.

They sighed together at length. Her tremors continued as long as he was inside.

His hand dropped away from the dagger. Alena would never know how close he had come to grabbing all the power now, and dealing with the consequences later.

He stepped back, and immediately went to the red sarcophagus, whispering contritely.

"Thanks for the cuddles," Alena called out behind him. "Asshole."

"I have no time for your wretched cuddling."

Chambers watched Alena approaching, gloriously naked and flushed from her pleasure. Her eyes and lips mocked him, but he knew she was all in with his plans. She had her own.

"Whatever you say, Father."

Her tone was full of snark.

"Alena, my dear, you should be careful. Our goals overlap. But if they didn't..." He left just enough unsaid.

He was more powerful than ever, and about to become even more so.

And if his goals and hers were to not coincide, then she was of little use to him now that Blackstone had seemingly solved the translation problem. Suddenly the possibilities of the last few decades were coming to fruition.

The voices in his head swelled to a chorus of discordant screams overlaid with the sound of a million bees, wasps, and hornets.

Even though it should have hurt his head, he realized that for the first time he was reacting differently. Now he was *listening.*

Now he was ready for his destiny.

He smiled at her such a grimace of hate and disgust and rage that he, himself, thought she would turn to dust at his gaze.

He strode away, leaving her naked, alone, and suddenly frightened among the dead.

Chapter Thirty-Six
1964

CHARLES CHAMBERS SENIOR had succumbed to the sadness his life had become since the third of his four children had been buried after bizarre accidents and circumstances. Running the mammoth oil company that bore his name turned into a chore, and he had increasingly foisted its day-to-day duties to his son, Alton.

The young man was more than capable of handling the company. This surprised Charles Senior because he had often felt Alton was the weakest of his offspring. The boy had spent his youth pretending to be a scientist and explorer, and Charles had decided he was just too childish. Serious work would not have been his strong suit. But then Alton had discovered a tomb in the middle of the desert of northern Egypt, and he had grown in size and maturity rapidly after that. But his siblings hadn't fared as well. Charles Junior, Cynthia, and Harrison had all fallen from grace in one way or another, and then had lost their lives in mysterious circumstances. Charles Senior had hired private investigators to delve into those circumstances far more deeply than police departments, but ultimately had come up dry. The deaths appeared strange, but they were judged to have been accidents.

Charles Senior had wondered why his eldest had committed suicide after one poor meeting, or how his daughter had managed to get lost on her way to the house she'd grown up in and slipped near the pond, cracking her skull wide open. Or how Harrison had come to be struck by a taxi on a New York City street... But ultimately his suspicions were either disproven or he was convinced to drop his inquiries for the sake of the company's reputation. He had done so, reluctantly, but his quest had left him uninterested in management and unwilling to continue as head of the company. He'd handed it all to Alton, fearful on one hand that the young man would run the company into the ground, and on the other that he would die in some bizarre accident soon and leave Charles Senior with no option other than a bullet in the brain.

To his surprise, Alton had taken the reins willingly and had immediately begun to turn the company around from the period of Charles Senior's negligence. Also surprisingly, Alton had thrived and had most definitely not come to the kind of strange and unexplainable end his siblings had suffered. Charles Senior's naturally suspicious and paranoid personality had soon fed him the idea that Alton had somehow engineered his siblings' deaths. After all, the young man now had complete control of a multinational corporation with nearly unlimited resources. Who needed a better motive for homicide? The problem was that Charles Senior had engaged two of the very best investigative firms, and all those professionals had found that Alton's alibis and indeed his whereabouts proved that he could not have had a hand in murdering his siblings.

Perhaps it was all a big coincidence, Charles Senior thought, and perhaps not. Either way, he could not prove anything, and, in fact, the company was indeed thriving under Alton's leadership. His further diversification into shipping and various forms of transport had taken the company to new heights. Alton had bankrolled some secretive projects he had minimally explained to his father, but Charles Senior had waved off his son's explanations.

"Do as you wish, Alton," he had said over drinks and cigars, a ritual that Charles still cherished despite his despondency. "It's your company now, and I trust you to handle it as I would."

Alton let his cigar burn. He hated the things. He said, "Father, I wanted to tell you what I am planning to do with—"

"Please! I don't care, don't you see? I have lost my children and nothing matters to me."

"You haven't lost me, Father."

"No, I have not. And that may be fate. Your destiny is to take over and make me and your siblings proud. I just wish to be kept out of your affairs. The company is yours, you know. You've signed the papers."

"So all you want to do is hang your head in despair, is that it?" Alton was surprised at his own harsh tone. "All you want is the benefits of the company, the trappings of wealth, without any of the responsibilities?"

"We have switched roles, haven't we?" Charles Senior said wistfully, watching his cigar smoke swirl above him. He drank some bourbon and his eyes teared up. "Should be me, reminding you of your responsibilities."

"Yes, it should."

"Well, I am finished with all that. Do whatever the hell you want with the company. I don't care."

"Just so long as I keep the dividends coming?" Alton's bitterness was obvious.

"I built it, I should benefit. But for everything else, please go to Gram. I trust that man like another son."

"Very well. As you wish, Father." Alton stood to leave, his cigar left to smoulder itself to death in the crystal ashtray. He finished his bourbon, however, which was a vice he had learned not from his father, but from Gram. "I won't bother you again."

Alton had been about to tell his father about his project to cut up the strange Egyptian tomb they had always kept secret and ship it overseas. He thought his father would be interested. He thought his father would care.

He had been wrong, he realized as he slammed the library door behind him, his anger amplified by the sound of the whispering voices in his head. He strode through the house and let the front door also slam on the way out. As he got into his car, a new Ford convertible named the Mustang, he saw his father's silhouette at the library window.

"Goodbye, Father," Alton muttered as he started the engine and roared away, tires spitting gravel behind him.

Later that night, as Alton thrust himself into a willing young woman he had met in a random bar, he spoke a series of phrases that had entered into his mind as if from nowhere. As they achieved orgasm, Alton's right hand took a surgical scalpel from its hiding place and slit the woman's throat. She gasped in shock and pain. When the blood fountained over them both, Alton recited another phrase as he watched the woman's life leave her eyes. They were glazed soon enough, and Alton found himself breathless and nearing exhaustion. He didn't even know her name. This was the most difficult of his increasingly effective attempts at Egyptian *sex magick.*

Difficult...and messy.

Alton decided he needed a right-hand man, someone he could trust implicitly. Someone who could help him with the occasional body disposal. He put out feelers and set about waiting.

Three days later, a phone call summoned him to the local police headquarters. His father, he was told with little preamble, had died.

The evening of their final argument, Charles Senior had drawn himself a bath. He had placed a half-filled bottle of bourbon and a used glass on the ledge. He was found by one of the servants, and the coroner's report indicated that at first it appeared that the oil magnate and financier had cracked his head on the tub's lip in a fall, and then, unconscious, had sunk under the water and drowned. An accidental death, the coroner ruled, having found no bruises on the body to prove he had been held under the water or tried to fend off an attacker.

Alton *had* held Charles Senior's head under water, but his hands had been nowhere near the old man and had left no marks. And his hands had indeed rammed his father's head against the tub's edge, though of that there would be no indication either.

When Gram came to see him, still tearful after the old man's funeral, Alton had been cold.

"You couldna come to you father's service?"

"I was busy trying to keep the company from sinking under me," Alton said less than graciously. "The old man's death sent our stock spiraling. I think ultimately it was more important I stay at the helm while the ship headed for the shoals."

"You sound like 'im, with your high-minded fancy metaphors, but you're no' like him atall, are ye?"

"I'm sorry you feel that way, Gram. Perhaps you should look for another position, if this one has become a problem for you."

His old friend stared at him, lower lip trembling. Alton stared back coldly.

"Well, I just might move on then, Mister Chambers. I have had an offer." Gram stood and turned away, but then turned back to look Alton in the face one last time. "I don't know what's happened to you, or your family, young *sar*, but I think something's not right. It's mighty convenient that your entire family's died around ye, leavin' you a fortune."

"What are you implying, Gram?" Alton's tone was cold, colder than his father's had ever been.

"Not implyin' a thing, but tellin' ye that even as I move on to Shell, I will keep an eye on ye from afar. Make damn sure you keep your nose clean, and if I hear anythin'—"

"Is that a threat?"

"Nah, I don't threaten. But it *is* a warnin' for old times' sake."

"Goodbye, Gram. Best of luck."

The older Scotsman looked at him and a tear squeezed out of his right eye. He wiped it away. Then he turned and strode out of Alton's office, which the new head of the company had already remodeled to his own tastes.

Three weeks later, Gram was crushed by a collapsing derrick on a newly drilled well in Kuwait. Afterward, witnesses said the derrick looked like it had been pushed, for it had been perfectly constructed and tested the very same morning. There was no wind, and no fault was found in the steel girders. It had merely toppled over onto the grizzled veteran, sparing everyone else on the crew.

Alton sent a white wreath to the funeral. He did not attend.

Chapter Thirty-Seven

SEVERAL FEVERISH DAYS had passed. Blackstone had been working in his room since before dawn, the ancient words demanding to be deciphered. The panels and their meaning—which seemed to gain clarity by the moment—played through Blackstone's brain, keeping him from sleep, and requiring a quiet and undisturbed place where he could focus completely, unlike his library workstation where Chambers might pop in unexpectedly or Alena might attempt to seduce him away from his work.

By the time Michelle Davenport joined him, he was awash in a sea of notes and papers. He held up one sheet of his developing "Rosetta dictionary."

He had been creating a secret notebook, a direct translation to the best of his abilities, of every panel or separate ritual he could identify. Each page included phonetic pronunciations, or his best guesses. It was rather thick by now, and he suspected that Chambers would want it immediately in his grubby hands if he realized Blackstone had gone so far as to create his own book of spells, as it were.

"I think I can read some of this now," he said as she entered his field of vision. He waved the sheets he'd been working on. "Maybe with an accent, but I think I have it."

He had neglected Michelle due to the intensity of Naira's frontal assault, but as he glanced at her now, he noticed that she also had gone out of her way to look especially alluring, with silk blouse half-undone, no bra, and rather more makeup than usual. Perhaps she had sensed his withdrawal and wanted to put a stop to it, but at the moment he was too excited by his work to respond.

"Let's hear it," she said. Her face registered some disappointment that he hadn't perked up at her arrival.

He shuffled his stack of note-covered paper into order as she flopped onto a club chair. He glimpsed creamy breast skin as she bent at the waist to sit. He looked away quickly, refusing to get caught ogling. Alton Chambers did enough of that for the both of them.

He went back to the sheet he had selected and began to read the guttural syllables, heavy on the Hs, that was so reminiscent of Hebrew, and yet so completely alien. He read slowly at first, stumbling a little, and then began to gather speed as his confidence grew. His pronunciation was based on educated guesses for a language that must have predated the pharaohs.

A language that, as far as he knew, no one else had heard, spoken, or documented for hundreds of years.

Michelle read along to the translation he had laid out according to his studies. "'*The Great God of all things comes from the sky in its infiniteness / And grants the beasts life and death / and all must obey who hear the Master's voice...*'"

"Sounds like an old record label," Blackstone added, chuckling.

"Huh?"

"Yeah, you're too young. Keep going."

"Okay... '*When they hear the sound on the lips of the Chosen...*'"

"'*And the eyes of the dead will open,*'" he finished the line, nodding. "Then?"

Michelle shrugged. "I can't make out... What's this phrase?" Her slender fingers traced the symbols on the photograph from which they were working.

"Looks like, '*The muscle's tears that flow.*'"

"The *muscle*?"

"I think they're using *muscle* as a stand-in for *heart*," said Blackstone. "But the next phrase seems to be, '*to the ground / where they wet the sand and call...*'"

"'Wet the sand?'"

"I'd substitute *moisten*, I think," said Blackstone, making a note on the sheet. "So then, '*Where they moisten the sand and call / To them all / come to Him who / Waits.*'"

"But what does it mean?"

"I would guess *moisten the sand* is a metaphor. Probably for *shed blood*."

"Okay, that sounds pretty gruesome."

"Life was cheap, what can I say."

Michelle nodded and went on. "And '*Eternity is but a day / For red tears are succor...*' Red tears?"

"Another blood metaphor? I don't know."

"Okay, so: '*Eternity is but a day / For red tears are succor.*'"

"'*To the dead, and the living,*'" Blackstone finished. "Read all of it back."

Haltingly, she intoned:

"*The Great God of all things comes /
from the sky in its infiniteness /
And grants the beasts life and death /
and all must obey who hear the Master's voice /
When they hear the sound on the lips of the Chosen /
And the eyes of the dead will open /
The muscle's tears that flow / to the ground
Where they moisten the sand and call
to them all / come to Him who /
Waits /
Eternity is but a day /
For red tears are succor /
To the dead and the living...*"

She let the last words linger for a long moment. Then: "This is certainly unusual in terms of an incantation, isn't it?"

"It really doesn't sound Egyptian at all. To my ears anyway. I agree. But since it's from that different *dialect*, or whatever it is, I would expect it to sound different."

"Read it in the original! I want to hear what it sounds like."

"What it sounds like to the best of my understanding," Blackstone corrected. He tried the first line in the guttural form he thought was at least close.

"Jesus, that's hot," said Michelle, unsnapping another button of her blouse. She reached down and touched herself.

"What the hell?" he said, looking up with a combination of shock and lust. She was flushed and her eyes seemed to widen at the sound of his voice.

"I don't know, but it's like your reading is suddenly making my pussy leak."

"Christ!" He grinned. "Let me read the rest of it then."

"Okay." Her voice had taken on a throaty quality. She was sitting on the nearby chair, but he noticed she had spread wide her legs and her hand was caressing the fabric of her jeans where her thighs met.

He read the whole piece, putting forth his best effort. The pronunciation seemed to just come to him, the heavy consonants and gutturals falling into a natural rhythm.

For a moment, the air seemed to vibrate and then fall still.

He thought he was hallucinating.

He began the incantation again, only this time from memory. It was as if the words had somehow burrowed into his brain, stuck on repeat. Or maybe someone was speaking them into his ear, moving his mouth like a ventriloquist's dummy.

Michelle was slowly crawling like a cat toward him, her eyes wide and her lips open and inviting.

Blackstone struggled with his belt and undid his pants.

By the time she reached him, their unnatural lust was unleashed. Michelle straddled him, and in moments they were rocking, the chair teetering precariously as he entered her and began thrusting desperately.

Their eyes locked and they were *compelled* to couple, as if the decision had not been theirs. As if they were being manipulated.

And it was *deja vu*, because he remembered feeling this way before.

He gave in to the sensation as she rose and fell on him and the moment turned to white heat. They groaned with the intensity of their union, flesh slapping flesh, sweat running in rivers down their slick bodies.

Blackstone continued to speak the words, chanting in rhythm to their thrusts. And he would have sworn Michelle was reciting the ritual incantation as well, in quiet breathy whispers. Even though she couldn't possibly know it as well as he did...

* * *

When the air vibrated and then stilled far down below in the Prep Room, a second ticked by without any reaction, and another.

But then a wave of motion rippled through the wrapped bodies laid out in various degrees of completion, accompanied by an onrush of hushed whispers rising and falling like the voices of a quiet choir.

In the grotesque almost-silence there was a butterfly-wing rustle as ancient digits twitched beneath their wrappings. Torsos attempted to clamber upright. Despite the tightness of the gauze, they struggled to arise, compelled by a force greater than any ever encountered. Wrapped feet touched the tiled floor, claw-like hands reached out to steady their jerky balance as the genderless corpses staggered away from their resting places, making scraping sounds only the dead could hear. The mummified corpses wandered aimlessly, but then, as if their eyes were still in place and working, they homed in on the chamber's doorway and flowed toward it, a phalanx of silent shambling forms.

The room was large. Thirty or more such forms soon clogged the space in front of the door, which they were unable to breach.

Their fingers tensed and loosened as a nameless rage compelled them to seek necks to squeeze and snap. They sought enemies to vanquish, scores to settle. They wanted their Creator, but they would take what they could find. If they could escape and locate the one who had summoned them, they would take that too.

Their eerie, silent determination was only thwarted by the reinforced metal door.

Their silence was counterpoint to the chorus of whispers, which rose and fell like waves on a beach. In time, a new ripple passed through the jerking bodies and they turned back to their resting places.

Inside the ruby red sarcophagus, something that had been motionless for centuries shifted ever so slightly.

Then dust motes settled. Only the scent of herbs and decay lingered.

Chapter Thirty-Eight

MICHELLE AWOKE.

Beside her, Blackstone lay sprawled out on the bed, knocked out by their intense lovemaking.

And it *had* been intense.

There hadn't been much love, only lust.

Fucking.

Though they'd had some wild sessions before, what happened the night before was incredible. She didn't really know what had gotten into her. She had literally been out of control, moving entirely on instinct. Her body had moved of its own accord while her mind...her mind...

She honestly didn't remember much of it. Just that James had used *that voice.*

It was still dark outside, that pre-dawn quiet. Maybe the best part of the day. She got up and stretched. Though she liked sleeping with James, she didn't like *sleeping with him.* Or anyone else, really. Having someone else in the bed with her made her feel somehow trapped. She enjoyed the freedom of her own space, especially when she was trying to sleep.

She slipped on her blouse and panties, gathering the rest of her clothes in the crook of her arm, her shoes in hand, and quietly slipped out the door and into the hallway.

Her plan had been to go back to her own suite, take a shower to wash off the night's activities, and curl up in her own bed for a few hours of deep restful sleep, but now that she was up she felt the urge to go wandering.

Recently it had become habitual—she had always had a fascination with big old houses, not to mention the lives of others, probably due to her interest in ancient history—and since she'd moved some of her things into the Chambers estate, she often explored the seemingly endless wings of the main house. And what a house! It was like having the museum to yourself after hours. One night she'd even found a room with an actual taxidermied lion and his ostrich companion and nothing else. Why? Who knew?

She placed her gathered clothes on the floor in the hallway outside Blackstone's suite and struck out in a random direction. If she happened to be caught by that creep Batten, she would just tell him that she'd gotten lost, which was easy to do in this house.

Now she quietly padded down the stairs like a cat in the dark.

* * *

"You're just in time, daughter," Chambers called out jovially. "I think you'll enjoy this very much."

Alena entered the security room and joined him behind a wide monitor. On it, an angular image of someone walking slowly, carefully, toward a door. It was obvious that the camera was using infrared technology, because the person was squinting in the near dark.

"Our friend, Miss Davenport, is exploring again."

Alena leaned closer. "She's half-naked!"

Chambers chuckled. "She wore him out, then didn't bother to fully dress when she went walking."

"And you didn't provide any...inducement?"

"None at all," he said with a straight face. "It was interesting though," he added. "They were working out an incantation that Blackstone translated, and after he read it aloud, she jumped him for all the world as if he'd given her an aphrodisiac."

"Or you?"

"Or me. Except I didn't. I want him to finish, not spend all his time fucking either you or her."

"Or my daughter," Alena added softly.

"Is he, now?"

"I suspect... She's a spiteful little bitch, and if she thinks she can stick it to me by screwing the man I'm screwing, then she will. Plus he's not bad looking, so..."

"Yes, well, that's your problem. She's yours to wrangle. You and I have...different needs. Her need seems to be to set you off. If she can rub your nose in it, she's happy."

Alena said nothing.

He flicked on a separate window and the large color video image it displayed was a pornsite-ready side shot of Blackstone's bed, with Michelle Davenport on all fours, face down and ass in the air. The professor stood behind her, thrusting, as she groaned loudly. The bed rocked.

"This was a little while ago, after they nearly broke one of the chairs." Chambers chuckled. "I'm certain we didn't have any oysters recently, yet they could barely stop long enough to change positions. This is one of their most compelling..."

"Damn her, I hate youth," she said, grimacing as she watched the flickering image.

"You are ever so jealous, my dear. Might as well admit it."

"I admit nothing." But unconsciously she licked her lips. "Just for that, it'll be a long time before I give you any access to my body."

"Ha! We'll see." Chambers froze the sex video in mid-thrust. "Meanwhile, enjoy this other show."

In the other screen window, the same Michelle Davenport was on full motion video peering in doors as she advanced down the wide central corridor.

The cameras were well-placed and well-camouflaged, so she had not spotted a single one. Chambers had followed her from the sweat-stained bed all the way down the stairs to the first floor and into the corridor. Now he felt a tingle as she advanced through an open door. Another click, and now they saw Michelle from inside the room in the harsh black and white of night-vision photography.

It was a second much smaller library that contained most of Chambers' occult works outside of the Egyptian pantheon. Most of which were priceless. Here he had hand-written spell books by the likes of Aleister Crowley and other mystics, and the deeply religious and individually painted tomes of medieval monks, alongside other arcane artifacts whose possession would have condemned Chambers to the stake in a less enlightened age.

"What if she doesn't pull the trigger?" Alena asked.

"I can open it remotely from here, dear," Chambers said, mousing a cursor over a series of buttons on the edge of the monitor.

Michelle tiptoed ahead, enticed by the bait Chambers offered to her or any other potential interloper. There, ensconced in a small alcove, backlit by hidden LED lights, was a statue of the Assyrian demon Pazuzu that he had acquired at an Iranian dig site while attempting to uncover the secrets of the Occupant's tomb. Secrets that he—with Blackstone's aid—was now very close to understanding. *Very close indeed.*

On the screen, Michelle leaned in to get a better look at the statue.

"She isn't going to touch it," Alena said, pouting.

"It's okay, daughter. Would you like to do the honors?"

"No, that's okay, Daddy, you can do it."

Chambers clicked the mouse. As he did, on the video monitor a large section of floor beneath Michelle Davenport dropped open like a trapdoor. With a shocked expression on her face, the young woman fell through the opening which glowed red from below.

Quickly, Chambers switched to another camera so they could watch the action unfold.

The floor seemed to flow in a wriggling motion, undulating. The night vision camera wasn't needed here, as the room was constantly lit in the hellish red glow of heat lamps needed to keep the cold-blooded pets alive.

The Egyptian cobra—the *asp* of antiquity—may or may not have poisoned Cleopatra, but these particular cobras possessed all their poison sacs loaded with neurotoxins and cytotoxins. And although normally docile, they were cranky when disturbed. The first thing Michelle would have seen when the pain of her fall diminished and her vision had adjusted to the red light, was a group of rope-like six- to eight-foot examples of the species, all of them standing up and displaying their hoods in anger.

And hissing.

On the screen, Chambers and his daughter watched fixedly as the meaning of the wriggling floor finally penetrated the shocked Michelle's slowed reflexes and she screamed, further annoying the nearest snakes, who began bobbing and weaving as their muscular bodies ate up the floor in their advance on the intruder.

Michelle screamed again, and Chambers smiled at the grin on Alena's face.

"*Watch,*" he mouthed.

She nodded, her eyes alight with glee and some kind of fever. She couldn't help herself—as she watched the camera feed, her hand caressed Chambers' groin. He was just as aroused as she.

* * *

Inside the asp room, Michelle sobbed from the pain of landing hard on the sand floor, and as the extent of the danger became obvious when she managed to slowly stand on her screaming ankles. She was lucky they weren't shattered in the fall, but while the sand might have saved them, it sure hadn't made the floor any softer.

Squashing the sharp pain into a corner of her brain, she looked up in a panic, but the fucking trapdoor had closed above her.

What the fuck was this?

Looking around her, heart pounding as her panic increased, she noted another door set into the wall. But it was at least ten, fifteen feet away.

And there were the goddamned snakes...

She hated snakes. Like most people, but possibly even more because she had seen several fellow students working on digs bitten by the sinister creatures. In the case of one certain student, they hadn't gotten to the snakebite kit in time. She remembered the grotesque look carved on the guy's features in death.

So she had learned to fear and hate snakes of all kinds.

And she wasn't sure, but she thought these particular snakes were indeed venomous. Their loathsome undulations signaled the evil of their intentions, and her throat constricted at the sight of their grisly shuddering as their muscles expanded and contracted to move their serpentine shapes across the floor.

Michelle sobbed once more, unintentionally, then realized she was riling up the approaching monsters. She had recoiled backward one step, and now took another slow step toward that other door. Another step. And then another step.

The snakes' approach seemed to slow as she put some distance between herself and the closest of them.

How far could they leap and bite?

Her breathing was ragged, but she attempted to regulate it in case the sound of her gasps was making them angrier.

The door. She *had* to reach it.

The fastest among them had wriggled through the sand to within five or so feet of her trembling, throbbing legs, and it was with relief that she found herself backed onto the doorknob. Slowly—but not *too* slowly—she reached behind her back, felt for the knob, found and grasped it.

Thank God!

She half-turned to face the door, which was set higher than the sandy floor—maybe a half-step up—keeping an eye on the long slithering shapes. They *were* still coming closer. They didn't seem fazed by anything she had done so far, but their eyes transmitted a kind of dead-soul hate for her.

The angry, insistent hissing was louder in her ears. The dread she'd felt as soon as she had seen them had intensified and now threatened to choke her and cut off her breathing.

But now she was at the door, and in a few moments she would be safe, able to breathe, and running down the long corridor and away from this horrible fucking place. She'd take Blackstone with her and consider the whole thing some kind of nightmare that was finally over. Now that his wife had left him, she could make a life with him somewhere far from here, where their combined knowledge and experience would be too much for some university or college to ignore and...

Yes, but get out first. Get the fuck out!

The snakes were still far enough away that she would be able exit the room, slam the door, and get the *fuck* out of this eerie basement and out of this *fucking* house of *fucking* horrors. If Blackstone didn't come with her, *fuck* him too.

She turned the knob.

It didn't move. She tried again.

Goddamn it!

Fuck...

The palm of her hand, slick with sweat.

No wonder.

She wiped it on her sheer blouse, forcing herself to do it carefully, looked over her shoulder and saw that the serpentine leaders were now barely three feet away, and they were coiling back like springs, readying for a strike. She thought she saw their venom-dripping fangs exposed. Those black soulless eyes stared into hers, *through* hers, willing her to stand stock-still and await her fate.

But she had to turn the knob.

Hand dry now, she turned it and...

It didn't move.

God fuck damn, it wasn't moving.

The fucking door was locked.

Would noise trigger an attack? On the other hand, they were close enough now that an attack was imminent.

She pounded on the door until her fists hurt. It was metal, or lined with metal, and it didn't take much pounding to make her fists throb too. The door didn't budge.

Turning back to face the serpents, she searched desperately for some way out, for some unexplored exit, for another door, a window, a chair to leap onto and try to pry open the damned trapdoor that had deposited her here.

Something.

Anything.

But the room was below ground, so there would be no window. The door behind her was impregnable, and there was no other door she could see. And nothing for her to climb on except a few stones and branches that the snakes could rest beneath, and those were too short to help her. Besides, they were all on the other side of the aggressive serpents.

Then, up in the corner, she saw a blink. *A red blink.* An LED, it had to be a fucking camera light. It blinked metronomically and mocked her with its equally soulless eye.

The hissing was loud in her ears, all around her. The bobbing heads encased in their hoods were phallic in shape, but deadly with their curved fangs clacking together in hunger and lust.

Damn you, Blackstone, you fucker, what did you do?

There was no answer but her own croaking dry-throated scream as the living cocks struck in an orgy of venomous orgasm, their fangs digging deep into her flesh a dozen times—two dozen times!—injecting their evil seed with abandon, the first wave falling away then to make room for those behind them, and the second volley of bites and slimy poison hurt a lot less.

Sated, lust expired, now bored, the cobras threw themselves to the side and slithered back into their corners.

The last thing Michelle saw was the red camera light blinking emotionlessly as the poison spread rapidly through her system.

Goddamn you, Chambers, you monstrous old fuck!

Had she shouted the words or thought them? It didn't matter. Nothing did.

How long did she have?

Even that thought was scattered, aimless, darkening.

* * *

"That was satisfying," Alena said. Her eyes were glued to the screen while her hand was wrapped around the girth of Alton's member, his warm seed oozing down over the backs of her fingers. She licked them clean.

"Yes it was," Chambers said, grinning.

He picked up his cell phone. "Batten, Miss Davenport seems to have fallen into the snake pit. Would you please retrieve her, administer the antivenom, bring her to the shrine, and make sure she stays put? Then please collect her clothes from the professor's door. Dispose of it, as she won't be needing it."

Alena was still licking her fingers. Chambers turned to her and said, "All is ready. We perform the ritual tonight."

"Why don't we do it now, Daddy?!"

"Because we must go to Senator McDonald's fundraiser today. We can tell everyone what exceptional people Dr. James Blackstone and Naira Chambers are. After all, they will be attending in our stead at future functions."

She spread her thighs for him and he lowered his head to her flesh.

Chapter Thirty-Nine

BLACKSTONE AWOKE WITH the late morning sunlight spreading across his room. Michelle was gone, which was no surprise as she rarely stayed with him until morning.

He lay in bed musing about the previous night. The lovemaking had been surreal. Intense. And completely uncontrollable.

They had felt compelled to mate. As if both had taken Viagra or something similar. Maybe it was just the excitement of the breakthrough? It was hard to tell.

But *something* strange had happened.

In fact, he hadn't quite fully grasped it at the time, but now in the morning light he had an epiphany. The *magick* incantation had somehow caused a surge in sexual energy. And maybe it fed off that energy as well. The panel after panel of sexual positions he had examined and translated, when appropriate, weren't just a key to the language, they were actually part of the ritual. *And a compulsive part.* The thought of it frightened him. The lack of control. The ritual controlling *him*, rather than him controlling *it*.

Mostly what frightened him was the realization that this wasn't just some crazy mumbo jumbo, or some cartoon bibbidi bobbidi boo, as he and Michelle had laughed about. No, this was the real deal. Now he knew why it was so important to Chambers to unlock the secrets of the tomb. Who could guess what the old man would do with dark magic at his disposal. And what if everything here was already tainted with it? What if *magick* explained all the sexual energy and the three women: Alena, Naira, and Michelle?

Dear God, Michelle. What had he gotten her into? He had to talk to her, to see if she'd experienced the same thing. Though he was sure that she had. He could picture her now, rubbing the crotch of her pants and crawling across the floor to him. Nearly assaulting him with her need.

Then another thought popped into his head. Perhaps he could have any woman he wanted by just saying a few words in that long-forgotten language. Perhaps he could...

He shook his head. No, that wasn't the kind of man he was, was it? Was *he*?

He jumped out of bed, picked up his carelessly discarded clothes from the night before, dressed hurriedly, and before dashing down to Michelle's suite, as an afterthought, grabbed his translations notebook. He couldn't let it just fall into anyone's hands.

Michelle's door was unlocked, and the room empty. She was nowhere to be seen, and there was no evidence that she had ever climbed into bed. No tell-tale drops of water to indicate a recently used sink or shower.

Surely she wouldn't have left without saying a word. Not after last night.

Then again, she had gone home on other occasions, not bothering with a goodbye.

He took a deep, steadying breath before heading downstairs.

He was approaching the window to see if Michelle's Honda was still parked outside when he heard Chambers and Batten talking as he passed the open doors.

"I have the car waiting outside, sir," Batten said in his usual supercilious tone.

"Just give me five minutes and I'll grab my notes and a coat. There's time."

"Of course, sir."

"Is the plane ready?"

"Fueled and waiting."

"I'll be right there."

Blackstone wanted to eavesdrop, but even as he slowed, Batten strode out into the hall and gave Blackstone a dirty stare. Chambers was right behind him.

"Oh, Blackstone, here you are. Alena, Batten, and I are heading to Washington to attend a fundraiser for Senator McDonald. We'll be back late tonight," Chambers said as he scooped up a coat from the elaborate wooden tree.

"Ted McDonald?" Blackstone said with obvious distaste.

"When you're in my position, you can't afford to play favorites, Blackstone. The best way to turn a profit in wartime is to supply both sides. Anyhow, we won't be home by dinner, but the staff will start at the usual time, so feel free to enjoy on your own. Or with my granddaughter, if she's even around."

Blackstone chuckled. "Yeah, she's hard to pin down."

"Oh, I don't know about that..." Chambers said with a broad wink.

What the hell does that mean?

And a meeting in Washington? What was *that* about?

The old man was already crossing the foyer and heading out the door when Blackstone asked, "You haven't seen Michelle around, have you?"

"Can't say that I have, Blackstone. Perhaps she had to go and recharge from all your late-night sessions," Chambers said, winking again.

What the hell?

What does he know? Blackstone wondered for the umpteenth time.

"I think I heard an older auto starting early," the old man added as an afterthought. "Perhaps that was Miss Davenport driving away."

"Huh."

"And, Blackstone," Chambers added while standing at the door, "be sure you're here when we get back, I have something to share with you. For all your hard work on the translations. A bonus, you might say." He grinned, and Blackstone thought his face resembled a skull.

Chambers exited, and Blackstone quickly crossed the hall and the foyer and stood next to one of the windows that overlooked the driveway's circle. He watched Chambers enter the black Town Car, Batten holding the back door open for him before the goon made his way to the front passenger door, stopping to look back at the house and smirk at Blackstone through the window before getting in. Blackstone was sure he saw Alena's leg, so she was already waiting inside. He watched the car making the far turn and heading down the long private road toward the main gate.

The trees in the wooded areas surrounding the Chambers estate were bare, blackened skeletal hands that protruded from the ground like giants emerging from their graves. A handful of leaves the groundskeepers had overlooked skipped across the lawn and driveway.

He thought he could see a corner of Michelle's rusty Civic parked on the garage's side slab. So she was here then. She wouldn't have walked—the compound was quite a distance from most anyplace.

He shook his head, confused. He remembered he was holding the notebook. More like clutching it, as if it were a life preserver and he was in the middle of a storm at sea. His hand was sweaty and aching from the effort.

When his Seamaster indicated fifteen minutes had passed, he gave it five more minutes, staring at a painting of colorful splotches. With Chambers and his minions heading for the airport, this was his best chance to get on the hunt. For Michelle and whatever else he might find.

Turning away from the window, he headed to the library to see if Michelle was there, or if she'd left him a message. Anything, really. Any sign that she was still around so he could talk to her about what had happened the night before. To see if his perception of the experience matched hers.

Their work area looked exactly as Blackstone had left it. No note from Michelle saying, "Had to go, see you later!" or, "Thanks for the great time!" or, "I love you." Just scattered books on translating hieroglyphics, a smattering of hand-jotted notes, and a few photographs of the tomb's panels spread out for easy viewing. The photos held entirely new meaning as his eyes lingered over them, and he felt a chill run through him. Somewhere behind him he heard papers rustling as if in a breeze. Or maybe it was the whisper he sometimes heard in his head.

He couldn't escape the irony of the fact that, though he had left numerous women without the least bit of concern, when they disappeared on him it was a different story. Now he was knotted-up with anxiety. First Laura left him and now Michelle. Somehow he hadn't realized that he cared this much.

He roamed the first floor of the house, searching for Michelle through quiet, empty, lavishly furnished rooms and wide hallways whose walls were decorated with priceless pieces of art. He rarely saw any of the house staff. They were like phantoms. Clearly they'd been instructed to be discreet, but right now he would have been happy to see anyone as he felt a sudden wave of loneliness and isolation. His exploration eventually led him to a pair of swinging doors which he pushed through and found himself standing in the manor's large and presently dim kitchen.

"Morning, Prof."

Blackstone turned with a start and spotted Naira leaning against a stainless-steel countertop, a bowl of yogurt in front of her, a spoon hanging from her fingers. "Naira, have you seen Michelle?"

She shook her head. "No."

"How about your mother?"

"Alena? Any port in a storm, huh? I'm pretty sure Mother Dear went with my grandfather on his political orgy trip. She's probably planning to do some trolling for new blood since the old blood's always *occupied...* She's an easy one to—"

"Never mind, Naira," said Blackwood, halting the young woman's diatribe. He was certain Alena had been in the Town Car. Her absence gave him one less thing to worry about. "I really need to find Michelle."

"Maybe she had to go home to recover from all your sweaty late-night work sessions."

"I'm serious, Naira. We had a breakthrough last night and I can't believe she would have just left. I need to talk to her about our discovery."

"Yeah, what did you discover? A second G-spot?" Naira asked, before placing the spoon slowly in her mouth, teasing. Then she licked off the white yogurt while staring at him with her limpid eyes.

For a brief moment Blackstone wondered... If he spoke the words of the spell aloud, would Naira crawl to him as Michelle had the night before? *And then what would she do?*

For a few seconds, he was tempted.

But no, this had to be some of that strange presence he kept feeling. It wasn't really him, was it?

"I'm serious," he insisted. "Have you seen her or not? Do you know where she is?"

"No, I haven't seen her," Naira said, setting aside the spoon, her tone almost mocking, not at all reflecting Blackstone's concern. "But I think I know how we can find out if she's still here, or where she is. The coast is clear, so... Come on, I'll show you."

Naira led Blackstone through the seemingly empty house and back into the main library. She strode up to one of the many bookcases, slipped a slender finger inside the edge on one side, and pressed a concealed button, causing the entire case to swing open. Inside was a short paneled hallway. He followed her and at the other end was another door, and behind it a windowless room crowded by a long table covered with an array of flat screens. Each of these monitors was divided equally into eight frozen images. The images were various views inside and outside the house.

Blackstone's jaw dropped. It was a security camera monitoring station. A secret one.

"Grandfather knows everything that goes on in his house," Naira explained. "That's why we never *did it* here."

He fell into a nearby chair and stared at the screens, quickly noting the camera view pointing directly at the bed in his suite. He shook his head. Now Blackstone was sure. The old man knew everything, as he'd sometimes suspected. He knew about him and Alena, and Michelle. Maybe he even had that jackass Batten trailing him when he left the compound. Blackstone could picture that bastard sitting in his car and watching as Blackstone visited his apartment, that shit-eating smirk plastered on his face. If that was the case, Chambers probably knew about his trysts with Naira as well. Hell, maybe they even had his apartment bugged. People with unlimited amounts of money could get away with just about anything. He should have learned by now. His more famous colleagues were no different.

"Are you okay?" Naira asked, shaking Blackstone from his shocked stupor.

"How long have you known about this?"

"Since I was a kid. I was here when they put in the cameras. 'For our protection,' he said."

Exasperated, with a knot the size of a bowling ball growing in his stomach, Blackstone said, "How do you work this thing?"

"I think you use one of those joysticks to control the cameras, and you can control the feeds with the mouse and keyboard," said Naira, pulling up a chair next to Blackstone and swinging out a tray.

"And where does it all go? Some sort of tape system?"

She laughed. "Where have you been for twenty years? It's all digital, stored on servers. Each camera has its own, so you can play back different feeds at the same time, assign them to specific monitors."

Jesus.

Blackstone's throat had dried up like the Egyptian desert he had once loved.

"Well, let's see some of what's on this fucking thing," he said. Maybe he could find out what had happened to Michelle.

She shrugged. "You sure?"

"I'm sure I don't have a choice," he said. He was feeling anxious now, that something was definitely wrong.

Together they started to review the video feeds.

Naira jiggled the joystick and one of the screens lit up with video of Blackstone looking out the window. She made it run in reverse to where he'd been talking to Chambers just before the old man and the ghoul had left earlier. The picture stopped moving.

"That's it?"

"That's all that camera picked up. Motion-activated, I think."

"I need to find Michelle, damn it," he muttered.

Naira tapped the keys and soon had several screens active, running in reverse. "We might pick her up on one of these," she said with a shrug.

Suddenly Blackstone felt nervous. He knew where this was leading. He gazed at his empty bed on that one screen.

Naira was running several more feeds, but there was no movement except Batten at one point slithering past on some mysterious errand.

They continued their journey back in time. Blackstone's eyes scanned the multiple camera views of scenes playing at medium-high speed in reverse.

In a minute they were watching a screen on which Blackstone was standing at his window as birds flattened themselves on the bloody glass.

"Stop! Play it forward," Blackstone said.

He relived the moment while his eyes roamed over the other camera feeds. He was almost dizzy, but he thought he'd seen something in the corner of his eye as another view had unspooled quickly backward.

There it was, Alena pleasuring herself on her bed, an array of feathers laid out before her spread legs. She took hold of one and then another, held them up to her face, even as she manipulated something not quite visible, her hand moving faster and faster, her head tilting back, her mouth open.

"Ew," Naira said, clearly disgusted watching her mother's antics. "Nobody should have to see *that*."

Blackstone tried to catch his breath.

So there was no doubt they knew about the *sex magick* incantations like the one he'd been working on, and how to use it, at least in a limited sense. *Well, not so limited*, he thought as he watched the birds on the other screen helplessly commit suicide as if their feathers in her hands commanded them to perform the ultimate sacrifice. His own face, shocked and frightened, was visible when he turned his head away from the window slaughter.

And Alena achieved her orgasmic peak at the same time the final flurry of suicides smacked themselves bloody inches from his window.

Blackstone suddenly felt dirty and used. Was this why Alena had always had the hots for him? To involve him in some kind of magical ceremony? She had eyed him right from the start. Was she using her wiles to keep him trapped here? Or maybe to aid in his understanding of the hieroglyphs? Was Chambers controlling it all? *Why?* What was their endgame? And what about Naira, what was her part in this? She seemed innocent enough; after all, now she was helping him with forbidden knowledge. Or was this all part of Chambers' master plan too?

And Michelle. Where was she? How could he have gotten her involved in all this?

Again a sound behind him caught his attention. Was it really behind him, or was it inside his head? He turned and saw nothing.

"I've seen enough," Naira said.

"No, keep going. I need to know what's happened to Michelle. Can you find her on this thing?"

The images flowed backward at a dizzying pace as Blackstone studied them. He wasn't entirely sure what else he was looking for. Anything to help explain the old man's motivation or to give Blackstone the upper hand. Anything to help him understand what the hell was happening.

"Wait, what's that? Go back, play this one," Blackstone said.

It was Chambers and Alena in Alena's suite. They were both naked and Alena was on her knees, enthusiastically fellating the old man.

"Ew, yuck!" Naira winced. "Jesus Christ, that's disgusting! My mother—and...*my grandfather?*"

Then, as the reality hit her, she retched once and a glob of half-digested yogurt landed on the shiny desk. She wiped her mouth with the back of her hand and seemed about to faint.

Even Blackstone was sickened, though he'd watched hours of incest porn. At least in those videos he'd assumed the people weren't actually brother and sister or mother and son, or whatever. But this was undeniably real. With each passing frame he felt even more duped and disgusted for allowing himself to be involved.

Judging from Naira's response, the girl had no idea this had been going on. Blackstone had a hunch that she had been kept in the dark about most of what was happening in the house. If it was troubling for Blackstone, these revelations must have been horrifying for her.

Now her skin was white and sweaty. "Are you all right?"

"Shit, I'm watching my mother blow her own father, how do you think I feel? How all right can that be?"

Part of him wanted to say something like, *Hey, all you Chambers have seemed weird from the first time I saw you.*

But he saw that it was the wrong thing to do. Accusing her of weirdness, despite her gymnastic act in his car, or her agile fucking in his own bed—*Laura's bed*—at home wouldn't win any points in the Tournament of Empathy. He put his hand on her shoulder, trying to be reassuring.

She looked up at him and her eyes were wet. "I'll be fine. Forget it, James. It's Chinatown."

Wham. The quote seemed to smack him in the face. Suddenly he wasn't sure he should be empathetic at all.

The images were still moving on the screen. Chambers ejaculated and Alena gleefully tended to him with fingers and tongue. He wondered where she was now. Would she burst in here, catch them, and—and what, kill them both? Or what? Maybe she'd just get on her knees and share him with her daughter. And Blackstone knew he would let her. He wasn't sure why, but here in this house he seemed unable to help himself, unable to keep from indulging his worst...

"Okay, stop it now," said Blackstone, partly to himself. "Just...go somewhere else. Today or last night, but other feeds. Look for Michelle, damn it."

Naira complied with cold, robotic movements.

A minute later, the video froze.

"There she is," Naira said. "Oh shit!"

"My God! What the— *Is she dead?*"

They watched as the on-screen Batten pulled a body out of a plain room with what, in a glimpse, looked like sand on the floor and rocks along its inner edge.

Naira's eyes were glued to the screen. "Looks like she got into the snake room."

"*The what?!*"

"Uh, Grandfather has a room full of Egyptian snakes down in the basement. It's part of his crazy pharaoh obsession."

Blackstone tried to wrap his mind around that. *Egyptian snakes?* He knew they must be cobras—though they were often referred to as asps. "Where the hell is that? How do we get there?"

256

"Sub-basement. We go down in one of the elevators." She looked at him and must have seen the panic rising on his features. "She's probably fine... Grandfather keeps antivenom on hand. I mean, he's not a killer..."

"That's just...*fucked up!* Who does this kind of shit?"

"Well, *you're* on his payroll," she muttered.

Blackstone let that go... After what they'd just seen Chambers and his daughter doing, no amount of accusations seemed relevant anymore.

He *was* worried, and had plenty of reason to be. If Chambers knew that Michelle had been bitten by venomous snakes, why hadn't he said so earlier? Why had he implied that she had left? Had they tried to hide her car? Why had they left as if nothing had happened? And what the hell did they intend to do with her? Or with *him,* for that matter?

The ghoulish image of Batten with Michelle on the gurney was still frozen, flickering on the screen, taunting him.

Had Chambers killed Michelle?

He had to face the fact that she might actually be dead, despite Naira's reassurance.

Was he to understand that there was a level *below* where Chambers had shown him the tomb, or was this section simply on the same level but somehow walled off from it? Blackstone remembered his dizzying experience in the tomb and wondered if the whole thing wasn't some kind of surreal nightmare cooked up after having ingested some kind of drug. Suicidal birds? Incest in the Chambers family? A whole Egyptian tomb reconstructed down below these floors?

He stared at the flickering picture that might well mean Michelle was dead. He wiped away a tear. *Damn it, Michelle, why did you leave this morning?*

"Go back further," Blackstone said, his jaw set. He *had* to see what had happened. Could Naira be wrong? She *had* to be.

Naira reversed the feed. They watched in horror as Michelle was indeed attacked by half a dozen of the largest Egyptian cobras Blackstone had ever seen, and then as she fell upward through a trapdoor.

A fucking trapdoor!

They watched her tiptoeing backward up the stairs and down the hall, backing through his door barely clothed. They watched her and Blackstone copulating uncontrollably on Blackstone's bed and then moving backward to where they'd started, on the chair.

He might have been embarrassed, but there was too much at stake. With each passing scene, Blackstone's anxiety grew worse. Nausea bubbled in his gut until he felt it throughout his entire body. He turned to look over his shoulder, swearing that he heard someone whispering behind him. Fearing that the family had doubled back and Chambers would walk in on them at any moment.

Or Alena.

Or that ghoul, and maybe killer, Batten.

"I've got to get down there," he said. He looked at the time code. The attack had happened hours ago. "It may be too late. If you're wrong about the antivenom, she's dead. That size snake, that many snakes... It's impossible to survive that. Can we get down there?"

"I have access to parts of those areas, but not the snake room. Or a couple other places. You have to take a separate elevator for that room. It takes a key card."

"Can you get one?"

Naira looked up, squinted in thought. "Grandfather is plenty paranoid about people getting down there. Paranoid, period. You might have noticed, maybe in some of your talks?"

"Sure, I have. I never thought any of that stuff would involve me. Or Michelle."

She made a face. *Not a fan of Michelle*, she seemed to say with her features. "Look, I can try to find one of his cards, maybe in his bedroom. Well, you know, his suite. No one here has just a simple bedroom."

He nodded, impatient. "Okay, okay, can you just go, please? She might still be alive!"

"I'm telling you, she's almost definitely alive!"

"It's the word *almost* I don't like. Please hurry, Naira."

She stood up reluctantly and left him to those alluring, disgusting, flickering images. His hand moved the joystick and they washed over him.

He wasn't sure how much time passed, but suddenly she was back in a cloud of healthy sweat and leather. He'd smelled the scent on her before. She must have ridden her horse early this morning. He wished he'd seen her. Instead he'd slept in, unaware of her, or of what had happened to Michelle.

"I couldn't even get in," she said. "His suite's locked up tighter than Batten's asshole."

"Goddamnit. What about your, er, your mother? She must have a card."

Naira pouted. "Who knows? She's definitely not home."

"I know she's not. But does *she* have a card?"

"Probably, but she'll have it with her." She dropped into the chair next to his and suddenly he felt heat where their legs touched. Neither of them pulled away. "I bet old Batten might have a card." She licked her lips.

He had to ignore her. "Let's try that. Can't hurt."

They left the room and she led him to Batten's door, in the wing opposite the family's.

Blackstone pledged to himself that if he could save Michelle, he was out of here. He'd go to the police. Goddamn that old man, he'd go to the police and spill the whole story.

Naira pushed on the door, and to his surprise it clicked.

Chapter Forty

"WHAT THE HELL?"

Naira chuckled and held up a key card she'd just tapped on the shiny black plate next to the door. "I found a master key!"

"Why in hell didn't you tell me?"

"I wanted to see your face when the door opened. I'm not sure this'll work on the elevator, but I figured we should look in here first anyway."

Blackstone swallowed his anger at Naira's naive youth, and also his fear about Michelle. Now that they were here, he did want to do some snooping.

There was enough light from the tall windows on one side of Batten's suite that they didn't need to flick on any lamps. The apartment was surprisingly tastefully appointed in true Scandinavian blond wood and textured tapestries, and Blackstone noted several small but relatively valuable paintings on the walls. Quickly they scanned every flat surface in the living area, then ducked into and out of the large galley kitchen, then headed for the bedrooms, which were off a separate hallway.

And there, in Batten's own bedroom, sitting on a small antique roll-top desk, was Laura's clock. Blackstone walked up rapidly and took it in his hands, turning it over and spotting the slight dent in the base that he knew well. She'd thrown it at him once.

"Son of a bitch," Blackstone muttered.

"What is it?" Naira had entered the room behind him.

"This is my wife's clock. It was on his fucking desk."

"You're sure?" said Naira, stepping up close.

"It might as well have a sign on it." He showed her the dent.

"Weird." She scanned the top of the desk. "Hey, there's an old pocket watch there."

"I noticed it," Blackstone said, still clutching Laura's clock.

"Yeah, and it looks just like the one Professor al-Amani used to flash around. He said it was an heirloom."

"Ahmed al-Amani?" Blackstone was almost certain he had met the man once, years before.

"He was your, uh, predecessor," she said. Then she stared at him, her eyes wide. "There's a bunch of other old watches and clocks sitting up here on top of the desk."

Blackstone scanned the nearby dresser and spotted a small jewelry organizer. It was full of cufflinks and masculine rings, as expected. But there were also several feminine pieces he was certain had been in Laura's jewelry box.

A chill went through Blackstone. *What the hell, is the bastard keeping souvenirs?* It sure as hell felt like the kind of shrine a serial killer might keep.

Batten had been in the Blackstone apartment, and he had felt free enough to take Laura's clock and whatever jewelry had grabbed his fancy.

Why did Batten feel so free?

There was only one answer that made sense, but he wanted to avoid it.

Blackstone felt a shiver start in his lower back and rise up his spine. He closed the jewelry organizer and replaced the clock in the exact position he'd found it. "We're leaving," he said grimly.

"What about the clock and things?"

"Later. First, we try that card on the elevator."

They left the majordomo's suite, and Blackstone felt his hands tingling.

What did this mean about Laura's disappearance?

Did it mean anything at all?

He answered his own question.

You know it does.

Laura was never expected to return.

Chapter Forty-One

BLACKSTONE NOTICED THAT it was getting darker outside. They had spent so much time watching the video feed and searching for the key that it was now getting on toward dusk. If they couldn't find Michelle soon, he would have to leave to get the police without her, taking Naira with him for her safety.

"I need some things from my rooms," he said. "Meet me at the elevator in ten minutes."

"Okay," she said. But she was pouting.

"What's wrong?"

"I was hoping... You know, like what you and Michelle were doing. These chairs are pretty strong..." She gave him her seductive look.

Blackstone's anger rose suddenly. "I'm going to find Michelle first! I'm not convinced she's still alive, but if you're right then I want her out of wherever he has her stashed. If you think fucking right now is more important..."

"Nah, hey, I get it. I'll meet you at the end of the hall where Grandfather's rooms are. The elevator's hidden there. I'll have to show you how to find it."

"Good." He stared at her. *Damn, she's so incredibly sexy.*

For a second, he almost reached out and tore off her clothes.

Stop.

Michelle.

Naira's limpid eyes were fixed on his, her glossy lips parted. The tip of her tongue peeked out between them. There was a sheen of sweat on her forehead and he wanted to lick it off and taste the saltiness of it.

It was as if sexuality oozed from the walls around here.

Tearing himself away, Blackstone tore through the secret hallway and stalked the halls to his own rooms, his groin aching with the wanting of her. Guilt ate away at him, but did nothing to reduce his lust.

Inside his suite, he opened a suitcase he had stashed in the main closet. There was some of his field gear, mostly things that could be classified as camping equipment, which he used over and over. He selected a large Maglite, checked the batteries, and tucked it into his belt. Then he opened a zippered case and took out the Smith & Wesson revolver he kept there. It was his "dig gun," used for handling the rattlers that haunted his primary American Southwest sites. He checked the cylinder, made sure there were six rounds in it, then tucked a speedloader with six more into his pocket. The gun itself went into his other pocket.

Now he was ready to face whatever in hell Michelle had been dropped into down in that hellish sub-basement. He still shivered when he thought of those lower levels, both his real visits and those in his nightmares.

Naira wasn't where she'd said she would be. No one in the hall, anywhere. "Goddamn it!" His heart was thumping in his ears.

He found her facing the screens in the secret room.

"What the hell are you still doing here?" he raged, realizing that it was getting closer to dinner time, and Chambers might be home soon. Didn't he have his own plane? That would cut two hours from landing to home. They just didn't have *that* much time.

She turned her ashen face toward him. "I was shutting down here when I spotted something. You'd probably better look at this." She had her hand on the joystick and nodded at a different screen. She averted her eyes from his.

He grunted his assent.

Naira played a recording of Batten moving a body on a gurney. *Another, different body, not Michelle.* Taking it to one of the mansion's multiple elevators, but Blackstone couldn't tell from the video which one. The old thug and the gurney disappeared, and it would take time to determine where and when they re-emerged. It was probably the same elevator Naira was going to locate for him.

She rewound the feed a little further, showing not much of anything they could make out in the distorted perception, until they saw a horrifying sight—a woman trapped in some kind of very narrow hallway or room. They couldn't see the woman's face, just the back of her head, the space so narrow that she couldn't even turn to face the camera. She was pounding on the wall as it moved. There was no sound, but that made the whole scene more terrifying.

Because the fucking wall was moving.

It gave Blackstone a flashback to his visit of the tomb, where he and Chambers had navigated a long and narrow hallway. But this one was made of metal as far as he could tell.

"What is this? Who is that?"

But some part of him knew. Blackstone felt pressure growing in the pit of his stomach.

"This room has a wall on tracks," she explained in a hoarse whisper. "Grandfather has all these crazy traps around the house. Like that trapdoor we saw Michelle fall through. It's all part of his obsession with that tomb. He tried to duplicate as much of it in the house as he could."

This sounded somewhat familiar to Blackstone. Hadn't Chambers told him as much at some point, or had that been a dream too? He couldn't be sure. In the back of his head, he heard the echoes of what sounded like the fluttering of moths' wings.

"Keep going back," he said. Blackstone's intuition was screaming at him. He felt as though he was onto something, yet he was afraid to pull the thread, unsure if his sanity would unravel too.

His eyes were glued to the monitors. Backward, the room expanded as the walls moved outward and then the woman exited it but he still couldn't see her features clearly in the dim light.

But he could see enough, couldn't he?

A small shape was moving backward through the shadows on one of the exterior cameras. It had only been a glimpse of an image, caught for a blink in one of the security lights, but that had been enough.

"Stop," Blackstone said, and then he hesitated. Did he really want to know?

You already know.

Naira put the image in forward motion and froze it. Blackstone stared at the screen for what seemed like a long time. His heartbeat was visible in the large vein on his neck. In his head it sounded like a thunderous bass line.

"What is it?" Naira avoided his eyes. "Who is it?"

"It's—it's my wife," Blackstone said in a tortured whisper. "It's Laura."

Chapter Forty-Two

THEY BOLTED FROM the security room to find the hidden elevator. They'd seen Batten taking the gurney to that very elevator most likely, after they'd witnessed Michelle's limp body being hauled out of the asp pit. Blackstone wondered what other horrors lurked down there that Chambers didn't want anyone to know about. *Until it was too late.*

As soon as Blackstone had the women, all three of them (for Naira was a victim too, wasn't she?), safely away from here, he would head to the nearest police station. There was more than enough video evidence saved to have Chambers and Batten arrested. Naira could probably download enough video files on a thumbdrive. From there the police could do the digging. Who knew what other messed-up endeavors Chambers had his hands in, the sick bastard.

Blackstone's hands were trembling, but he wasn't sure which was worse, his anger or his panic.

In the back of his mind, he bid farewell to his dreams of financial security and fame. Good thing he'd banked most of what he had been paid already.

When they arrived at the head of the master's suite, it was clearly the swankier portion of the house if the artifacts on display here were any example: statuettes, pottery, jewelry, scrolls unfurled behind glass, massive wall hangings depicting gods and pharaohs that looked as brilliant as the day they'd been painted. Miniature obelisks. Golden implements for the Afterlife. Where had Chambers acquired all these, and how? And how had he managed to sneak them all into the country?

Blackstone wished idly that he could have spent a month just cataloguing the items displayed in this one hallway.

His mind wandered as Naira counted aloud with each step. He followed robotically, his thoughts unfurled.

Were they keeping Michelle down there? If so, why? Wouldn't it have made more sense to take her to a hospital? Were they afraid she would spill their secrets, like the exotic snake pit? That didn't make sense, did it? Why endanger anyone with deadly snakes at all? He *had* to assume Naira was right, that Michelle was still alive. He had called and texted her, with no response. Maybe they realized Michelle knew too much about the incantations? If that were the case, then what would they do to *him*? After all, he knew more than she did. And he had the notebook.

And Laura, what had they done to *her*? If that was her on the outside video and in the moving wall room, were they keeping her here too? Why had she come here? She'd been home to gather her things. And she'd sent him all that incriminating information on Chambers. So she had come here to see *him*, broken in, and—what, fallen into another of the old man's traps? Or perhaps they had brought her here? The tangle of possibilities and motives was too large, the knots too tight.

"Did you find it yet?" he asked.

"Not yet," Naira said as she stopped in the hall, her counting finger in the air. "But almost... Twelve, thirteen. Here it is!"

It was a panel like all the others, except a framed papyrus parchment crowded with glyphs was centered upon it. Naira reached in front of him and touched what appeared to be a knot in the wood, and the whole panel slid out and sideways. An old-fashioned elevator door stood in front of them.

Batten had swung that gurney in here.

For a split second he had a sense of impending doom... He remembered something Chambers had told him in an uncharacteristic avuncular moment. *There's more than just hidden panels, Blackstone. You shouldn't stray there either...*

Then they heard a metallic click, and the floor dropped out from under him.

Instinctively he spread out his hands, seeking something, anything, to grab.

Perhaps his experience in caverns and tombs had given him a built-in survival mechanism. But he wasn't thinking about that now. In fact, he wasn't thinking of anything.

His elbows hit—*hard and painfully*—a lip of floor that remained between the trapdoor and the elevator, and he hung there suspended in space, clinging desperately to the polished wood floor with his forearms, terrified that the slightest move would send him plunging into the pit below. The Maglite slipped from his belt and went flying down, crashing with the sound of shattered glass.

"Oh my God!"

It was Naira, yelling from where she had fallen aside, just barely missing the drop trap. A few inches closer to him and she would have plummeted with him. She'd reached in front of Blackstone because he'd stood closer to the panel, not knowing its exact location.

She leaped to her feet thanks to her spectacular fitness and was able to grip one of Blackstone's arms, relieving some of the pressure of his weight trying to drop him straight through. She screeched, "Grab my arm, Prof!"

He did, and while he thought his forearm muscles would burst into flames, slowly he was able to use her steady grip and standing leverage to lift himself back into the corridor, where they both collapsed onto the floor. Looking down into the square hole and past the two trapdoor elements, they could see the array of stainless-steel punji sticks rising from the floor of the pit, where they appeared to be set in concrete.

"Jesus fucking Christ." Blackstone's voice was barely more than a hoarse whisper. He didn't think he had any more voice than that.

"Are you all right?" A sheen of sweat on her forehead gave her a sort of jungle panache that he found decidedly attractive. Even with punji sticks ready to skewer his guts, he thought, he could be turned on by this spectacular young woman.

He wiped sweat he suddenly realized was pouring from him from out of his eyes. He took one last glance down and saw in his mind's eye what he would look now, if not for... Yeah, those sharp-pointed spears were set so close together he'd have been a fucking human pin cushion.

"Uh, let's get out of here," he said. He stood, unsteadily at first, and gave the pitful of spikes a wide berth as they stepped away. He kept an eye first on the spikes and then on the black square opening as if they might rise up and give pursuit.

The elevator door was still open a few feet away, mocking them with its trivial ordinariness.

They stepped inside the car and Blackstone wondered if its floor would now give way. That was a Bond movie stunt, wasn't it? Not for the first time, he saw Chambers as a cartoon supervillain, except he wasn't so comical now, was he? The floor did not move, and he sighed with relief when she closed the old-timey iron grate and tapped the black plate that engaged the motor. In a few seconds they were headed down, the car sounding a lot quieter than it looked like it should.

Blackstone remembered now that he had been in this same elevator with Chambers at least once. Or had he dreamt it? If he had been, the sliding panel had been open and he hadn't been aware of the elevator's secretness.

There were two levels beneath the house, the basement and a sub-basement. They decided to start at the former. He supposed the tomb was located in the sub-basement, but his recollection was hazy at best.

After visiting Batten's suite and viewing the video evidence, he had no doubt that something had indeed happened to Laura. Any hope that she had just been scared off and left town, or that she had just left after realizing that their marriage was unrepairable, had been extinguished. Batten had done something with her and then had stolen the clock as some type of grisly memento.

Didn't serial killers take *trophies*?

Blackstone shuddered.

The car came to a surprisingly smooth stop, and Blackstone pulled open the grate. Part of him expected a new booby-trap, but nothing happened. They looked at each other, then stepped out into a semi-circular foyer crossed by an ornately paneled hallway. Once again, Blackstone was struck with a wave of *deja vu*, or maybe he was just panicked. His whole experience with the Chambers house and brood had been a little off from the start, but it had grown more and more bizarre over the passing weeks, and now it was completely off the rails. Hell, off the rails and plummeting into the depths of an endless void. He wasn't sure his sanity could handle much more. Or his body, if he found any more of the old man's traps.

He gripped his notebook like a life preserver. He was lucky it hadn't landed at the bottom of the pit, but he had tucked it inside the waistband of his pants behind his back. He could never let Chambers get his hands on it, not after what he'd experienced with Michelle. Blackstone could only guess at the power the glyphs represented, but if what he'd felt was an example...then it was potentially much too dangerous.

Once the authorities were involved, they would probably confiscate all of Chambers' ill-gotten artifacts. Maybe before they fled the house Blackstone would be able to grab some of the photos of the wall panels so he could complete the translations.

Blackstone shook his head to clear it. What was he thinking? Taking the photos? This was no time to be considering something like that. He heard another voice inside himself that wasn't his, scratching at the inside of his skullcap. There was a constant sound in his ears, like leaves rustling in the wind, rushing water, or...that eerie whispering choir.

The voices scared him. They didn't sound human.

Chapter Forty-Three

THEY CHOSE THEIR direction by instinct, deciding to go down the right branch. Though still opulent, with tiled floors and ornate wallpaper, it was clearly a step down from the main house's interiors. The hallway was narrow compared to those above, and it lacked many of the mansion's decorative elements. What it lacked mostly was doors. The corridor seemed to stretch endlessly with no doors in sight. Blackstone's memory of the lower level—or levels—he had seen was hazy. Had he been here? Or had they been fever dreams?

Naira led the way, her body language not nearly as assured as he was used to. He followed along beneath the glow of fluorescent lights set at regular intervals in the drop-tile ceiling. Soon they came to a ninety-degree bend in the hall. Turning the corner, they found a series of doors set into the walls.

"I'm not sure about where we're heading," she called out over her shoulder. "But I think this is where those trap rooms are."

She was right. The first door they tried with the master key opened to a warm red glow.

In clear view, there was the side-to-side slithering motion of one of Chambers' asps crossing the sandy floor. Blackstone slammed the door shut, but not before also noticing the tell-tale drag marks in the sand near the door where Michelle's limp feet had rested as Batten hauled her from the room. He patted the revolver in his pocket, nervously. They were definitely in the right area. Now they'd have to try to figure out where Batten had gone.

The next door was on the opposite side of the hall. Inside it was dark and loud. They flipped a switch and overhead lights slowly flickered on. It was a huge, deep, mechanical room, and while Blackstone was no engineer, he guessed it was the mansion's HVAC systems, clearly a recent update, for the face of the furnace was shiny and modern-looking. He turned the lights off and they moved on.

The next door down the corridor bore a sign: *Prep Room.*
Blackstone stopped and stared at it. A shudder worked its way up his
back and straightened his neck hairs. Not sure why, but he saw his hand
trembled as he reached for the door while Naira tapped the lock plate.

What the hell? Blackstone thought feverishly. *What's he prepping?*

Dread spread throughout his body as if it were a transfusion. The
door sighed open.

The smell was so strong a memory that he suddenly felt shaky,
unsteady on his feet.

Natron smells like salt and sodium bicarbonate for the most part,
but large quantities of natron have a strong almost sulfuric smell that,
mixed with the smell of drying corpses, cannot ever be forgotten.
Blackstone had once visited a "mummy factory" in the narrow backroads
of Cairo's *casbah*-like quarter, where unscrupulous merchants created
their own mummies to sell illicitly to unsuspecting buyers of equally
unsettling motives.

And this "Prep Room" smelled the same.

He flicked on the light and his senses reeled in horror. Taking one
step inside, he already knew what he had found.

Having completely forgotten Naira, and the drone in his ears
obscuring the sound of her apprehensive voice, he took a second
hesitant step.

Three oblong, vat-like tubs, in two of which fresh bodies reposed,
partially covered in umber crystals.

As he approached, he saw that one was Laura.

His breath caught in his throat and bitter bile gushed into his mouth.
He put a hand up to cover his lips. She had been gutted and spread
open, her body cavity carefully packed with the natron that would
dessicate her, just like in the Egyptian mummification process. Her eyes
were lifeless, open, glassy.

Blackstone's nostrils and eyes poured helplessly onto his cheeks and
face.

Laura.

He sobbed explosively.

His nose clogged, he opened his mouth and felt his gorge rising.

He turned away, toward the second vat, and his knees were
suddenly floppy. He reached out for the cold edge of the vat to steady
himself. Touching it made him break down again, tears leaking from his

eyes like twin waterfalls. He'd kept the thoughts at bay since seeing the video, but now his head was full of them.

"Jesus! Holy shit, is that—?" Naira gasped suddenly, clasped her hand over her eyes and nose, and quickly backed out of the room.

Tears ran down Blackstone's cheeks now and he forced himself to ignore them. He tried to collect himself.

In the second vat, an older man, so obviously of Middle Eastern descent that he resembled a pharaoh, lying there as if ready for the Afterlife. Or he would have been, if his features had been in repose. He was indeed the scholar whose face Blackstone recognized from years before. But his face was frozen in what must have been a scream of terror, his eyes wide open black pits.

Ahmed al-Amani.

He had indeed been Blackstone's predecessor here at the compound, someone who had definitely not simply *left.* His body cavity showed signs of strange mauling.

But by what?

Invisible jackals?

Blackstone remembered his dream.

The third vat was empty, but how long would it be before Michelle or Blackstone himself rested in it?

He looked around and saw the canopic jars for organs and the other implements of mummification. The oil bath, the natron baths. This was a charnel house.

Blackstone shivered.

He'd never expected to find Laura like this, and now that she was dead he felt immense guilt at how he had thought of her. *Lot of good that'll do her.*

Emotionally spent, but now also starting to panic, he realized he had unconsciously walked around the tables and their gruesome cargo.

He looked up, startled, when Naira opened the door. "It's getting late," she said, trying hard to not face the reclining figures. "We've got to get on with it."

"Where does this go?" Blackstone pointed to the rear of the room, where another door hinted at further horrors. "Could this be where they took Michelle?"

Her lovely face drained of color, Naira stepped inside, her eyes facing up and away from the center of the room. "I don't know. I've never seen any of this...this... *Shit.* Is my grandfather a murderer?"

"I'm afraid so," he said. "And Batten. And I'm not quite sure about your mother." And then he realized that, technically, he had no real idea whether Naira was innocent in all this. Just because she *seemed* to be shocked and horrified...

She was shivering in the chilled air, but he could see it wasn't just that.

"Let's take a look in case he's got Michelle stashed in there... Then, if it's a fucking closet, we can go back to the hallway."

He had to stop lying to himself. Michelle wasn't going to be in a hospital room behind the damned Prep Room. He knew it, but he didn't want to admit it.

Still, he *needed* to know where the secondary exit led.

"Okay." She nodded too rapidly. She wanted out.

He took one last look at Laura's corpse and wished he could apologize for his faults. But it was too late now, wasn't it?

Blackstone opened the door at the rear of the grim chamber. His wife's not-so-final resting place. He didn't want to know any more. He had no real desire to see what else this dungeon of horrors contained, but he had to try to find Michelle before she ended up just like Laura.

Chambers was a monster.

A murderer and a monster.

There was no other explanation.

The door led to yet another level of horrors.

According to the sign, it was the Tomb Room, in which every wall was lined with niches reminiscent of those found in catacombs the world over. In each niche a mummy reposed, and by their shapes and sizes, Blackstone decided they had been processed at various ages. There were children-sized mummies, too. At a glance, he determined that the mummies all smelled the same, the result of having undergone the Chambers method, he assumed. A second look revealed that some of the cadavers still needed to be wrapped, but would be done at that point. They were strangers to him, and there were many.

Blackstone's nose twitched at the musty smell, though it was at least somewhat relieved by the scent of the sacred spices.

"Who are they all?"

He was startled. He'd forgotten about Naira again.

"I don't know. I think they may be people Chambers killed over the years. Maybe both him and Batten. Michelle can't be here, these people have all been mummified. She wouldn't be ready yet..."

"I told you, I'm sure she got some antivenom."

"You also said your grandfather wasn't a killer..."

She lowered her eyes. "I didn't know," she whispered. "I just thought he was—"

"Eccentric?"

She nodded, sadly. Glanced at the walls covered by mummies. She was crying.

"There's another damn door," he said brusquely. He pulled on its knob as if he were running from the devil himself. Finally it opened, and Blackstone stumbled out into the hallway, delirious with grief.

The corridor was wider here, lit by electric torches every few feet. There were long rows of ornate tables holding more canopic jars, perhaps filled with the organs of the mummies in the room they'd just left. Overhead, curved brick arches reminded him of medieval sewers.

This was exactly like the corridor in his dream. Or what he had thought was a dream. He wondered if here he would find the chamber filled with a circle of sarcophagi. And was the tomb nearby?

He turned to Naira. "We have to find Michelle. I have to save her if I can, and then we'll get out of here. Better leave this door open, in case we need to retrace our steps. Or I'm not sure we can find our way back to the goddamn elevator."

She was still shivering, but she nodded. The door would have swung shut, but she moved a carved wooden seat a few inches and propped it in the doorway.

"Save? *Who* will you save?"

Naira screamed. The voice had come from nowhere.

Chapter Forty-Four

BLACKSTONE WHIRLED ABOUT, his hearing suddenly muffled as if the unexpected voice had wiped out all other sound. He did, however, hear and feel the rapid beating in his arteries.

It was Alton Chambers.

But...how?

The old man was dressed in ceremonial robes, his head covered by a traditional *nemes* headdress and golden crown adorned with an asp, all symbols of a pharaoh's power and station. If he hadn't been so old and pale, he might have been able to pull off the pharaoh thing, but on his frame it appeared almost comical. The robe reminded Blackstone of many extant Aleister Crowley photographs. On the old man's left stood Alena, dressed in similar robes minus the headgear, though the robes flattered her appearance. Her erect nipples were obvious under the sheer cloth. Her face was in full Cleopatra mode, and Blackstone, to his chagrin, felt a stirring interest. To the old man's right stood Batten in his normal attire, his face caught somewhere between a snarl and a smirk. Batten and Alena both brandished handguns, which they were presently aiming at Blackstone.

"The senator's fundraiser ended early. Why, you wonder? Some sort of sudden illness. Frankly, I wouldn't be surprised if he's been poisoned. No, not surprised at all. But before that, he whispered my name into several very influential ears. So, mission accomplished, as they say. After all, McDonald is on his way out, and it's time for a much better candidate to come along... There's a bright future for his replacement, believe me." He nodded with certainty. "Well, it looks like we've arrived just in time for the fun part of the evening we had planned. What's wrong, Blackstone? I must say, you don't look so good. Have you been eating well enough? I would have thought so." He glanced sideways at his daughter, who made a smirk and tossed her hair.

"Y-Y-You'll never get away with this, Chambers." Blackstone winced. Even to his own ears, his whining words sounded ridiculous.

His eyes found Naira's, and she looked away and then down. Apparently to *her* ears, too. Her hands were trembling, Blackstone noted, even though she should have felt safe.

The old man laughed. "I've been getting away with this for years, Blackstone. It is *his* will. All of this, from the beginning, was *his* will. Come along," he said, motioning back down the hallway from where he and his minions had come. "I'm going to make James Blackstone the most powerful man on Earth in a few short steps. Shame you won't benefit, really, but it's still quite an honor."

Blackstone hesitated, weighing his options. They had no idea he was armed. Was he even capable of swashbuckling if it didn't involve a naked woman?

Alena would be easy enough to overpower if he could reach her without being killed first. Of course, they were probably going to kill him anyway, right? He didn't want to entertain the thought, but he could hardly afford to dismiss it. He'd seen too much. He knew too much. After watching the video playback, Blackstone was aware that Chambers had to know he'd cracked the code of the hieroglyphs. Blackstone was no longer necessary. Now Chambers could probably finish the translations himself. *And he was keenly aware of his notebook, riding behind his back. Could he keep it hidden there? Would the old man—or Batten—pat him down?*

Chambers seemed to sense Blackstone's trepidation. "You want to see your lovely assistant, don't you? Come along, she's waiting for us."

"What about Laura?" His voice came out loud and hoarse as he fought for control. Was he really unnecessary now? No, he still had knowledge the old man needed. He forced himself to believe it. "Why did you have to kill my wife?"

Chambers nodded. "Truthfully, she made that decision for me. It wasn't enough that she tried to warn you in person and with her amateur *dossier.* She broke into the compound with the intention of...well, I don't know, rescuing you? From yourself? From your greed? From me?" He shrugged. "We'll never know."

"You m-monster!"

Chambers chuckled. "If only you knew how pathetic you look and sound. Not professorial at all. Now let's move, please. Despite your sad feelings about Laura, who was much more attractive than I'd expected really, I'm certain right now your mind is on the lovely Michelle. So come along, she is still with us."

Furious, Blackstone grudgingly followed the old man. What choice did he have? He trudged between Alena and Batten who were leaning against opposite walls, their handguns aimed at Blackstone's gut. Their sickening smirks filled Blackstone with added rage. He contained it. If he kept his cool long enough, maybe he'd find a way out of this...this *nightmare.*

Chambers led them back to the elevator, with Blackstone followed by Batten and finally Alena bringing up the rear with her daughter.

Blackstone wasn't sure if Naira was a prisoner or not. But she didn't seem to be in as much danger as he was. She did share the family name, after all.

"Your work has really been sensational, Blackstone," said Chambers as they walked. "The way you figured out the pictograms and then were able to translate the much more complex hieroglyphs was quite inspiring. I enjoyed watching every bit of it. You could have had a career as a code breaker."

They stopped at the hidden elevator.

"You are a sick fucking bastard, Chambers. Jesus Christ, *Laura...* You didn't have to *kill her!*"

"No. No, I didn't. Quite frankly, I wanted to. I enjoyed feeling her *ka* escape while I was fucking her."

No longer able to control his rage, Blackstone sprang at Chambers.

He was just able to clutch Chambers' robes in his fists when he felt the barrel of Batten's pistol pressed against his head.

"Back off." Batten's voice was a snarl.

Blackstone relented, defeated, releasing Chambers and taking a step back. He hoped that now he might be able to draw his weapon, having been once thwarted so easily.

"She didn't have a choice," said Chambers. "Fucking me. If that makes you feel any better."

"I suppose it's also true that you murdered your sister and brothers. And your father."

"Well..." Chambers began, as he opened the elevator door. "That really should be a story for another day. Pity you won't be writing my book after all. It's your fault, you know. You solved the glyphs much more quickly than I expected. Sorry, Blackstone, it would have been nice to have more time to talk. I rather like you. You remind me of...me.

But Alena and I are anxious to get things going, and as you know, I don't have all the time in the world. Yet."

They all entered the long, narrow car, and Blackstone wondered if this would be his best opportunity to use his gun. His indecision caused the moment to pass, and Batten's gun poked him in the stomach. Any move and he'd be gut-shot.

The elevator rattled its complaint at the overload as it slowly headed one floor lower, to the bottom-most level of the mansion.

"Where were we?" said Chambers, his face blank. "Oh yes, my siblings. I guess I played a part in their deaths, though I wasn't completely aware of it at the time. Later I made the connection. I was the conduit, not the instigator. I realized that it was him, the Occupant, through me. Much of it I can't completely grasp, even now. My father... I didn't kill him as much as put him out of his misery. After the deaths of Charles Junior and Cynthia, all he did was mope. I believed he didn't much care what happened to Harrrison—and to me—though now I'm sure Harrison's death added to his misery."

The elevator stopped with a *clang*, and Chambers opened the door.

As they stepped out, Blackstone was struck with a wave of vertigo. He stumbled against the wall to regain his bearings.

They were standing in a round space like a foyer. The corridor split the foyer and extended in two opposite directions. The walls were paneled in some medium-dark wood, and Blackstone was certain he recognized it as one of the places he had seen in the dream that hadn't been a dream after all, and it certainly wasn't a dream now. The tomb beneath the house and the otherworldly blood-red sarcophagus *were* real, no matter how confused he had been for a while.

"Professor, don't try to play games with me," Chambers said. "There is nothing wrong with you. At least not yet."

Blackstone tried to catch his breath. He stammered, "I...I...I...I..."

"Well, *J-J-J-James*," Chambers mocked, "I thought you had outgrown your stutter long ago."

How did the old man know about that?

"It's nice when you can relive a bit of your childhood, isn't it?" Chambers continued his mockery.

"I...I...I...I can't...*breathe.*"

"Of course you can, Professor. Just calm down. We'll be with Michelle very soon now. I can't have your stuttering interfering with the incantation. Take a minute and catch your breath."

Blackstone tried to comply, but his head was swimming as he tried to process all the grief, rage, confusion, and fear. All while trying to formulate an escape plan to save Michelle and Naira. And his own miserable neck. Not to mention figuring out what the fuck was going on right now. He took the opportunity to study his situation through slitted eyes.

Alena and Batten held their guns steady—their barrels aimed at him seemed larger than life. Naira was unwatched, but what could she do? Chambers checked his watch and rolled his eyes.

"Come on, Professor," said Chambers. "Time to go. Follow me."

Blackstone pushed off the wall and took a few tentative steps before regaining most of his faculties. He let Chambers lead him to his almost certain doom, like a lamb to the butcher.

They travelled through the dizzying maze of brick arches until Blackstone was hopelessly lost, and then they arrived in the massive chamber where the sand half-covered the reconstructed tomb itself. They filed into the tomb's claustrophobic entrance. Though the space only took two at a time, the drawn guns spurred him and Naira through and into the terror of the narrowing hallway. In what Blackstone had come to think of as his dream, Chambers had told him that at one time the walls were designed to move, trapping those who entered. But it hadn't been a dream, had it? For here they were again. Now Chambers led the way, and Blackstone was forced to follow by Batten, who was close enough behind to keep his gun leveled at his head. When the passage narrowed to the point that they were walking sideways, Blackstone thought about trying to fight. But behind Batten was the shaken Naira, and behind her was her mother with the other gun. Shooting inside this small space would turn it into a slaughterhouse, no matter who pulled the trigger.

They exited the slightly curving hallway into a more spacious chamber, one that didn't match Blackstone's memory of the place. Their flashlights made menacing shadows that loomed over them like silent gods. It was time to try and make some kind of play.

"What is it, Chambers?" Blackstone asked. "What is the thing in the tomb? I know you know more than you've told me. You must know more."

"I'm not sure that I know more than you, Blackstone, and yet I have gleaned a few things in all my years of study, the decades I have spent in its company. I also have some personal theories about the Occupant, his nature, how he fits into life's puzzle. Some of these theories arose from long years of contemplation, while others appeared to me as visions. Ever since that fateful day trying to rescue the oil rig, I have had many visions." He paused. "I'm not sure I know more than you, but I'll tell you what I do know."

The old man was panting now as he spoke. Blackstone could feel it, too. It was more than just the silica floating in the air like a swirling haze. There was a charge in the atmosphere and a tingling in his loins. They were getting close. He could picture the red sarcophagus, recalling it in vivid detail.

Chambers went on, warming up. "Humans have created religions to counterbalance their deep-seated certainty that there is nothing beyond their puny existence. Their fear of death—the end of everything, the end of their participation in the world, the great unknown—sparked their need to provide themselves a fantasy world filled with immense possibilities for an afterlife that would be comparable to this life, and most likely better. And the Egyptians, so well-known for their obsession with death... In reality, their obsession was the Afterlife, or their vision of what it would be, which is why, as you know, they furnished their dead with all the necessary goods for a rich future in the land of the dead."

He was in his element now, his head tilting as his eyes roved over the few painted panels that remained and the bland spaces where he had removed them.

"But think, *think* if their obsession was tinged with the knowledge that some—some perhaps known to them, others perhaps not—were indeed *different* from them. These others were not bound by the end of things that bound everyone else, including their pharaohs—*as much as they would have denied it!*—no, they were not bound, for they were true immortals. They were not from here, you see, not from our world..."

Chambers turned his head to look back at Blackstone while he spoke, the flashlight Batten held high in his left hand—while the gun in his right targeted Blackstone—illuminating the old man's face. The professor was sure he could see that the billionaire was frothing at the mouth. Spittle dripped onto his ornate robes. He was unwinding, losing himself in his diabolical fantasies.

"And they had what the Egyptians and everyone else wanted," continued Chambers. "They had *immortality.* They did not face the long night, they did not need to rot in a hole or a cavern or even inside a pyramid, for their lives would indeed continue forever. Forever, that is, as long as they had one resource, a single element, a single obstacle to what was otherwise an immortal existence."

Chambers paused.

For effect, Blackstone thought.

"They needed blood. *Human blood.*" The old man's eyes were wide, as if he were riding a heroin high.

"Think of it! As long as a supply of blood was available, then these beings would go on forever. They could be considered gods by the men who surrounded them, and who wanted what they had. One such being was finally identified as a god, but instead of being celebrated, one day the men around him decided he was an evil god, a god of wickedness and terror. They claimed he left empty husks of their fellows and acted drunkenly upon the imbibing of their blood. He was vainglorious and yet was not a pharaoh, although he was as rich as one. He should have been one, and indeed *would* have been, if not... The people turned against him and betrayed him. He should have been crowned an immortal pharaoh, but his behavior had prevented it, so their response was to treat him as a pharaoh in death, if not in life. They poisoned his blood supply by tainting his slated victims with a potion. And then, when he was rendered helpless, they put him through the process, removing his organs and his brain and drying his body in natron and wrapping him in gauze."

Blackstone interrupted. "It's a fascinating story. What does any of this have to do with you, Chambers? With us?"

"He's immortal, Blackstone. They didn't realize that he was *still* immortal, even after they mummified him."

"What are you saying? Are you saying that...*that thing*...is still alive?"

"In a way, yes. Yes, it's still alive. Maybe not in the realm of the flesh, but in spirit...the Occupant is very much alive. And he lives through me. All of this has been possible because of him. And more will become possible. He wants me to be pharaoh. He's told me as much from the beginning, when I first found him. I can hear him speak to me. I hear him now. Can you hear it, Blackstone? Can you hear the voice?"

"You're insane, Chambers! Listen to yourself!" But Blackstone *could* hear the voices whispering in the back of his head. *Calling to him.*

It was the whispering choir, and its volume ebbed and waned like an aural tide.

"We will soon see, Blackstone."

They left the narrow passage, following Chambers through another maze until they reached the central chamber and its Stonehenge-like concentric circles of sarcophagi. But they didn't seem to be in the original tomb anymore. Blackstone was confused, yet he recalled this chamber as clearly as if he'd been here a hundred times.

Who had told him the sarcophagi were occupied by Chambers family members going back generations?

Was it Alena?

He thought it was, but he wasn't sure which portions of his memory were real and which were fantasy and dream images.

Before he knew it, the small group had slipped through the claustrophobic rings of "stones." There, on a raised altar in the center of the room, lay Michelle, apparently unconscious. She was stripped naked, an IV bag hanging from a pole beside her, its needle deep in her flesh and held in place on her arm with several strips of white tape. She was bathed in the eerie red glow of light refracted through the countless rubies that encrusted the Occupant's intimidating standing sarcophagus, which loomed over them a few yards away.

But hadn't the massive red sarcophagus stood within the tomb's royal chamber when Blackstone had seen it?

He swore it had been in its own regal chamber inside the tomb the young Chambers had discovered by falling.

"Here she is, waiting for us, just about to wake up," said Chambers, spreading his arms wide to accentuate his proclamation.

Naira hissed in surprise. Or panic. Alena stood behind her, as if keeping her in line.

"What have you done to her, you monster?" Blackstone took two steps in the direction of the altar, but stopped. He wasn't sure Batten wouldn't just shoot him.

"I've saved her, Blackstone. She had a little mishap with a few of my *pets*. As I'm sure you're well aware from watching the video playback that led you down here. We've given her the critically needed antivenom and a mild sedative to help her rest. That's all. She's in perfect health. For now. And she'll remain healthy and alive so long as you're cooperative. Do you feel cooperative, Blackstone?"

He wanted to tell the old man to fuck himself, but Blackstone knew he didn't have any leverage. With Naira and himself at gunpoint and Michelle incapacitated, probably unable to arise from the altar and run, what choice did he have?

"What do you want, Chambers?"

"I just want you to read a passage from that notebook you're hiding in your sweaty pants. Oh yes, I'm well aware that you've deciphered the necessary incantations. Just read and you shall be richly rewarded."

Chambers threw off his ornate robes and stood before them naked save for his Egyptian headdress. His impressive penis twitched as it began its rapid transformation from flaccid to erect, and despite the circumstances, Blackstone was shocked to feel his own loins tingling with activity. Then the old man mounted the dais and stood at the end of the altar, where Michelle's feet rested. It was like a scene out of a horror movie or porn, and it should have been amusing, if only he hadn't been aware that it was all too real.

"Now begin, Blackstone."

"Begin what? What do you want me to do?"

"Read the spell of immortality and transformation. I believe you called it body-switching."

"I don't know what you're talking about!" Blackstone lied, stalling for time. What was the old man trying to do, switch bodies with Michelle? Or...with *him*?

And what did Alena want?

Suddenly he understood why Naira was here. Both of them, lured here to give father and daughter new bodies? And thereby achieve immortality?

Would it work?

Somehow, Blackstone knew it would. He had seen enough.

But what would the Occupant gain?

"Come now, Blackstone. I've been watching you, watching your progress day after day, reading your notes while you were preoccupied with your assistant and my lovely daughter. Or while you slept with the help of a mild sedative. Yes, we did that." Chambers pulled Michelle's unconscious form toward him as he spoke, dragging her body across the stone slab until her buttocks lined up with the platform's edge, her limp legs hanging down on either side of Chambers. "Oh, there's no harm, it's just *bibbidi bobbidi boo*, isn't it? Now read, Blackstone."

Sedative? They'd been drugging him! No wonder he had trouble discerning dreams from reality. That explained why his memories seemed so slippery, why time itself was so hard to pin down.

Alena stepped forward and brought her handgun to bear on Blackstone's head. "Read, lover," she whispered. Her lips dripped red as she mouthed the words. He knew her well enough to know she was highly aroused. Her pupils were dilated, her skin lustrous with the blood just under the surface. And she held the gun with obvious familiarity.

After all this, she was still indescribably desirable.

Blackstone's hands trembled as he pulled the notebook from his waistband and flipped through its pages, his mind a blur as he tried to come to grips with what was happening. He cleared his throat and began to read the guttural translation, having little idea how he knew the pronunciation of the words in a long-dead language. But the voices in his mind seemed to help him along.

" *The Great God of all things comes /*
from the sky in its infiniteness... "

Almost immediately Alena was at his side, rubbing the crotch of his trousers.

"And grants the beasts life and death /
and all must obey who hear the Master's voice..."

She was whispering—almost moaning—the words into his ear as he read them.

"When they hear the sound on the lips of the Chosen /
And the eyes of the dead will open..."

Now she was grinding her groin against his thigh, her free hand tracing the shape of his erection. He was enthralled by the pleasure of her stroking in juxtaposition with the painfully tight fabric holding his straining passion at bay.

"The muscle's tears that flow / to the ground
Where they moisten the sand and call
to them all / come to Him who /
Waits..."

The words seemed to come on their own now as Alena's touch distracted him from the page, and his eyes rolled back in ecstasy. Blackstone continued the incantation as if it had grafted itself to his subconscious. He no longer needed to see the words he had transcribed.

"Eternity is but a day /
For red tears are succor /
To the dead and the living."

It wasn't just Alena's hand bringing him to new heights in pleasure. The sensations racked his whole body as wave after wave of delight moved through him, as if the room itself was resonating with sexual energy. He began the incantation again, its syllables creating a cadence that matched the rhythm of Alena's movements and kept time to the titillating pulse that surrounded them. The very space around them throbbed with raw sexuality.

Blackstone looked up through lids made heavy by uncontrollable ecstasy, the notebook all but forgotten as the words formed on his lips unbidden. On the altar, Chambers was thrusting himself into Michelle's sexual center. The lust-filled energy of the room seemed to have awakened her from her sedated slumber as her hands now gripped the edges of the stone slab and her hips rose compliantly to meet the old man's thrusts.

His glance shifting momentarily to his right, Blackstone could see Naira bent over and grasping her ankles, her knees straight, her feet spread apart, her short skirt thrown up over the curve of her buttocks. There behind her was the monstrous Batten, rutting, his pants hanging just above his ankles. One hand still held the other gun, while the other pulled Naira's head back by the hair. Her face was alight with—it wasn't exactly pleasure, but something more akin to spiritual satisfaction. But her eyes were glazed as if she'd been drugged. Batten's reward for loyalty?

It wasn't just Blackstone incanting the arcane spell; they were all doing it, as if they'd practiced this chant for weeks.

He might have gone for Alena's gun, except he couldn't think clearly. He was being overtaken by pleasure as she worked his belt loose, freed him, and went to work with religious zeal. The gun's barrel she thrust into his side as both an action born of lust and essentially a threat that she could gut-shoot him at any time. Blackstone flashed briefly on the thought that she might actually *prefer* to do so upon his release.

"*The Great God of all things comes /
from the sky in its infiniteness /
And grants the beasts life and death /
and all must obey who hear the Master's voice /
When they hear the sound on the lips of the Chosen/
And the eyes of the dead will open /
The muscle's tears that flow / to the ground
Where they moisten the sand and call
to them all / come to Him who /
Waits /
Eternity is but a day /
For red tears are succor /*

To the dead and the living..."

They spoke-chanted the words over and over, casting the spell. Blackstone's passion was at its peak, but he felt as if he could remain at the edge of climax forever, as if he were leaning over an impossibly high cliff, barely able to keep himself from toppling off the edge but unable to pull himself back to safety.

He suspected the sexual energy that surrounded them was stealing the power of the shuddering orgasm that should have been racking his entire frame with its release, and feeding it back through them, the tension rising in the chamber until it was its own entity. This was occurring to everyone whose lust was being harvested, control having been ripped from them until they were merely animalistic channels for the revived *sex magick* of the ancients.

The temperature in the dank chamber seemed to have risen to one hundred degrees or more. It now resembled the distant desert that had once sprawled above this tomb. Sweat rolled off their bodies in sheets as their uncontrollable lecherous thrusting and grunting rose in an almost unbearable crescendo.

This has to be hell, Blackstone thought.

And yet it also has to be paradise...

After an unknown amount of time, as it all had slowed while Blackstone stood trembling at the precipice of rapture, a shuffling sound pulled him from his trance.

"Goddamn it, Blackstone!" Chambers screamed suddenly, as he pulled away from Michelle and turned to face him, rage etched on his grotesque, inhuman features. "You are reading the wrong incantation!"

Blackstone looked down at the notebook in his hand incredulously.

Chambers was right.

Somehow he'd landed on the wrong page and read an invocation about eternal life, not the transformation spell Chambers had demanded. It was the same spell he had read to Michelle the night before.

Behind Chambers, Michelle had somehow awakened and swung her legs down over the side of the altar and was standing tentatively on shaky feet like a newborn doe. She cupped her hand on her face, confused or pained, or both. Her eyes were glazed, but she was smiling, having caught the lust wave that had rippled through them all inside the bizarre chamber.

Alena suddenly stepped away from him, straightening her robes. She seemed embarrassed by her total lack of control, but yet she held the gun on him still. Though he noted her grip seemed weak.

This was the time, Blackstone thought. Slowly, he started digging in his pocket, where no one had yet noticed the weight of his own gun. He'd shot enough snakes and the occasional coyote while out in the Southwest, and regular sessions at the range had made him a better than passable shot. He bet Chambers didn't know *that.*

He reached for his Smith & Wesson.

Batten, half-naked, was pulling away from Naira, who seemed hypnotized by the chant or otherwise unable to track what was happening. Blackstone swore he would get her and Michelle out of this house of grotesque horrors.

Now was the time. His hand gripped the gun's butt and he started to draw it from his pocket. He had six rounds, and then six more in the speed-loader.

Then the screaming started.

First there was Batten's foghorn scream.

Moments later, Naira also started screaming uncontrollably.

For the briefest instant, Blackstone thought Batten was being attacked by *children,* but his senses quickly coalesced and he realized the children were actually *mummies.*

The entire tomb was crawling with lurching, bandage-shrouded corpses, their covered eyes somehow making them more terrifying.

They appeared on all sides, emerging from the rings of sarcophagi and, judging by their number, from the old man's mummy room as well. And they must have been at least as strong physically as they had been in life, as two of the undead creatures—one on each side—had grabbed Batten's throat, their bony fingers tearing through his flesh. After her initial scream, Naira had shrunk from Batten's vicinity, shrieking as she watched. In moments his dress shirt, jacket, and tie were drenched in a spreading crimson stain. A red jet arced from his throat in a gurgle. Another of the things had sunk its teeth into Batten's hand, causing him to drop his gun. It clattered between the rows of sarcophagi, disappearing in the deep shadows they cast. At the sight of the bleeding, Naira scrabbled across the sandy floor to Blackstone's side as if he could protect her.

But Blackstone froze, his brain attempting to assess what could not be, and yet what played out in front of him.

God! Had *they* done this? Had the spell and ritual reanimated these long-dead husks? How was it even possible? Though many looked ancient, dry and shrivelled, others looked fresh— obviously Chambers' most recent handiwork. The oldest had degraded...they were not much more than skeletons wrapped in decomposing filthy cotton linens.

Even Chambers was stilled, struck dumb and staring at the terrible invaders of his sanctum.

This was the opportunity Blackstone had been waiting for. He dropped the notebook and pulled the Smith & Wesson from his pocket.

He drew a bead on Alena, as she had the second gun, but she was clearly not a threat at the moment. Alton's beautiful daughter was in awe—or perhaps shock—as she stood wide-eyed and slack-jawed, staring at the chaos unfolding around them. It was a miracle Blackstone wasn't in the same state, but his survival instinct had kicked in despite the nightmare reality in which he found himself.

He scrambled to his feet and surveyed the surroundings. Nothing made sense. He was a child who had been thrown into the deep end of the pool. And he could easily drown.

One of the horrors staggered toward him, its arms outstretched with homicidal intent. Its barely gauzed-over empty eye sockets that stared blindly and emotionlessly into oblivion drilling holes through Blackstone's soul.

He raised the gun and fired into the thing's head. The report seemed strangely muffled in the chamber.

The top half of the mummy's skull vaporized, exploding in a puff of bone dust.

It did not relent, its clawed murderous fingers still stretching toward him.

Blackstone stepped back to avoid the creature's reach. A thought, flashing briefly: *You kill fictional zombies with a bullet to the brain, but how do you kill mummies?*

Of course! The heart.

The one vital organ left inside the mummy was its heart, so it could be weighed in the golden scale of Osiris against Ma'at's feather, that they might know if the dead would proceed to the Field of Reeds or if Ammut would consume their soul.

Blackstone pointed the gun at the ghoul's chest, pulling the stiff trigger. As soon as the bullet passed through the mummy's heart, the thing collapsed to the floor like an old sack of bones with a sound like bowling pins bouncing down the alley.

Noticing two of the swaddled corpses coming up behind Alena—who was still transfixed— Blackstone stepped up and shot them both. They fell into heaps of bones and wrappings, kicking up plumes of dust and decay.

Alena looked into his eyes and Blackstone could see the unadulterated joy there. She laughed insanely and put a hand on either side of Blackstone's head. "We did it! We did this!" she said, raving. She forced his gaze at the mummies who were reveling in Batten's blood. They seemed to be drinking it, and it almost looked as if it were reviving them. Their emaciated limbs were gaining mass. Their rawhide skin gained a sheen of moisture, as if the blood itself were restoring them.

"*James!*"

Blackstone heard the sheer terror in Michelle's voice. He ripped himself away from Alena's grasp and turned to see that Michelle had somehow stepped down from the dais and was now on the floor of the chamber, trailing her IV tubing and recoiling from a pale undead monster. Chambers still stood above her, naked, his mouth open in a continuous scream and his hands covering his ears as if he was trying to keep sounds or voices from entering his skull.

James Blackstone froze as he recognized the advancing corpse. Due to a particularly horrifying and ironic twist of fate, it was Laura—whose reanimated gutted body stood reaching for her rival in life, Michelle.

Laura, her dead face twisted into a rictus of hate.

His Laura.

Blackstone swallowed hard, his mouth dry, his guilt rising like vomit in his throat. It was his fault. *He* had caused this. He had done this to her. He had done it to both of them. His weak will in the face of his desires. His lustful ways. His disregard for others as long as he was getting what he wanted. Now he stood paralyzed, trying to gather the will to shoot Laura. He'd already destroyed her heart once. How could he destroy her again?

But Michelle was still alive. She still had a chance.

Blackstone finally lifted his gun and aimed. But the loves of his life had aligned themselves in such a way that Michelle was now blocking his sight of Laura.

"Michelle, down!" he shouted.

She heard him and dropped to the chamber's hard floor below.

Suddenly the dead but very mobile Laura was in his sights, and he squeezed the trigger twice, aiming for her gutted chest right where her heart was located. He closed his eyes to avoid the sight of her body collapsing as if poleaxed.

"Damn it, Blackstone! Look what you've done!" Chambers yelled down at him. Unlike his daughter, who seemed drunk on mystical power, Chambers was furious. Spittle dribbled down the old man's chin as he shook his fists in the air.

Rage overtook Blackstone. But before he could raise his firearm to gun the old man down, they both heard the deafening noise of stone grinding against stone. They froze.

Two reconstituting mummies were pulling open the enormous lid of the ruby-encrusted sarcophagus, the resting place of the Occupant. When the coffin was wide open, the animated corpses stood aside, flanking it. The interior of the sarcophagus was filled with shadows and it took Blackstone a few seconds to make out its contents.

There stood the mummy for whom the entire tomb was built, and then moved and rebuilt.

The mummy's arms were crossed over his chest in the standard position, but instead of the scepter and flail of a Pharaoh, he held a dagger in one hand and a chalice in the other. There was no doubt as to the mummy's gender, because his groin area was grotesquely enlarged to proclaim his abnormal endowment. He wore a *nemes* that once heralded his rank, but now it was tattered and faded, matching the dull brown tone of the Occupant's taut, wrapped skin. A moment passed before the thing twitched and thousands of years of accumulated dust and sand stirred. He took a first tentative step forward, but quickly gained his footing. He tossed the dagger and chalice aside as if, after clutching them for millennia, he couldn't stand to hold them one moment longer—and began to walk. He moved slowly at first, awkwardly dragging one foot behind him, but gained agility by the instant. In three steps, he was striding purposefully toward the dais where Chambers still stood beside the altar. Though the lighting in the tomb was itself odd, the shadow cast beneath the feet of the Occupant was something wholly *other.* For while it lacked any cohesive form, what little of it did take shape resembled numerous writhing, segmented insect legs.

Chambers stared at the Occupant and his shadow, his expression a blend of adoration and utter joy. Alena stood on Blackstone's left, daintily clasping all her fingers together as if she were witnessing Jesus

Christ walking from the tomb. A little farther back, Michelle's body was still crumpled on the ground where she had fallen, perhaps mercifully unconscious. Naira was on his right, disbelief and fear etched on her features. Blackstone imagined that hers was very similar to his own expression. He half-expected to wake from this nightmare in his bed, with Laura at his side. As much as he prayed, he knew it wasn't to be.

The Occupant climbed the steps, strode directly to Chambers and placed his claw-like hand on the old man's head. Chambers gasped. His eyes widened as if they were being *filled* with visions.

Now is the time! Now, kill him now!

Realizing he'd emptied his revolver, Blackstone snapped open the cylinder and clumsily ejected the spent cartridges. Then he fumbled in his pocket for the speed-loader and managed to drop in the new rounds despite his shaking hands.

Blackstone's notebook lay near his feet where it had fallen. It opened as if it were caught in a strong wind, the pages fluttering until they came to rest open to the page denoting the body switching spell that Chambers had wanted.

Though he couldn't make out the complicated translations, the words of the spell began to form on Blackstone's lips. He could hear them clearly in his head and his mouth moved as if it were being controlled by someone else. *Perhaps it was*, he thought, wracked with terror. Yet his lips and tongue continued to form the sounds.

No sooner had the first syllables formed on Blackstone's lips than the Chambers women were suddenly at his side, sinking to their knees. Alena stroked him beneath the fabric of his trousers while Naira worked the button and zipper to free him from his confines. They were incanting the esoteric *magick* along with him as if they were caught in a new lust-induced trance.

Meanwhile, Chambers was groaning, almost screaming. His hands were clawing on the Occupant's wrapped arm, perhaps trying to remove the ancient deity's own hand from his head, or perhaps he was desperately holding it there.

The women were now fellating Blackstone in unison, mumbling the spell into his hardened flesh, taking turns engulfing his length and working the sides of his shaft with their lips and tongues. His glans was a purple bruise, his veins so engorged with blood that they were nearly black. Alena's luxurious robes had fallen open, exposing her naked body, and Naira had lost her skirt. The two women were fingering each other even as they pleasured Blackstone, rubbing each other's slickened sex with abandon.

Blackstone was awash in rising ecstasy. His mind emptied as the pleasures of the flesh came to encompass everything around him. He still spoke the spell, but he barely heard himself.

The surviving mummy horde had formed a misshapen circle around Chambers and the Occupant, enclosing Alena, Naira, and Blackstone also within their perimeter. They were chanting silently, but Blackstone could hear them in his head. He could hear the Occupant too, feeling his presence inside of him.

Somehow he managed to lift the revolver again and aimed for the monster's chest, then took the shot.

The wrapped creature began to dissolve into powder, as if it were being sandblasted into oblivion. His limbs slowly turned to sand until just his arm remained in Chambers' grasping hands. Then just a hand on the old man's head. Finally, there was a flash of light on Chambers' forehead, and the Occupant blinked out, having returned entirely to dust.

A ripple passed through the standing mummies and they collapsed to the floor as if their hearts had been pierced at exactly the same moment.

The chanting stopped dead in mid-phrase.

Alena and Naira stood slowly as if awakening from a trance. Alena picked up her robe and Naira tried to straighten the bits of clothing she still wore. Their motions were sluggish with exhaustion. Blackstone wobbled where he stood.

Chambers turned to face them. He seemed different. Somehow more powerful, confident, charismatic. *Terrifying.*

"Come to me, daughter," Chambers said, reaching for Alena.

"Yes, lover," she responded, but she hesitated.

"It's all right. Come to me."

Slowly, after glancing at Naira and Blackstone, she complied.

Mounting the dais, Alena dropped her tangled robe to the floor and embraced her father.

Chambers put his lips to his daughter's neck and began to kiss her. Alena sighed with pleasure. Then he opened his mouth and began sucking her white skin. Alena moaned as they shared the embrace altogether too long. Almost imperceptibly at first—so much so that Blackstone tried to blink it away—Alena started changing. Her flesh, so firm for her age, rapidly began to sag. Her mostly pepper salt-and-pepper hair turned a brilliant white. Meanwhile, Chambers' bald spot filled in and the lines on his wrinkled face seemed to smoothen and disappear. In a few moments, Alena was transformed into a bent-backed centenarian.

"*Mother!*" Naira screamed, then clapped a hand over her mouth.

Alena had become an ugly, twisted hag. She seemed to be ready to drop dead of old age.

Chambers smiled broadly at his granddaughter and the purchased professor. His canine teeth had elongated into fangs, and a single drop of blood wound its way down his chin and fell to the floor, followed by another.

Blackstone knew this wasn't Chambers. They had chanted the transformation ritual and what stood before them now was no longer Chambers, it was the ancient blood god who had been sealed in his tomb for thousands of years, somehow reborn in Chambers' skin which was now regaining youth. He seemed to be trying on the Chambers body like a shirt, shrugging his shoulders and cracking his neck.

Blackstone lined up his gun to dispatch this new version of the demon.

The creature that had been Alton Chambers laughed heartily. Blackstone heard its chortling not only in his ears, but inside his skull.

"Professor Blackstone," it said, its voice reverberating through the chamber and through Blackstone's head. "I believe we still have a contract." Then he added: "The portal is open."

"Fuck that," Blackstone said, and he fired once. Twice.

The Chambers-thing's eyes opened wide and glazed over. The body carrying the Occupant crashed down to the floor in a heap and turned rapidly to dust.

"*The portal is open.*"

But now the voice wasn't male, it was female. It was Alena's voice.

Blackstone, shocked, realized that Alena's aging had reversed and suddenly her body was youthful again, bursting with sexuality, her breasts thrust out in defiance and pride. Her nipples were huge, erect, and Blackstone once again felt the heat of lust.

Alena smiled at him.

"Professor, I believe we do still have a contract," she said, her full lips forming the words carefully, still trying them out. "But it will indeed require restructuring."

Blackstone fired again. And again. He fired until the hammer fell on an empty cartridge.

Alena's chest was bloody, four rounds having found their marks. Her eyes bored into his and she smiled crookedly. Grimaced.

Then she also collapsed, and her body's dust joined that of the others.

"And fuck you too," Blackstone muttered. "Restructure *that*." He dropped the hot revolver.

He turned and saw that Naira stood transfixed by the sight of her mother and grandfather turned to dust in front of her.

"My God, my God..." She turned away from him, her head hanging.

Blackstone took her limp hand. Over her shoulder he saw that Michelle was struggling to her feet, still trying to remove her IV tubing. Her face was ashen, her normally alluring body bruised and scraped bloody. He could barely believe she was alive. "Michelle, are you all right?"

She nodded, fat tears squeezing between her eyelids. "Get me the hell out of here, James. *Please*."

Blackstone helped her straighten up, then led her away from the altar. They joined Naira where she stood, and he put his arms around both their bodies. Together, they stepped away from the carnage caused by the Occupant.

It's over.

Heading for the elevator—wherever it was from here—he led them through a narrow opening between two of the family sarcophagi, Michelle behind him, Naira bringing up the rear.

It's finally over...

Blackstone heard a loud *Snap!* and whirled in time to see Michelle's dead body hitting the floor, her head canted at an unnatural angle. Behind her, Naira smiled widely, her youth suddenly reinvigorated and refreshed, her ripe body now exponentially more alluring than her mother's had been.

"The portal is open," she said, and now the words came easily from her lush lips. "Professor, we must talk of the restructuring. We have much work to do."

Then she laughed, long and hard, her voice echoing through the chamber. It was no longer the voice of a young woman.

Around the dais behind them, the piles of bones reconstituted like a film running in reverse. The mummies arose and approached.

Like a royal escort.

The thing that Naira had become laughed again, only now all of its shuffling acolytes joined in.

Blackstone listened to the choir of laughter inside his head until he realized that he was laughing with them.

Insanely.

Epilogue
Six Months Later

THE OCCUPANT RECLINED in its golden throne overlooking the revelry and excess all around. It had ordered the throne—reminiscent of one it had enjoyed in a previous incarnation—created by melting down a number of its old treasures from eons ago. What are antiquities to a being that lives forever?

Beneath it—in the great room of the old Chambers mansion—naked human bodies intertwined lustily. The perfumed scent of incense that filled the air couldn't conceal the miasma of sweat and sex. The naked string quartet playing in the corner of the room was drowned out by the choir of grunting and lustful panting from the sea of flesh.

The mansion had become a mecca for the world's elite. The rich, the powerful, the famous, the talented, the connected...all clamored for a spot on the list of attendees. A chance to enjoy carnal pleasures with the stable of young nubile females and males that the Occupant had procured for their amusement. They didn't need to know about the numerous cameras situated around the house. They wouldn't find out about those until the Occupant needed something from them.

It had learned a great deal from its last life on the throne. It was far better to rule from behind the veil.

The Occupant squeezed Naira's right breast in its hand, teasing its nipple hard. It liked this new body; it was more luxurious than the last one. Then again, anything would seem luxurious after spending thousands of years locked in that dehydrated old husk.

Now that the portal was open, it would be able to invite more of its kind over the threshold. There was plenty of willing flesh for everyone. This world was a banquet waiting to be devoured.

Speaking of which, where was Blackstone? It was getting thirsty.

* * *

Blackstone haunted the old tomb. What had once seemed so enigmatic and improbable was now well-worn and intimate. In his hands he clutched the Occupant's old chalice and dagger. The dagger had a fresh, crisp edge, sharpened like a razor. He could feel his master's pull inside his head. Once mysterious whispered supplications were now harsh commands.

Around him, the old dead shuffled on bandaged feet. Ghosts.

Old man Chambers had once venerated this place. Now it was just storage for the unwanted. A forgotten hole where it kept the things it didn't want to think about. It was a tomb.

Blackstone made his way through the narrow passageway, the one Chambers had once told him was a trap for unwary robbers. He knew now that it had indeed been a trap. He no longer needed a flashlight to find his way through it, he knew the passage by rote. His feet shuffled through the sand as if it were all he'd ever known.

In the place where a ring of sarcophagi had once stood like the *moai* of Easter Island were now stacks of cages holding the young men—mostly men—and some women too, that the Occupant had shipped over from third world countries. These were the ones deemed unfuckable. But the Occupant had other uses for them.

Blackstone fished a set of keys from his pocket and unlocked the nearest cage. Inside, a young man—a boy, really—who was chained to the cage's wall looked at him innocently, his eyes pleading.

Blackstone knew just what the boy wanted. Because it was what he wanted, too.

With a flash of gold, Blackstone opened the boy's carotid artery with the dagger's blade, catching the first gush of crimson in the ancient chalice. It filled quickly. Then the boy deflated, falling to the cage floor, the rest of his life running along the cracks in the stonework and soaking into the sand.

Blackstone was jealous.

Nearby mummies gravitated to the pool, lapping up what they could. Hungry to be whole again.

Blackstone left the place without looking back. He had obligations.

He carried the chalice in his cupped hand, careful not to spill a drop.

Master would be pleased.

END

Acknowledgments

David Benton

I'd like to acknowledge W.D. Gagliani, whose interest in Egyptology and love of the craft led to the creation of this book.

W.D. Gagliani

Much of this novel found its shape during the first year of the pandemic, so I'd like to recognize some of the high rotation music coming through the "cans" on my ears during that long summer: Genesis, Tangerine Dream, Mike Oldfield, Spock's Beard, Ennio Morricone and Jerry Goldsmith soundtracks, as well as (of course) classic Yes, and ELP.

I'm especially grateful for the songwriting and compositions of Eric Woolfson, whose 1978 album *Pyramid* (by the Alan Parsons Project), which I first heard in its entirety on a late night radio broadcast that summer, was surely at least partly responsible for awakening my own latent interest in Egyptology and all things pyramidical, laying a subtle foundation that led me from reading about *The Book of the Dead*, Egyptian magic, and the search for immortality, to the plotting of this novel.

Since our creative lives are jigsaw puzzles, I'd be remiss if I didn't also mention *The Anubis Gates*, the 1983 Philip K. Dick Award-winning novel by Tim Powers, as a defining influence. I can honestly say it changed my writing life by exposing me to a whole other kind of fantasy I had never before encountered.

And, most importantly, I'd like to acknowledge my long-time friend and collaborator Dave Benton, whose ideas and enthusiasm for this novel led to the book you hold in your hands...

Thank you all!

About the Authors

The creative team of **David Benton & W.D. Gagliani** has published the award-nominated novel *Killer Lake* as well as *Acolytes of the Dead*, plus fiction in anthologies such as *THE X-FILES: Trust No One, SNAFU: Dead or Alive, SNAFU: An Anthology of Military Horror, SNAFU: Wolves at the Door, A Fistful of Demons, Dark Passions: Hot Blood 13, SPLATTERPUNK: Fighting Back, Past Indiscretions: The Best of Splatterpunk Zine, Zippered Flesh 2, Malpractice, Masters of Unreality,* etc., along with venues such as *DeadLines* and *Splatterpunk Zine*, plus the Amazon Kindle Worlds *Vampire Diaries* tie-in "Voracious in Vegas." Some of their collaborations are available in the collections *Starless and Bible Black* and *Mysteries & Mayhem.* Their Western novellas *Blood Trail* and *Blood Vow* were written as by Rex Masters.

David Benton is the author of the eco-terror novel *Fauna*, as well as other solo short works in Horror and Dark Fantasy. Outside of his writing he's worn many hats, finding employment variously as a warehouse worker, landscaper, printing press operator, cheesemaker, bricklayer, and janitor (*long nights, impossible odds...*). He is also a working musician whose most recent albums with the band CHIEF are *Chief II* and the double-length work *The Galleon*.

W.D. Gagliani is the author of the horror-thrillers *Wolf's Trap* (a finalist for the Bram Stoker Award in 2004), *Wolf's Gambit, Wolf's Bluff, Wolf's Edge, Wolf's Cut, Wolf's Blind*, the thrillers *Savage Nights* and *The Judas Hit*, plus the novellas *Wolf's Deal, Wolf's Call*, and "The Great Belzoni and the Gait of Anubis." He has published fiction and nonfiction in numerous anthologies and publications such as *Robert Bloch's Psychos, Fearful Fathoms, Undead Tales, More Monsters From Memphis, The Midnighters Club, Extremes 3: Terror On The High Seas, Extremes 4: Darkest Africa,* and others, and e-zines such as *Wicked Karnival, Horrorfind, 1000Delights, Dark Muse,* and *The Grimoire*. His fiction has garnered six Honorable Mentions in *The Year's Best Fantasy & Horror* (one of which, the story "Starbird," is also available on audio from Amazon). His book reviews and nonfiction articles have been included in *The Milwaukee Journal Sentinel, HorrorWorld, Cemetery Dance, CD Online, The Writer* magazine, *The Scream Factory, bare bones, Science Fiction Chronicle, Chizine, Flesh & Blood, BookPage, BookLovers, Hellnotes,* and many others, plus the books *Thrillers: The 100 Must Reads, They Bite,* and *On Writing Horror*. His Western action novella, *Chaco's Gold*, was written as by Tom Ferris.

Contact:
www.wdgagliani.com
www.facebook.com/wdgagliani
@wdgagliani.bsky.social
www.facebook.com/david.benton.7509

Amazon Author Pages

https://www.amazon.com/stores/W.-D.-Gagliani/author/B002BMHHPQ

https://www.amazon.com/stores/David-Benton/author/B004Q7C902